"No, I am not!" I glared at Lord Winterdale, indignant that he could even suggest such a thing. "As a matter of fact, I wrote to all of the other men and told them that I had destroyed the evidence that Papa had collected on them."

He reached over and put a hand on Cato's bridle, forcing us to stop. "Did you really destroy that evidence?" he asked incredulously.

"Yes, I did."

His incredulous look did not change.

"Not a brilliant move, Miss Newbury," he said sarcastically. "Who are the other men on that list?"

"Well . . . the Earl of Marsh," I said.

"Wonderful. The Earl of Marsh, Miss Newbury, is one of the most dangerous and unscrupulous men in all of London. In fact, the only man I know who is probably more dangerous than Marsh is me."

Please turn the page for raves for Joan Wolf's latest published romance . . .

"Joan Wolf's THE GUARDIAN, like Charlotte Brontë's *Jane Eyre* and Daphne du Maurier's *Rebecca*, has an element of suspense and mystery [and] echoes yet another master of the female first-person point-of-view, Louisa May Alcott. . . . Engrossing . . . with a large cast of interesting and individual characters, an intricate and believable plot, mastery of period details, a fallible but untarnished hero, and a storyteller heroine who lets the reader into the deepest recesses of her tormented heart."

—Lee Gilmore, *Romance Reader*
(Web site magazine)

"Romance writing at its best."
—*Publisher's Weekly* on *The Guardian*

"Delve beneath all the layers of the marvelous characters in the book and discover love, deceit, hatred, envy, mystery, forgiveness, great danger, and passion. It's one heck of a story that will keep you turning the pages far into the night."
—*The Belles and Beaux of Romance*

"Told in a poignant, intelligent manner . . . this is a highly charged tale that will stay with the reader long after the book is put aside."
—*Rendezvous*

BOOKS BY JOAN WOLF

The Gamble

JOAN WOLF

WARNER BOOKS

An AOL Time Warner Company

Cover design by Diane Luger
Cover art by Stanislaw Fernandez
Hand lettering by David Gatti

Warner Books, Inc.
1271 Avenue of the Americas
New York, NY 10020

Visit our Web site at www.twbookmark.com.

 An AOL Time Warner Company

Printed in the United States of America

First Printing: May 1998

10 9 8 7 6 5 4 3 2 1

For Catherine Coulter—thanks, babe, for all
the good advice

CHAPTER

one

BELIEVE ME, IT IS A DEFINITE SHOCK TO DISCOVER that one's father was a blackmailer.

This happened to me one rainy Friday afternoon, about ten days after my father's death. The rain was beating heavily against the library windows and the room smelled strongly of the coal-burning fire and of old leather book bindings. I was going through the drawers of Papa's desk to clean them out wh en I found the documentation.

When at first I realized what I was holding, I was horrified. There were five victims identified on Papa's list, four of whom he had caught cheating at cards and one of whom he had found cheating on his wife (an heiress). There was a file of the evidence he had accumulated against each victim and an accounting of the amount of money that Papa had succeeded in squeezing from each of them as well.

It amounted to quite a substantial sum.

I sat back on my heels and stared at the papers I had heaped on the old red Turkish carpet in front of me. I had never harbored any great illusions about my father, but I must admit that I had not thought him capable of this.

Next I wondered where all the money had gone to.

If he had put some of it aside for his daughters, I thought bitterly, then Anna and I would not find ourselves in the dreadful situation in which we now stood.

I got to my feet and went to the windows to look out at the rain-drenched garden, my mind once more running over that situation, like a child lost in a maze, hoping that somehow the next turn would be the one that would lead her out.

My father had been Lord Weldon, of Weldon Hall in Sussex. As he had no sons, the title and the estate were entailed upon a cousin of his, whom I had met twice and whom I disliked intensely. Now that my father was dead, the victim of a bludgeoning by a London thief, my sister and I found ourselves almost totally dependent upon the new Lord Weldon (who had a mouth like a fish and who had once tried to kiss me with it) for our welfare.

It was not a situation that I liked.

As I stared out at the rain, a scheme began to form in the back of my mind. I turned back into the room, and before I quite knew what I was doing, I had scooped up the blackmail evidence, stuffed it back into its folder, and fled up the stairs to the privacy of my own room.

I didn't get a chance to look at the folder again until after dinner, which Anna and I took by ourselves in the dining room, as we had ever since my mother had died five years before. Papa had rarely been home, preferring to spend his time in London, where the gambling was more easily come by.

After Anna had gone to bed, I went upstairs myself, spread all the incriminating papers out on my bed, and read through everything carefully. My father had collected quite an impressive file on each of the men he was squeezing, including newspaper clippings about the various activities of his victims. I suppose this helped him to know when it would be most profitable to ask for money. The files made for interesting, if sordid, reading.

In every case the evidence against each man was fairly solid. If it hadn't been, I suppose the victims would never have paid up.

I dragged an old oak chair across to my bed, made five neat piles of the papers spread out upon my ancient tapestry bedspread, and began to read through everything again.

Mr. George Asherton was the first candidate I looked at. Papa had caught him playing with a deck of shaved cards at Brooks's, one of the premier clubs for gentlemen in London. I read on and discovered that Mr. Asherton was an elderly bachelor who lived with his mother.

Next came Sir Henry Farringdon. Sir Henry was the man who had married an heiress from the city. Evidently her father had tied her money up well enough to keep Sir Henry on leading strings and he couldn't afford to let his wife find out about the pretty little dancer he was keeping on the side.

As soon as I saw that Sir Henry was married to a Cit, I lost interest in him. A wife with no social connections was useless to me.

My father's next victim was the Earl of Marsh. In many ways he fit my needs. He was married. His wife was impeccably aristocratic and moved in the best social circles. But reading between the lines of the *Morning Post* articles my father had clipped, I could see that his reputation was extremely unsavory. Seriously unsavory. I wasn't sure that I wanted to trust myself to a man like that.

Next came Mr. Charles Howard. About eight months ago my papa had caught Mr. Howard using a strategically placed mirror to cheat at cards. Mr. Howard was young, though, with young children. I didn't think he would be of much use to me.

Then there was the Earl of Winterdale. In many ways he seemed to be the perfect choice. One thing struck me as odd about him, however. Unlike the other victims, he had not made a payment to Papa for over a year.

Then a piece of information from the *Post* struck me like a bolt of lightning from the sky. This season, the Winterdales were presenting their daughter, Lady Catherine Mansfield, to the *ton*.

Perfect! I thought. If Winterdale was already presenting his daughter, I saw no reason why I couldn't easily blackmail him into presenting me as well.

I had no idea why Lord Winterdale, who from all of the information Papa had gathered seemed to be an extremely wealthy man, had found it necessary to cheat at faro, but evidently he had. Perhaps some men just did it for the excitement, I thought. Anyway, my papa had caught him and had been squeezing him for quite a while.

I narrowed my eyes thoughtfully, went through the file again, and decided that Lord Winterdale was my man.

If you are thinking "like father like daughter," I cannot blame you. It is a small excuse, I suppose, that I was only going to blackmail one man instead of five, but that I had every intention of blackmailing that man there was no doubt.

I bundled all the papers back into the folder before one of the housemaids came to help me undress for the night. After she had left I got into the bed that had been mine since I had been old enough to leave the nursery, but I didn't sleep. Instead I pulled the coverlet up over my shoulders and settled down to spend the rest of the night listening to the rain tap against the window while the following thoughts chased round and round in my brain:

How much money did I have at my immediate disposal?

What conveyence would I use to get to London?

Where would I stay when I got there?

Would Anna be safe while I was gone?

And finally, what would I do if the Earl of Winterdale refused to be blackmailed and threw me out of his house?

The rain came down and my thoughts churned around and around in my sleepless mind.

What would Frank say when he learned what I was doing? I had already told him that I could not marry him, that a soldier's life would never be suitabie for Anna, but I knew he hadn't believed me.

If he learned that I had gone to London, he would go berserk.

Well, I would worry about that when it happened.

I turned restlessly onto my other side and my thoughts veered off in another direction. I could probably marry old fishmouth, I thought. The big advantage of that course of action would be that Anna and I would be able to remain at Weldon Hall. The even bigger disadvantage, of course, was that I would have to let old fishmouth do more than kiss me.

The thought of that was so repugnant that the dangers of a trip to London seemed positively pleasant in comparison.

As the light began to creep into my room, and the rain to slow outside my window, I rolled onto my back and flung my arm across my forehead.

I thought firmly: *This is the only legacy Papa has left to me and it would be fainthearted of me not to use it. If I*

*fail, then I will simply come home, and Anna and I will be
no worse off than we were before I left.*

I quoted to myself the lines of the Marquis of Montrose that I always summoned up when I needed to find
courage:

> He either fears his fate too much
> Or his deserts are small
> That puts it not unto the touch
> To win or lose it all.

Tomorrow, I thought resolutely, I would see what I
had to do in order to get myself to London.

After breakfast I had my chestnut mare saddled and
rode over to see Frank's father, Sir Charles Stanton, our
local squire. After Weldon Hall, Allenby Park was the second most important house in the neighborhood, and I had
been in and out of it all my life. It was a typical gentleman's home, built of yellowish brick and standing in small
but pretty grounds, which were blooming now with early-
April flowers: daffodils, alyssum, cowslip, and violets.

When I rode up the graveled drive, Lady Stanton was
standing at the foot of the shallow front stairs. She told me
that Sir Charles was in the stable, then mounted into the gig
that was waiting for her and drove smartly off. I followed
her directions and rode around to the back of the house,
where I found Sir Charles admiring a new litter of spaniel
puppies that were nested amidst the straw in one of the
stalls.

"Ah, Georgie," he said in greeting. "Ain't these a
pretty sight?"

"They're adorable," I said with a smile, going down

on my knees next to him. We fussed over the puppies for a while, exchanging some of our favorite dog stories, and then I asked if I might talk to him. He invited me to accompany him back to the house, where we walked in the side door and went into his office, a male bastion of chestnut-paneled walls and ancient oak furniture. It was Sir Charles's favorite room, the one place where his wife did not care how much mud he tracked in on his boots.

I sat in the chair that faced his desk, and he regarded me with the steady gray eyes that he had given to Frank. "How may I be of service to you, Georgie?" he asked.

I trotted out the lie I had prepared. "I received a letter yesterday from a firm of solicitors in London, Sir Charles. Evidently Papa had done some business with them in the past and they have asked to see me. It is necessary, therefore, that I go to London and I was hoping that you might recommend a respectable place where I might stay."

He said immediately, "Nonsense. If these solicitors wish to see you, then tell them they must come to Weldon Hall. There is no reason for you to have to go to London."

"They write that I must come, Sir Charles," I insisted. "Considering my circumstances, I do not think that I can afford to neglect any possibility that might mean an improvement in Anna's and my situation."

He contemplated me in silence for a moment, his gray eyes thoughtful. Then he said, "I know you have been left in an awkward position, my dear, but surely the solution to that must be as clear to you as it is to me. It was obvious that your cousin was much taken with you when he visited here last Christmas. A marriage between the two of you would have the eminently desirable effect of giving both you and Anna a home. And not just any home, but the home you have known for all your lives. Now I ask you, what could be better than that?"

"Sir Charles," I said pleasantly, "I would rather spend the rest of my life spinning wool in a factory than marry my cousin. He has a mouth like a fish."

Sir Charles's level brows, also like Frank's, drew together. "Now, Georgie, I know that you and Frank are fond of each other, but . . ."

I interrupted him. "This has nothing to do with Frank. I have told Frank that I will not marry him and I mean it. It is not possible for me to attach myself to a military man as long as I have the responsibility of Anna."

Sir Charles looked relieved. He liked me, but he did not want his younger son to marry a girl with no money. I didn't blame him at all.

Because he liked me, however, he felt guilty about that relief, and so he told me about Grillon's Hotel.

I went to Anna's room after dinner the following evening, when I knew that Nanny would be there, and broke the news that I would be leaving for a while. Anna was upset.

"I won't be gone for long, dearest," I said to her, "and Nanny will be here with you, you know."

"But I want *you*, Georgie," she wept. Anna's weeping always broke my heart. I knew that what I was doing was for the best, however, and I steeled myself and soothed her as well as I could.

Nanny didn't help.

"I don't know what this nonsense is about London, Miss Georgiana," she said crossly. "What do you need to do in London that can't be done here?"

Find someone to marry me, I thought, but the words

remained unspoken. I smiled. "I have business to attend to, Nanny. Don't worry, I will be staying at Grillon's, which is a perfectly respectable hotel. It was recommended to me by the squire himself. I will write to you the moment that I get there so that you will know that I have arrived safely. Do not fret yourself about me. All will be well."

Nanny's sour look was not precisely a vote of confidence, but she did not wish to upset Anna any more and so refrained from further comment.

"As always, you will do what you wish to do, Miss Georgiana," she said tartly. "What is new about that?"

I must admit that the stagecoach ride to London was excessively uncomfortable. Sir Charles had wanted me to take the mail, but the coach was cheaper, and saving money was definitely an object with me, so I had booked seats on the coach for myself and Maria, one of the Weldon maids. It was going to look odd enough for me to arrive at Grillon's unattended by a gentleman; it would never do to be unattended by a maid.

So it was that Maria and I found ourselves squashed inside the London stagecoach with two men who looked like merchants, a fat woman who took up far too much of her share of the seat, and a tall, skinny man whose knees kept hitting mine and who kept apologizing for the entire six hours it took us to make the journey. The coach felt as if it had no springs at all and we were jolted unmercifully, even though the road was good. The food we were offered at the two stops we made was inedible: mutton roasted to a cinder and gritty cabbage at one inn, and rare boiled beef and waxy potatoes at the other.

I was horribly nervous about what I was going to do, however, and the distractions of the ghastly journey were actually rather welcome. Inevitably, though, our destination was finally reached and at midafternoon we entered the outskirts of London.

Maria's eyes were bugging out of her head as we drove deeper and deeper into the city. I thought ruefully that I probably didn't look any less astonished. We were, after all, both country girls and neither of us had ever seen so many people or so many carts and carriages in one place in all of our lives.

Maria and I took a hackney from the coaching inn where the London stage ended its journey to No. 7 Albemarle Street, the address of Grillon's Hotel. I had sent ahead to book a room, so I was expected.

The hall of the hotel was as grand as the ballroom of a nobleman, with great crystal chandeliers and polished green marble floors. The clerk behind the desk did not look happy to see me. Obviously he did not think that I fitted the elegance of the surroundings.

He flicked his eyes quickly up and down my person, taking in my old mulberry pelisse and hat. "Miss . . . Newbury?" he said haughtily.

I gave him a return look that was even haughtier. I do not like to be sneered at. "I am Miss Newbury," I announced, "and I require to be shown to my room immediately, if you please. I have had an excessively tiring journey."

We stared at each other for a few more moments, and then his eyes dropped away from mine. I had won.

I have always found that perseverance pays off.

"Of course, Miss Newbury," the desk clerk said in a more conciliatory tone. "I will have someone show you up immediately." He motioned to a white-wigged lackey who was lurking close by. "Take Miss Newbury and her maid up to her room, Edward." He twitched his lips in a semblance of a smile. "I hope your stay with us is a pleasant one, ma'am."

I nodded graciously and swept off after the footman. Another lackey trailed after us, carrying my portmanteau.

I did not sleep very well that night. My whole body felt bruised and battered from the stagecoach ride, but I was so worried about my interview with the Earl of Winterdale that I felt wound tighter than a spring.

Over and over I rehearsed the coming scene in my mind.

He had to know that Papa was dead, and he must be wondering and worrying about what had happened to the evidence Papa had been holding against him. I thought that my appearance would not come as a complete shock to him.

I wondered what he looked like, this wealthy earl who was dishonest enough to cheat at faro. According to Papa's file he was forty-eight years of age and he had one son and two daughters. The son was twenty-seven. The eldest daughter was twenty-three and married. The daughter who was being presented was my age, nineteen.

This was not the kind of man who wanted his world to know that he was a cheat. I thought that there was an excellent chance that he would agree to have me presented with his daughter.

But I would feel better when tomorrow's interview was over.

CHAPTER

two

I AWOKE TO THE UNACCUSTOMED NOISE OF TRAFFIC on the street. The day outside my hotel window looked as bright and as clear as I supposed the morning ever got in London. I breakfasted in my room at eight, then paced the floor for several hours, waiting for eleven o'clock, which I judged to be a decent hour to pay a call on a town gentleman.

Maria helped me to dress carefully in the outfit I had bought for Papa's funeral, a black broadcloth walking dress with a cape. My brown hair is as straight as rain, and there is little to be done with it except wear it on top of my head in a coronet of braids. My black straw bonnet with its black ribbons fit over it neatly, however, and my boots were well polished and my leather gloves immaculate. I took Maria with me for propriety's sake and gave the hackney driver the address in Grosvenor Square, in which I had discovered Mansfield House was located.

I was so sick with nervousness as we drove through the London streets that I scarcely noticed the bustle of the city that was going on around me. Over and over again I practiced what it was that I was going to say to the earl. Over and over again I imagined his reply, imagined the various responses I might make.

I tried very hard not to think about how sinful was the act I was planning to do.

Grosvenor Square was a square of mostly brown-brick buildings with red dressings and stone cornices and a formal garden in the middle. Number 10, Mansfield House, was a large Palladian-style edifice, about twice as wide and consequently twice as imposing, as the other houses that surrounded it. I couldn't help but wonder why someone who was wealthy enough to own such a house would cheat at cards.

Several steps led up to the front door, and my heart began to beat dangerously fast as I ascended the staircase and lifted the impressive brass knocker.

It was opened very quickly and a footman in green-velvet livery stood there, regarding me and Maria with obvious surprise. I supposed that in London, unknown ladies did not come calling at the home of a gentleman.

"Yes?" he said.

"I am here to see Lord Winterdale," I said firmly.

The footman looked flustered. On the one hand, my obvious mourning made it pretty clear that I was neither a dancer nor an opera singer. On the other hand, what was a single young lady, accompanied only by a maid, doing on the doorstep of Lord Winterdale's home?

A moment later another man in livery, who was clearly the butler, appeared behind the footman. "That will be all, Charles," he said to his underling. The newcomer turned to me. "Lord Winterdale is not at home," he said coldly, and began to close the door in my face.

"He will be at home to me," I said grimly, and stuck my foot in the door. "Please have the goodness to inform his lordship that Miss Newbury, the daughter of Lord Weldon, wishes to speak to him."

The absolute certainty in my voice, not to mention my foot in the door, shook the butler for a moment.

I took advantage of his indecision, and said haughtily, "I would prefer to wait indoors, and not on the doorstep, while you inform Lord Winterdale of my presence."

After another moment, the butler opened the door a fraction wider. I stalked in, with Maria creeping after me.

Directly inside the door was a grand entrance hall, which opened up into a magnificent circular staircase. The butler did not take us farther into the house, however, but ushered us into a small anteroom set off by round columns that opened off the entrance hall to the right.

"Wait here, and I will see if his lordship desires to see you," he said abruptly.

I watched as he moved in a stately fashion across the black-and-white marble tiles of the anteroom. Once he had left, I felt some of the tension drain out of me.

"Lor'," Maria breathed, "this is certain a grand house, Miss Georgiana." She looked around the room, with its huge portrait of an elegant eighteenth-century gentleman hung over the alabaster fireplace, its pale green walls, and its marble floor, and once more her eyes were bugging out of her head.

The only furniture in the room was a gilt table under the large front window. There were no chairs.

I took a long breath and went to stand beside the fireplace, which was not lit.

I waited for almost half an hour and I can tell you that my temper was quite hot enough to keep me warm by the time the butler returned and informed me that Lord Winterdale would see me. I didn't say anything about the wait, however, just left Maria behind in the anteroom and followed the butler down the passageway, past the magnificent staircase. Another anteroom was directly at the end of the passageway, and I caught a glimpse of a huge glass portico opening off it to the back of the house. Before we reached the anteroom, however, we halted at a door to the right of the passage.

The butler pushed open the door and announced, "Miss Newbury, my lord," and I walked into what was obviously the library.

A thin, black-haired young man, standing next to a shelf with a book in his hand, half turned to glance at me. I looked around the room for the earl and saw no one. I looked again, but there was no one else present.

A dreadful suspicion rocked me. "Surely you can't be the Earl of Winterdale!" I blurted. "The Earl of Winterdale is old!"

The black-haired young man came across to the big mahogany desk and put down his book.

"I assure you, Miss Newbury, that I am indeed the Earl of Winterdale," he said in a cool, contained voice. "I have been the earl for the last fourteen months, ever since my uncle and my cousin were killed in a sailing accident off the coast of Scotland."

"Oh no!" I wailed, not believing my bad luck.

"I apologize if my succession to the title has caused you any distress, but I assure you that it was quite out of my control," this new earl said, finally lifting his head to look at me fully. I detected a tinge of amusement in his cool voice and I looked at him more closely, trying to see if it might be possible after all for me to salvage something from this unexpected development.

How blue his eyes were! It was the first thought that struck me as I looked into his face. Next I noticed his eyebrows. These were not level and steady like Frank's, but arched and reckless.

This, I thought positively, was the face of a gambler.

How unfortunate that I didn't have any evidence against *him*.

I did still have the evidence against his uncle, however. Perhaps, I thought, this new Lord Winterdale would have enough family feeling not to wish to see his name dragged through the mud that my revelations would inevitably produce.

I clasped my gloved hands tensely in front of me and decided that it was worth a try.

I straightened my shoulders, and said, "I have come to tell you, my lord, that upon going through my father's papers after his death, I discovered that he had been blackmailing a number of gentleman of the *ton* whom he had discovered cheating at cards."

As you can see, I believe in being blunt.

The reckless black eyebrows lifted slightly higher.

"As I have not been cheating at cards, Miss Newbury," he said mildly, "of what possible interest can such a revelation be to me?"

I frowned. He was not making this any easier for me.

"One of the men Papa was blackmailing was your uncle," I said baldly.

Lord Winterdale pulled out the chair behind his desk and sat down, regarding me steadily with those brilliant blue eyes of his. He did not invite me to take a chair, which I thought was excessively rude.

I scowled at him. "This is a very serious matter, my lord. Your uncle paid my father a great deal of money to keep his mouth shut about this matter."

"What a delightful man your father must have been," the earl said lightly. "However, I still fail to see what my uncle's peccadilloes have to do with me."

I was furious about his comments about Papa. "Your uncle wasn't any better than my father!" I said hotly.

He shrugged as if the matter was of supreme disinterest to him.

I took a few steps toward the desk where he was so rudely sitting. "I have come to see you because I have read in the paper that Lady Winterdale is presenting her daughter Catherine this Season. When I read the notice I thought that Catherine was the earl's daughter. Am I correct in assuming that Lady Winterdale is your aunt and that Catherine is your cousin?"

He nodded gravely. "You would be correct in assuming that, Miss Newbury."

Really, it was outrageous of him to keep me standing here like this. As if I were a servant or something! I said nastily, "I do not think that either Lady Winterdale or Catherine would care for the *ton* to discover that Catherine's father had been a cheat, particularly at a time when Lady Winterdale is trying to find a husband for her."

His eyes narrowed, and for the first time I noticed how hard his mouth was. "Are you now threating to blackmail *me*, Miss Newbury?" he asked in a voice that was downright scary.

I thought of Anna and forced myself to meet that dangerous blue stare. I lifted my chin. "Yes," I said. "I am."

An exceedingly uncomfortable silence fell between us. I shifted from one foot to the other and tried to keep my chin in the air.

Finally he said silkily, "May I ask if you are squeezing the rest of your father's victims or am I the only unfortunate soul to find myself the object of your attention?"

I could feel myself flush. "I am not blackmailing anyone else. I only chose you because I saw in the paper that you were presenting your daughter—at least, I thought she was your daughter—and I thought I might convince you to present me as well."

He looked amazed. "Present you? I cannot present a young lady, Miss Newbury."

"I know that," I said crossly. "I was hoping you might persuade your wife—or rather your aunt—to present me along with your cousin. It wouldn't be that onerous a task, after all. All she would have to do would be to include me in the schemes she has already arranged for Catherine."

A little silence fell as he drummed his fingers on his desk and looked at me. The sun slanting in the window behind him fell on hair that was as black as a raven's wing.

"Why do you wish to have a Season, Miss Newbury?" he said at last.

I replied with dignity, "For the usual reason, my lord. I need to find a husband."

He leaned back in his chair. "And you have no female relative of your own who might be persuaded to perform this service for you?"

I said regretfully, "Every Newbury I know is poor, and it costs money to have a London Season. You see, Weldon Hall is entailed and Papa had only two daughters, so Anna and I have found ourselves without a home. Consequently, I need to marry, and it seemed to me that my best chance of doing that was to come to London and have a Season."

He said, "In short, Miss Newbury, you are a fortune hunter."

I corrected him. "I am a husband hunter, my lord. I don't need a fortune; a respectable man with a respectable home will suit me very well."

"Respectable men do not marry blackmailers," he said.

I flinched.

He continued remorselessly, "Moreover, as I said before, *I* am not the one who is presenting my cousin. Her mother is doing that, and I rather doubt that my aunt will wish to bring you out alongside Catherine. The comparison between the two of you would not be to Catherine's advantage."

I bit my lip and wondered if I could possibly blackmail *Lady* Winterdale. She certainly would not like the truth about her late husband to come out at such a delicate time.

When I lifted my eyes again to Lord Winterdale, I was amazed to see that he had a completely different expression on his face. The hardness was gone and those reckless eyebrows were slightly drawn together. He got up from his chair and came over to stand in front of me. As he approached I had to restrain myself from backing up. He was not an exceptionally large man, but he was certainly intimidating.

"Take off your hat," he commanded me.

I stared up at him in bewilderment.

He lifted his hands as if he would do it himself, and I hastened to untie the ribbons and lift my bonnet from my head.

He lifted my chin and stared down into my face.

I looked back unwillingly, caught in the intense blue of his eyes.

"Hmmm," he said. Then he grinned. Not pleasantly. He turned my face to the left and then to the right, his eyes narrowed with calculation.

All of my life I have been called a pretty girl, but believe me, mine was not the sort of face that would launch a thousand ships. It is heart-shaped, not oval, and my hair and eyes are brown. My sister is the one who is truly beautiful, not I.

Lord Winterdale said, "By George, I believe I'll do it."

By now his eyebrows were looking positively dangerous.

"Do what?" I asked in bewilderment. "Bring me out?"

"Make a push to have my aunt bring you out, at any rate," he said.

I looked at him suspiciously. "What has changed your mind? A minute ago you were making nasty comments about my being a blackmailer and making me stand while you sat there like a sultan looking at a harem candidate."

"My, my, my," he murmured. "A blackmailer who wants to be treated politely. That is certainly something new."

"Have you had much experience with blackmailers, my lord?" I asked sarcastically.

"Don't be unpleasant, Miss Newbury," he said. He tapped my cheek with his finger. "It doesn't become you."

I opened my mouth to reply, but a knock came on the library door and the butler opened it and looked in.

"Lady Winterdale has arrived and wishes to speak to you, my lord. I just thought I would let you know in case the young person was still with you."

"Thank you, Mason."

"Shall I ask Lady Winterdale to wait, my lord?"

"Not at all," Lord Winterdale said blandly. "Show her along to the library."

The butler's face was impassive as he backed out of the room.

The earl put his hand on my arm. "Now, Miss Newbury, if you will come over here, I think we can success-
fully hide you behind this drapery," he said.

I stared at him in amazement. "You want me to hide
behind the drapery?"

"I think it will be very much to your advantage to do
so," he replied.

He looked as if he were enjoying himself enormously.

The drapery he was referring to was a gold-velvet af-
fair that hung on either side of the tall, narrow window that
was behind the library desk.

"Quickly!" he said, and his voice was so imperative
that I scurried across the floor and slipped in behind the
gold velvet. It tickled my nose and I tried to press back
against the wall to get away from it. The earl arranged the
folds so that they covered my feet.

Thirty seconds later I heard the library door open and
a woman's perfectly modulated, excessively well bred
voice said, "There you are, Philip. I must speak to you."

"Ah, Aunt Agatha. How lovely to see you this fine
morning. How may I serve you?"

The exchange between the two people in the room on
the other side of the velvet curtain was entirely pleasant and
civilized, but I knew instantly that they didn't like each
other.

Lady Winterdale said, "I wish to discuss with you the
date for Catherine's come-out ball."

"Sit down, Aunt Agatha," Lord Winterdale said pleasantly.

I thought darkly that it was nice to see he didn't keep
every female standing while he sat and stared at them.

There was the rustle of silk skirts as his aunt presumably took one of the chairs in the room. Once she was

seated, the earl said blandly, "I appreciate your seeking my advice, of course, but I hardly see what the date of Catherine's come-out ball has to do with me."

"Philip! Of course it has something to do with you! We are having it at Mansfield House, after all."

Silence from Lord Winterdale.

"Aren't we?" Lady Winterdale asked sharply.

"I was not aware of such a plan," Lord Winterdale said.

"Of course we are having it here," Lady Winterdale snapped. "Mansfield House is one of the few houses in London that has a ballroom. I had Eugenia's come-out ball here, and I fully intend to have Catherine's as well."

"Ah, but when you had Eugenia's come-out ball, my uncle was Lord Winterdale. Now I am. There is, you will admit, a difference."

This time the silence was on Lady Winterdale's part.

Finally she said, "Philip, are you telling me that you will not allow me to have Catherine's come-out ball in this house?"

She sounded as if she might explode.

"I didn't say that," Lord Winterdale returned. "Precisely."

"Then what did you say? Precisely?"

Lord Winterdale appeared to veer off in another direction. "I have just received a letter from an old friend of my father's. He tells me that one of my father's friends, Lord Weldon, has died recently and left his two daughters penniless. In his will, Lord Weldon unfortunately named me to be their guardian."

"You!" Lady Winterdale said. I could hear the horror in her voice. "You are twenty-six years old. You are not fit to be anyone's guardian, Philip. You can't even govern yourself."

Lord Winterdale said sarcastically, "Believe me, my dear aunt, compared to Lord Weldon, I am a paragon of virtue."

I could hear silk rustle as Lady Winterdale shifted in her chair. "Well, what has all this to do with Catherine's come-out ball, pray?"

"This is what it has to do with Catherine's come-out ball," said Lord Winterdale. "I want you to present Miss Newbury with Catherine, Aunt Agatha, and take her around with you during the Season."

Lady Winterdale's reply was crisp and immediate. "This is impossible. Utterly impossible. I know who Weldon was, and he was almost as disreputable as your late father. I want nothing to do with any daughter of his."

I could feel my hands ball into fists. The fact that she was right about Papa did not make me feel any less inclined to hit her.

"That is unfortunate," Lord Winterdale was saying regretfully. "If you would present Miss Newbury, I was thinking that you and Catherine might move into Mansfield House for the Season. That, of course, would save you the cost of renting a house. You would also have the use of the Winterdale town carriages as well, which would be another savings."

I could almost hear Lady Winterdale toting up sums in her head. Then she said in a hard voice, "Let us get our facts straight, Philip. If I present this Miss—what is her name?"

"Miss Newbury. I do not yet know her first name."

"If I present this Miss Newbury of yours, then you

will allow Catherine and me to live, rent-free, in Mansfield House for the duration of the Season."

"That is correct."

"You will allow me to use the ballroom to introduce Catherine to the *ton*."

"That is correct."

Another rustle of silk. Then, "Who will pay for the come-out ball?"

"I will," said Lord Winterdale.

Lady Winterdale heaved a regretful sigh. "It just isn't feasible, Philip. Weldon died quite recently, I believe, and the girl must be in mourning for at least six months. It is impossible for her to have a Season this year."

"I realize that this would be true under normal circumstances," Lord Winterdale said, "but the circumstances surrounding Miss Newbury's situation are scarcely normal. She is virtually destitute, Aunt Agatha. If she does not find a husband, she will find herself thrown on the parish."

Well, I didn't think things were quite as bad as that, but it certainly didn't hurt for Lord Winterdale to make my plight sound as pitiful as possible.

"I am certain that if you throw the mantle of your enormous consequence over her, that the *ton* will overlook her lack of mourning," Winterdale said coaxingly.

"I don't know about that," Lady Winterdale said dubiously. "The rules for mourning are very strict."

"As you said earlier, everyone knows the worthlessness of Weldon. Surely there will be some pity for his daughter. Particularly if you sponsor her, my dear aunt."

"Hmmm," said Lady Winterdale. It sounded to me as if she were beginning to come around. "What does she look like? Is she presentable?"

"I believe she will be reasonably presentable once her

wardrobe is spruced up a little," Lord Winterdale returned blandly.

Reasonably presentable indeed!

I heard Lady Winterdale get up and begin to walk around the room. From what I had heard during the course of this interview, I didn't care for her any more than Lord Winterdale appeared to, but I began to pray that she would accede to this scheme of his. I wouldn't mind posing as his ward if it would get me what I wanted.

At last Lady Winterdale said, "What a mercy it is that I did not put a deposit down on that house in Park Lane."

"It must have been meant," Lord Winterdale said smoothly.

"Well then," Lady Winterdale said briskly, "as the Season opens in a few weeks, Philip, I think it will be important for Catherine and me to move into Mansfield House as soon as possible. We have a great deal of shopping to do."

"By all means, Aunt Agatha. You will let me know the date, and I will arrange to have Miss Newbury move in at about the same time. I am certain that she and Catherine will get along splendidly."

"I suppose I shall have to take her shopping with us," Lady Winterdale said sourly.

"If you don't wish to be ashamed of her, certainly you will have to take her shopping."

I was irate. I thought the dress I was wearing was perfectly acceptable. Certainly it was in style in Sussex.

"Who is going to foot the bill for these clothes, Philip?"

"You may have the bills sent to me," came the easy reply.

"What about Catherine's new clothes?" Lady Winterdale said tentatively. "You know how slender is my widow's portion."

"My dear aunt, my uncle left you very well provided for, as well you know. However, I will be happy to foot the bill for Catherine's clothes as well."

"Well, well, well." Lady Winterdale sounded excessively happy about all of this. "I should like the ball to be at the beginning of the Season, Philip, so that Catherine is immediately distinguished from the rest of the girls who will be crowding the marriage mart this year."

"Choose the date, Aunt, and the ballroom will be at your service," said Winterdale.

I could scarcely believe that I was hearing all of this. Things were proceeding beyond my wildest dreams.

After a little more discussion between aunt and nephew in regard to the come out, Lady Winterdale made her departure and I was allowed to step out from behind my drapery. I stood there in front of it and looked at him.

"You heard what transpired, Miss Newbury," Lord Winterdale said blandly. "Are you satisfied?"

"I am very satisfied, my lord," I said slowly. "What is it that you wish me to do now?"

"Where are you staying at the moment?" he asked.

"Grillon's."

"Well you can't remain there alone. Nor can you come here until my aunt is installed to chaperone you. I suggest that you go home and wait until I write to tell you that it is proper for you to return to Mansfield House."

I nodded.

"Where is Weldon Hall?"

"It is in Sussex, my lord."

"You must give me the direction." He moved to his

desk, sat down and picked up a pen. I gave him the direction to Weldon Hall and he wrote it down.

"I don't think that it will take very long for Aunt Agatha to move in," he said ironically, "so I would be prepared to return quickly."

I nodded.

He blotted his paper and looked up at me. "Well, I think that will be all, Miss Newbury," he said. He did not get out of his chair. "By the way, what is your first name?"

"It is Georgiana, my lord."

He nodded. "Miss Georgiana Newbury."

He wrote it down, as if he would forget it if he did not do so.

I said coldly, "I have been wondering what caused you to change your mind so abruptly, my lord. You were ready to show me the door, and then all of a sudden I was hiding behind the drapery and discovering that I was your ward."

"I did it to annoy my aunt, Miss Newbury," he said with a devilish lift of those reckless eyebrows. "I confess that I expect to derive a good deal of pleasure from seeing her fury this Season as she is forced to escort you around with Catherine."

I thought that Lady Winterdale was a woman who had lost both her husband and her son under tragic circumstances and surely deserved a little more consideration than was being shown her by her nephew. However, since I was the beneficiary of his heartlessness, I held my tongue.

I said instead, "It sounds to me as if you will be spending a great deal of money on this presentation. Is it worth it?"

"Oh yes, Miss Newbury," he said. "Believe me, it is."

CHAPTER
three

I RETURNED TO GRILLON'S IN A VERY PECULIAR FRAME of mind. I should have been delighted, I thought. After all, had I not achieved everything I had come to London to achieve? I was going to make my come out in society under the sponsorship of a lady of impeccable connections and reputation. I would have an opportunity to meet a great many eligible young men, and surely one of them would like me well enough to make me an offer, and surely I would like him well enough to feel that living with him would not be an eternal penance.

I *was* delighted, I told myself. But the truth was that I was also infuriated. I had never, in all my life, met anyone who had so instantly set up my back as the Earl of Winterdale.

Really, he was quite the rudest man I had ever met. Writing my name down as if otherwise he would forget it!

Why, he had not even inquired about how I had traveled to London. Doubtless I would have to return home on the stage, and then, when he deigned to write to inform me that the time was appropriate for me to return, I would be forced to travel back to Grosvenor Square on the stage as well. With all the clothes that he had insulted dragged along with me inside my portmanteau.

With one part of my mind I knew that I was being unreasonable, that it was unfair to expect a man whom one was blackmailing to behave toward one as if one were a lady. But the fact remained that I thought he was insufferable.

The rest of the afternoon stretched out before me emptily, and I decided that rather than kick my heels in a boring hotel room, Maria and I should see some of London. I particularly wanted to see Westminster Cathedral, but Maria was so eager to view Madame Tussaud's wax collection, which was presently being exhibited in London, that I didn't have the heart to deny her, and we went there. I, after all, would be returning to the city. Maria would probably never see London again in her life.

The full-sized wax figures of famous historical characters, displayed in lavish costumes, were utterly amazing. Maria and I had a grand time, oohing and aahing at the astonishingly lifelike representations, until an odiously intrusive man, with an oily, ungentleman-like manner, began to talk to me and would not go away.

"Is this fellow bothering you, ma'am?" I heard a soft, masculine voice say from behind me.

I turned to find myself looking into the hazel eyes of a young gentleman dressed in the blue morning coat and buff pantaloons of the upper classes.

"I ain't bothering the lady," the odious man said. "I'm just pointing out some of the best parts of the exhibit to her."

"I told you that I did not wish to speak to you, sir, and you would not go away," I said coldly. "You most certainly are bothering me."

"Take yourself off, then, and leave the lady alone," the newcomer said in a commanding, aristocratic accent.

After a moment's hesitation, the odious one slunk off, and the gentlemanly young man turned to me with a very nice smile. "So young and lovely a lady should not be at a public exhibition without a gentleman escort, ma'am. If you have your carriage with you, I will undertake to escort you to it safely."

It was very nice to hear oneself called a young and lovely lady, particularly when one had only just been called *reasonably presentable* by other obnoxious parties.

"I am afraid I did not come by carriage, sir," I said regretfully. "My maid and I took a hackney cab."

"Then you must allow me to fetch a hackney for you now." He must have seen the resistance on my face, because he added hastily, "That is, if you have seen the entire exhibition?"

"Well . . . I believe Maria wished to look at the figures of the Roman emperors," I said.

"Then allow me to escort you," my rescuer said immediately. "My name is Sloan, ma'am. Lord Henry Sloan."

I held out my hand. "How do you do, Lord Henry," I said graciously. "I am Miss Georgiana Newbury."

"Miss Newbury," he returned with a charming smile. "I am honored to make your acquaintance."

The rest of the afternoon was extremely agreeable. Lord Henry was a very pleasant young man, and he had many interesting and amusing tales to tell of the historical figures featured by Madame Tussaud in her collection.

He seemed to be delighted when I told him that I would be making my come out this Season.

"That means I will be seeing you again," he said. "I reside at my father's house during the Season and we shall be forever running into each other at balls and things."

I wasn't quite sure who Lord Henry's father was, but I didn't like to betray my ignorance. Fortunately, he clarified the matter for me almost immediately.

"My father is the Duke of Faircastle, you know."

"Oh," I said faintly. "Of course."

"And who will be presenting you, Miss Newbury?" he asked in the nicest possible way.

We were standing waiting for the hackney Lord Henry had summoned to cross the street to us, and I looked down to smooth an imaginary wrinkle from my skirt.

"Lady Winterdale," I mumbled.

"I beg your pardon?"

"Lady Winterdale," I said more clearly.

"Good God," he said.

I looked up. I met his nice, ordinary hazel eyes, and said, "I am Lord Winterdale's ward, you see, and he has asked Lady Winterdale to present me along with her daughter, Lady Catherine."

Lord Henry stared at me. "You are Winterdale's *ward*?"

"Yes," I said stonily.

"And he has actually inveigled Lady Winterdale into presenting you?"

"Yes," I said again. "You see, my father left my sister and me virtually penniless, Lord Henry, and consequently I must marry. Lord Winterdale was very kind, and he persuaded his aunt to present me, even though I should technically be in mourning for at least six months."

"I wonder how the devil Winterdale managed to do that?" Lord Henry murmured. He answered himself almost immediately. "He must have offered to foot all the bills."

I could feel the color flush into my cheeks. "As a matter of fact, he did."

Lord Henry grinned. It was a pleasant smile, not wicked, like the smile of another person I could name.

"I can foresee that we can look forward to a very interesting Season this year," Lord Henry said lightly. "Ah, Miss Newbury, here is your hackney now. Allow me to assist you inside."

Maria went first, and I followed. When once we were established inside, Lord Henry lifted his hand to close the door. Before he did, however, he leaned inside and said, "Allow me to give you a piece of advice, Miss Newbury. Or perhaps I might instead call it a warning. Lord Winterdale is never kind."

He withdrew his shoulders from the carriage and closed the door. "Grillon's," I heard him tell the driver, and the cab moved off.

Lord Henry raised his hat to me as the cab went by.

When I walked into the front hall of Grillon's the desk clerk told me that a message had arrived for me two hours earlier. I took it up to my room and unfolded it there. It read:

My carriage will call for you tomorrow morning at eight o'clock to take you back to Sussex. Winterdale.

When I had left Mansfield House this morning I had been vastly annoyed that he had not made any arrangements for my travel. Now I was annoyed that he had made arrangements without consulting me.

I am usually a very reasonable person. I didn't know why this man had managed to have such an irritating effect on me, but I told myself that I was going to have to learn to curb my feelings. If I was going to live under the same roof with Lord Winterdale during the two months that the Season lasted, I was going to have to learn to ignore him.

Unfortunately, he did not seem to be the sort of man it was easy to ignore.

My return journey to Sussex was far more pleasant

than my original journey had been. Lord Winterdale's coach was well sprung and the velvet squabs inside were deliciously comfortable. The food when we stopped was very different as well: a good soup and fresh fish at one inn and perfectly cooked roast lamb at another. We even had time to finish our meals before we had to get back on the road.

I had two weeks at home before the letter arrived from Lord Winterdale informing me that his chaise would be arriving in two days' time to bring me back to Mansfield House in London. Rather to my own surprise, I was relieved to receive the summons. It was becoming increasingly difficult to answer the questions of my friends about Lady Winterdale's sudden desire to give me a Season.

Nanny had been shocked because I was not mourning my father.

Anna was miserable because I was going away again.

Sir Charles and Lady Stanton were very worried that I was going to be taken advantage of by Lord Winterdale.

"I will tell you bluntly, Georgie, that he does not have a good reputation," Sir Charles had told me when I had gone to visit them to impart my news. "He inherited the title a year or so ago after his uncle and his cousin were unexpectedly killed. His own father was a dissolute bounder who dragged him around the cesspots of Europe all the while the boy was growing up. He's respectable now, of course. Any man with the Winterdale wealth and title would be respectable. But I would not like to see any daughter of mine living under his roof."

We were sitting in the parlor at Allenby Park, having tea. At least, Lady Stanton and I were having tea. Sir Charles was having something stronger.

"What about Lord Winterdale's mother?" I asked Sir Charles. "Did she travel around Europe with him as well?"

Sir Charles poured himself a little more hock. "His mother died when he was quite young, I believe. I don't know why his father didn't give the boy to some female relative to look after, but apparently he didn't."

Lady Stanton offered me another piece of bread and butter. "I remember that there was some scandal attached to the marriage," she offered. "His mother was only the daughter of a country clergyman or something." She frowned. "I seem to recall that there was an elopement." She folded her lips. "Suffice it to say, Georgiana, that I do not think it is a wise move for you to put yourself under the power of a man like that."

I put my teacup back on the small mahogany piecrust table in front of my chair. "I am not going to be alone with him," I said. "His aunt and his cousin will be there, after all, and his aunt will be in charge of me. I will be very well chaperoned."

Sir Charles scowled. "You are a very pretty girl, Georgie. Who knows what the scoundrel might have secretly planned?"

I folded my hands in my lap. "Sir Charles," I said patiently, "as things stand, I have very few choices. I must find a home for Anna and me, and in order to find a home, I must first find a husband. You must agree that I have a better chance of finding someone to marry me in London than I do in our small village in Sussex."

We looked at each other. We all knew that Frank wanted to marry me, and we all knew that they did not want him to.

"You should marry your cousin," Lady Stanton said. Her fresh-colored countrywoman's face was set sternly. "It would not take very much to bring him up to scratch, Georgiana. We all could see that clearly when he visited Weldon Hall last Christmas."

"I think my cousin is repulsive," I said firmly. "He kissed me last Christmas, and I almost got sick to my stomach."

Lady Stanton frowned and put down her teacup with a small click. "He should not have done that."

"Well, he did. And it was disgusting." I took another bite of bread and butter.

"It takes a while for a young girl to grow accustomed to a man, Georgiana," Lady Stanton said.

"I didn't at all mind Frank kissing me," I said boldly. "In fact, I rather liked it."

The squire groaned, got to his feet and went to look out the window. Lady Stanton gazed at me in obvious distress.

"Don't worry," I said to them. "I am not going to marry Frank."

"It is not that we don't like you, Georgie," Sir Charles said, turning to look at me. "It is just that all of my own money is tied up in Allenby Park, which as you know will be going to Edward. Frank needs a wife with some money of her own if he is to make a career in the military."

"I know that," I said.

"I am afraid that your lack of a portion might affect your chances in London as well," Lady Stanton said worriedly.

I knew this and I had already begun to think that perhaps I could squeeze a few thousand pounds out of Lord Winterdale for a dowry.

How quickly one becomes accustomed to a life of crime.

"I have some of Mother's jewelry that was left to me," I lied. "Perhaps I could sell that."

The Stantons sighed. They had been good friends to me for many years, and they didn't like this scheme at all, but they really didn't have any alternatives to offer.

"If for any reason at all you find that things are not going as you think they should, write to me and I will come and fetch you home immediately," Sir Charles told me.

I smiled at him. "Thank you," I said, grateful for his kind offer but at the same time bitterly aware that Weldon Hall was not home to me anymore.

The night before I left Weldon Hall I burned all the papers relating to my father's blackmailing scheme—including the papers incriminating Lord Winterdale. I had always known that I would never use Papa's evidence against any of his victims. If my threat had not succeeded with Lord Winterdale, I would have burned the evidence anyway.

I then penned short notes to each of the four victims I had not approached personally. I thought it would be sensible to keep the notes as uncomplicated and as unrevealing as possible and so I wrote:

Dear (here I put in the appropriate name), You will be relieved to know that a certain file of papers which I discovered in my father's desk after his death has been disposed of. Very truly yours, Georgiana Newbury.

I regarded this note and was pleased with my own delicacy. I had written enough to reassure the victim, but if by chance the note should fall into the wrong hands, my words were enigmatic enough to keep the victim safe from exposure.

I went to bed and tried very hard not to think about how much I was going to miss Anna.

The following morning found me once more on my way to London, this time comfortably ensconced in the earl's chaise and being treated like a queen at the various posting inns we graced with our business.

I think I was even more nervous on this trip than I had been before, when I had been riding the stage and going forth to face what I had thought was an elderly Lord Winterdale. I had too many things to think about now, and not enough distractions to occupy my mind in other directions.

For one thing, even though I had spent the last two weeks spouting lies to my friends about how amiable a man Lord Winterdale was, the fact remained that he was not amiable at all. The truth of the matter was, he was young and irritating, and most of all, he was intimidating.

He had no cause to love me, of course. I was blackmailing him, for God's sake. But it had been made abundantly plain to me in the short time that I had spent in Mansfield House that it was not going to be fun pretending to be Lord Winterdale's ward.

Then there was Lady Winterdale, who was being blackmailed to present me by Lord Winterdale. I could already tell that she would not like me, nor did I expect to like her.

Catherine, her daughter, was probably a haughty girl who would look down her nose at a country bumpkin like me.

It had to be done, though, I told myself resolutely as we passed through the countryside on the outskirts of London. As I had said to Sir Charles and Lady Stanton, I

needed a home, and in order to find a home, I needed a husband. Blackmail was an ugly thing, and Lord Winterdale
was probably going to make my stay in London as miserable as he possibly could, but I had no choice but to take
advantage of the opportunity that my father's criminal activities had offered me.

By the time I got to Mansfield House in Grosvenor
Square I was quite miserable. I tried not to show it, however, as I marched up the steps and rapped sharply on the
brass knocker.

The door was opened by the same green-velvet-clad
footman who had opened it upon my previous visit. His response to me this time was somewhat different, however.

"Miss Newbury," he said, "we have been expecting
you." The door was opened wider. "Come in."

And so, for the second time in my life, I entered the
grand green marble entrance hall of Mansfield House.
"Lord Winterdale is not here at the moment, nor is Lady
Winterdale," the footman informed me. "I believe Lady
Catherine is at home, however. Allow me to send for her."

"Thank you," I said.

This time I was escorted into the room to the left of
the hall, a drawing room not an anteroom. A sign, I
thought, of my elevated status in the house.

The drawing room was decorated in shades of pink
and claret and had three large, crimson-draped windows
that looked out upon the street. A collection of delicate,
pink-upholstered chairs circled the marble fireplace, and a
crystal chandelier hung from what looked like an Angelica
Kauffmann–painted ceiling. A rosewood cabinet with brass
mounts, a secretaire-bookcase, and a rose-colored sofa and
a pair of armchairs were the other furniture in the room.

I perched very carefully on the edge of the silk-uphol-stered sofa, folded my hands in my lap, and waited.

Five minutes later a girl of about my age came into the room. Her hair, an indeterminate shade of brown, was worn in a cluster of curls around her ears, and she wore spectacles. She was very thin and the look that she gave me was not at all haughty. In fact, it was rather shy.

"Miss Newbury?" she said in a small, timid-sounding voice.

"Yes," I said, standing up.

"I am Catherine Mansfield. I believe we are to be pre-sented together."

I had not expected Catherine Mansfield to look like this. I smiled and crossed the room, holding out my hand. "I am very glad to meet you," I said. "It is so kind of your mother to do this for me."

Her head was down and she lifted it briefly to give me a quick, fleeting look. Behind the spectacles I saw that her eyes were a very pretty shade of blue. She took my hand in a quick yet pleasantly firm grasp. "Yes," she said faintly. "I am sorry that Mama is not here just now. I will be happy to show you to your room."

"Thank you," I said. "I would like that."

At that moment a tall robust woman came into the room behind Catherine. "You must be Miss Newbury," the newcomer announced in a commanding voice. "I am Mrs. Hawkins, his lordship's housekeeper." She looked at Catherine dismissisively. "I will take Miss Newbury to her room, Lady Catherine."

"Y . . . yes, of course," Catherine said.

I think it was the girl's stutter as well as her air of helplessness that spurred me to do what I did. After years of looking out for Anna, my maternal instincts are very well developed. I stepped forward, and said imperiously, "That is very kind of you, Mrs. Hawkins, and of course I am delighted to make your acquaintance. Lady Catherine has already said that she will take me to my bedroom, however." I glanced at Catherine and smiled. "It will give us an opportunity to get to know each other a little."

Mrs. Hawkins looked at me in stunned silence. Obviously she had not expected his lordship's little ward to have the nerve to question her authority. I had had the running of my father's house for too many years, however, to allow myself to be ruled by a tyrant of a housekeeper.

"Come along, Lady Catherine, and you can show me where I am to go," I said more quietly, moving toward the drawing-room door. Catherine followed along behind me rather like a duckling trailing after its mother.

Once we were outside in the huge green-marble hall, I stopped and turned to Lady Catherine with a smile. "Now I must follow you," I said.

"This way," she replied, in a voice that was a trifle stronger than the one she had used in the drawing room. She led the way to the grand circular staircase that I had passed once before on my way to the library to meet the earl. The staircase was painted white, with a polished wood railing, and in the roof above the third story was a large window which allowed for natural illumination during the day.

"This house seems to be very large for a London town house," I commented chattily as we began to climb the wide staircase. "Most of the houses I have seen look to be much narrower."

"Yes, it is actually double the width of most houses. That is why my grandfather was able to fit in a ballroom on the second floor," Lady Catherine said. We had finished climbing the first flight of stairs now and were stopped on the second landing, and she gestured to a set of wide double doors across the way. They were closed. "That is the ballroom there, and back behind the staircase there are two other drawing rooms as well as an anteroom that looks over the back garden."

She spoke of the house with great familiarity, I thought, and then I remembered that she had probably grown up here.

"The bedrooms are on the third floor," Catherine said in a toneless voice, and she turned back to the staircase again. The third floor when we reached it was far less grand than the floors below, consisting as it did of a simple passageway with doors opening off either side.

We began to walk down the passageway. "This is my bedroom here," Lady Catherine said, pausing outside a door about halfway down the hall. She hesitated, then bit her lip. "Do you know, I am afraid I did not ask Mrs. Hawkins what room she planned to put you in, Miss Newbury."

"Do you think it would it be all right if I had the room next to yours?" I asked.

"Well . . ." She was tentative, unsure. "I suppose that would be acceptable. If Mother approves, of course."

"I don't know anyone in London, you see, and it would be such a comfort to be close to a friend," I said, and boldly pushed open the door and went into the aforementioned bedroom.

It was a perfectly delightful room, with blue-painted walls, a white stucco fireplace, and an old blue Turkish rug on the floor. There was a door in the right wall that presumably led into a dressing room. The bed was large and hung with blue silk draperies, and a comfortable-looking print-upholstered chair was pulled up before the fireplace. Two small windows were set high in the wall, presumably to place them above the house next door. One of the problems with London town houses was that they were set so close together that it was difficult to get light in the long sides of the buildings.

"This room is lovely," I said.

The rattle of keys announced the approach of the housekeeper from the end of the passageway.

"Oh oh," I murmured, "here comes the dragon."

Lady Catherine stared at me in fascination.

Mrs. Hawkins appeared in the bedroom door and remained there, blocking our view of the passage with her height and heft.

"This is not the room Lady Winterdale had planned to give to Miss Newbury," she announced to Lady Catherine.

Catherine swallowed. "Er . . . what room had my mother chosen, Mrs. Hawkins?"

"The yellow room."

Catherine looked distressed, and I guessed that the yellow room was probably the least desirable bedroom in the house.

Let me explain here that already I did not like Lady Winterdale. I had not liked her from what I had learned of her from her conversation with her nephew, and I liked her even less as I saw how pitifully she appeared to have intimidated her daughter. I also did not like this Mrs. Hawkins. I am not someone who sets a great deal of store by my own consequence, so the yellow room would not have bothered me at all, but it didn't take a genius to see that poor Catherine needed a champion.

"I do not at all care for yellow," I announced. "I believe I would rather remain here."

The housekeeper looked at me grimly. "May I remind you that this is not your house, Miss Newbury? I believe that Lady Winterdale's wishes must take precedence over yours."

"This is not Lady Winterdale's house either, Mrs. Hawkins," I replied sweetly. "The house belongs to Lord Winterdale, and I am certain that his lordship will not want his ward relegated to a room whose color is unattractive to her. Particularly if there is another, more desirable, room available."

Mrs. Hawkins and I stared at each other for a long moment. Then a faint flush stained her forehead and she looked away.

"Very well, Miss Newbury," she said stiffly. "I will have your portmanteau sent up to the blue bedroom."

"Thank you, Mrs. Hawkins," I said, smiling graciously.

I always believe in being a good winner.

CHAPTER
four

AFTER MRS. HAWKINS HAD MADE HER DEPARTURE, I looked away from the door to find Catherine staring at me with a mixture of wonder and fear.

"That . . . that was very brave of you, Miss Newbury," she said.

"It was very ill-mannered of me, I'm afraid," I replied ruefully. "I am a guest in the house and I really should not have overruled your mother's choice of a bedroom for me. It is just that Mrs. Hawkins's attitude rather put my back up. I do not deal well with people who condescend to me."

Catherine sighed profoundly and pushed her spectacles back up on her nose. "She frightens me to death," she confessed. "But I am very glad you stood up to her, Miss Newbury."

I said impulsively, "I would like it exceedingly if you would call me Georgie. I do so hope that we are going to be friends. After all, we will be spending a great deal of time together this Season, will we not?"

Lady Catherine replied, "I would like to be your friend, Georgie, and of course you must call me Catherine. But I fear that I won't be much of a companion for you. I would so much prefer not to be making this come out, you see, that I'm afraid I don't have much enthusiasm for it."

"But why don't you want to come out?" I asked in

profound surprise. Most girls would give their eyeteeth to have a London Season.

Catherine looked extremely dejected. "Well, for one thing, Mama is determined to puff me off with all sorts of pomp and circumstance, and I know that I shall be a failure. No one will want to marry me, and Mama will be angry, and . . ." She drew in a deep, unsteady breath and added in a hurry, "and to tell the truth, I'm not at all sure that I want to get married anyway."

Once more I stared at Catherine with surprise. Every girl's ambition was to get married.

"And if I absolutely must make my come out, I don't want to stay in this house," Catherine finished miserably. "I'm afraid of Philip."

Silence fell as Catherine stared at the blue Turkish rug. I traced the carving on the mahogany bedpost with my finger and thought of Sir Charles's warnings.

"Is there any particular reason why you are afraid of your cousin?" I asked carefully.

"He is always so cynical," Catherine said. "I never know if he means what he says or if he is being sarcastic."

"Oh." Sarcasm I could deal with, I thought; attempted rape I could not.

I leaned my shoulder against the bedpost and said quietly, "Catherine, why should you think your come out will be such a failure?"

"Because I'm ugly and stupid and I wear spectacles," came the immediately reply.

I stared at her in dismay. "Catherine! What a terrible thing to say of yourself!"

"It's true," she said stubbornly. She lifted her eyes from the rug and looked at me. "You'll find a husband, Georgie. You have soft shiny hair and big brown eyes

and a nice smile and you don't wear spectacles." She
pushed her own spectacles back up on her nose. "I don't
think Mama will be very happy about presenting you
alongside of me, but I don't mind. It will be nice to have
a friend."

"I will be happy to have a friend as well," I said. And
I meant it.

I met the Countess of Winterdale for the first time in
the downstairs drawing room as we were waiting to be
summoned for dinner. She was seated on the rose-colored
sofa upon which I had sat earlier that afternoon, addressing
herself to her nephew, who was leaning against the wall
next to the alabaster fireplace. Lord Winterdale listened in
silence, regarding her with an ironic expression on his
face.

Catherine was seated next to her mother, looking as if
she were trying to become invisible.

"Good evening," I said as I walked into the room.

"Ah," said Lord Winterdale in the cool, faintly sarcastic voice that I remembered and that Catherine feared, "here
is Miss Newbury now. Allow me to present my ward to
you, Aunt Agatha. Miss Newbury, Lady Winterdale."

"My lady," I said and went up to her and curtsied. "It
is very kind of you to bring me out with Catherine, and I
wish to thank you," I continued politely.

Lady Winterdale had a pointy nose, a pointy chin, and
a thin mouth. She looked mean. She did not acknowledge
my introduction but turned the whole upper part of her
body toward Lord Winterdale, glaring at him in outrage,
and said, "I thought you told me she was *reasonably presentable*."

Even though I did not look at him, I could feel his blue eyes fixed upon me.

"Well," he said appraisingly, "I think she is."

I will not let him irritate me, I thought. I turned to face him at last and said very gravely, "Thank you, my lord. You are too kind."

The reckless eyebrows flew upward. "Really? That is not a virtue of which I am often accused, Miss Newbury."

The wretch looked as if he were enjoying himself.

The blue eyes returned to Lady Winterdale and he said amiably, "Are you taking the girls shopping tomorrow, Aunt Agatha?"

Lady Winterdale looked as if she might be going to have an apoplexy. "Do you really expect me to buy clothes for this . . . this person, Philip?"

I dug my nails into my palms in my effort to keep my mouth shut. I could not afford to alienate this wretched woman. I needed her too much.

"I thought we had agreed that you would buy sufficient clothes for a Season for Miss Newbury, and for Catherine, too, of course. And as I also told you, Aunt Agatha, you may have the bills for both girls sent to me," Lord Winterdale returned.

One could almost see the monumental struggle going on inside of Lady Winterdale. On the one hand she didn't want anyone who was going to take attention away from Catherine coming out with her, but on the other hand she didn't want to foot the bills for the come out either.

To my relief, greed won out.

"Very well," she said tightly. "Tomorrow we will go shopping."

I couldn't prevent a smile of satisfaction from spreading over my face. I had no idea why Lord Winterdale so

disliked his aunt, but it was working very much in my favor
that he did.

The dining room at Mansfield House was large and
elegant. The three apses on each of the long walls were
filled with marble statues of classical origin, and the walls
themselves were painted a pale green. The doorways, windows, and the chimneypiece of white alabaster were distinguished by the beauty, simplicity, and elegance of their
detail.

The food served by the Mansfield House chef was
equally splendid. We had Soupe à la Bonne Femme, fried
perch, rolled beef steaks, and pineapple in mould for
dessert.

Unfortunately, the company was not in the same class
as the food and the surroundings. Lady Winterdale held
forth in solitary monologue as one course succeeded the
other. Ostensibly, she was addressing Lord Winterdale,
whom she called "dear Philip," but "dear Philip" did not
appear to pay attention to a single word she spoke. He ate
his meal as if he were not very hungry and as if he couldn't
wait to be somewhere else.

In truth, I couldn't blame him.

Over the rolled steak, Lady Winterdale began to discourse about the ball. "I should like to schedule it for April
18, Philip," she said. "That will put us right at the beginning of the Season. No point in waiting, is there?"

Lord Winterdale looked bored. "The date is entirely
up to you, Aunt Agatha. I only ask that you tell Mrs.
Hawkins. She will be the one who will be most inconve-
nienced by so large a party."

"You forget, Philip, that Mrs. Hawkins and I were together for many years," Lady Winterdale said tightly. "You

do not need to tell me how to get along with my old house-keeper."

For the first time I felt a pang of sympathy for Lady Winterdale. It could not be easy for her, having to beg her nephew for the use of the house she had long reigned over as mistress.

A flash of brilliant blue darted from Lord Winterdale's eyes as he shot a quick glance at his aunt. "If you remember, I offered to get another housekeeper and relinquish Mrs. Hawkins to you, Aunt Agatha. You did not wish to employ her."

Lady Winterdale drew herself up. "I cannot afford to pay Hawkins's salary out of my widow's portion."

Lord Winterdale's mouth curved sardonically. "I might believe that sad tale if I were not privy to exactly how much money my uncle did leave you, Aunt Agatha. So please don't cry poverty to me."

"I have my old age to think about," Lady Winterdale said with tragic dignity. "I have the future of my child."

Lord Winterdale's black eyebrows flew upward in exaggerated surprise. "Good heavens, have I been mistaken all along? I thought the whole purpose of this Season was to find Catherine a husband so that her future would be secured. Are you planning to keep her single so that she can serve as a nursemaid to yourself, Aunt Agatha?"

Poor Catherine, who had spoken not a word during the entire dinner, put down her head and looked as if she would like to slide under the table.

It was time for a diversion, so I said to Lord Winterdale, "I believe I met an acquaintance of yours the last time I was in London, my lord. Do you know Lord Henry Sloan?"

He turned away from Lady Winterdale, a predator

briefly distracted from his prey. "Yes, I know Lord Henry. Where did you meet him, Miss Newbury?"

"I met him at Madame Tussaud's exhibit when I was last in town. He was very gallant and rescued me from the attentions of a most unpleasant man."

The faintest of lines appeared on Lord Winterdale's brow, and I could see him turning his mind back to my last visit to London.

"You only came to London with your maid," he said abruptly. "What the devil were you doing at Madame Tussaud's?"

The remains of the rolled steak and the side dishes were cleared from the table, the cloth was removed, and the pineapple moulds were brought in.

I said, answering Lord Winterdale's last question, "Maria and I went to look at the exhibit, of course. I wanted to go to Westminster Cathedral, but Maria was so anxious to see Madame Tussaud's that I gave in. I must say, I was glad I did. It was fascinating."

No one at the table appeared to be terribly interested in Madame Tussaud's, however. What did seem to exercise their attention was the fact that I had gone there unescorted.

"Miss Newbury, I will not present you if you continue to behave in so ill-bred a manner," Lady Winterdale informed me, putting down her dessert spoon.

"What was happening that Sloan felt that it was necessary to rescue you?" Lord Winterdale asked abruptly.

"Oh, nothing terrible," I assured him. "A young man of the merchant classes kept following me around trying to impress me with his knowledge. I wasn't frightened or anything; I was just annoyed. Lord Henry saw what was happening, however, and soon sent him about his business."

"Very gallant of Lord Henry indeed," Lord Winterdale said with that sarcastic tone in his voice that so intimidated Catherine.

"I thought so," I replied spiritedly. "He showed us around the exhibit himself and I told him that I was your ward, my lord, and that I would be making my come out this season with Lady Catherine."

"You told him you were my ward?" The sardonic look on Lord Winterdale's face was very pronounced. "And what did he say to that?"

"Oh, he just said that we would doubtless be seeing each other as he was spending the Season at his father's house."

"Lord Henry is only the younger son of a duke, but I believe he is to inherit some small amount of money from an uncle," Lady Winterdale said. "He might be an eligible *parti* for you, Miss Newbury."

"Have you ferreted out the financial dirt on every bachelor in London, Aunt Agatha?" Lord Winterdale asked ironically.

"It is the duty of a mother," Lady Winterdale replied with majestic calm.

Lord Winterdale's eyes went to Catherine, who had spoken not a single word during the entire meal. "True," he said, not even trying to hide his amusement.

I said to Catherine, "Have you ever been shopping in London before, Catherine? I haven't."

Lady Winterdale answered, "Of course Catherine has been shopping in London, Miss Newbury. She is not a little nobody from the provinces. Her father was the Earl of Winterdale, and until the tragic accident that took his and her brother's life, she lived in London. In this house!" She glared in loathing at the present Lord Winterdale.

He looked back, and what I saw on his face frightened

me. It must have frightened Lady Winterdale, too, because she looked away from him quickly and turned her pointy nose in my direction.

She said, "I do not believe I have ever learned how you came to be my nephew's ward, Miss Newbury. Surely it seems odd that a man as young and as . . . ah, shall we say, notorious . . . as my nephew should be made the guardian of two young women."

I remembered what I had heard Lord Winterdale tell her when I was hiding behind the drapery in the library and said glibly, "My father was a good friend of Lord Winterdale's father, you see. That is how it came about."

Lady Winterdale looked incredulous. It came to me that this was a reaction I was going to have to deal with all Season long. Perhaps Lord Winterdale and I could come up with a better tale.

I tried again with Catherine. "What is your favorite color, Catherine? Mine is pink."

"Catherine looks well in blue," said Lady Winterdale. "It matches her eyes."

I said evenly, "I believe I asked Catherine what her favorite color was, Lady Winterdale, not you."

Lady Winterdale's nose and chin became pointier than usual, and she looked so surprised by my impertinence that she did not reply.

Catherine said in a small thin voice, "Mama is right, Georgie. Blue is my favorite color."

"Then perhaps we can get a come-out dress in blue for you and one in pink for me," I said cheerfully.

"Miss Newbury, obviously you are unaware of the fact that young girls at their first ball always wear white," Lady Winterdale said, clearly pleased that she could once again score over the "little nobody from the provinces."

Lord Winterdale stood up. "This has been such a delightful family dinner, but I fear that I must tear myself away. Have a pleasant evening, ladies, discussing the ways in which you are going to spend my money tomorrow."

The three of us watched in silence as he walked toward the door. His hair was as black as his evening coat, and as I observed his lithe dark figure, the image of a panther came irresistibly into my mind.

For the first time I fully understood Sir Charles's comment that he would not want any daughter of his residing under Philip Mansfield's roof.

After dinner was over, the three of us ladies retired to the green drawing room, which was one of the less formal drawing rooms on the second floor. It was lined with portraits of family and friends and the paneling on the wall was painted a pale green with white trim. There were half a dozen gilt armchairs with green-tapestry embroidery scattered around the room, a pianoforte in one corner, and a harp in the other. There was a rosewood writing desk between the tall, green-silk-hung windows and a rosewood sofa table in front of the green-silk sofa.

"Catherine will play the pianoforte for us," her mother announced as she ensconced herself in one of the tapestry chairs. "She is very good on the pianoforte."

I waited for Catherine to creep timidly toward the pianoforte, but she surprised me by approaching it with more authority than I had ever seen her display. She sat down on the bench, arranged her skirt, turned to me, and asked, "Is there anything in particular that you would like to hear, Georgie?"

"No," I answered. "Play whatever you like, Catherine."

She flexed her fingers, placed them on the keys, tilted

her head for a moment as if she were listening to an un-
heard note, and began to play.

I sat as one transported. This was not the kind of playing every young miss learns in the schoolroom. Even I,
who am not notably musical, could hear that this was the
real thing.

"That was absolutely wonderful, Catherine," I said
when she had finished. "You didn't tell me you were a musician."

My words were simple, but Catherine flushed with
pleasure. She said, "The pianoforte is not in perfect tune. I
shall have to ask my cousin if I might have it seen to."

Nothing could have made it clearer to me how important the pianoforte was to Catherine than her willingness to
brave Lord Winterdale to ask for something.

"She would play the pianoforte all day long if I did
not make her stop," Lady Winterdale announced, partly
with pride and partly with annoyance. "She has quite ruined
her eyesight from peering at the notes."

"I don't peer at the notes, Mama," Catherine said. "I
have told you that many times."

Lady Winterdale waved her hand, dismissing her
daughter's words as unreliable. "I have never approved of
your spending five and six hours a day practicing, but it did
keep you occupied while you were a girl. You are a young
woman now, however, and there will be many other things
to occupy you while you are making your come out into society." Lady Winterdale gave her daughter a gimlet stare.
"It is always desirable to make a good impression with an
instrument, Catherine, but you must take care that people
don't think you *odd*."

I stared at Lady Winterdale in astonishment. Couldn't

she see what a brilliant musician she had in her own daughter. Wasn't she proud of Catherine?

Catherine's eyes were downcast. She looked quite desperate. "No, Mama," she said.

The tea tray came in and both Catherine and I sat and listened to Lady Winterdale discourse on the day she had planned for us tomorrow. We would go to the shops on Bond Street during the morning. "That is the time for ladies to shop," Lady Winterdale informed us. "The shops belong to the gentlemen after two and it would not do for us to be seen on Bond Street then."

This seemed odd to me. In a country village one could shop at any time one wished, but I wasn't going to question Lady Winterdale's superior knowledge.

"In the afternoon, we will write out the invitations to the ball," Lady Winterdale said. "And I must begin to see about ordering the flowers and arranging for the food. We must serve only the best champagne. And I believe I shall have lobster patties for supper."

I thought of all the money that the shopping expedition and the ball was going to cost Lord Winterdale and wondered again what he must hold against his aunt that causing her any kind of discomfort was worth it.

CHAPTER
five

WE SPENT A WEEK SHOPPING UP AND DOWN BOND Street. I had never in my life seen so many pretty clothes and I have to confess that I enjoyed myself hugely. We bought morning dresses to wear for when gentlemen called upon us at home in the morning and walking dresses and pelisses to wear if we should go on an expedition outdoors in the afternoon. We bought carriage dresses to wear should we go for a drive in Hyde Park and both Catherine and I got a new riding habit to wear should we prefer to ride. Needless to say, all of these garments required matching bonnets and boots, for which we visited a variety of Bond Street milliners and bootmakers. Then we shopped the Pantheon Bazaar for gloves and stockings.

I must confess that I took to shopping like a duck to water. While it would have been much nicer if I had not been forced to bear the company of Lady Winterdale, whose personality definitely did not improve upon further acquaintance, and whose taste I had constantly to overrule, as it was execrable, I had been poor all my life and nothing could destroy my pleasure in the lovely and elegant garments that began to fill the great mahogany wardrobe in my dressing room.

Unfortunately Catherine did not share my pleasure. Nothing could have been clearer to me as we bustled from shop to shop, that she would much have preferred to be at home playing the piano. She did play the pianoforte for us after dinner, but her mother always made her stop after an hour, and it was so apparent that an hour was not enough for her that my heart ached for her pain and frustration.

It was becoming more and more obvious to me that Catherine needed to marry a man who loved music, who would be proud of her talent and who would let her practice for as long as she chose.

There had to be such a man somewhere in this vast city, I thought. We would just have to find him.

I saw little of Lord Winterdale during the two weeks before the ball, except for an occasional glimpse as he went into the library or left the house completely. He dined at his club most nights, leaving his three female guests to their own company. I thought this was excessively rude of him, but then I had come to expect rudeness from Lord Winterdale and I tried not to let it irritate me. After all, I told myself firmly, if it was not for him I would not be making my come out at all.

I also reminded myself that he did get someone in to tune the pianoforte for Catherine, which led me to hope that perhaps he was not as utterly insensitive as he appeared.

I had been thinking and worrying about the story he had concocted about my being named his ward, and on the day before the ball I managed to catch him in the library before he disappeared for the day so that I could discuss my concern with him.

I opened the door to find him sitting at his desk, going through an extensive pile of what looked like bills. I felt the faintest twinge of guilt as I thought that they were probably the bills for our many shopping expeditions.

"Yes, Miss Newbury?" he asked, looking up as I said his name.

"Might I speak to you for a moment, my lord?" I asked politely.

"Come in," he said, folding his hands on top of the pile of papers and preparing to bestow upon me the honor of his attention.

The Mansfield House library was not as grand as the rooms in the rest of the house. The bookshelves that lined the room were made of chestnut wood and the walls above them were painted a dark gold. The ceiling and the moldings were painted white and the Turkish rug on the floor was green and gold and red. The fireplace was the most impressive thing about the room. It was dark green marble and above it hung a picture of a thoroughbred on Newmarket Heath that looked as if it had been painted by Stubbs.

I advanced now into the room and this time I did not wait to be invited to sit before I took the green-velvet-covered armchair that was placed on the far side of Lord Winterdale's desk.

He looked at me, his thin, hard face expressionless, his startling blue eyes steady. "What do you wish to see me about, Miss Newbury?" he asked.

"I don't think this story you have concocted about my father naming you as my guardian is going to fly, my lord," I said bluntly. "Lady Winterdale has mentioned her skepticism to me several times, and I have a suspicion that I am going to hear similar comments all Season long. I fear that it might very well affect my chances of catching a husband."

"I see," he said. His hands moved slightly, drawing my attention to the thin-boned, strong, ringless fingers resting on the huge pile of bills. He asked courteously, "And do you have any other suggestions as to how we might account for the fact that I requested my aunt to bring you out?"

As a matter of fact, I did have another suggestion. "I thought that perhaps we might say that my father had named your *uncle* to be my guardian, my lord," I said. "Your uncle appears to have been a perfectly respectable man, and my being named his ward would cause no great surprise. Then, we could say that after your uncle died you felt it incumbent upon yourself to take over your uncle's responsibility to me." I looked at him, proud of my invention. "How do you think that sounds?"

A flash of amusement showed in his eyes. "Damned peculiar," he said immediately.

I gave him an affronted stare. I had, of course, heard the word *damn* many times, but it was not very nice of him to say it to me. Nor did I like his disparagement of my idea.

He continued as if he had not seen my outraged look at all, "To put it bluntly, Miss Newbury, outside the gambling tables, your father and my uncle did not move in the same social circles. I cannot imagine any circumstances under which my uncle would agree to take on the indigent daughters of a notorious gambler as his wards."

I felt myself flush. "Your uncle was scarcely a paragon, Lord Winterdale. He was a card cheat, after all."

"Ah, but the *ton* does not know that, do they?" he returned blandly. "Nor do they know that he was being blackmailed by your father. All they know was that he was, as you say, an extremely respectable man—which, regrettably, your father was not."

His words made me angry, but reluctantly I had to admit that they also made sense. "But it sounds so suspect that Papa would have left Anna and me the wards of a twenty-six-year-old man, who, from what I understand, has an extremely disreputable reputation!"

Those reckless eyebrows lifted, and I said with dignity, "I am sorry, my lord, but that is what I have heard from everyone I have talked to. It just looks . . . suspect."

He shrugged, a supple, elegant gesture. "I am afraid there is nothing we can do about it, Miss Newbury. We must just rely on my Aunt Agatha's undoubted respectability to counteract my own regrettably disreputable reputation. And I can assure you that while Aunt Agatha may be a dragon, her consequence in good society is enormous. She is a personal friend of several of the patronesses of Almack's, and this ball she is throwing will be attended by all of the most important people in London."

I bit my lip. "I don't like her," I said. "Haven't you noticed how horrid she is to Catherine?"

"No one is forcing you to go through with this come out if you don't choose to, Miss Newbury," he said. His eyes drifted pointedly to the pile of bills under his hands. "If I remember correctly, it was you who blackmailed me, not the other way around."

"You don't have to keep reminding me of that," I said irritably. "I can only assure you that I did what I did out of necessity, not desire."

He gave me a cool, ironic look that only increased my ire. The fact that he was in the right and I was in the wrong was utterly infuriating.

Then he said unexpectedly, "Do you ride?"

I could feel my whole face light up. I had had to leave my beloved mare Corina down at Weldon Hall, and I missed her more than I could say. "Yes," I said, "I do."

"Would you like to come for a ride in the park with

me this afternoon? It is a fine day, and I have a nice sensible gelding in the stable whom you could ride."

Nice and sensible also sounded boring, but I was so happy at the thought of being in the saddle again that I didn't object. "A ride sounds wonderful," I said sincerely.

"Very well. I will tell Fiske to have the horses ready for us this afternoon. Be in the stable yard a little after four."

For the very first time since we had met, I gave him a real smile. "Thank you, my lord," I said. "That will be absolutely lovely."

He looked back at me, his face inscrutable, and did not reply.

As in many of the homes in Grosvenor Square, the stables were immediately behind the house, separated from the terrace by a small garden. I arrived in the stable yard at exactly four o'clock and stood looking around with curiosity.

The stable building and the carriage house took up most of the available space and were built of the same brown brick as was the house. I thought with pity of the poor horses confined within the stable with no place to be turned out for exercise or fresh air. It must be hard to be a horse in London.

As I was standing there, two men leading saddled horses came from within the stable building into the yard. To my surprise, I saw that one of the men was Lord Winterdale. He was smiling, and for the first time since I had met him his unguarded face looked as young as I knew he was.

The man who was holding the other horse, obviously the Head Groom, saw me and said something to Lord Winterdale. The smile disappeared from his lordship's face, he nodded, and the groom began to lead a very solid-looking bay gelding in my direction.

"Good afternoon, Miss," he said. "I'm Fiske, his lordship's Head Groom, and this is Cato. He's a real gentleman, Miss, and wise to London traffic. You won't have to worry about a thing. He'll take care of you just fine."

I patted Cato's thick glossy neck. He was in excellent condition, but he was clearly no longer young. "Hello there, fellow," I said.

Fiske led Cato to the mounting block and I mounted into the sidesaddle, hooking my knee around the horn and arranging my skirts. I was wearing my old habit, as the new one Lady Winterdale had ordered for me was not yet ready.

Lord Winterdale walked his horse over to me, and I stared with reverence at the beautiful black thoroughbred mare he was riding. She had a perfect white streak down the middle of her face, but the rest of her was like black silk. Her neck was long and arched, her shoulder ideally sloped, her legs perfectly clean, her hindquarters well muscled. This was a horse who was not only well looked after, she was also obviously well ridden.

"What a beauty!" I said sincerely.

"This is Isabelle," he replied with the friendliest look I had yet gotten from him. "She has already been out this morning, so she should be perfectly content to walk and trot."

"I can assure you, my lord, that I am perfectly capable of riding to more than a walk and a trot," I said testily. "In fact, at home I have even been known to gallop over fences."

"Have you indeed?" he murmured, as if he didn't believe me.

I ground my teeth and held my tongue.

He looked at me more closely. "Good God, didn't Aunt Agatha buy you a riding habit? I'm sure there was a bill for a riding habit in that enormous pile on my desk this morning."

I said very calmly, "Lady Winterdale did indeed purchase a new riding habit for me, my lord. It is not yet ready, however."

He was looking at the habit I was wearing as if it was a rag.

"There is nothing wrong with this habit," I said indignantly. "It is excessively comfortable, I'll have you know. The new one Lady Winterdale ordered for me will not be half as pleasant to ride in."

A flash of genuine humor lit Lord Winterdale's thin, dark face. "Haven't you learned yet, Miss Newbury, that the more comfortable a garment is, the more unfashionable it is likely to be?"

It was astonishing how intensely attractive his face became when that cold ironic look was replaced by warmth. The change was brief, however, and as we turned to leave the stable yard I was once more confronted by his chill, hard profile.

It was a short walk from Grosvenor Square to the Oxford Street entrance to Hyde Park and as we entered in under the trees I smiled with delight. The busy streets of London were exciting, certainly, but there was no doubt that I had missed the green beauty of the country.

"The usual promenade of the *ton* does not begin until about five," Lord Winterdale informed me, "so we have a brief respite before the paths become too clogged with traffic to do anything but stop and socialize with the people who are here only to be seen."

"Can we go for a canter?" I asked eagerly.

He gave me a speculative look. Then, "Why not?" he said. "I think you can trust Cato."

His disparaging remarks on my horsemanship annoyed me no end, and I didn't wait for him to say anything more before I asked the bay gelding for a canter. He moved off smoothly and after a minute Lord Winterdale appeared at my side on Isabelle. The two horses cantered along side by side under the greening oak trees, and I rode easily in a forward seat the way I did at home when I rode cross-country with Corina.

The path along the Hyde Park lake called the Serpentine was fairly empty at this hour, and we were able to increase our speed. Cato surprised me with his enthusiasm, and our horses stretched out side by side in a nice long gallop. When finally we pulled up I laughed and patted Cato's warm neck and Lord Winterdale looked at me with surprise and approval.

"You do ride well," he said.

It was absurd how delighted I was by his compliment. "Thank you, my lord," I said. "I would ask you to send for my own mare, but she is used to being outdoors all day long, and I'm afraid the confinement of a London stable would be detrimental to her health."

As we rode back the way we had come I found that the park was beginning to grow crowded with fashionable carriages and well-turned-out men and women on horseback. All of the horseflesh was sleek and shiny and all of the carriages sparkled with cleanliness. The men and women were dressed in the height of elegance. The men wore immaculate buff breeches and polished riding boots with black or brown riding coats; the women's outfits were more varied: from curricle dresses and pelisses, to the kind of full-skirted riding habit that Lady Winterdale had ordered for me.

It was an incomparably rich-looking scene and, truthfully, I found it slightly intimidating. Was I mad to think that one of these aristocratic, elegant-looking gentleman was going to want to marry *me*?

Lord Winterdale and I were walking our horses side by side, each of us thinking our own thoughts, when we were approached by a young woman on a chestnut horse who was accompanied by a gentleman riding a handsome bay.

"Lord Winterdale," the woman said in a well-bred, faintly husky voice. "How delightful to see you. You so rarely ride in the park at this hour."

"Miss Stanhope," Winterdale returned. "How do you do. May I present my ward, Miss Georgiana Newbury. Miss Newbury, this is Miss Helen Stanhope and her brother Mr. George Stanhope."

Miss Stanhope was extremely beautiful, with satiny black hair and long green eyes. She was wearing a green habit that matched her eyes exactly.

"How do you do," I said with a friendly smile. "It is very nice to meet you Miss Stanhope, Mr. Stanhope."

Miss Stanhope gave me a look that was noticeably cool. On the other hand, her brother's smile was extremely amiable. "A pleasure to make your acquaintance, Miss Newbury," he said. "It certainly came as a shock to the *ton* to learn that Winterdale had acquired a ward, but I can see that you will be a very welcome addition to our social circle this Season."

"Thank you, Mr. Stanhope," I said. "Will you be coming to our ball tomorrow evening?"

"We certainly shall," Mr. Stanhope said. He had black

hair like his sister, but his eyes were a less brilliant green. "May I hope that you will save me a dance?"

One of my terrors about tomorrow's ball had been that no one would ask me to dance, so now I gave Mr. Stanhope a big, relieved smile. "I should be delighted to save you a dance, Mr. Stanhope," I said. "Thank you for asking me."

"And I hope you will save me a dance, Miss Stanhope," Lord Winterdale asked politely.

That lady bestowed upon him a far more restrained smile than the one I had given to her brother. I noticed that she answered rather quickly, however. "Of course, my lord. Shall I pencil you in for the quadrille? Or would you prefer a waltz?"

"What about both?" Lord Winterdale said.

Miss Stanhope could not conceal her pleasure with this arrangement and agreed to accommodate him with both those dances.

"Will there be waltzing at the ball?" I asked in surprise. We did not waltz in the country, and I did not know the steps.

"There will be no waltzing for you, Miss Newbury," Miss Stanhope informed me patronizingly. "You may not waltz until one of the patronesses of Almack's approves you, you know."

Almack's was the most exclusive club in London, known colloquially as the marriage mart, and even a country bumpkin such as I knew the importance of attending the balls at Almack's.

I asked apprehensively, "What if they do not approve me?"

"If they do not approve you, then you will not get a voucher for Almack's, and if you do not get a voucher for Almack's, you will not be invited to any of the balls that are given by the best people in London," Miss Stanhope informed me. "In short, you will be relegated to the second-best society." She looked down her aristocratic nose at me. "It is very difficult to please the patronesses, I am afraid. They do not like young girls who deviate from behavior that is considered socially correct."

I knew immediately that she was referring to my lack of mourning for my father.

"I believe my aunt has already spoken to Lady Jersey and Countess Lieven about getting vouchers for my cousin and my ward," Lord Winterdale said coolly. "I do not think that they will have a problem being approved for Almack's."

Miss Stanhope could not quite conceal her annoyance, and I could not quite conceal my relief.

Evidently Lord Winterdale had been correct when he had said that his aunt's consequence was enormous.

Then I wondered when he had spoken to Lady Winterdale to ascertain this information. He was certainly never around the house when I was there.

"Are you enjoying London, Miss Newbury?" Mr. Stanhope asked me.

I laughed. "Well, all I have seen of it so far is Bond Street, but I must say that I have liked that very much indeed."

Miss Stanhope's cool green eyes took in my worn gray habit. "You did not purchase that habit on Bond Street, I hope?"

I was beginning to dislike Miss Stanhope exceedingly, but I tried very hard to hold on to my temper. "My new habit was not yet ready, so I am wearing my old one," I said.

Lord Winterdale said, "I can assure you, Miss Stanhope, that once Miss Newbury mounts into the saddle, no one will notice what she is wearing." He turned to me and smiled. "Miss Newbury has quite the best seat I have ever seen on a woman."

For the second time that afternoon, the hardness had melted away from his face, and I saw youth and a hint of sweetness that was inordinately fascinating. Then, as before, it was gone.

We parted from the Stanhopes a few moment's later, and though a number of people waved to Lord Winterdale as we trotted back along the path, he did not stop again.

CHAPTER

SIX

WHEN I AWOKE THE MORNING OF THE BALL, IT WAS raining. This was depressing as I knew that Lady Winterdale would certainly consider the weather a personal affront to her, and when I went down to breakfast I quickly discovered that this was indeed so.

"The streets become so dirty in London when it rains," she was complaining to a silent Catherine, as I came into the dining room. Lord Winterdale was, as usual, absent from the breakfast table.

"Fortunately, no one who will be coming to the ball tonight will have planned to come on foot," Lady Winterdale went on as she made her way through a plate of ham and cold fowl. "We shall have to make certain that our footmen have plenty of umbrellas to escort our guests safely from their carriages into the house. But there can be no doubt that this rain is a decided nuisance. I am seriously displeased."

I took a plate of eggs and a cup of coffee from the sideboard. The dining room was gloomy, lit only by a few candles set on the table and the sideboard. The great crystal chandelier, which provided the light for dinner, was never lit during the day.

I said, "Perhaps the rain will let up by this evening, ma'am."

"I certainly hope that it will," said Lady Winterdale

majestically. "Now, Catherine, I want you to make certain that you have your hair washed today. I will send Melton to do it for you. And take a nap this afternoon. It is important for you to be fresh this evening. Gentlemen do not like to see girls who have circles under their eyes. Dinner will commence at six-thirty and the ball at nine and you girls will probably not see your beds much before two o'clock this morning."

I thought this sounded very exciting. The few dances I had attended in the country had always ended promptly at eleven.

Catherine said, "Shouldn't Georgie have her hair washed, too, Mama?"

Lady Winterdale gave me an austere look. "I am afraid that I cannot spare my dresser to you as well as to Catherine, Georgiana. If you wish to have your hair washed, perhaps one of the maids will do it for you."

"I am sure that Betty will help me, my lady," I said cheerfully. Betty was one of the chambermaids, and she had been acting as a lady's maid for me whenever I needed her.

Lady Winterdale compressed her lips and nodded.

"Is there anything I can do to help you today, Lady Winterdale?" I asked. I had not realized how tremendous an undertaking a ball the scale of the one Lady Winterdale had planned would be, and all of the work had fallen upon Lady Winterdale's shoulders. All Catherine and I had been allowed to do so far was to help write out invitations.

"You can help me by keeping out of my way, Georgiana," Lady Winterdale replied grimly.

Very briefly, my eyes met Catherine's and we both looked away.

"Yes, ma'am," I said, and began to eat my eggs.

After luncheon Betty brought a basin of heated water to my room and we washed my hair. After the fourth rinse with fresh heated water, she pronounced it clean of soap, and I wrapped it in a towel and dried it as best I could. Then I put a dry towel around my shoulders and combed my hair so that it fell rain-straight halfway down my back. There was nothing more to be done until it dried.

I went next to Catherine's room and found her undergoing the same procedure at the hands of Melton, Lady Winterdale's dresser. Melton was one of those superior servants who have a very exaggerated sense of their own worth, and she had begun by treating me as if I were less than the dirt beneath her feet. I do not take kindly to such treatment, however, and Melton and I had had words. We had since achieved a kind of truce; neither of us liked the other, but we were icily polite.

I sat down in a chair and waited for Catherine to be finished. Unlike mine, her hair had curl and I thought that she would look well in one of the new shorter styles. Lady Winterdale liked her hair bunched in front of her ears, however. I thought it only called attention to the thinness of Catherine's face and took attention away from her best feature, which was her eyes.

Catherine would have liked to cut her hair also, mainly because it would require less trouble to arrange. Unfortunately, this was one more issue on which she was not able to stand up to her mother.

Once Catherine was done, I suggested, "Why don't we go down to the green drawing room and you can play the piano for me while our hair dries?"

The girl's face lit to beauty. "Oh Georgie, that would be wonderful." Then the light died out. "But Mama said I was to take a nap."

"You can't nap with a wet head," I said practically. "And besides, your mother is so busy that she won't even notice what you're doing." I got up from the small silk-upholstered chair that was placed before Catherine's fire. "Let's go."

The drawing room was damp and chilly, and I had one of the servants add some coals and stoke up a nice warm fire for us. Then I pulled one of the tapestry chairs over in front of the fireplace and settled down to listen to Catherine play.

She played for three hours and while I listened I thought about many things. I thought about home, about Anna, about Frank, about the ball. About Lord Winterdale. Both Catherine and I had perfectly dry hair by the time Lady Winterdale finally came hustling in to shoo Catherine upstairs so that she could get dressed. A number of very important people were to dine with us before the ball, two of whom were patronesses of Almack's, and Lady Winterdale was most anxious for Catherine to make a good impression.

It also became clear to me that she was apprehensive about Lord Winterdale's behavior. "I hope Philip makes an effort to converse with at least a semblance of politeness," she said to me as Catherine put away her music. "He is the host this evening, and it will behoove him to exert himself to show a degree of civility to his guests."

"Surely Lord Winterdale will be polite in his own house, ma'am," I said in surprise.

"Who knows how far Philip will go to embarrass me," Lady Winterdale replied acidly. Her pointy nose quivered, and the uncomfortable idea occurred to me that his aunt was not the only person whom Lord Winterdale might like to see embarrassed this evening.

Good God, I thought with momentary panic, could his willingness to host this ball have been part of a diabolical plan to get revenge on Lady Winterdale and me? Was he going to do something tonight to humiliate the both of us?

Surely not, I answered myself. Surely no one would go to such expense just to cause embarrassment to someone else.

"Come along, Catherine," Lady Winterdale said. She turned to me as a definite afterthought. "You too, Georgiana. Time to think about getting dressed. I am sure that Betty will help you."

"She has said that she would," I returned. I didn't leave the room immediately, however, but went over to close the cover of the pianoforte. I was standing there, staring worriedly at the instrument and thinking of Lady Winterdale's words about her nephew, when I heard someone at the door. I looked up and saw him standing there watching me.

"Miss Newbury," he said. His eyes flicked over me, lingering on my loose hair. By now it was perfectly dry and hung around my shoulders like a mantle.

I could feel myself flush. "Catherine and I had our hair washed for the ball and then we came down here so that Catherine could play the piano while it dried," I explained.

He nodded and advanced slowly into the room. I stood with my back against the piano and watched him approach me. He stopped perhaps two feet away and said, "I presume that my estimable aunt has everything well in train for this evening?"

Raindrops sparkled on his black hair and the shoulders of his caped driving coat.

"Yes." My voice sounded oddly breathless, and I

cleared my throat. "I see that it has not yet stopped raining."

"No, it has not."

Then he did a shocking thing. He reached out, took a strand of my hair and ran his fingers along the length of it, all the way from my ear to its evenly cut ends. His touch was frighteningly enjoyable. "Your hair feels like silk," he said.

"It doesn't curl," I babbled. "Not even a curling iron works on it."

"What does that matter?" he said. "It is beautiful the way it is." My heartbeat began to accelerate dangerously. He was looking at me out of narrowed blue eyes and I pressed back harder against the piano. I could feel the top of it digging into my backbone.

"My lord," I said a little desperately, "I think it is time for me to go upstairs and get ready for dinner."

He was close enough to me that I could smell the dampness of rain on his skin and hair. After what seemed to be a long time, he nodded and stepped back, giving me room to get by him.

"Certainly," he said indifferently.

As I climbed the stairs, I wasn't sure what bothered me the most about our encounter: his attention or his indifference.

I had picked out my ball gown myself, and it was beautiful: an ivory-colored high-waisted frock trimmed with a bias fold of pink satin up each side of the front. The epaulet sleeves were also edged with pink satin and fastened in front of the arm with small satin buttons. The decolletage of the neckline was certainly lower than what I was accustomed to, but I thought it made me look quite satisfactorily sophisticated.

Betty was very helpful, getting me into the dress and doing up all the back-fastenings. Then she fixed my newly washed and shining hair into an intricate arrangement of braids on the top of my head.

I had a small string of pearls that had belonged to my mother and a matching pair of pearl earrings, and these I put on. I was standing in front of the cheval glass, admiring myself unashamedly, when there came a knock on the door. Betty went to answer it and returned carrying a bouquet of pink roses.

"'Tis from his lordship, Miss Newbury," Betty told me with glee.

I should not have been so thrilled. I told myself that I would be expected to be carrying a bouquet, that he was only playing his role in sending it, but the fact of the matter was, I was thrilled with those roses.

Betty came over to give me the bouquet and while she was doing that Melton came to my door and announced that Lady Winterdale would like me to come downstairs to be ready to greet the dinner guests.

I turned away from the mirror, drew a long breath to unfluster myself, and went out into the passageway.

Lady Winterdale and Catherine were just ahead of me, walking toward the stairs. I caught up with them at the landing and Catherine turned to look at me.

"Georgie!" she said. "You look beautiful."

I smiled at her. "Thank you, Catherine. So do you."

Her dress was a white frock with blue satin trim and I noticed that she was carrying a bouquet of white roses tied with bouquet blue satin ribands. The white did not really become her, and the dress's decolletage made her look too thin.

I wished that I and not Lady Winterdale had been able to choose Catherine's dress.

Lady Winterdale was regarding me with tightened lips. "Did you paint your cheeks, Georgiana?" she asked ominously.

"Of course not, Lady Winterdale," I replied in surprise. "If I am rather flushed, it must be from excitement."

She did not look as if she believed me.

We began to go down the stairs, Lady Winterdale and Catherine side by side with me trailing along behind them. When we reached the second floor the ballroom doors were flung wide open and for the first time I was able to see the magic that Lady Winterdale had wrought.

The room was banked with white roses. She must have scoured all the greenhouses in the vicinity of London in order to get the enormous amounts of roses that bedecked that room. They were gathered in huge vases along the walls and in smaller vases around the ten elegant white columns that marched around the room. The ballroom had two magnificent crystal chandeliers and a polished oak floor and the circular columns were trimmed with gilt. Tonight the Mansfield House ballroom looked and smelled like a summer garden.

"Oh, my lady," I said reverently. "It is magnificent."

"I think it will be remembered," she replied with justifiable complacency. "Now, come along down to the front drawing room girls. Our dinner guests will be arriving shortly."

We turned back to the staircase and went down to the first floor of the house, where the dining room had been set for dinner. There would be a supper served later during the ball, but that would be laid out upstairs on the ballroom floor in one of the drawing rooms.

Lord Winterdale was standing at the window looking out at the rain when we came into the drawing room. He turned when he heard us.

"Ah," he said, "good evening, ladies. You are all looking in great beauty tonight."

His blue eyes went from his aunt, to Catherine, to me. They did not linger on me, and I suppressed a stab of disappointment. I had thought I looked particularly nice.

"I must thank you, Cousin Philip, for the bouquet," Catherine was saying shyly. "It is very pretty, and it matches my dress perfectly."

He gave her a brief nod. "I am glad you like it, Catherine." He paused, then added, "It becomes you."

She gave him a doubtful look.

I said, "I, too, must thank you for my bouquet, my lord." I succumbed to curiosity. "How did you know what colors our dresses were?"

"I asked my aunt," he replied briefly.

The sound of the knocker on the front door reverberated clearly into the drawing room. Lady Winterdale drew herself up, and the image of a knight girding himself to go into battle flashed into my mind. I repressed a smile and my eyes went to Lord Winterdale. He, too, was looking at his aunt, but the expression in his eyes was not at all humorous.

Once again I felt a flash of apprehension about how Lord Winterdale would conduct himself this evening.

The most important part of any dinner is the food, of course, and Lady Winterdale and Cook had spent many hours in deep discussion before coming up with the follow-

ing menu, which was served the evening of the Winterdale
Ball. I reprint it in full for those who are interested in such
things:

SOUPE A LA BONNE FEMME
LE POTAGE A LA BEAUVEAU

LE TURBOT, SAUCE AU HOMARD
LE DOREY GARNI D'EPERLANS FRITS
LE SAUMON A LA GENEVOISE

LES POULARDES A LA CONDE
LE DINDIN A LA PERIGUEUX
LES FILETS DE PERDREAUX SAUTES
A LA LUCULLUS

LE JAMBON DE WESTPHALIE A L'ESSENCE
LE CUISSEAU DE PORC A DEMI SEL
GARNI DE CHOUX
HAUNCHE DE VENAISON

PETITS PUITS D'AMOUR, GARNIS DE CONFITURES

LES GLACES

LES FRUITS

All of this food was served by eight footmen wearing
the green-velvet livery of Lord Winterdale, and as the various courses were served and removed, the guests con-
versed politely with the dinner partners whom Lady
Winterdale had placed upon either side of them.

I was seated between an elderly gentleman, who ate

as if he had never seen food before in his life, and Lord Henry Sloan, my knight-errant of Madame Tussaud's. Lord Henry was looking very elegant in his evening wear, and we had a very pleasant time chatting about the various activities that I might enjoy during my stay in London.

The surprise of the night, however, was Lord Winterdale, who proved himself to be an absolutely delightful host. The ladies on either side of him were utterly undone by his seemingly effortless charm. I watched as his black head bent toward Lady Jersey, one of the patronesses of Almack's. He said something, and she laughed and gave him a look that could only be described as coquettish. His eyes gleamed a pure sapphire blue.

As I watched he gave her a devastating smile, then he turned his attention to the lady on his other side, the Countess Lieven, another of the all-important patronesses. The Countess was well-known for her haughtiness, but it took less than a minute before she, too, fell a victim of Lord Winterdale's deliberately wielded magnetism.

How clever he was, I thought. And how dangerous.

Once more the predatory image of a panther slipped into my mind.

At last dinner was over and we went upstairs for the ball itself. Lord and Lady Winterdale and Catherine and I formed a receiving line at the top of the stairs, and people were introduced to Catherine and me before they proceeded into the brilliantly lit ballroom.

It soon became clear that Lady Winterdale's ball was going to be one of the great successes of the social season. People were packed onto the staircase waiting to get up to the second floor, and word came to us that the entire of Grosvenor Square was lined with carriages waiting to reach the front door so that their occupants could alight.

Lady Winterdale beamed as she said again and again,
"Allow me to introduce you to my daughter, Lady Catherine Mansfield, and to my nephew's ward, Miss Georgiana
Newbury." Catherine and I curtsied and curtsied and
smiled and smiled. It was delightful.

Then it was time for us to enter the ballroom and
open the dancing. I had another shock as I came in the
door and saw the room packed with people in full evening
regalia. The smell of the roses and of the many different
perfumes the women were wearing assailed my nostrils so
intensely that I almost stepped back. All of the wall
sconces were lit and the huge crystal chandeliers shed the
light from hundreds of candles onto the dance floor.

Lord Winterdale took Catherine out to the floor and
some earl I had never heard of escorted me. The line
formed up behind us, the music started, I curtsied to my
partner, and the dancing began.

Everything about the ball went perfectly until after
supper, which I ate with Lord Henry Sloan and a few other
young people in the yellow drawing room. I had looked
around for Catherine to see if she wanted to join us, but
she had been nowhere in sight, so we had gone along to
the supper room without her.

After the dinner I had eaten I hadn't thought I would
want to eat again, but the lobster patties were delicious and
I actually found myself hungry. I had some punch with the
patties and Lord Henry drank champagne, which he pronounced to be of the finest quality.

Not for the first time it occurred to me that this ball
must be costing Lord Winterdale a fortune.

After we had finished supper we returned to the ballroom. I was standing with Lord Henry and another young

gentleman when Lady Winterdale approached me with a rather heavyset, middle-aged gentleman.

"Georgiana," she said, "allow me to introduce Mr. George Asherton to you."

The name immediately set off an alarm bell in my head. Mr. Asherton was one of Papa's victims.

Mr. Asherton bowed, and I distinctly heard the creak of a corset. "Miss Newbury," he said. "I was a friend of your late father. I wonder if I might have the honor of this dance."

It had never occurred to me that I might meet one of Papa's victims in the course of my London stay. I had certainly no intention of seeking any of them out, and I had assumed that none of them would desire to meet me.

Evidently I had been wrong.

"Certainly," I said a little nervously, and allowed Mr. Asherton to lead me to the floor.

It was a country dance fortunately, and consequently there was little opportunity for us to talk. The next dance was a waltz, however, and since I could not dance the waltz, I was forced to stand in front of one of the ballroom columns with Mr. Asherton and listen to him talk.

He began by saying, "I received your communication, Miss Newbury."

"Mr. Asherton," I interrupted. "Please believe me when I say that there is no need for us to discuss this matter further. I can only deplore what my father did to you and assure you that the incriminating papers have been destroyed. The matter is over."

His round chubby face seemed oddly unlined for a man his age. It was also very pink. He said, "I would much have preferred to receive the papers back, Miss Newbury.

It is a little disturbing to have to rely on your word that they are destroyed."

I bristled, and said a little grandly, "I can assure you, Mr. Asherton, that my word can be trusted."

"Perhaps it can be, but you must confess that my experience with your family has not been a positive one," Mr. Asherton replied grimly. "Certainly it has not inclined me to trust anyone bearing the name of Newbury."

I glared at him. "I don't want any money from you, Mr. Asherton. What more can I tell you?"

Lord Winterdale's voice broke in on our tête à tête. "Ah, there you are, Miss Newbury. I was hoping that I might claim you for the next dance."

I looked at him in relief. For one thing, we had not yet danced, and to be truthful this had somewhat put my nose out of joint. And secondly, I was grateful for any interruption of my conversation with the creaking Mr. Asherton.

"Of course, my lord," I said.

Lord Winterdale stood with us for a few minutes until the waltz had finished, and then we were able to leave Mr. Asherton by the pillar while we took the floor.

"You looked distressed, Miss Newbury," Lord Winterdale said as we stood side by side in the midst of the line of dancers. "Is everything all right?"

"Yes," I said briefly.

He gave me a speculative look. "Asherton wouldn't by any chance be one of the other chaps your father was blackmailing?"

I gave him a cautious look. "Why should you think that?"

"He has a reputation for playing high and he is not wealthy," Lord Winterdale replied bluntly. "I should think that the temptation for such a man to cheat would be great."

Before I could reply to this comment, the orchestra started up again, and Lord Winterdale took my hand in his. His grip was light and impersonal, but I felt again the odd shock his touch on my hair had produced.

What was the matter with me, I thought in annoyance. This was not the man for me to get all silly over. I had watched him in action at dinner. The other women at the table might have been fooled, but I had seen through his performance. He had used his personal charm and magnetism with all the conscious deliberation with which someone else might use a weapon.

I pitied the poor woman who lost her heart to such a man.

The steps of the dance brought us back together again, and he frowned down at me. "We can't go out onto the terrace together; there are too many people watching us tonight. But I think we need to talk. Do you think you could get out of bed for a ride in the park tomorrow morning?"

"Of course I could," I answered promptly.

"Good. Be in the stables at seven," he said.

I glanced up at him. His brows were drawn together, his mouth was hard.

What was bothering him? I wondered.

"All right," I said. "I will see you at seven."

CHAPTER

seven

It was three o'clock before I saw my bed and it seemed like I had scarcely closed my eyes before Betty was awakening me at six-thirty. I struggled out of bed, however, got dressed in my old habit, and made my way to the stables, yawning the whole time.

Lord Winterdale was already there, looking disgustingly alert and awake. He wore a russet-colored riding coat this morning and brown-leather breeches, attire that was more suited to the country than to the elegant requirements of London. Cato was ready for me once more, and my erstwhile guardian and I set off through the London streets, which were quite amazingly busy for such an early hour.

Fruits and vegetables were piled on wagons which lumbered through town on their way to the Covent Garden market; fishmongers were carrying the purchases they had just made at the wharves to their various shops; and haunches of freshly slaughtered meat were bleeding through the bottoms of wicker baskets as they were driven by cart into the butcher shops. The myriad number of people who inhabited London had to be fed, and this was the hour at which their food was moved.

Isabelle was much more fidgety than she had been on our last ride, jumping when a milkman's truck rumbled up beside her and cantering in place when a big wagonload of fodder hay came lumbering by.

"She's actually getting better," Lord Winterdale informed me. "When I first brought her to London she regularly tried to put me under the wheels of the wagons going by. Now she just dances around."

"Do you take her to the park every morning?" I asked.

"Yes. She needs exercise and she can't get it in the afternoon in that fashionable parade that fills the park from five o'clock onward. And before five there are too many children around for me to feel that it is safe to gallop her full out. So we come in the morning, when the park is empty."

"Why don't you leave her in the country, where she can get all the exercise she needs?" I asked curiously.

His answer surprised me. "Because I would miss her, and I think that she would miss me. We've been together for four years, Isabelle and I, and we suit each other. I don't want to ride another horse."

It was the first time that I had ever heard him express affection for another creature.

We entered the park as before from the Oxford Street entrance and immediately our surroundings underwent a magical change. Deer grazed under the budding trees, and the city seemed to disappear magically, like Atlantis sunk beneath the waves. A slight morning haze hung in the air, giving the light a particularly diffuse and pearly look that was extremely lovely.

"Shall we gallop?" Lord Winterdale said.

"By all means," I replied readily, and our two horses took off down the path at the same time, stretching out in full gallop, obviously enjoying themselves. Isabelle easily pulled away in front of me, but Cato kept going, impressing me with his gameness and his general good condition.

We went around half the lake at a flat-out gallop,

coming back to a canter as we circled the top of the Serpentine and turned down the other side. By the time we came down to a walk I was feeling wide-awake and full of energy and not at all as if I had had only four hours sleep the previous night.

We walked the horses side by side on a loose rein and when Lord Winterdale remained silent I couldn't contain myself any longer, and asked, "What was it that you wished to speak to me about, my lord?"

He patted Isabelle's glistening black shoulder and turned to look at me. "How many men was your father blackmailing?" he asked.

I thought about telling him it was none of his business, but then I met his eyes and changed my mind. "Five, including your uncle," I admitted.

He was hatless, and the breeze blowing off the lake ruffled the black hair on his forehead. Two deer gazed at us serenely from beneath the trees to our left. He asked, "And who were they?"

I hesitated at that. "I don't think I should tell you."

His black brows drew together. "I think you had better tell me, Miss Newbury. Particularly, I think you had better tell me why George Asherton should have sought you out last night. Did you get in contact with him at all? Are you trying to blackmail the rest of those men, the way your father was?"

"No, I am not!" I glared at him, indignant that he could even suggest such a thing. "As a matter of fact, I wrote to all of the other men and told them that I had destroyed the evidence that Papa had collected on them. I said that they could consider themselves free men, that I would never bother them with what I knew."

He reached over and put a hand on Cato's bridle, forcing us to stop. The horses stood side by side on the path, and Lord Winterdale and I looked at each other. "Did you really destroy that evidence?" he asked incredulously.

"Yes, I did."

His incredulous look did not change, and I began to feel defensive.

"Surely it was the right thing to do. I had no intention of using the information, and I thought that Papa's victims would be relieved to know that it no longer existed. That is why I wrote the letters, to let them know that the evidence was destroyed and that they were now safe."

"Jesus Christ," he said. "How could you have been so stupid?"

By now I was partly angry and partly frightened. "What do you mean, I was stupid? What should I have done?"

"Tell me," he said. "What did Asherton want with you last night?"

"He wanted the evidence Papa had against him," I said. "He said he didn't think he could trust my word that I had destroyed it."

"Precisely," Lord Winterdale said. We were still standing side by side, and a squirrel ran across the path close to the horses' legs. Isabelle began to jig and Lord Winterdale patted her again and spoke softly to her. I stared at him in astonishment. I had not thought his voice capable of sounding so gentle.

Then he looked back at me and when he spoke the gentle note was quite gone. "Allow me to tell you, Miss Newbury, that Asherton is not going to be the only victim who feels that way. None of those men are going to feel safe until they have the incriminating papers in their own hands."

I had never thought of that. I bit my lip. "But I don't have the incriminating papers anymore. I burned them."

"Not a brilliant move, Miss Newbury," he said sarcastically. "Not a brilliant move at all."

I said furiously, "So I made a mistake. I'm sorry if I don't have much practice at blackmailing."

"Really? I have found you to be remarkably gifted," he replied suavely.

I glared at him but didn't answer. Unfortunately, there was nothing I could say.

He took note of my obvious frustration and said with hateful satire, "Ah, but you are not doing it for yourself, are you? You are only concerned for your little sister."

He began to walk Isabelle forward, and Cato followed without my even asking him. I seethed in silence.

Finally Lord Winterdale said, "Who are the other men on your father's infamous list?"

I glanced at him and didn't answer.

"You had better tell me," The hard, ironic tone I so disliked was very evident in his voice. "After all, I am your guardian and consequently am supposed to be in charge of your welfare."

"You are not my guardian, my lord, and we both know it," I returned emphatically.

He lifted those reckless eyebrows. "Then what am I, Miss Newbury?"

I could feel a flush stain my cheeks. "Well, I suppose you are my pretend-guardian," I muttered.

He looked at me as if I were two years old. "Then, as your pretend-guardian, I think you ought to tell me the names of those men."

"Oh very well," I said a little sulkily. "Besides Mr. Asherton there was Sir Henry Farringdon."

He gave me a surprised look. "I did not know that Farringdon gambled."

I said reluctantly, "I believe it was more a matter of a . . . ah friend . . . that Lord Henry did not want his wife to know about."

"Sophie Henry," came the instant reply. "Of course. Poor Farringdon was afraid his wife would find out about Sophie and then her father would cut off his funds."

"How did you know this Sophie Henry's name?" I demanded suspiciously.

"Oh, Sophie has been about the town for years," came the easy reply. "She used to be a diamond of the first water, but she's come down a bit lately. Farringdon doesn't have the money that her earlier protectors had, but he kept her in a certain style. The fact that he was keeping her on his wife's money would probably have caused his father-in-law to cut off his allowance. I can see where Farringdon would prefer to pay up than to have that happen."

It was not at all proper for Lord Winterdale to be discussing the ladies of the *demimonde* with me, but I was aware that our relationship was not precisely the ordinary one of gentleman to lady. I decided that, under the circumstances, it would be somewhat hypocritical of me to protest.

I said instead, "The next one of Papa's victims was Mr. Charles Howard."

He scowled. "Charlie Howard? I knew he was a gambler, and a weak fool to boot, but I hadn't thought it was as bad as that."

"Yes. He wrote Papa a number of truly pitiful letters, but I am afraid that Papa was not moved. He squeezed him for almost thirty thousand pounds."

"Howard could not possibly afford to pay thirty thousand pounds."

"He wrote to Papa that he was going to have to get the money from a moneylender."

The branches overhead rustled in the breeze. The air smelled of grass and trees, and the daffodils and daisies and cowslips and buttercups that waved in the grass along the lake were as sunny as the morning.

Lord Winterdale said, "Miss Newbury, allow me to tell you that your estimable father was a scoundrel."

I sighed mournfully. "I am afraid that he was."

We were approaching the end of the lake. "And who was the last recipient of his tender mercies?" Lord Winterdale asked me a trifle grimly.

"The Earl of Marsh," I said.

Silence. Then, "Would you repeat that, please?"

"The Earl of Marsh," I said.

"Wonderful." This time the sarcasm in his voice was like dripping acid. "That is truly wonderful. The Earl of Marsh, Miss Newbury, is one of the most dangerous and unscrupulous men in all of London. In fact, the only man I know who is probably more dangerous than Marsh is me."

"The information Papa had collected on him was not pleasant," I said in a small voice.

"Did you write to Marsh also and tell him that you had burned the papers pertaining to his cheating?"

"Yes," I said in an even smaller voice than before.

He cursed. I winced. Then I put my chin in the air.

"I think you are making a mountain out of a molehill," I said. "When time passes, and these men see that I am going to make no demand on them, then surely they will feel that they can rest easy."

"Don't you think that they will deduce that you are

making demands on me?" he said. "As you yourself have pointed out, there is no sensible reason for your father to have appointed me as your guardian. Of course there is gossip about it—which is why I said that we should not go out together on the terrace last night. If there is any thought that you might possibly be my mistress, your reputation will be destroyed."

I stared at him in horror. "Your mistress! Why should anyone think that I am your mistress?"

"Because that is the way people's minds work," he replied. "And because, to be perfectly honest with you, Miss Newbury, my own reputation is not quite spotless."

He was staring ahead, directly between Isabelle's ears as he spoke, and I looked at his hard, taut profile and thought that at that moment he looked more alone than any human being I had ever seen.

We arrived back at Grosvenor Square at eight-thirty, and by then I was starving. The dining room was still in a state of disarray from the evening before, however, and Lord Winterdale ordered food to be brought to the library. Almost as an afterthought, he invited me to join him.

A footman set up a sofa table for us in front of the fire and another footman carried in a tray of eggs and pork chops and muffins. There was also hot chocolate and coffee. I had chocolate and eggs and Lord Winterdale had two pork chops and coffee.

We ate in silence. Finally, as I was wiping my mouth with a napkin, I said ruefully. "I cannot believe how much food I have consumed these past two days. First the dinner, then all those lobster patties, and now these eggs. If I am not careful I will get as fat as a pig."

As I am reed-slim, this was a blatant lure for a compliment. I didn't get one.

"I believe it is more difficult for ladies to keep their figures in town than it is in the country," he said. "Men have the options of exercising at Gentleman Jackson's boxing saloon, or Angelo's fencing establishment, but all ladies can do is shop." He lifted an eyebrow at me. "And that you do very well."

I gave up on the compliments. "Well, I will do my best to get myself off your hands as soon as I can, my lord. I did dance with quite a number of young men last night, and several of them asked if they might call upon me today."

"I noticed that you were quite occupied," he said. "Catherine, unfortunately, was not as successful in collecting admirers."

I frowned. "Wasn't she? I looked for her when I went into supper, and I couldn't find her."

"She spent a bit of time sitting with the chaperones," Lord Winterdale said. His face was unreadable.

"Oh no, poor Catherine," I said. "Lady Winterdale will be furious."

"Yes, I rather believe she was." He actually sounded pleased, and I glared at him.

"If Catherine wasn't dancing, then why didn't you introduce partners to her?" I demanded. "You certainly seemed to know everyone who was in that room. You could have made sure that Catherine always had someone to dance with her."

"That was her mother's job. My job was to speak to all my guests and to dance with all the dowagers. Which I did with scrupulous politeness, Miss Newbury, and I can assure you that it was not fun."

I said stubbornly. "Still, it wouldn't have taken a great

deal of time for you to have introduced a few of your friends to Catherine."

"I didn't have to introduce young men to you," he said.

"Catherine is quieter than I am. She doesn't put herself forward. She needs *help*." My glare increased. "You deserted her just because you wanted to infuriate Lady Winterdale, didn't you? That is why you forced her to present me along with Catherine, so that Lady Winterdale would be humiliated by seeing her daughter outshone by a nobody from the country." I jumped to my feet. It was impossible to glare any harder, but I tried. "It's true, isn't it. *Isn't it?*"

He looked back at me, his eyes clear as a summer sky, his face imperturbable. He said softly, "Would you prefer that I sent you back to the country? I am perfectly prepared to do that if that is what you want."

What I wanted was to slap his too-good-looking face, but I wasn't stupid enough to try that. Instead I said, "I think you are despicable," and stalked out of the room.

I think you are despicable.

Strange words coming from a blackmailer to the man she was blackmailing, perhaps, but I thought that they were true. He had used me for his own purposes, which was to infuriate and possibly humiliate Lady Winterdale. To be honest, I didn't care about Lady Winterdale, but I did care about Catherine.

I went upstairs and knocked on Catherine's door and when her voice told me to come in, I entered a little tentatively.

"Good morning," I said. "Have you recuperated from our late-evening revels?"

She was sitting up in bed drinking a cup of chocolate. Her brown hair was loosely pulled back into a single braid and she wasn't wearing her spectacles. I thought she looked almost pretty.

Those horrible ringlets that Lady Winterdale insisted on, I thought. We had to get rid of them.

"Sit down, Georgie," she said, gesturing to the bottom of her bed. I sat on the edge of it and looked at her with concern, searching her face for unhappiness.

She seemed much the same as always.

"Did you have a good time last night?" I asked carefully. "I looked for you when I went in to supper but you were nowhere to be been."

"I went in earlier than you, I believe," Catherine said. "Mama forced the son of one of her bosom friends to escort me. We were not in the supper room for long."

She sounded resigned not resentful.

"Did *you* have a good time?" she asked me.

"I had a marvelous time," I answered honestly. "But then I like parties, and you don't."

"I don't, really," Catherine admitted. "Even if I were as popular as you, I still wouldn't like them. I don't like talking to people I don't know. It's too much trouble."

I grinned at her. "I know. You would rather be playing the pianoforte."

She sighed. "Yes. I would."

My grin disappeared. "Still, Lord Winterdale should have made sure you danced all the dances. It was your come-out ball more than mine."

"Philip doesn't like me because of Mama," Catherine said simply.

I leaned forward. "I can understand why there might be little sympathy between Lord Winterdale and your mother," I said. "They are both very strong personalities. But there is more between them than simply lack of sympathy. There seems to be active dislike—I might almost go so far as to say animosity. Is there any particular reason for that?"

"Yes," Catherine replied sadly, "I am afraid that there is, Georgie. You see, Philip's mother died when he was only eight years old, and directly after the funeral his father asked his older brother, who was my own father, if he would take Philip and raise him with his own children at Winterdale."

Catherine reached over and put her cup of chocolate on the beside table. "At the time, that seemed the only course of action that would benefit Philip," she continued. "My Uncle Jasper was sadly unstable—he was an inveterate gambler, you know—and with his wife gone, the chance of Philip having any kind of a normal, respectable life with my Uncle Jasper was virtually nonexistent. I think that everyone just assumed that my father, as head of the family, would take Philip in."

Catherine tugged on her braid. "Well, my papa was willing to have Philip, but my mama was not. She disapproved of Philip's mother for having eloped with my Uncle Jasper and, needless to say, she disapproved exceedingly of my Uncle Jasper. She said that Philip was bound to have been corrupted by his parents and that she didn't want him in the same house with her own children. Eventually Papa gave in to her, as he always did, and told Uncle Jasper that he would not be able to take Philip."

Catherine stared at the counterpane over her lap and refused to meet my eyes.

"This decision, of course, threw Philip on the mercy of his father, and from the little that I heard from my brother James, Philip's life was neither easy nor respectable. I myself never met him, of course, but I must say I can't blame Philip for his animosity. It would be strange indeed if he thought he owed our family anything at all."

I stared at Catherine thoughtfully, ruminating on all that she had told me. It explained a great deal about Lord Winterdale's willingness to sponsor my come out, I thought. It also made me feel more sympathetic toward him.

What a terrible thing to do to a small boy, I thought indignantly. What a life he must have led.

"Did your cousin go to school, at least?" I asked Catherine.

She shook her head. "He didn't go to school in England, at any rate. Perhaps he went somewhere on the Continent."

"How did Lord Winterdale's father die?" I asked curiously.

Catherine put her cup down on the tray that was laid across her lap. "I'm not supposed to know this, of course, but he was shot. It happened somewhere in Belgium, I believe. Supposedly someone caught him cheating at cards."

Oh my God. I shut my eyes.

How Lord Winterdale must hate and despise me, I thought. True, he was using me for his own ends, but still . . . to have lost his father in such a way, and then to have me show up on his doorstep trying to blackmail him for a similar offense.

"How old was he when his father was killed?" I asked Catherine.

"I remember that James told me about it on his eighteenth birthday, and Philip is a year younger than James," Catherine replied. "That would have made him seventeen."

It occurred to me that Lord Winterdale had good reason to wear that locked-away look he had. The world had certainly not been kind to him during his boyhood years.

CHAPTER
eight

FIVE BOUQUETS OF FLOWERS WERE DELIVERED TO THE house for me that morning, and none for Catherine. I thought that Lady Winterdale was angry enough to say that she would no longer sponsor me. When the bouquets were followed up by gentlemen callers, however, and I managed to arrange for one of them to take Catherine for a drive in the park during the afternoon, Lady Winterdale seemed a little more reconciled to keeping me on.

The man I picked for Catherine was older than the rest of the group sitting in Lord Winterdale's front drawing room. His name was Mr. John Robertson, and he seemed to be more sensible and settled than the younger men who were gossiping and joking and flattering me in a way that made Lady Winterdale frown so direfully.

I had danced once with Mr. Robertson last night, and he had told me that I must be sure to see Kean at the theater and to attend the opera as well. I had immediately marked him as a possibility for Catherine.

My own chosen driver was Lord Henry Sloan. I had liked him when he rescued me at Madame Tussaud's, and I liked him even more every time we met. He was amusing and easy to be with and his voice was never sarcastic. I wore my new fawn-colored carriage dress and an An-goulême straw bonnet with a high fluted crown and broad front brim. The ribbons were pink and tied on one side with a dashing bow.

We drove along the same path in Hyde Park, upon which I had ridden with Lord Winterdale earlier in the morning, only now the park was crowded with the *ton*. No one galloped; a decorous trot was the fastest pace one could manage in that flock of people. Lord Henry's phaeton was extremely elegant, and he stopped it frequently to speak to people whom he knew or whom I had met at the ball the previous evening. It was a thoroughly delightful outing.

I saw Catherine twice, and she seemed to be enjoying herself as well. Once she was even talking.

There was no sign anywhere of Lord Winterdale.

He did make an unusual appearance at dinner, however, and as the soup was being served, he said to Lady Winterdale, "I assume you are taking these two chits to Almack's tomorrow evening."

Lady Winterdale signaled to Catherine that she was to sit up straighter. "Of course we will be going to Almack's," she replied majestically to her nephew. "I officially received our vouchers this morning from Sally Jersey."

Lord Winterdale took a sip of his turtle soup. He swallowed it, and said, "I also assume that you expect that they will shortly be given permission to dance the waltz."

"Catherine will be given permission, of course." Lady Winterdale looked down her pointy nose at me. "And Georgiana, too, I suppose, if she continues to behave with decorum."

I tried to look as decorous as one can with a mouthful of turtle soup.

Lord Winterdale also looked at me. "Do you *know* how to waltz, Miss Newbury?" he asked bluntly.

I swallowed the soup, and admitted, "I am afraid that I do not."

"Good heavens," said Lady Winterdale. "How can this be?"

"After all, it is a relatively new dance, ma'am," I said reasonably. "Lady Stanton, the wife of our local squire, thinks it is fast, and so we never dance it at home."

All of the points on Lady Winterdale's face seemed to draw together and quiver. "A squire's wife?" she said. "What can a squire's wife possibly know about what is or is not fashionable?"

"In our part of the world, Lady Stanton is the arbiter of fashion, and she does not approve of the waltz," I replied.

"Well, this will not do, Georgiana." Lady Winterdale put down her spoon. "If one of the patronesses introduces a gentleman to you for the waltz, and you must refuse because you do not know the steps, I shall be humiliated."

I put down my own spoon.

"If dancing the waltz is so important, my lady, I don't see why I cannot learn it," I said spiritedly. "I was watching the way it was done last night, and it did not seem extraordinarily difficult to me."

"The ball at Almack's is tomorrow evening. There is no time to engage a dancing master." She looked at Lord Winterdale, who appeared to be the only one at the table who had managed to finish his soup. "Are you going out this evening, Philip?" she demanded.

"I have an engagement at Brooks's," he replied.

"You will not be leaving for your club for at least an hour after dinner," Lady Winterdale announced imperiously. "If I have Catherine play the piano, I do not see why you cannot engage to teach Georgiana the waltz."

The reckless eyebrows lifted in incredulity. "In an hour?"

"She has assured me that she is a quick learner."

As a footman removed my unfinished soup, Lord Winterdale looked at me. "Are you game to try, Miss Newbury?"

For some reason, I could feel my breath coming short. The reason Lady Stanton disapproved of the waltz was because it required the gentleman to take his partner into his arms.

"Why not?" I said with an attempt at lightness. "It can't do any harm to try."

Lord Winterdale did not remain in the dining room to drink his port after dinner, but went with us upstairs to the green drawing room where Lady Winterdale had instructed the servants to roll up the rug. Catherine took her place at the piano, and Lord Winterdale and I walked out together onto the middle of the exposed oak floor. Lady Winterdale took a seat on one of the green-tapestry chairs along the wall and prepared to play the chaperone.

"We'll walk through it first, Miss Newbury," Lord Winterdale said. "Just follow my lead."

I nodded nervously.

He took my right hand in his, put his other hand on the back of my waist and held me lightly.

I was shocked by the jolt of feeling that went through me at the touch of his hand on my waist. I swallowed and lifted my left hand to rest it on his shoulder.

"Now," he said, "the waltz is a three-step count. If you will follow me, we will count out loud: one two three, one two three, one two three."

We moved off across the room, his hand on my waist

compelling me to follow him, my feet almost of their own volition making the three-step pattern he was dictating.

I stumbled once and fell against him. He was solid as a rock. Scarlet stained my cheeks. "S . . . sorry, my lord," I stuttered.

"That is perfectly all right," he replied evenly. "You are doing very well."

After we had gone once more around the room doing this, and I was following him more easily, he said to Catherine, "All right, Catherine, play something for us."

Catherine struck up the opening bars of a waltz that I had heard played the previous night at our ball, and Lord Winterdale tried to swing me into motion. I stiffened and stuck.

"Relax your waist, Miss Newbury," he said softly. "Don't fight me, just follow my lead."

I glanced at Lady Winterdale to see her reaction to this comment, but she wasn't looking at me at all. She was looking at Catherine.

I made myself relax and felt myself drawn slightly closer to Lord Winterdale. We danced two steps and he swung me around a turn. Giddily, I followed.

I don't think I have ever in my life been so conscious of a man. Even when Frank had kissed me—and he had held me considerably closer than Lord Winterdale was doing now—I had not felt like this.

I tried to think of Frank.

"God, Georgie," he had groaned. *"I love you so much. There has to be a way we can manage to get married."*

His arms had been around me, and I had been standing with my cheek pressed into his shoulder. I had felt inef-

fably sad. "There isn't, Frank," I had said. "There just isn't."

Lord Winterdale said, "You are doing very well, Miss Newbury."

I immediately tripped. His hand on my waist tightened to support me. "You shouldn't have complimented me," I said breathlessly. "It was bad luck."

"You are dancing too close together," Lady Winterdale announced from her chaperone's chair. "Georgiana must be able to follow her partner without hanging all over him."

I jumped away from Lord Winterdale as if I had been scalded.

Lord Winterdale stopped and turned to face his aunt. "Miss Newbury tripped," he said.

Catherine stopped playing.

"Following the steps is not quite as easy as it looked," I admitted.

Lady Winterdale waved her hand. "Well, don't stop yet. You have at least another half an hour before you must leave for Brooks's, Philip. Another half hour's practice can only be beneficial."

Lord Winterdale glanced down at me and for a moment I thought I saw a glint of humor in his eyes. "It will help to exercise away all those excess pounds you have been putting on, Miss Newbury."

Devil, I thought ruefully. That will teach me to fish for compliments from Lord Winterdale.

"Very well, my lord," I said. "I will do my best not to step on your feet."

"Thank you," he said.

He took my hand. He put his other hand on my waist.

I put my hand on his shoulder. Catherine started to play, and once more we moved down the floor.

The waltz, I thought, was a very wicked dance. I quite saw why Lady Stanton wouldn't allow us to perform it in Sussex.

Lady Winterdale actually managed to engage a dancing master for me for the following afternoon, so by the time we arrived at Almack's that evening I felt as if I would not utterly disgrace myself if I was indeed allowed by the patronesses the felicity of performing the waltz.

Once more I had a wonderful time arraying myself for the dance. Really, I thought, I had never realized how much I would like nice clothes. I had never before owned anything but extremely simple cotton round gowns, so I had never had the experience of looking and feeling really grand. The dress I was wearing this evening was a gossamer-light frock of ivory silk, simply stitched with gold thread and with gold-covered buttons down the back and on the sleeves. I had a gold fan to carry, and Betty twined small gilt roses in my braids. I couldn't wait to get to Almack's.

What a disappointment! Ever since I had arrived in London, Almack's had been talked about as if it were some kind of sacred shrine, and I was expecting something really splendid. However, when we finally reached the assembly rooms on King Street, St. James, all I saw was a simple building with undistinguished brickwork and a staid pedimented Ionic doorcase marking the entrance. The second story sported six windows with round arches, which Lady Winterdale informed me graced the ballroom. The whole place looked excessively dull.

The inside wasn't any better. When finally we reached

the famous ballroom I saw nothing but a huge, spare room with a terrible floor.

"Why on earth do people want to come here so desperately?" I said in a low voice to Lord Winterdale who, rather to everyone's surprise, had actually agreed to escort us to our first Almack's ball.

He was garbed in the dress that was decreed by the Ladies Committee as being correct for entrance into the club: knee breeches, a white neckcloth, and black dress coat with long tails. But as he looked arrogantly around the room I felt as if the civilized outer show of the man was not quite successful in disguising the inner predator.

He said cynically, "They want to come because the patronesses succeed in keeping so many people out. The power they wield in society is quite amazing. They have even rejected peers of the realm, and once they did not let the Duke of Wellington in because he was not dressed correctly."

"How on earth did you manage to get in?" I blurted. Then I clapped my hand to my mouth. "Oh, dear, I did not mean to say that. I am so sorry, my lord. It just seemed to pop out of my mouth. I do most truly beg your pardon."

The smile he gave me was so bleak that it almost brought tears to my eyes. "The Winterdale fortune is known to be very handsome, and I am unmarried," he said. "Almack's is not known as the marriage mart for nothing, and the patronesses are not utter fools. They would like to see me attend more frequently, as a matter of fact, but the truth is that I can't stand the place."

I was silent. I did not know what to say.

A young man appeared before me wearing a happy smile. "Miss Newbury, it is nice to see you again." He turned to my guardian. "Winterdale. The patronesses will be in heaven to see that you have shown up."

Lord Winterdale looked even more cynical than before.

The young man, whose name was, of all things, Mr. Loveday, said, "May I hope that you will give me a dance, Miss Newbury?"

"I will be happy to, Mr. Loveday," I said graciously. I smiled. "Lady Catherine is here also, on the other side of the room with her mama. I am sure that she would be happy to give you a dance as well."

Mr. Loveday looked at me. I looked back.

"Of course," he said. "I shall be certain to ask her."

"I believe she is free now," I said.

He shot a look at Lord Winterdale. Then, with palpable reluctance, he smiled, nodded, and took himself off to Catherine.

As soon as he was out of earshot, Lord Winterdale demanded of me, "Are you planning to make all of your partners dance with Catherine?"

"If it looks as if she needs my help, then I will help her," I replied tartly. "Unlike *some* people, I don't want to see her standing around partnerless. It is humiliating for her."

His eyes were on Mr. Loveday, who was now speaking to Catherine. Lady Winterdale was beaming. "And you don't think it will be humiliating for her to learn that you have forced all of your own admirers to dance with her?"

"There is no reason for her to know that. I certainly have no intention of telling her."

He turned back to me. "Miss Newbury, London's male society is a very small world. We get together at our various clubs, at Tattersalls, at Jackson's, at Angelo's. We talk to each other, Miss Newbury. It will not be long before word is out about what you have done. And let me tell you, that will be far more humiliating to Catherine than being a wallflower could ever be."

I frowned at him. He looked back, his eyes incredibly blue in the poorly lit grimness of Almack's ballroom.

"Do you really think so?" I asked doubtfully.

"I know so."

I felt very distressed. "But what can I do to make sure that Catherine has partners? Her mother has bought her a whole collection of dresses that do not become her at all, and she makes her wear her hair in that dreadful style. And Catherine is shy. She needs help."

There was a pause. The musicians were getting ready to play. Lord Winterdale said resignedly, "I will make sure that Catherine has partners, Miss Newbury. And unlike you, I will do it in a way that will not humiliate her."

I gave him my warmest smile. "Thank you, my lord. That is very kind of you. I am grateful."

He looked back at me and a muscle twitched in the corner of his jaw. "It's nothing," he said.

"There you are, Miss Newbury," said the familiar voice of Lord Henry Sloan. "I thought that this corner of the room was glowing more brightly than the others."

I laughed and turned to greet Lord Henry, and while I was doing that Lord Winterdale walked away.

Halfway through the evening, the moment arrived that I had been preparing for all afternoon. Lady Sefton, one of the patronesses, appeared in front of me with a gentleman who had attended our own ball, and presented him to me as a partner for the waltz.

My partner's name was Lord Borrow. He was very big and very burly—a huge bear of a man. I thought that if

I got my foot under his by mistake, I was going to be in serious trouble.

As we went out to the floor I said a little nervously, "I have only just learned the steps of the waltz, my lord, so I am afraid I might be a little clumsy."

"Nonsense, nonsense," he said. He smiled down at me from his great height. I could not imagine dancing with this huge creature. Lord Winterdale, whose height was but five or so inches above my own, suited me far better.

Fortunately, the waltz did not go as badly as I had feared. Lord Borrow was lighter on his feet than I would have thought possible, and I managed to perform all the steps correctly.

"Just as I thought," Lord Borrow beamed at me when we had finished. "You are lighter than a feather, Miss Newbury."

"Thank you, my lord," I said a little breathlessly.

I saw Lady Winterdale beckoning me from across the room and I excused myself from Lord Borrow and made my way over to my chaperone.

"Georgiana," she said, "I should like to present Mr. Howard to you. Mr. Howard tells me that he is a friend of some distant cousin of yours and would like to meet you."

Charles Howard, I thought with a flash of panic as I recognized the name. This was the man who had been forced to go to the moneylenders in order to pay Papa his blackmail money.

Dear God, I thought in dismay. *I hope he, too, does not want his evidence back.*

"I wonder if I might take you in to supper, Miss Newbury," Mr. Howard said courteously. "That would enable us to exchange information about our mutual friends."

"All right," I said a little helplessly. I looked around

for Lord Winterdale, but at the moment he was nowhere in sight. I had seen him earlier, dancing with Miss Stanhope. In fact, I had noticed him dancing twice with Miss Stanhope, an act which I understood was a signal of particular attention. He had also danced with Catherine.

He hadn't asked me to dance once.

I don't need Lord Winterdale, I told myself crossly. *All I am going to do is sit and have supper with Mr. Howard. There is nothing wrong with that.*

With these thoughts in mind, I accompanied Mr. Howard into the room next door, where tables were set up and food was being dispensed.

The food was on a par with everything else about Almack's. It was dreadful. I had tepid lemonade, stale cakes, and a thin slice of bread and butter. My mind was not on my tasteless supper, however, but on Mr. Howard, who began to talk as soon as we were seated.

"I received your letter, Miss Newbury, and I must confess that it did little to reassure me. In short, I would much prefer to have the papers your father was holding over my head in my own possession than to rely on your word that they have been destroyed."

Mr. Howard was a thin, fair young man with droopy blue eyes. His fingers picked nervously at the bread and butter on his plate. "I have had to go to the moneylenders to pay your father, and the interest is killing me," he said desperately. "I don't see how I am to pay them back. I absolutely refuse to pay you any more blackmail, Miss Newbury. I just want to make that clear."

"I don't want any blackmail money from you, Mr. Howard," I said sharply. "Please believe me when I say that. In fact, if Papa had left any money, I would have tried to pay you back. But he did not leave any money, unfortunately, and so you are going to have to deal with the moneylenders yourself. You can rest assured, however, that you will be receiving no further demands from me."

He did not look reassured. "Your father left you with no money?"

I sighed. "Not a penny, Mr. Howard. That is why I have come to London without observing a period of mourning. I need to find a husband."

Twin spots of color stained his thin cheeks. "If you don't find a husband, you can always fall back on blackmail, can't you, Miss Newbury?"

"No, I can't!" I glared at him. "I burned the evidence. What do I have to do to convince you of that?"

He stood up. "You can't, Miss Newbury. I knew your father too well to believe anything his daughter might say. But you may believe me when I tell you that I will pay you no more. Good evening."

He rose from the table and departed from the room, leaving me sitting alone. I was very upset.

Lord Winterdale had been right, I thought with dismay. I should never have burned that evidence.

CHAPTER

nine

LORD WINTERDALE DID NOT RETURN TO GROSVENOR
Square with us but went on to Brooks's with a friend. Lady
Winterdale, Catherine, and I went home together in the car-
riage *sans* our gentleman escort.

"I must say," Lady Winterdale pronounced as the
Winterdale town carriage rolled along through the deserted
London streets, "I am more pleased with Philip than I can
ever remember being. He was actually quite attentive this
evening, introducing a number of eligible young men to
Catherine. It was quite obliging of him."

Catherine said with a distinct shudder, "I wonder
where they found that orchestra. The music was terrible."

Lady Winterdale surged on, ignoring Catherine's remark and commenting extensively on all of the various
men with whom her daughter had danced. It amazed me
how she knew almost to the penny how much each of those
men was worth.

When finally she stopped to take a breath, I managed
to interject, "What do gentleman do at Brooks's anyway?"

Lady Winterdale turned to answer me with distinct
disapproval. "They drink and they gamble, Georgiana. That
is what gentleman do when they are in London. When they
are in the country they ride and shoot as well as drink and
gamble. Gentlemen, unfortunately, have very limited inter-
ests."

I sighed. I didn't like men who drank and gambled. My papa had been very good at both those things, and I had always sworn that I would never marry a man like my papa.

Like it or not, I thought gloomily, I was going to be associated with men who gambled. Already two of Papa's victims had sought me out and while neither Sir Henry Farringdon nor the Earl of Marsh had been present at our ball or at Almack's this evening, I was very much afraid that I would be making their acquaintance as well.

I thought of Lord Winterdale's comment about the Earl of Marsh being a dangerous man. I thought of the ugly innuendos in my father's file about the man and shivered. I did not want to meet the Earl of Marsh alone.

Perhaps, I thought, I had better speak to Lord Winterdale about this. After all, I was living under his roof. He was supposed to be my guardian. Wasn't it his duty to protect me? He could scarcely do that if he spent all his time drinking and gambling at Brooks's.

As I got ready for bed at two in the morning, I realized that Lord Winterdale had not invited me to join him in the morning for his regular ride in the park. I attributed the stab of disappointment that went through me to the fact that I had enjoyed the exercise extremely.

Perhaps he had thought that I would not like to arise regularly at such an early hour after being out so late the night before.

I decided that when the opportunity arose, I would mention to him that I didn't mind getting up early at all. I would tell him that the fresh countrylike air had been invigorating. Perhaps then he would invite me to ride with him again.

As it was, we ladies breakfasted at ten and by eleven a

group of gentlemen were sitting in the front drawing room, conversing and drinking the tea Lady Winterdale offered. Instead of a drive in the park that afternoon, however, Lord Henry Sloan invited me and Catherine to a three o'clock concert at his mother's.

"My mother is quite musical, and she puts these small concerts together for a few friends who enjoy music as well," Lord Henry said lightheartedly. "I thought that you and Lady Catherine would enjoy it, Miss Newbury."

Catherine's fingers were pressed together so tightly that they were white. "I should enjoy it very much, Lord Henry. Thank you," she said.

I gave him a glowing smile. "We will be delighted to go," I assured him. "Thank your mother very much for inviting us."

The usual light luncheon was served at one and there was still no sign of Lord Winterdale. We were just finishing at the table when I heard the sound of the knocker and then the faint creak of the heavy front door as a servant opened it.

Lady Winterdale frowned. "I must instruct Mason to have that door attended to. It should not squeak like that."

The dining-room doors were open and so we could hear Mason's own voice as he said in his most cold, formal, and disapproving fashion, "Yes, madam? May I be of service to you?"

"Is this Lord Winterdale's house?" came a voice with a distinct Sussex burr.

My heart leaped into my throat.

"Yes, madam, it is," Mason replied, his voice even colder and more disapproving than before.

"I want to see Miss Georgiana Newbury," the voice said firmly. "It is very important."

I pushed back my chair, almost knocking it over in my haste, jumped up, and ran out into the hall. Two people were standing on the doorstep, a small, square woman with a gray bonnet tied firmly under her round chin and a tall, slim girl with glorious golden hair and the face of an angel.

"Nanny!" I cried. "Anna! What are you doing here?"

"Oh Georgie!" Anna slipped by the butler and came running down the hall to throw herself into my arms. "That man came and I didn't like him at all. I wanted you!"

I held my seventeen-year-old sister in my arms and soothed her with the skill of many years of practice. She was actually slightly taller than I, but her bones were so fragile that she felt like a child.

I looked around the golden head toward Nanny. "What man?" I said.

"Your cousin, the new Lord Weldon, arrived to take possession of his inheritance. He was not pleased to discover that you were gone, and he was not very kind to Anna." Nanny's face was ferocious. "Anna was very upset, and I decided that the only thing to do was to take her away. You had written me to say that everthing was going well for you here in London, Miss Georgiana, so this is where I decided to come."

By now Lady Winterdale and Catherine had come out into the hall from the dining room.

"Who are these persons, Georgiana?" Lady Winterdale asked in an ominous-sounding voice.

"My sister and her nurse, Lady Winterdale," I said in as pleasant a voice as I could manage. "Apparently there has been some trouble at home. Perhaps we could all go into the drawing room and sort it out."

Lady Winterdale's eyes lingered pointedly on Nanny, who was not the type of person her ladyship was accustomed to entertaining in her drawing room, but I shepherded my two visitors firmly forward and into the room, where we could have some privacy from the ears of the servants.

As soon as the door was firmly closed behind us, I said, "First of all, Lady Winterdale, allow me to present my sister, Anna. Anna, make your curtsy to Lady Winterdale."

With all the naturalness and prettiness of a young child, Anna curtsied, and said softly, "How do you do, Lady Winterdale. I am happy to meet you."

Lady Winterdale gave Anna a long, hard look. Her voice was stiff as she replied merely, "Thank you."

"And this is my friend Catherine, Anna," I said next.

Catherine gave my sister the warmest smile I had yet seen upon her face. "How lovely to meet you, Anna," she said. "What pretty hair you have."

Anna beamed. She was very proud of her hair, which was like spun gold. "Thank you, Catherine," she said. She turned to me. "I like Catherine," she said. "She's nice."

I was immensely grateful to Catherine. "Yes, she is."

There was the sound of a step in the hall and then the drawing-room door, which I had closed so firmly, opened and Lord Winterdale stood upon the threshold. His eyes went directly to me, and there was a frown line between his black brows. "What is this I hear of your sister arriving in Grosvenor Square?"

"She just arrived a few moments ago, my lord," I said.

I spoke with a semblance of calm, but my heart began to thud with fear that his hard, sarcastic manner would hurt Anna's sensitive feelings. I reached for her hand. "My lord, may I present my sister, Anna." Reassuringly, I squeezed the slender hand that rested within my own. "This is Lord

Winterdale, Anna. I have been living here in his house while I have been in London."

Anna looked from me to Lord Winterdale. She was never very comfortable with men and now she whispered a little nervously to me, "Is he nice, Georgie?"

I saw the look of shock that came across his face as he realized the situation with Anna, but it was gone as quickly as it had come. He smiled and came across the room to stand in front of her, but he did not come so close that he would frighten her. "Miss Newbury never told me that she had such a pretty sister," he said easily.

She gave him a tentative smile, and then she curtsied.

Thank God he wasn't a bear of a man like Lord Borrow, I thought thankfully. Anna would have been terrified.

I said, "And may I also introduce Mrs. Pedigrew, whom we always refer to as Nanny."

He looked at the little gray wren of a woman who had been such a rock of support to me over the years. "I am very pleased to meet you, Mrs. Pedigrew," he said. "How nice that you have decided to visit Miss Newbury in London."

Thank you, I thought with a combination of surprise and profound gratitude. *Thank you.*

He looked back at my sister. "I have an idea, Anna. Would you like it if Catherine took you upstairs and let you pick out which bedroom you would like to have for yourself? Once you have done that you can come back downstairs and tell me and I will have it all arranged for you."

"Won't that be fun, Anna," Catherine said enthusiastically. "I will show you my bedroom and Georgie's bedroom and then you can decide which bedroom you want for yourself."

Anna was intrigued by this prospect and held out her

hand to Catherine with simple trust. The two of them walked out of the room. Lord Winterdale went over and closed the door. "Now," he said, "we can talk."

"My God," said Lady Winterdale with horror, "is she *simple,* Georgiana?"

Anger ripped through me. It never got better. Everytime that question was asked, I wanted to murder the person who had asked it.

Nanny said in her Sussex burr, "There was nothing at all wrong with Miss Anna when she was born. It was an accident that made her the way that she is, poor lass."

Lord Winterdale asked me, his voice very quiet, "What happened?"

I said, without expression, "She was on the back patio at Weldon Hall, playing with a hoop, when one of my father's big wolfhounds came galloping along and knocked her over. She hit her head on the edge of the stone. She was unconscious for a week. She was four years old when it happened, and her mind has never grown any older since then."

"What a tragedy," he said. His words were spoken without any overt fervor but for some reason I could feel tears sting behind my eyes.

"Yes." I added what I always said when this subject came up. "My only consolation is that she seems to be content." I gave him an anxious look. "But it is very important that her tranquility not be disturbed, my lord. She is happiest in surroundings that are peaceful and familiar. If people stare at her, or make remarks, she knows that something is wrong and it upsets her."

"Which that miserable man was doing," Nanny put in angrily. "Would you believe it, Miss Georgiana? He had the nerve to say that Anna was a booby. Right in front of her he said it!"

"I am sorry I was not there," I said fiercely. "I would have dealt with him properly, that disgusting fishmouth."

"Er . . . fishmouth?" said Lord Winterdale.

"He has a mouth just like a fish," I said furiously. "All wet and slimy. He tried to kiss me once. It was disgusting."

"Georgiana!" said Lady Winterdale in horror. "I am seriously disturbed by your language."

I ignored her and turned to Nanny. "It is too soon for any of the men I have met here in town to come up to scratch, Nanny. The Season has barely begun, after all." I began to pace back and forth in front of the alabaster fireplace. "God, but I was hoping that my cousin wouldn't come to Weldon Hall until after he had leased his own house in Berkshire!"

"Georgiana," said Lady Winterdale dangerously.

Nanny completely ignored her. "Well come he has, Miss Georgiana, and we can hardly ask him to leave. He is the new owner, after all."

I shut my eyes briefly. What was I going to do with Anna? It was my worst nightmare come true. We were homeless.

Nanny said prosaically, as if what she was asking was perfectly normal, "Perhaps Lord Winterdale wouldn't mind if Miss Anna and I remained here with you until our future is settled, Miss Georgiana."

I bit my lip and looked with distress at Nanny's weathered, kindly face. I realized that she thought that Lord Winterdale was my guardian. She had no idea that I had blackmailed my own way into his house.

At Nanny's suggestion, all of the points on Lady Winterdale's face drew together. She drew herself up to her full, imposing height. "That is impossible," she said.

From his post by the door, Lord Winterdale said blandly, "Of course you and Miss Anna are welcome to remain at Mansfield House, Mrs. Pedigrew."

My eyes flew to him, but he wasn't looking at me. He was looking at Nanny, and his face wore a smile of such genuine sweetness that my heart quite turned over.

I swallowed, and managed to say, "Thank you, my lord. Anna will be no trouble, I promise you."

He looked back at me and lifted his black brows and the sweetness was gone from his face. "Of course she will be no trouble," he said. "She is a child, after all. What trouble can she possibly be?"

Lady Winterdale, who was still smarting from having her nephew overrule her, said, "You cannot allow it to be known among the *ton* that she is here, Georgiana. What man is going to marry you if he realizes that you have a simple sister to drag along as excess baggage?"

I wanted to kill her. I said in a strangled kind of voice, "Lady Winterdale, the only reason I have come to London to find a husband is because I need a man who will offer Anna the tranquil and settled way of life that is necessary for her. If this were not so, I would just have married Frank Stanton and gone off with him to follow the drum."

Lord Winterdale said, "Who is Frank Stanton?"

I opened and closed my fingers, trying to relax them from the fists that they had clenched into at Lady Winterdale's words.

"He is the son of the local squire near my home in Sussex. Frank and I have known each other forever and he has wanted me to marry him ever since he returned from the Peninsula. But I cannot drag Anna around from one military post to another, and so a marriage between us is impossible."

"I see," he said. His face was inscrutable.

There was a light knock on the door behind him and he turned to open it. Catherine and Anna stood upon the threshold.

"I have picked out the room next to yours, Georgie," Anna said as she came into the room. She gave a little skip before she got to me. "It is very pretty."

Lord Winterdale said to Nanny, "Do you usually sleep close to Miss Anna, Mrs. Pedigrew?"

"Indeed I do, my lord," Nanny replied. "The poor lamb has nightmares sometimes, and I like to be near."

"Then I will instruct my housekeeper to prepare the bedroom on the other side of Anna's room for you," Lord Winterdale said.

"Philip!" The outraged voice came from Lady Winterdale. "You cannot put a servant on the same floor as the rest of us."

"Nanny is not a servant," I said stoutly. "She is family."

Lady Winterdale gave me a withering look. "That, my dear Georgiana, is about as outrageous a statement as I have ever heard, even from you."

"If you do not wish to sleep on the same floor with Mrs. Pedigrew, then you are perfectly free to leave Mansfield House, Aunt Agatha," Lord Winterdale said pleasantly. "Perhaps that house in Park Lane is still for rent for the Season?"

Silence descended upon the drawing room.

How he must hate his aunt, I thought. First he took me in and now he was taking in Anna and Nanny, and it was all done to annoy Lady Winterdale.

"Nothing is for rent anymore, unless one wants to go into the outer reaches of the suburbs," Lady Winterdale said at last. "You know that perfectly well, Philip."

"Well then I suggest that you learn to accept Mrs. Pedigrew, Aunt Agatha, because she is staying," Lord Winterdale said in a hard voice.

Anna pressed herself close to me, upset by the harsh tones of the voices in the room.

"Is everything all right, Georgie?" she asked me in a frightened voice. "Why is the man angry?"

I saw Lord Winterdale take a deep breath. He said in a much milder tone, "I am not angry with you, Anna, and I am sorry if I frightened you."

She gave him a timid smile.

"Are you hungry perhaps?" he asked even more gently. "Would you like something to eat?"

"Oh yes," she replied eagerly. "Do you have hot buttered muffins, my lord?"

Hot buttered muffins were one of Anna's favorite foods. She could eat them any time of day.

"I am sure that we must," he said. "I shall ask Mason to consult with cook. In the meanwhile, why don't you let your sister help you to change your dress, and when you have done that your luncheon will be ready."

Anna beamed.

The door knocker sounded once more, and this time it was Lord Henry Sloan come to collect Catherine and me to go to his mother's concert. It did not take a great deal of persuasion on my part to convince Catherine to go without me, and if Lord Henry was disappointed that he had only Catherine to escort, he concealed it beautifully. My estimation of him went up as he drove off with Catherine to the duchess's afternoon concert while I devoted myself to taking care of my sister.

The journey from Sussex had tired Anna out and after she had eaten I persuaded her to lie down for a nap. When I came back downstairs again, Lord Winterdale was waiting for me.

"Let us go into the library, Miss Newbury," he said. "I think that we need to talk."

"Yes," I sighed. "I suppose that we do."

We took our usual places, Lord Winterdale behind the desk and I in the chair on the other side of it.

"Why did you never tell me about your sister?" he started out by asking.

I gave a small shrug. "I never hid from you the fact that I have a younger sister for whom I am responsible. I never mentioned Anna's . . . problem . . . because I didn't think it was relevant."

"It is relevant in one way," he returned. "Much as I dislike agreeing with my aunt on any subject, I am afraid that she is right about one thing. A younger sister in perfect health can be expected to marry one day and leave your protection. Obviously, this is not the case with Anna. She will be your responsibility for as long as she lives."

"I don't mind that," I said hurriedly. "I love her. She is not a burden to me."

"Of course she is a burden," he said impatiently. He held up his hand. "Now, don't get all heated up. I am not saying that you don't love her. But my aunt is right when she says that Anna is going to make it more difficult for you to find a husband."

I scowled. "I don't see why. You have seen her, my lord. She isn't *violent*, for heaven's sake. She is just like a four-year-old child."

"Yes, but she is not four, Miss Newbury. How old is she anyway?"

"She is seventeen," I said reluctantly.

"Seventeen, with the mind of a four-year-old. There is a stigma attached to such a childlike creature, Miss Newbury, no matter how lovely she may be. Look at this cousin of yours, calling her a booby to her face."

"I would like to kill that man," I said fiercely.

"Yes, that was perfectly obvious from the expression on your own face when Mrs. Pedigrew told you of it," he said dryly.

I drew in a deep, ragged breath. "He must have made life exceedingly unpleasant if Nanny felt that she needed to take the drastic step of removing Anna from Weldon. Please let me tell you, my lord, how grateful I am to you for allowing Anna and Nanny to stay here." I rubbed my forehead and eyes, which had begun to ache. "For years it has been my greatest fear, that I would not be able to provide a home for Anna."

The brilliant blue eyes were steady upon my face. "Your father did not leave you with any means of support?"

I gave him a crooked smile. "No. He left the estate, which is both entailed and mortgaged, to my cousin. There was nothing left for Anna or me."

"Is your cousin married?"

"No, he is not. I must admit that he has shown signs of interest in me, but the thought of being married to a man like that, of being forced to submit to his embraces . . ." I shuddered. "When I found the evidence of my father's blackmailing scheme, I determined that I would rather try that instead."

One eyebrow quirked. "This is the cousin with a mouth like a fish?"

"Yes," I said.

He leaned back in his chair. "What men have you met in London so far whom you do like?" he asked bluntly. "Lord Henry Sloan?"

"He seems very nice," I agreed. "He lacks a certain seriousness, perhaps, but he is certainly a very agreeable companion."

He drummed his fingers on the arms of his chair. He had beautiful hands with short and immaculate nails. I always noticed nails because I bit mine.

"Sloan is not wealthy, but he is expecting to inherit a decent little property from an uncle, I believe," Lord Winterdale said.

"That is what he told me," I confessed.

The fingers drummed some more.

"What about Borrow?" he asked next. "He is quite well off, and he made a point of getting Lady Sefton to let him waltz with you."

"Lord Borrow is too big," I said firmly. "He would intimidate Anna."

Once again up flew an eyebrow. "Precisely how big is the gentleman you are looking for?"

"Well . . . about your size, my lord," I said. "Big enough to be reassuring but not big enough to intimidate."

He looked briefly amused.

Then, "What about Stanhope?" he asked. "Didn't I see him dancing with you twice last night?"

"Yes," I said, my mind going to the two dances he himself had danced with Mr. Stanhope's sister.

"Stanhope has a nice little fortune," Lord Winterdale told me.

"I thought he seemed rather cold. Anna needs someone who will show warmth to her."

"*You* can show her warmth, Miss Newbury," he said. "Your husband need only be pleasant and provide her with a home."

He must have seen my disagreement on my face, for he added bluntly, "You can't afford to be too choosy, you know. Girls who have no portion and who are encumbered by a permanent dependent are not likely to be snatched up on the marriage mart, no matter how pretty they may be."

It was a brutal thing for him to say and a brutal thing for me to listen to. Unfortunately, it was the truth.

I felt my lip quiver and I put my hand to my mouth and pretended to cough so that he should not see how close I was to tears.

He straightened some papers piled on the desk in front of him and changed the subject. "I saw Charlie Howard at Almack's last night with his wife. Did he seek you out by any chance?"

I bit my lip. "Unfortunately, he did." I told him all about my conversation with Mr. Howard over the stale cake in Almack's supper room. "It seems that you were right, my lord, and I made a grave mistake in burning that evidence. But there is nothing I can do about it now. The deed is done."

He scowled at me. "What is your schedule of activities for the rest of the week?" he demanded.

I told him.

"You'll meet Marsh when you go to the ball at Wrenham House," he said with certainty. "Lady Marsh and Lady Wrenham are bosom bows, and the Marshes will be sure to be there. What night is that ball again? Monday?"

"Yes, my lord," I returned.

"I'd better come along," he said. "Marsh is a nasty piece of work, and I don't want you running into him by yourself." His eyes glittered. "Not that there is much that he can do to you surrounded by half of London's most elite society, but I still think it would be better if you met him while you were in my company."

I smiled at him. "Thank you, my lord." I laughed a little unsteadily. "I seem to be saying that a great deal lately, don't I?"

"It makes for a pleasant change," he replied blandly. "It is not a phrase I have heard very often in my life."

He stood up, an unmistakable and rude signal that our interview was over. "Please don't hesitate to ask my housekeeper for anything you might need for Anna."

"Yes, my lord," I said stiffly. I stood up also. "Thank you," I repeated, and turned to leave the room. I glanced back at him once, just before I went out the door. He had sat back down at his desk and was looking at the top paper on the pile that was stacked there. Again I had that powerful impression of his solitariness that had struck me before.

I closed the door quietly behind me and made my way upstairs to look in on Anna.

CHAPTER
ten

CATHERINE CAME BACK FROM THE CONCERT PRACTI-
cally radiant. She confided in me that Lord Henry had told
his mother that Catherine was a musician and that the
duchess had insisted that Catherine perform for the assembly.

This didn't surprise me, as it was I who had told Lord
Henry to ask his mother to do just that.

"You can imagine how horrified I was, Georgie,"
Catherine told me. "I had nothing prepared. I haven't practiced in weeks. I was certain that I would disgrace myself."

"I am sure that none of those things happened," I said.

"Well, I most certainly did not play my best, but people were very kind," she replied. Behind the spectacles, her
eyes were like stars. "In fact, they made me play another
piece."

I smiled at her. "What you need, Catherine, is to become a part of London's musical society. That is your natural milieu."

She heaved a despondent sigh. "Yes, but unfortunately Mama doesn't see things the way you do, Georgie.
She wants me to be fashionable."

"Were there any eligible young men present at this
musicale?" I asked hopefully.

Catherine shook her head. "The only men under the
age of fifty were the duchess's sons."

As the only one of the duchess's sons I ever saw at *ton* parties was Sir Henry, the other son must be very young. This was not promising news, and I sighed.

Catherine brightened. "The duchess is having another musicale next week, however, and she invited me to come and play."

"That is wonderful," I said warmly. I thought that even Lady Winterdale would allow Catherine to play the piano if she was invited to do so by a duchess.

The next few days went by relatively smoothly. When I was at home Anna stayed very close to my side, and I realized how much her sense of security had been shaken by this unaccustomed change in her residence.

Lady Winterdale had decreed that she did not want Anna to appear in the downstairs drawing room during the morning hours when Catherine and I entertained visitors, and I did not try to gainsay her on this subject. I did not feel that I had the right to do anything that might stand in the way of Catherine's making a good match, and so I told Nanny to make certain that Anna remained out of the way during the hours between eleven and one.

Three days after Anna's arrival, however, she appeared in the doorway of the drawing room accompanied by Lord Winterdale.

"The weather is very fine this morning and I am going to take your sister to see the milkmaids and the cows in Green Park, Miss Newbury," he said to me. "We will not be gone for long."

The four gentleman in the room had gotten to their feet and were looking at Anna with dazed admiration. I made a quick decision to dispense with introductions.

"How lovely," I said warmly. "You will like the cows, Anna. They are particularly pretty."

Anna's eyes lit upon Catherine. "I left a surprise for you in your room, Catherine," she said. Her beautiful blue-green eyes sparkled. "Something I made for you myself."

"Did you, Anna? How wonderful," Catherine said. "I can't wait to see what it is."

A voice from the hallway said, "The carriage is waiting, my lord."

"Come along, Anna," Lord Winterdale said. "I can't keep my horses standing, you know."

To my amazement, Anna skipped happily over to his side. She nodded wisely. "I know. That is what Frank always says."

He took her elbow to turn her toward the door, but she artlessly slipped her hand into his. I could hear her asking him a question about the cows as they went out the front door.

There was a horribly embarrassed silence in the room after they had gone. Lady Winterdale looked thunderous.

Once again, Lord Winterdale had managed to make his aunt furious. I was quite certain that his appearance with Anna had been deliberate.

Catherine broke the heavy silence by saying, "I wonder what it was that darling Anna could have made for me."

"Good God," said Lord Borrow. "Did you say that she is your *sister*, Miss Newbury?"

"Yes," I said.

It was Lady Winterdale who rushed into words to explain that Anna's childishness was the result of an accident, not heredity.

"She is such a beautiful girl," Lord Henry Sloan said to me. "What a pity that such a thing should have happened to her."

"Yes," I said. "It is something we have had to learn to

live with, however. And she is really no trouble. She is like a perpetual four-year-old child, that is all."

He had come to ask me to drive out with him in Hyde Park that afternoon, and since he had seemed so sympathetic to Anna's plight, I suggested that perhaps we might include her in our outing. I had been worrying that Anna was not getting enough fresh air.

Lord Henry was not comfortable with my idea.

"You know how people stop to talk to one another during that hour," he said. "It will be impossible to keep your sister from being a topic of gossip if we take her driving through Hyde Park. Really, Miss Newbury, I do not think that it is a good idea."

He must have read the look on my face.

"Besides," he said hastily, "there is not room in my phaeton for three people." He brightened as an idea struck him. "I suggest that your sister take her outing in the Winterdale town chaise. That way there will be plenty of room for her and she will be able to see the parade of the *ton* without feeling uncomfortable about having to talk to people."

"Perhaps that is a good idea," I said expressionlessly. "Anna does not cope well with a lot of new people all at once."

"May I pick you up this afternoon at five, then?" he asked eagerly.

"No," I replied. "I rather believe that I will go with Anna."

At four-thirty in the afternoon, when I was entertaining Anna by playing spillikins with her in the upstairs yellow drawing room, Lord Winterdale came into the room wearing the drab coat with three tiers of pockets, huge pearl buttons, and blue waistcoat with yellow stripes that signified a member of the Four House Club.

He looked at me in surprise. "It is a fine spring afternoon, Miss Newbury. I felt certain that you would be driving in the park."

"Lord Henry invited me, but I decided not to go," I said coolly.

He looked at me consideringly. I had a feeling that he guessed what had happened between Lord Henry and me earlier. However, all he said was, "Have you been indoors all day?"

I repressed a sigh. "Yes, I am afraid that I have." Lady Winterdale had taken the town chaise to make some visits with Catherine, and I had not desired to accompany them.

"Well, if you will be ready in half an hour, I will engage to take you and your sister driving in the park," he said pleasantly.

Anna jumped to her feet. "May I drive your horses, my lord? Like I did this morning?"

"Perhaps," he replied. "But first you must change your dress."

"I'll go find Nanny," she said eagerly, and left the room in a hurry.

I got to my feet, leaving the spillikins spread out across the baize-covered games table. I had been rethinking my earlier proposal to Lord Henry, and now I said, "I don't know if it is such a good idea to take Anna to the park during the fashionable hour, my lord. I don't want people staring at her."

He replied soberly, "The word about her affliction cannot yet have spread very far. People who notice her this afternoon will notice her because she is an extremely beautiful girl. And that is why I think it is important that she be seen, Miss Newbury. You do not want the misinformation to go around that she is some kind of deformed freak."

"Of course she isn't a freak!" I said hotly.

"It is important for people to see that. That is why I took her to Green Park this morning and that is why we are going to drive in Hyde Park this afternoon."

I was conscious of a stab of disappointment. I had been hoping that he had taken Anna to the park that morning out of kindness.

"Very well, my lord," I said quietly. "Perhaps you are right."

"Then go and change your dress, and I will have the carriage at the front door in half an hour."

We took the barouche to the park rather than the phaeton, as the phaeton seated only two and the barouche would seat four. Lord Winterdale drove instead of a coachman and Anna sat next to him and every once in a while he pretended to let her hold the reins. I sat opposite to the two of them, in a seat that had my back to the horses.

As usual, the park was filled with a glittering array of horseflesh and humanity. Anna's beautiful eyes grew huge as she took in the spectacle.

"Look at that man with the little doggie!" she cried with delight, pointing to a dandyish man driving his phaeton with a poodle perched beside him.

Lord Winterdale looked disgusted at the precious sight but he made no comment as Anna craned her neck to follow the man and the dog as he passed beside and then behind us.

"Nanny made me leave my dog back at Weldon," Anna said sadly as she turned to face forward once again. "I hope *that man* isn't mean to him."

"You can be sure that Harris will take good care of Snowball," I assured her.

Harris was our butler and had been at Weldon forever.

Lord Winterdale said, "Do you see the carriage coming toward us, Miss Newbury? That is Sir Henry Farringdon and his wife."

I turned my head and stared at the gaudy yellow equipage that was approaching our barouche. The tall man who was driving was elegantly dressed in a blue coat, fawn trousers, and Hessian boots. The woman seated beside him was short and plump, and she wore a carriage dress with far too many frog fastenings down the front. The feather in her hat was too long and too curly and too blue.

This was the fifth man whom Papa had been blackmailing besides Lord Winterdale, Mr. Asherton, Mr. Howard, and the Earl of Marsh. Sir Henry was the only one of the lot whom Papa had not caught cheating at cards; he was the one who had been caught cheating on his wife.

When Sir Henry caught sight of Lord Winterdale he slowed his carriage. My head was still turned in his direction and I could feel Sir Henry's eyes burn into my own. He looked back to Lord Winterdale and signaled to him to stop. Lord Winterdale drew up his horses.

"Hallo, Farringdon," he said. "I haven't seen you in a while." He nodded to the plump, overdressed little woman who sat beside her husband. "Lady Farringdon. May I introduce my wards, Miss Newbury and her sister, Miss Anna Newbury."

I nodded and produced the required smile. Anna was staring at Lady Farringdon's feather in utter fascination.

Nature had not been kind to Lady Farringdon and unfortunately she had done nothing to help along the good points that she had been blessed with. Her peacock blue carriage dress was truly dreadful.

Sir Henry was looking at me with an extremely strained expression on his face. I sighed to myself. Here was another one who was obviously worried about what I might be able to hold over his head.

I gave him a reassuring smile.

His eyes looked even more strained than before.

Lord Winterdale said abruptly, "I don't like to keep my horses standing for more than a minute. Good day to you, Farringdon, Lady Farringdon."

"So nice to meet you," I said.

"I like her feather, Georgie," Anna said as we drove off. "Do you think I could have a feather like that one?"

"You can have a feather to play with, not to wear," I said.

Anna turned to Lord Winterdale. "That lady's dress was the exact same color blue as your eyes, my lord," she said. "It was pretty. Too bad she was so fat."

"Anna," I said despairingly, "how many times have I told you that it is not polite to talk about the way people look."

"I didn't say it in front of her, Georgie," Anna said indignantly. "I said it to you and Lord Winterdale."

Lord Winterdale said, "We are coming to a nice straight stretch of the path now, Anna. Would you like to drive the horses again?"

"Oh yes!"

He handed her the ends of the reins while he himself kept ahold of them farther up. Anna slapped the ends and clicked her tongue and looked extremely happy.

I smiled. "What a good driver you are, darling," I said. "You make me quite jealous."

We returned home in time to change for dinner. Lady Winterdale had tried to get Anna banned from the dinner table as well as from the downstairs drawing room, but once again Lord Winterdale had overruled his aunt. As there was nothing wrong with Anna's table manners, Lady Winterdale had found nothing concrete to complain of to her nephew. This annoyed her excessively.

After the unusually domestic morning and afternoon he had passed, I had been hoping that Lord Winterdale would join us for dinner. Unfortunately, this was not to be the case. His place at the end of the table was empty as usual.

After dinner Lady Winterdale, Catherine, and I went to an unusually boring rout at some friend of Lady Winterdale's. We were home and in bed by midnight.

On Friday night we went to a ball at the Castletons'. As usual, my dance card was filled, but Lord Winterdale's strictures had made an unwelcome impression on me and as I evaluated the men I danced with as potential husbands and protectors for Anna, I began to have serious doubts as to their suitability.

Very few of them inspired me with any confidence in their steadiness or in their concern for more than themselves and their own amusement.

I also began to wonder how many of them were interested in me beyond my being an entertaining and pretty girl to dance with at a ball. As Lord Winterdale had so tellingly pointed out, I was scarcely the most desirable prize on the marriage mart.

Lord Winterdale was not present at the Castleton ball.

On Saturday night we went to a ball at the Pomfrets'. I danced with many of the same men as I had the night before, as well as Mr. Asherton, the first one of Papa's victims who had sought me out.

Mr. Asherton asked me directly about Anna, so word was evidently getting out.

"I am not going to blackmail you so that I can take care of my sister, Mr. Asherton," I said fiercely as we swung around the room in a waltz to the tune of his creaking corset. "You must believe me. I do not have any evidence!"

His chubby face looked grim, and I deduced that he didn't believe a word that I was saying. It was very frustrating.

Lord Winterdale did not attend the Pomfret ball either.

Really, I thought with annoyance, what did the man do with himself? Surely he couldn't spend every evening at Brooks's drinking and gambling.

Sunday afternoon I decided to take Anna to see the Royal Menagerie at the Tower of London. Nanny came with us, and Lord Winterdale, whom I actually caught for a moment in the hall as he was on his way out, recommended that we use his curricle for the trip across London.

The day was fine and as we walked across the landing where in the past so many famous prisoners had been brought in by boat, my first impression of the Tower was not that of a gloomy and doom-ridden place but of a picnic grounds filled with a holiday gathering.

It appeared that half of London with its young had decided to spend a delightful Sunday afternoon visiting the Tower of London. The grounds inside the grim stone walls were packed with people, most of them respectable-looking, middle-class citizens dressed in their Sunday finest.

I was disappointed. I had been expecting an atmosphere more appropriate to a place that had seen so much suffering and death.

However, as we toured the different areas of the famous prison that were open to the public, my imagination was able to supersede the pleasant reality of the present and call up what it must have been like several hundred years ago, when the only human presences in this grim place were prisoners and their guards. I could almost see Sir Walter Raleigh, that captive panther of a man, pacing restlessly back and forth along the wall that had been the only place allotted him for exercise during all the many years he had been kept in prison here.

The panther simile immediately brought to my mind the picture of another lithe, dark man, an image which I instantly tried to banish from my thoughts. Instead I dragged Anna and Nanny over to the group of people that were crowded around the small area in front of the chapel where two of Henry VIII's wives had been beheaded.

Anna was not interested in Henry's unfortunate wives, however, and she tugged at my hand to indicate that she wanted to move on to look at the menagerie, and this is where we went next.

It was not very impressive. The animals were housed in a deep pit, which must once have been part of a protective ditch for the Tower when it was a royal residence, and the total menagerie consisted of one mangy-looking lion, an elephant, and two grizzly bears.

Truth to tell, I felt sorry for them, they looked so ill kempt and listless.

Even Anna was uncertain. "They don't look very happy, do they, Georgie?" she asked me.

"No, they don't," I said. There was a large crowd of people around the pit, and I edged closer to the low wooden fence that surrounded it and looked down. It was pitiful, really, I thought. I didn't know what I had expected, but it hadn't been this.

I was standing above the lion's part of the pit and all of a sudden he looked up from his melancholy stare into space.

"Hello there, fellow," I called to it in a friendly voice. "How are you?"

I thought his eyes moved to find me and I leaned out farther. "What a handsome boy you are," I crooned, although he was not handsome at all, poor thing. He looked as if he had some sort of skin disease.

There was a good-sized crowd behind me as I was leaning over the low wooden rail, and suddenly someone knocked into me. Hard. I lost my balance and began to tip forward. I grabbed for the railing to right myself, and I would have been all right were it not for the hand on the small of my back that shoved me beyond recall. Then I was tumbling down the steep rocky side of the pit in what seemed to be an endless fall. I landed on the bottom, bruised, shaken, and ten feet from the lion.

I scrambled to my feet, my breath coming hard.

From what seemed to be a long way away I could hear screaming, and in a dim part of my mind I recognized that the screams belonged to Anna. But the main part of my mind was focused on the animal in front of me, who appeared to have awakened from his listless stupor now that someone had come to join him in his captivity.

I stopped breathing.

I can't let him sense how terrified I am, I thought. *Once animals sense fear they attack. Oh God, oh God, oh God. Be calm, Georgie. Be calm.*

Anna kept screaming.

The lion opened its mouth and roared. The stench of its breath nearly knocked me down.

I must have courage, I told myself. I was shaking all over.

The lion took a few steps in my direction.

"All right, Miss," I heard a voice saying. "I'm going to throw him a bit of meat, and then we'll put the ladder down into the pit. Can you climb up it on your own?"

I nodded. I could have climbed the Matterhorn if it meant getting out of that cage.

A few seconds later a huge haunch of meat came flying down into the pit, in the corner farthest away from me. The lion turned immediately and went to get his meal.

The keeper lowered a long wooden ladder down into the pit and my foot was on the first rung before the lion had taken his first bite of meat. I hiked my skirts up past my ankles and climbed that ladder as if all the devils in hell were after me. When I reached the top, a weeping Anna threw herself into my arms.

Nanny was right behind her. "God Almighty, Miss Georgiana," she kept saying, "God Almighty."

The lion's keeper was extremely annoyed at my stupidity in falling into the pit. "You mighta been kilt, and then what woulda happened to me?" he said. "And what woulda happened to poor Leo?"

I apologized as coherently as I could and managed to get myself, Nanny and a still semihysterical Anna into the barouche. Fortunately it was an open carriage, because I smelt most dreadfully of the lion's pit.

The carriage deposited us on the doorstep of Grosvenor Square and we went in the front door. The first person I saw as I came into the hall was Lord Winterdale, who appeared to be on his way to the library. He turned when he saw us.

"How was your outing to the Tower?" he asked courteously.

"Oh, Lord Winterdale," Anna cried, "Georgie fell into the lion's cage and was almost eaten up!"

That certainly got his attention.

"It's true," I said. "Fortunately I was rescued by an intelligent keeper. He threw the beast some meat to distract him while I climbed up the ladder to safety."

"I think you had better come along to the library with me and tell me all about this," he said a little grimly.

I gave him a smile that was not quite steady. "I rather think I had better have a wash first and change my clothes."

He looked me up and down, taking in the stains on my new green pelisse. His blue eyes darkened noticeably.

"All right," he said tersely. "Come along when you are ready. I will be waiting for you."

I went upstairs with Nanny and Anna, relieved to know that there was one person at least with whom I could share the whole truth of how I came to be pushed into that cage of death.

CHAPTER
eleven

I HAD BETTY FILL THE TUB AND SCRUBBED MYSELF IN front of the fire until my skin was red. Then I dressed in a pale blue afternoon dress and went down to the library to confront Lord Winterdale.

He was seated at his library desk, going over a ledger book. It occurred to me that he appeared to spend a great deal of time on business matters.

He did not stand up when I came into the room, a usual sign of his rudeness, but folded his hands on his papers and gestured me to my usual chair.

"Now," he said, "tell me precisely what happened."

"Somebody pushed me," I said. "I was standing on the edge of the lion's pit, and perhaps I was leaning out a bit too far, but somebody definitely bumped into me. Then they put a hand on the small of my back and pushed, sending me over the rail and down into the lion's pit."

For the first time I felt tears filling my eyes. "I have bruises all over my shoulder and my back," I said, with a quiver in my voice. "Then the lion roared at me." The quiver got even more pronounced. "His breath smelled horrible."

"Don't cry," Lord Winterdale said in a tense, angry voice. A muscle twitched in the corner of his jaw. "I shall dislike it intensely if you cry."

I struggled to hold back my tears, trying to substitute

indignation instead. Really, I thought, I had had an extremely frightening experience. I thought I was entitled to a few tears. It wouldn't have hurt him to spare a compassionate word for me. It wouldn't have hurt him to give me a comforting hug.

He did neither of these things, however. Instead he sat there, looking at me out of unsympathetic blue eyes and waiting for me to compose myself. There was a white line around his nostrils.

When I was breathing more evenly, he said, "I gather that you have no idea who this person was who pushed you?"

I shook my head. "It was very crowded around the menagerie, and there were a lot of people behind me. At first, when someone bumped me, I thought it was an accident. I grabbed for the rail, and I would have been able to right myself, but then someone put his hand on my back and pushed me right over the fence. It was quite deliberate, my lord. I have no doubt of that."

He swore softly.

I said in a very small voice, "Do you think it might have been one of those men whom Papa was blackmailing?"

"I think it is very likely," he returned. "Unless you have enemies of your own you have not told me about, Miss Newbury?"

I shook my head.

He stared at me, drumming his fingers on the arm of his chair. He looked very tense.

"What is to be done?" I asked in the same small voice as before.

"Get you married off as quickly as possible so that you are under the protection of your husband," he replied instantly. "Until that desirable goal is accomplished, however, I suppose that I had better keep an eye on you. God knows what you have stirred up with those stupid letters of yours."

A surge of healthy anger washed through me. I could feel my cheeks grow pink. "I thought I was behaving honorably," I said. "But then, to you all honorable behavior probably seems stupid."

"Shall we get this straight once and for all, Miss Newbury?" he replied. "It is you who are blackmailing me, not the other way around."

I replied grandly, "I am not blackmailing you, Lord Winterdale, and well you know it. It is you who are blackmailing your aunt." I stood up before he could. "And I'll have you know that I don't need your solicitude. I am perfectly capable of taking care of myself!"

On this truly stupid note, I swept out of the room.

We stayed home on Sunday night so I did not have to worry about someone trying to harm me. Lady Winterdale and Anna and I spent the evening listening to Catherine play the piano. The Duchess of Faircastle had quite taken Catherine up, and even Lady Winterdale felt that she could hardly snub a duchess by refusing to allow her daughter to attend her afternoon musicales.

I kept asking Catherine if any interesting young men appeared at these musical afternoons, but she always shook her head and said that the only men present were the duchess's sons. As I knew Lord Henry was there only because his mother demanded it, I didn't harbor any false hopes about Catherine's finding a possible husband at the Faircastles'.

Anna loved listening to Catherine play. I had never

before realized that my sister would enjoy music, and it was a great pleasure to watch her lovely face as she listened to the beautiful notes of Mozart come pouring out from beneath Catherine's talented fingers.

My mother had been musical, I remembered. Anna must have inherited her love of music from Mama.

Lord Winterdale did eat Sunday dinner with us, but he did not participate in much of the conversation. Then, after drinking a glass of port in solitary splendor in the dining room after we ladies had gone upstairs to the drawing room, he disappeared.

Back to Brooks's no doubt, to drink and gamble some more.

Monday night was the night of the Wrenham ball, the ball where Lord Winterdale had said I was likely to meet the Earl of Marsh. To my great relief, Lord Winterdale appeared at dinner dressed in full evening regalia and announced to his aunt that he would be accompanying us that evening to the Wrenhams'.

Lady Winterdale pronounced herself to be amazed.

"How is this, Philip? You are like a shadow in your own house for weeks on end, and then you appear out of nowhere to escort us to a ball! I am stunned."

"To succeed in stunning you is a feat indeed, Aunt Agatha," Lord Winterdale said sarcastically. "You usually are so certain of everything."

Lady Winterdale glared at him down the width of the dining-room table. The chandelier glinted on her gold turban, which she was wearing to match the gold embroidery in her purple silk gown, "You are not as witty as you think you are, Philip," she said.

He looked up from his chicken, a look of blatant surprise on his face. "I'm not?"

I looked at his flying black eyebrows and glinting blue eyes, and the first inkling of a very unwelcome knowledge began to insinuate itself into my mind and my heart.

I pushed it away.

"Anna, darling," I said, "would you care for some of these delicious green beans?"

"Oh yes, thank you, Georgie," Anna said, and one of the footmen hurried to bring the side dish to her.

The servants loved Anna. How could they not, I thought, resolutely keeping my mind on my sister. She was the sweetest child who ever lived.

Wrenham House was in Hanover Square and, like most of the town houses in London, it was too narrow to have a ballroom so Lady Wrenham had had the rug taken up in her upstairs drawing room and the dance was held there.

I came into the room with Lady Winterdale, Catherine, and Lord Winterdale, and looked around me.

The same faces that I had seen at every ball since I had come to London looked back.

I sighed.

"Bored already, Miss Newbury?" Lord Winterdale murmured in my ear.

"Not bored precisely," I returned in a low voice. "It is just that one keeps seeing the same people over and over again."

"Well, here comes someone who does not appear bored to see you," Lord Winterdale said, and I saw Lord Borrow lumbering his bearlike way across the dance floor in my direction.

He bowed in front of me, made a civil acknowledgment of my guardian, and asked me to dance. I accepted, of course, and he led me out to the floor for the opening quadrille.

The ball proceeded as most balls had proceeded since I came to London, with the big difference that this time Lord Winterdale was there, and I could feel him watching me. I never once caught him doing it, but I could feel it, and for some reason that made my blood run faster and my nerve endings tingle.

About halfway through the evening a couple I had never before seen came into the drawing room. I saw Lady Wrenham rush to the wide double doors, and she stood in conversation with the newly arrived woman for a few moments while the man stood silently beside them, his eyes roving over the scene in front of him.

We were between dances, and I was standing in front of the crimson-draped windows with Mr. George Stanhope, waiting for the music to start up again. "Who are those people who just came in?" I asked him, trying to sound as if I were merely casually interested.

"That is Marsh," Mr. Stanhope replied. There was a very cold look in his green eyes and a very disapproving expression on his face. "My advice to you is to stay away from him, Miss Newbury," he warned me. "He is not a nice man."

Lord Marsh appeared to have a universally delightful reputation.

"He doesn't look like a bad man," I said, and this was true. I had rather expected the Earl of Marsh to be a forbidding-looking fellow, with a swarthy and dissipated face. This man was very fair, and even from my position across the room I could see that his eyes were light.

Mr. Stanhope muttered something about looks not being everything, and I agreed.

It took Lord Marsh precisely fifteen minutes to seek me out. My hostess, Lady Wrenham, presented him to me as an old friend of my father's, and when he asked me to dance I could scarcely refuse.

It was a waltz.

We went out onto the dance floor, and he put his hand on my waist and took my hand in his and looked down into my face. He was about as tall as Lord Winterdale, and up close I could see the threads of gray that had dimmed the bright gold of his hair. His eyes were almost colorless, a pale gray-green, and there was something about them that did not look right.

I looked around for Lord Winterdale and didn't see him.

Damn, I thought crossly. Where was he when I needed him?

"And how are you enjoying your Season, Miss Newbury?" Lord Marsh said to me.

"Very well, my lord," I replied tersely, once more searching the room for Lord Winterdale.

"It was so kind of Lady Winterdale to sponsor your come out, was it not?" he said. "And so strange. One does not usually think of Lady Winterdale as being kind."

He was smiling a little, the look on his face that of a cat who is playing with a mouse.

I said, "Lord Winterdale is my guardian, Lord Marsh, and Lady Winterdale is sponsoring me to oblige him."

He laughed.

It was a soundless laugh, and it didn't reach his eyes. I have to admit that it was frightening. He was indeed an excessively unpleasant man.

He was mercifully silent for the remainder of the dance, however, and as soon as it ended I turned away from

him to flee to the shelter of Lady Winterdale's chaperon-
age. But Lord Marsh's fingers closed around my bare arm
beneath the puffed sleeve of my pale pink evening frock
and held me next to him.

"I wish to speak to you, Miss Newbury," he said.
"Come along with me to a place where we can be private."

"No!" I said in panic, and tried to pull away. Once
more I looked vainly around the room for Lord Winterdale.

Lord Marsh's fingers bit into the flesh of my arm with
cruel pressure. "Don't cause a scene, you stupid little
bitch," he said in a low and vicious voice. What made his
words even more frightening was the fact that he was smiling when he said them.

He urged me forward and I went with him, thinking
that he was right, that I did not wish to cause a scene, and
that the other drawing room on the floor had been set up as
a supper room and so I would surely be protected by the
presence of other people.

We didn't go into the supper room, however. Lord
Marsh went directly across the hall, pushed open a closed
door, and pulled me into the small anteroom that was dis-
closed. He shut the door behind him and said in a voice that
sent shivers up and down my spine, "Now, then, let us talk
about that evidence."

I thought of that hand pushing me into the lion's den
and my heart began to pound with terror.

Lord Winterdale's voice said from the darkness of the
anteroom's far corner, "Let us do that, Marsh. And take
your hands off my ward."

Lord Marsh dropped his hands, swung around to face
Lord Winterdale, and cursed.

I took the opportunity of being free to run across the
room to Lord Winterdale's side.

A little silence fell as the two men sized each other up. Then Lord Marsh said, "Was Weldon blackmailing you, too, Philip?"

I must confess that his use of Lord Winterdale's Christian name stunned me.

"Not me, my uncle," Lord Winterdale replied briefly.

"The saintly Winterdale?" Lord Marsh asked incredulously.

"It appears so. At any rate, our innocent Miss Newbury here found all the blackmailing evidence after her father died. Instead of returning the evidence to the victims, however, she stupidly burned it, thinking she was doing a good deed to all concerned."

"Or she says she burned it," Lord Marsh replied in a harsh voice.

"Oh, I don't think there is any doubt that she burned it, Richard," Lord Winterdale said amiably. "She wouldn't have sent those notes out if she hadn't. She would just have put the screws on you, like her father did."

Richard. I felt another jolt as I realized that these men were on far closer terms than Lord Winterdale had ever let on to me.

"She must have put the screws to you," Lord Marsh was pointing out. "I cannot imagine any other reason for you to be taking up an insipid little schoolroom miss. She is scarcely your type, Philip, you must admit."

I could feel my hackles go up. Insipid little schoolroom miss, indeed!

"I am doing it to get back at my aunt, of course," Lord Winterdale replied pleasantly. "You cannot imagine how much pleasure I have derived this Season from watching her squirm as Catherine is continually passed over in favor of my ward."

Lord Marsh looked skeptical. "If she is not blackmailing you, then how did Miss Newbury come to your attention in the first place?" he demanded.

"Oh, I went to see her," Lord Winterdale said easily. "My uncle's books showed a record of payments to Lord Weldon, you see, and I wondered about them. So I sought Miss Newbury out myself and she told me about what she had found among her father's papers."

I was enormously impressed by this clever account of how we had come to meet.

"And you decided to present her in order to annoy your aunt?" Lord Marsh said.

"That is right," Lord Winterdale replied.

Lord Marsh said silkily, "Do you know, Philip, I have known you for a long time, and I find that I do not believe you?"

Lord Winterdale shrugged. "Believe me or not, it is the truth." He took a step forward, closer to Lord Marsh. "And believe this also, Richard," he said. "If you pose any danger at all to Miss Newbury, you will have to deal with me."

"Ah," said Lord Marsh. He contemplated Lord Winterdale for a moment in silence. Then, "Is that a warning?" he asked.

"Yes," said Lord Winterdale grimly, "it is."

I moved infinitesimally closer to him.

Lord Marsh gave his chilling, mirthless smile. "I will remember that," he said. "And now, I believe I must return to the ballroom. My wife will be wondering where I am."

"A very good idea," Lord Winterdale said pleasantly, and we stood in silence as Lord Marsh opened the door and left the anteroom, closing the door behind him once more.

The only sound in the room after Lord Marsh had departed was my own accelerated breathing. "He didn't believe you, my lord," I said at last.

"Perhaps not, but I gave him something to think about," Lord Winterdale returned grimly.

I said tentatively, "It sounded as if you know each other well."

He shrugged. "I did not frequent the most salubrious places in my boyhood, Miss Newbury. I know a lot of men like Lord Marsh."

I thought of what Catherine had told me of Lord Winterdale's youth and felt ineffably sad.

We stood in silence for a minute, wrapped in our own thoughts, and absently I began to rub my arm where Lord Marsh had gripped it.

"What is wrong with your arm?" Lord Winterdale asked sharply.

I glanced down at my skin below my puffed pink sleeve. The anteroom was only lit by a few wall sconces, but even so Lord Marsh's fingerprints were quite clear on my white flesh. Doubtless they would turn to ugly dark bruises the following day.

"Lord Marsh grabbed me and made me come with him," I said. "His fingers dug into my arm."

Lord Winterdale lifted his hand and lightly touched the bruises with his right forefinger. It was as if a bolt of lightning shot through me at his touch.

He dropped his hand, stepped away from me, and said with an attempt at lightness, "You will be a mass of bruises if you don't take care, Miss Newbury."

I gave him a wobbly smile. "Thank you, my lord, for being here. I don't know what would have happened had he managed to catch me alone."

He nodded. "Speaking of being alone, we had better

return to the ballroom before people begin to notice we are missing. I'll go first and get Catherine to come and accompany you back. It won't do for people to think that we have been together."

I must confess, I found it discouraging the way he was so determined to keep his distance from me. Once again, he hadn't even asked me to dance.

I swallowed my pride, and said, "You dance with Catherine, Lord Winterdale. Why don't you dance with me?"

"I told you the answer to that before," he returned impatiently. "You are supposed to be my ward. Any hint of a romantic entanglement between us would be extremely detrimental to your reputation. It is wisest for us to keep apart."

"I can't imagine how one dance could lead people to imagine that we are romantically involved," I said spiritedly.

"You have plenty of beaux to dance with, Miss Newbury," he replied with finality. "You don't need to dance with me."

The rest of the ball was discouragingly tedious. The only good thing was that my regular partners, Lord Henry Sloan, Lord Borrow, and Mr. George Stanhope, were all very attentive and did not seem to be put off by their discovery of the existence of Anna. In fact, they all made a point of telling me that they were sorry they had reacted so badly to her appearance at Mansfield House, and they attributed their behavior to surprise.

I supposed I should be happy that it looked as if Anna was not going to prove an obstacle to my chances of bringing one of my beaux up to scratch as a husband.

I had no idea why I should be feeling so depressed.

In an unusual move, Lord Winterdale saw us home from the Wrenham ball. Then, once he knew we were safely in the house, he got back into the coach and left. On his way to Brooks's, no doubt, to gamble and to drink.

The more I saw of him, the more I realized how disreputable he really was. Tonight had only compounded matters when I had discovered that he was on first-name terms with one of the most notorious rogues in England.

I went to sleep and dreamed about him, which annoyed me no end. Lord Winterdale was nothing to me, I thought, as I awoke in the morning. I needed to concentrate on the men who were likely to marry me and provide a home for Anna.

CHAPTER
twelve

THE FOLLOWING AFTERNOON, I ACCOMPANIED CATHERine to one of the Duchess of Faircastle's musicales. Catherine had been looking prettier than usual lately, with color in her thin cheeks and a sparkle in her eyes, and I thought it was the greatest mercy in the world that she had been taken up by the duchess's musical set.

Of course, it would have been even better if there had been a young man associated with these musical afternoons at Faircastle House, but from what Catherine kept assuring me, there was not.

Faircastle House was in Berkeley Square, and the duchess had turned the front upstairs drawing rooms into a music room, complete with pianoforte, harpsichord, and harp. Because of Anna's arrival, I had not attended one of these musicales before, and I looked around me with curiosity as I came in the door.

It was an excessively simple yet elegant room. The walls were painted a pale lemon yellow and the silk draperies that framed the two tall windows were a deeper shade of lemon than the walls. The polished wood floor was bare, and the three instruments were arranged along one of the long walls, with three rows of gilt chairs arranged to face them. There was a white-marble fireplace behind the row of chairs and on the other short wall were two sofas, both of which were upholstered in a watery green silk.

Lord Henry came over to greet us as soon as we came into the room. He was followed more slowly by another man, who as he came closer I saw had the same hazel eyes as Lord Henry but who looked to be a good ten years older.

"Miss Newbury," Lord Henry said, "may I make you known to my brother, Lord Rotheram."

I curtsied to the man who, from his title, I knew must be the heir to the Faircastle dukedom. "How do you do, my lord," I said.

He gave me a courteous smile. Looking at the fine lines that fanned out from the sides of his eyes, I thought suddenly that he had the look of a man who has suffered.

"We are so pleased that you could join us this afternoon, Miss Newbury," he said. "We have heard so much about you from Lady Catherine."

I looked at his somber clothes and realized with a slight shock of surprise that the man was in mourning. This must be why I had not seen him at any of the social functions Catherine and I had been attending these last few weeks, I thought.

"I am very pleased to be here, my lord," I returned quietly.

To my great delight, Lady Winterdale had not accompanied us today, choosing instead to spend her afternoon at some sort of dowagers' tea party, where the guests would no doubt rip apart every single person of their acquaintance. Away from the overbearing presence of her mother, Catherine was like a different person. She almost glowed. After the harpist was finished and Catherine was asked to play, she rose with quiet confidence and gave us a performance that displayed more feeling than I had ever heard from her before. Technically she had always been superb, but out from under the shadow of Lady Winterdale she allowed her own natural feelings a fuller rein.

It was not until after the musical part of the afternoon was over and we were all partaking of tea in the second drawing room, that I tumbled to the real reason for Catherine's astonishing transformation. She and I were sitting together on two rosewood chairs against the wall, when she happened to glance away from me and caught sight of Lord Rotheram approaching us holding a plate of small cakes.

Her whole face lit up.

Aha, I thought with a burst of insight. *So that's the way the wind blows.*

I thought back and remembered all of Catherine's nonchalant comments that the only young men who were present at the duchess's parties were her dutiful sons. As I had heard Lord Henry talk occasionally about his two younger brothers, I had always assumed that it was one or both of those young men, who were too young to go out in society, who had been present at the musicales.

Of his elder brother, Lord Henry had said nothing.

I wondered uneasily if Lord Rotheram were married. If he were, that was certainly a potent enough reason for Catherine's holding her tongue.

Lord Rotheram had reached us. "May I offer you something to eat?" he asked with gentle courtesy. He held out the plate to Catherine. "Lady Catherine?"

Catherine took a piece of bread and butter and looked at him as if he had given her the world.

He turned to me. "Miss Newbury?"

"Thank you, my lord." I accepted a small piece of lemon cake.

The three of us remained talking for a few moments about music and I could not help but notice how comfortable Catherine appeared to be with this duke's heir. I looked again at his somber clothes and wondered. No one else in the ducal family appeared to be in mourning.

Lord Henry joined us and it did not take much effort on my part to detach him from the other two.

"Is your brother in mourning?" I asked as soon as we were out of earshot of Lord Rotheram.

Lord Henry's mobile face took on a look of unusual gravity. "Yes. His wife died nine months ago, poor chap."

"How very sad," I said. "She must have been very young."

"Twenty-seven," Lord Henry said. "The deuce of it was, she suffered for a long time. It was dreadful for her, of course, but it was also dreadful for Edward to have to watch it. I'm glad my mother managed to convince him to come to London. He needed a change of scene, even if he can't go to regular social events for another three months."

No wonder Lord Rotheram looked sad, I thought. And no wonder Catherine had said nothing to me about him. With his wife dead less than a year, he did not sound as if he was likely to be a potential beau.

It was the night for Almack's weekly ball, and I must say I dressed with a good deal less enthusiasm than I had dressed for my first visit to that august place. In fact, I was beginning to find this whole business of husband-hunting a bore. For some reason, I was feeling restless and irritated, emotions which had rarely beset me before I came to London.

Perhaps I was a country girl at heart, I thought. Perhaps once I found a husband and could retire into the country with Anna, my old serenity would return.

For some reason, this scenario did not appeal to me as much as I thought it should.

Lord Winterdale did not accompany us to Almack's, and I danced with my usual coterie of admirers and tried not to look as bored as I really was.

One surprising thing did happen at Almack's that evening, however. Lord Borrow told me that his mother was coming up to town the following day. With a smile that I thought was just a trifle patronizing, he informed me that she would like to meet me.

I must confess, he caught me off guard. I had not thought that he could really be serious about me, but it seemed as if he was. He would not be desiring to present me to his mother otherwise.

I accepted his invitation, of course, but I have to confess that I was not as happy as I should have been at the prospect of an offer from Lord Borrow. The man was just too confoundedly big.

I woke up early the following morning, feeling heavy-eyed and depressed. On impulse, I peeked into Anna's room next door and found her wide-awake and having a cup of chocolate at the small table in front of her fire.

"Do you want to walk in the park while it is still quiet, Anna, and see the ducks on the lake?" I asked impulsively.

Her lovely face broke into a smile. "Oh yes, Georgie. I don't *like* being indoors so much."

At this moment, Nanny came into the room.

"I know, darling," I said to my sister. "I know you are happier in the country, and I hope that soon we will be able to remove there." I thought of Lord Borrow and repressed a shiver. "But you will like going for a walk in the park this morning, won't you?" I asked my sister.

"You cannot go to the park alone, Miss Georgiana," Nanny said firmly. "Not in London. It isn't safe."

"I'll ask one of the footmen to accompany us," I said.

Nanny looked doubtful. "Have you spoken to his lordship about this, Miss Georgiana?"

"He won't mind," I said with confidence. "Now, if you will help Anna get dressed, Nanny, I will get dressed myself."

Anna jumped up and down and clapped her hands. "Oh good, oh good, oh good," she said. "We're going out!"

I felt a pang of guilt. How confined she must have been feeling, poor child. I leaned over and kissed her petal-soft cheek. "Let's see who can get dressed first," I said.

She laughed gleefully. Anna loved contests. Before I was out of the room she was urging Nanny to lay out her clothes.

It was eight o'clock in the morning when Anna and I set out from the house accompanied by Robin, one of Lord Winterdale's larger footmen. The morning was almost like a morning in the country. The sky was a clear cerulean blue and the air was fresh, with just a hint of the softness of the burgeoning spring.

We were precisely at the place where Oxford Street enters the park when we met a fashionable town chaise that was driving briskly along Park Lane. We waited for it to pass before we crossed the street to enter the park, but instead it stopped in front of us. The door, which bore a crest I didn't recognize, opened, and a man jumped out. He stepped in front of us, further blocking our way.

"Miss Newbury," he said with a lift of gray-blond eyebrows. "What are you doing out at such an early hour? May I offer you my escort home?"

My heart began to hammer as I looked up into the

strange light eyes of Lord Marsh. "No, thank you, my lord. It is very kind of you, but my sister and I are going for a walk in the park."

I moved as if to step around him, but he moved as well, continuing to block my way. "Your sister?" he said, looking at Anna. "I did not know that you had a sister, Miss Newbury."

Anna looked back at him with the candidness of a child. She looked so perfect, so untouched standing there in the early morning light that I felt fear clutch even more strongly at my heart.

I knew from reading my father's pile of evidence that the earl's reputation with young children was vicious. He was the very last person I wished Anna to meet.

"Do you like to go out in the morning too, sir?" she asked him with the politeness Nanny had taught her."

He gave his mirthless smile. "I am afraid that I am coming home, not going out, my dear. A late night at Brooks's, you know."

Anna turned to me, her eyes huge. "He's been out all night, Georgie," she said. "Imagine that."

The earl's eyes were glued to Anna now, and I was desperate to get her away from him. I watched him take in the exquisite shape of her head, the perfect oval of her face, the childish grace which marked her every move.

"We must be going, my lord," I said firmly. "If you would be so kind as to stand out of my way."

"You are certain that I cannot see you home?"

"I am certain," I said grimly. Anna, uneasy with the tone of my voice, slipped her hand into mine and clung tight.

Marsh's eyes noted the childish gesture. "I wonder

that your guardian allows you to come out by yourselves like this," he said.

I didn't say anything.

He tipped his fair head inquiringly. "But then, perhaps Winterdale doesn't know."

"Good day to you, Lord Marsh," I said.

Once more he bestowed upon me that chilling smile. "Good day to you, Miss Newbury." He produced a deep bow for Anna. "And good day to you, my dear. It was indeed a pleasure to meet such a lovely girl as yourself."

Anna, still clinging to my hand, smiled back a little uncertainly. She had clearly sensed that I did not like Lord Marsh.

Marsh climbed into his chaise, gave the word to his coachman to proceed, and the vehicle moved off. I took a deep breath, feeling profoundly shaken by what had happened.

"Don't you like that man, Georgie?" Anna asked as we walked through the entrance and into the park.

"I don't think he and Lord Winterdale get along very well," I returned cautiously. "It would probably be wisest for the both of us to stay away from him, Anna."

"Why don't they get along?" Anna asked. "Did they have a fight?"

"I think so."

Anna looked thoughtful. Then two deer appeared in the grass at the side of the road and her attention was distracted. We did not talk about Lord Marsh for the remainder of our walk.

Lord Winterdale was waiting for us when we returned from our walk about two hours later. I sent Anna upstairs and trailed after him into the library, not at all liking the anger that I could see so clearly in the rigid set of his shoulders. He did not sit down behind his desk as usual, but stood under the Stubbs painting in front of the fireplace and glared at me.

"Are you mad?" he demanded. "There are four men loose in London who you know are out for your blood and you go walking by yourself in the park at the loneliest hour of the morning? Unescorted? Did you want to find yourself pushed into the Serpentine this time?"

Because I knew I was in the wrong, and because I didn't want to admit it, I stupidly did not tell him about our meeting with Lord Marsh.

"Eight o'clock in the morning is a very busy time in London," I defended myself. "The only people who are not out of bed are the very people whom I have been avoiding! Anna and I were perfectly safe. And I did take Robin with us, my lord. He is certainly big enough to fight off anyone."

"The people you have been avoiding are often just *coming* home at eight o'clock in the morning, Miss Newbury," he said angrily. "It was not at all unlikely for you to have been seen on the streets by someone like Marsh."

Stupidly, once more I said nothing.

"Well," he said at last in a voice whose anger had moderated slightly, "it seems as if no harm has been done." His blue eyes held mine. "But don't be so foolish again."

I said, "It is that Anna is finding this stay in London so confining, you see."

"I realize that, but perhaps that particular problem will soon be resolved." Lord Winterdale leaned his shoulders against the mantlepiece. "I had a talk with George Stanhope last night and he asked my permission to pay his addresses to you."

I stared at Lord Winterdale in shock. "He did?"

"Yes, Miss Newbury, he did. I asked him if he was aware of the fact that you had no portion, and he said that he was. He also told me that he is aware of your responsibility to Anna and he will undertake to offer her a home for the rest of her life." He shrugged. "In short, Miss Newbury, this appears to be precisely the offer you were hoping for. I queried Stanhope about his own expectations and, as I thought, they are very handsome. He has a nice property in Derby and ten thousand a year—more than adequate for your purposes, I should think."

I stared at him in stunned amazement.

"Well?" he said irritably. "What is wrong?"

I said, "Last night Lord Borrow told me that his mother wanted to meet me."

He gave me a smile that was as wintry as his name. "You appear to have made a resounding success, Miss Newbury. I congratulate you. If you would like me to interview Borrow as to his expectations, I shall be glad to do so for you."

I said numbly, "I didn't expect either Lord Borrow or Mr. Stanhope to be the ones who would come up to scratch."

"Ah," he said softly. "You were hoping perhaps for an offer from Lord Henry?"

I had not been hoping for an offer from Lord Henry. I knew that suddenly, finally, and terrifyingly. I stood there in the Mansfield House library, looking at Lord Winterdale, and at last the knowledge that I had been trying so hard to evade pushed itself irresistibly to the front of my mind.

I didn't want to marry any of my three suitors.

I pity any woman who loses her heart to Lord Winterdale.

I remembered thinking that on the evening of my

come-out ball, when I had seen how effortlessly and how carelessly he had charmed his female guests.

I had never dreamed then that I would be one of those women whom I pitied.

He was looking at me now, with his reckless eyebrows flying like flags, and I realized how much I loved to look at him, how much I missed him when he wasn't around, how much his clever brain stimulated mine, how much . . .

"Are you in love with Lord Henry?" Lord Winterdale asked me, his voice harsh with impatience.

Get a hold of yourself, Georgie, I commanded myself sternly. I squared my shoulders like a soldier coming to attention. "No, my lord, I am not in love with Lord Henry. It is just that I have always thought that his personality seems more suited to Anna. However, if Mr. Stanhope is willing to offer her the shelter of his home, then of course I will entertain his offer."

I felt like crying as I said this.

"You're certain you wouldn't prefer Borrow?" Lord Winterdale said. "I believe you will find that his income is even more substantial than Stanhope's."

"As I told you when first I came to see you, I am not a fortune hunter," I said sharply. "Mr. Stanhope seems to be a very pleasant gentleman. I am sure that I will grow accustomed to being married to him. One day."

He made a restless movement with his hands and then folded his arms across his chest as if he was forcing them to be still. "Still regretting this Frank fellow, eh?"

I blinked in surprise. Then I shook my head. "I always knew that union was impossible, my lord. It doesn't do to regret what cannot be, you know."

The smile he gave me was wry and full of unexpected

pain. "I know it well, Miss Newbury," he said. "I know it well."

Lady Winterdale was furious when she learned that I was about to receive an offer of marriage from Mr. Stanhope. Over the luncheon table she scolded Catherine for not making enough of an effort at the parties we were attending.

"You must show more animation, Catherine," she exhorted her daughter. "Look at Georgiana. She has nothing to offer a man except a pretty smile, and she has managed to secure an offer." She looked at me. "Not that Mr. Stanhope is a brilliant *parti*, Georgiana. His fortune is but respectable. However, he is certainly a notable catch for *you*."

"He seems very nice," I said with a regrettable lack of enthusiasm.

Catherine, who it appeared to me was evincing more and more of an ability to ignore her mother, gave me a searching look through her spectacles. "I must say, you don't sound very enthusiastic, Georgie. Don't you love him?"

I toyed with the slice of cold roast beef on my plate. "He's nice enough, Catherine," I said. "I am certain that we shall deal very well together."

Catherine looked both worried and unconvinced.

Lady Winterdale bestowed upon me one of the few approving looks I had ever won from her. "A very sensible attitude, Georgiana," she said. "This business of love is all very well for the lower classes, but when it comes to marriage a girl needs to look at the realities. I can assure you, any well-brought-up girl would find love in a cottage very unpleasant indeed."

"Yes, ma'am," I said listlessly, and pushed my roast beef to the side. I did not feel like eating.

Mr. Stanhope presented himself precisely at two o'clock in the afternoon. Lady Winterdale took him into the library and sent for me. As soon as I came into the room she departed, saying with an archness that did not become her at all, "Well, I will leave you two young people alone for a few moments, then."

The door closed behind her and I looked at Mr. Stanhope. He was standing in front of the fireplace, under the Stubbs painting, and he immediately struck me as an interloper. His hair might be black, but his brows were boringly level and his eyes were light green, not blue. He smiled at me. "I think you must know why I am here, Miss Newbury," he said.

I made myself smile back. "Yes," I said, "I think I do."

He came across the floor and took my hands into his. No shock of awareness leaped through my blood at his touch. He said soberly, "I hope very much that you will marry me, Georgiana. I have come to love you dearly, and my life would seem very empty indeed if I never saw your smile again."

It was scarcely a declaration of great passion, but I did not think he was a passionate man. Perhaps that was just as well, I thought. It would have been more difficult being married to a man like Frank, who would have known that something was missing in me that should have belonged to him.

I said stiffly, "You do me a great honor, Mr. Stanhope. I shall try to be a good wife to you."

He gave me the warmest smile I had ever had from him and said, "My name is George, Georgiana."

That made me laugh. "We sound like a pair of dogs."

He put up his hands and cupped my face gently between his palms. Then he bent his mouth to mine.

His lips were cool and I felt none of the disgust I had experienced when old fishmouth had kissed me. I closed my eyes, and let him keep on kissing me, and thought desperately that perhaps it wouldn't be so bad being his wife.

A knock sounded on the door and Mr. Stanhope lifted his head and stepped away from me just as Lady Winterdale swept back into the room. Mr. Stanhope smiled at her and said a little breathlessly, "Lady Winterdale, I am happy to tell you that Miss Newbury has done me the honor of agreeing to be my wife."

Lady Winterdale gave me a sour look. "I wish you very happy, Georgiana. You are a very lucky girl."

I didn't feel lucky, however, I felt miserable.

George took a ring out of his pocket and slipped it on my finger. It was an absolutely huge diamond. It weighed my finger down.

"It is magnificent," I said. I gave him the brightest smile I could conjure up. "Come," I said, "let's go into the drawing room. I want to break the news to Catherine."

CHAPTER
thirteen

GEORGE AND I AGREED NOT TO FORMALLY ANnounce our engagement until after I had paid a visit to his family at his estate in Derby. This delay suited me very well, although when I informed Lord Winterdale of our plans, he disagreed. He thought the notice should be sent to the newspapers as soon as possible in the hope that it might reassure all of Papa's blackmail victims. I could understand his reasoning, but I found his eagerness to be rid of me excessively depressing.

That evening at Almack's I told Lord Borrow that I would not be able to meet his mother. He was not pleased.

"Does this mean that I should shortly be expecting to hear an announcement about your engagement?" he demanded.

We were standing together in front of one of the windows in the ballroom waiting for the next dance to form up.

"Yes," I said quietly. "We are not making it public just yet, but I certainly do not wish to give you or your mother a false idea of my situation, my lord."

"Who is it, Sloan or Stanhope?" he asked abruptly.

"Mr. Stanhope," I replied.

He looked down at me and for a moment his chocolate brown eyes wore the expression of a wounded animal. I felt terrible.

"Well, then," he said in a strangely staccato voice, "I see that I must wish you happy."

"Thank you," I replied, not knowing what else to say. "You are very kind."

The rest of the week passed in much the same way as usual: morning visits and shopping; afternoon musicales, receptions, and drives in the park; and evening balls. Ironically I saw George less than I usually did as he had gone into the country to break the news of his engagement to his parents.

I did endure one very chilly visit from George's sister, who was obviously not pleased with her brother's choice of a bride. I devoutly hoped that Miss Stanhope would soon find a husband of her own (one who was not Lord Winterdale) and so remove herself from my vicinity.

Several days before I was due to leave for my visit to George's home in Derby, I pleaded a headache and declined an invitation to accompany Lady Winterdale and Catherine to a garden party at a famous house outside of London. Instead I paid a quiet visit to the circulating library to collect some books to take with me into the country. I returned to Grosvenor Square to find Nanny waiting for me in the front hall in a state of hysterics.

"Thank God you have come home, Miss Georgiana," she cried. "I didn't know what I should do. Miss Anna has been kidnapped!"

I could feel the blood congeal in my veins. "Kidnapped?" I repeated. "What on earth do you mean, Nanny?"

The two of us were standing in the middle of the entrance hall, and I could see Mason standing by the dining-room door, while the footman who had let me in was still at his post by the front door. Nanny, who was usually so careful not to say anything in front of the servants, had clutched my arm and was rushing on, "After you left for the library, she went outdoors to the park in the middle of the square to get some air. I've let her go out there before. The Spenser children from Number 12 play out there often. But this time, when I looked for her an hour later, she was gone."

"You let her go out alone?" I asked incredulously.

"No, of course not!" Nanny's eyes, which had always reminded me of raisins they were so small and so dark, were full of fear. "Mary, one of the housemaids, was watching her. But, oh, Miss Georgiana! Someone hit poor Mary over the head and she still has not recovered consciousness!"

I knew then that Anna had truly been kidnapped, and I also knew who had taken her. My stomach heaved.

"Where is his lordship?" I asked, looking around the entrance hall as if I might find him hiding in a corner.

It was Mason who answered, advancing down the hall toward me from his position by the dining room. "I have sent footmen all over town to look for him, Miss Newbury. We are hoping to see him shortly."

"Have you sent for a doctor for Mary?" I asked Nanny distractedly.

"That we have." Tears began to stream down Nanny's worn face. "Oh Miss Georgiana, why would anyone want to take Miss Anna?"

At that moment, the front door was pushed open and Lord Winterdale came striding into the hall. He saw me and for a moment I could have sworn there was a flash of relief in his eyes. Then he scowled. "What the devil is going on here?" he demanded. "I've just had three of my footmen converge upon me at Jackson's boxing saloon. What is this dire and urgent matter that requires my immediate attention?"

I said in a voice that was almost as hysterical as Nanny's had been when she greeted me, "Anna has been kidnapped, and I know it was Lord Marsh who took her!"

He went very still. Then he said, "Come into the drawing room," and went to hold the door for me. We both went inside and he closed the door again, shutting out Nanny as well as the servants.

Lord Winterdale threw his hat and his gloves down upon the rosewood cabinet and said grimly, "How do you know it was Marsh?"

"Because we met him the other morning when we went for a walk in the park. I didn't tell you, my lord, but you were right—he was coming home as we were going out and he stopped us at the bottom of Oxford Street." I felt myself swept by anguish. "His eyes were all over Anna," I said.

Lord Winterdale cursed.

"Oh God, oh God, oh God," I said desperately. "What will he do to her?"

"Nothing, if I can catch him in time," Lord Winterdale returned grimly. "How long has she been missing?"

"Nanny said she went out to the park in the middle of the square just after I left for the library, and that was at eleven o'clock. Nanny did not discover that she was missing for an hour, so she could have been taken any time between eleven and twelve."

He nodded. "All right. Let us hope that he doesn't have that long a start."

"Will he have taken her to his house here in London?" I asked fearfully, thinking that if he only had to take her a mile away, he had plenty long enough to do his damage.

Lord Winterdale began to pace like a panther up and down the middle of the pink-and-blue Persian rug. The sunlight from the window slanted in and caught the crystal drops in the chandelier, reflecting rays of rainbows on his coal black head. "I doubt it. His wife is in town for the Season, and he is unlikely to be using his London house for any nefarious purposes while she is around."

"But she may not be around today," I said, and I could hear that the note of hysteria had crept back into my voice. I paused, trying to get a grip upon myself. "There is a huge garden party out at Staine House this afternoon. I'm sure Lady Marsh will be going there."

"Even if she is not on the premises, her servants are," Lord Winterdale pointed out. "And Marsh is cagey enough to realize that if he is actually caught with Anna, he will be called to account by the law. She's not a little girl from the gutter about whom no questions will be asked. No, he'll think himself far safer at his country estate than he will be in London. That way it will be easy to use her and then to get rid . . ."

He must have seen my face because he broke off abruptly. "Don't worry, Miss Newbury, it won't come to that. I will go after him immediately." He went to the door, threw it open and shouted, "Mason!"

The butler hurried into the room so quickly that I knew he must have been hovering just outside in the hall. "Yes, my lord?"

"Send to the stables and have the grays put to the phaeton. And tell them to be quick."

"Yes, my lord."

Lord Winterdale strode across the room to pick up his gloves, and I said, "I am going with you."

He stopped and turned to look at me. "No, you are

not. Marsh's main seat is near Winchester and even driving fast, which I will certainly be doing, it will take me over five hours to get there. That is too long a ride for you in an open carriage."

"My lord," I said in a level tone, "if you do not take me in your carriage, then I will steal one of the horses from the stable the moment you are gone and follow you in the saddle."

Our eyes met and held. He saw my resolution and said in a voice that was surprisingly mild, "You have always been a consummate blackmailer."

I didn't even flinch. "When we find Anna, she will need me."

He hesitated, then nodded once. "There can certainly be no doubt of that. All right, Miss Newbury, you may come. The horses should be at the door in ten minutes' time. Go and get yourself ready."

We made a quick stop at Lord Marsh's town house in Berkeley Square and Lord Marsh's butler told Lord Winterdale that his master was at his club. Lord Winterdale then paid a visit to the stables behind the earl's house, where he discovered that both the town chaise and the barouche, a partially covered type of carriage, were gone.

"The Head Groom told me that Lady Marsh took the town chaise to the party, but Marsh took the barouche. Said he had some important business to attend to in the country and would be back in two days' time."

"Then the butler lied," I said.

"The butler probably does not know yet, and probably won't know until Lady Marsh returns from the garden party. Marsh certainly wouldn't have wanted his butler giving me information as to his real whereabouts should I tumble to the fact that it was he who took Anna."

He was threading his way through the streets of London as he spoke and I sat quietly beside him and let him concentrate on his driving. The phaeton was a light carriage, and he had his four magnificent grays hitched to it. There was no doubt that we would be able to make better time than Lord Marsh, whose horses were not as good as Lord Winterdale's (no one's were) and who was driving a heavier carriage.

Ironically, we left London on the same road that we would have taken if we had been going to Staine House, where the garden party was being held that afternoon. Neither of us spoke as the grays cantered steadily along the highway that would take us steadily southwest into Hampshire.

We had set out at one-thirty in the afternoon and by four we were on the Hampshire border. At five-thirty we were at Basingstoke, where we stopped briefly to water the horses and for Lord Winterdale to drink a glass of beer and me a glass of lemonade.

We occasioned a bit of notice at the inn in Basingstoke. Lord Winterdale, of course, was less of a novelty than I was. The sight of a gentleman traveling the highway in his phaeton was not unusual. It was definitely unusual for a young lady to be accompanying him.

Not for the first time I worried what was going to be the outcome of this adventure for me.

Resolutely, I pushed the thought from my mind. I had had no choice. As ever, Anna's need had to come before mine.

We set out from Basingstoke and turned south, toward King Alfred's capital of Winchester. Resolutely, I turned my attention to the countryside, which, in this part of the world was gentle, with no high hills or deep valleys. Indeed, the most notable part of the landscape was the hedgerows with which the country was honeycombed. Under these irregular borders of copse-wood and timber I could see spring primroses and anemones and wild hyacinths. I stared at them and tried not to let awful pictures of Anna and Lord Marsh form in my mind.

The grays were tired by the time we turned off the main road and trotted slowly down the lane that Lord Winterdale said would take us to Marsh Hall. I was tired, too, and very cold. It was a cold that went deeper than the mere chill a drop in the temperature can produce, however. This cold went right through to my bones.

For five long hours I had been praying that we would catch Marsh and Anna on the road, and we had not done so.

It was almost seven as we turned into the great iron gates that suddenly loomed beside the road and began the last part of our journey up the graveled drive.

"What if he isn't here after all?" I said to Lord Winterdale, trying not to betray my despair. "What if he's taken her to his hunting box? Or to another one of his estates?"

"We shall soon know the answer to those questions," came the comfortless reply. His profile was hard and bleak against the pink-tinged sky.

"Oh God," I said. "I have been praying and praying that we would come up with them on the road."

"I know. So have I."

I began to shiver. "What if he has raped her? She'll never get over it."

"If he has raped her, I will kill him," Lord Winterdale said calmly. "Let us hope that we are in time, however.

Don't make yourself ill until we know what our situation is."

I stared at him. *I will kill him.* He had said it as rationally as one might say, I will invite him to dinner. My shivering became worse.

At that moment, we rounded a turn in the drive and the house came into view. All I noticed at the time was that it was a rather strange conglomeration of diapered brickwork and an array of mullioned and transomed windows, which suggested a Jacobean house, with a hipped roof and gleaming central cupola, which was more characteristic of the reign of Charles II. I was scarcely in the mood to evaluate the architectural idiosyncrasies of Lord Marsh's abode, however, and sat, tense and rigid on the seat next to Lord Winterdale, as we pulled up to the front door and Lord Winterdale leaped down to knock imperatively on the front door. I scrambled down from the phaeton by myself and went to stand beside him.

After a wait of at least two minutes, it was opened by a butler who looked at Lord Winterdale with an expression on his face that could only be described as put out.

"I am the Earl of Winterdale," his lordship said commandingly, "and I am looking for Lord Marsh."

The butler looked even more put out. "Lord Marsh is not here, my lord. He is in London."

My heart dropped into my stomach. After all this, we had made the wrong move. Anna wasn't here after all.

My shivering became even worse. What were we going to do now? Where could she be?

Oh Anna, I thought in despair. *This is all my fault. I should have married old fishmouth and kept you safe in Sussex.*

"I believe we will come in and look for ourselves,"

Lord Winterdale said, and pushed his way past the butler into the house. I followed in his footsteps.

The butler was outraged. "You can't come bulling your way in here, my lord," he said.

"Yes, well I just have, haven't I?" Lord Winterdale replied. He began to walk toward the carved pine staircase that stood in the center of the great hall. He ran up stairs, calling Lord Marsh's name in a voice that was dangerous enough to send an icy chill up and down my spine.

He was gone for perhaps five minutes and when he came downstairs his face was absolutely bleak.

"He's not here," he told me. "Nor is there any sign of Anna."

I felt all the color drain from my face, and my shivering became uncontrollable. I pressed my hands to my mouth.

"Oh my God," I said, "what are we going to do now?"

He came over to me, took off his greatcoat, and draped it around my shoulders. Then he ran his fingers through his hair. "You must have been right," he said. "He must have taken her to one of his other estates."

The dreadful pictures I had been trying to suppress came to my mind, and I clenched my eyes shut as if I could deny them access. I clutched Lord Winterdale's coat around me. It was warm from his body but still I could not seem to stop shivering.

"We will have some tea," Lord Winterdale said to the butler. "And some food as well. The lady is frozen and needs some nourishment."

"I'm not hungry," I protested. "I couldn't eat a thing."

"You're both hungry and exhausted," he said. "Come into the dining room and we'll have something to eat and see if we can come up with another plan."

I thought with despair that it was too late for another plan, but I let him steer me into the dining room and sat down across from him at the table, his heavy, caped coat still draped around my shoulders. The surly butler brought us a pot of hot tea and a plate of cold meat. I couldn't eat the meat, but the hot tea tasted good and I drank two cups and was grateful for its warmth.

We sat for an hour at the table, evaluating our options, which looked grimmer and grimmer the more we discussed them. It was already too late to return to London, even if Lord Winterdale's horses had been fit to make the journey. He himself was looking grimmer and grimmer when we heard the sound of the knocker being pounded on the front door.

Both Lord Winterdale and I jumped to our feet and moved out into the hall as once more the crabby butler made his way to answer the knocker's summons. The door opened and there, on the doorstep, stood one of the Winderdale grooms.

"Oh, my lord," he said with enormous relief as he spied Lord Winterdale. "I am so glad that I have found you! I have brought you news that Miss Anna has been found."

I took a single step forward. "Found?" I asked. "Is she all right?"

"Yes, my lady. Miss Catherine brought her home, and she is perfectly fine."

Black spots suddenly appeared before my eyes and a strange humming began to sound in my ears. I blinked and I blinked but the spots did not go away. I tried to take a deep breath, but it didn't seem to help, and for the first time in my life, I fainted dead away.

I awoke to find myself lying on a sofa with Lord Winterdale sitting beside me. He had my wrist in his hand and his fingers were on my pulse. I opened my eyes, stared up into his intensely blue eyes and said unsteadily, "What happened?"

"You fainted. It's nothing. Just remain where you are for a few more minutes, and you will be fine."

Then I remembered what had happened. "Is it true?" I asked, fearful that I had dreamed the whole thing. "Is Anna really all right?"

"Yes, she is. Apparently all the while that we were chasing her into Hampshire, she has been safe and sound at Mansfield House in town."

I raised myself up a little from the pillow that had been propped under my head. "Then she wasn't kidnapped at all?"

"Oh yes, she was kidnapped all right. I have here a letter from Catherine. Would you like me to read it to you?"

"Yes, please," I said, and subsided back onto the sofa to listen. Lord Winterdale began to read:

Dear Georgie and Philip, I hope this letter reaches you in time for you to turn around and return to London before night falls, but I want you to know that Anna is back home again, and she is perfectly all right.

The garden party at Staine House was a terrible bore and I told Mother that I wanted to leave early because I had a headache. Our carriage was coming out of the local road that leads from Staine House onto the main highway to London when a barouche came racing by us, going at what I can only describe as a dangerous rate of speed. Mother and I were inside the chaise and so we could not see the occupants of the barouche of course, but Williams, who was driving, was certain that he spied Anna pressed up against the back of the covered part of the carriage. You know how she likes to wear her hair loose like a child, and there are very few girls who have that beautiful spun gold hair of hers.

Mama was furious that we had almost had an accident because of the barouche and she opened the window to give Williams a piece of her mind. That was when Williams said that he had seen Anna in the carriage.

I rolled down the window on my side and told Williams to go after the barouche.

Needless to say, Mama was furious, but I had a bad feeling in my stomach, Georgie. I thought that if we were wrong, and it wasn't Anna, we could just apologize and no harm would be done. But if it was, and someone was trying to kidnap her to make Philip pay a ransom to get her back, then I would never forgive myself if I had let her go.

Williams, bless him, listened to me and not to Mama and we took off after the barouche. We might not have caught up to it if it hadn't got stuck behind a haywagon on the road. Lord Marsh (for it was he who was the driver!) tried to pass the wagon, but there was not enough room and he overturned the barouche into a ditch at the side of the road. Anna was stunned and bewildered when we came up with her, but otherwise she is unharmed.

So that is the situation here at home. Nanny is taking care of Anna and Mama is having fits that you are out driving around the countryside with Philip unchaperoned. Please come home as quickly as you can.

"Thank God," I said. "Oh, thank God."

He nodded and stood up. I wished he would have stayed where he was. I tried to sit up and realized for the first time that his coat was draped over me like a blanket. I said unsteadily, "I have never fainted before in my entire life."

He ignored that comment. "My Aunt Agatha is right, Miss Newbury," he said. "It is imperative that we return to London as soon as possible. Your reputation would be wrecked should it be known that you spent a night with me unchaperoned."

I looked at him doubtfully. "Isn't it a little late to start out for London now, my lord?"

"Unfortunately, it is." Distractedly, he ran his fingers through his hair, disordering it so that one black lock fell over his forehead.

He said, "I think our best choice is to remain here at Marsh Hall for the night and to start back to London early tomorrow morning. Marsh is hardly going to say anything about this little adventure, and if we are back in Grosvenor Square before ten, there is no reason for anyone to know that we have been gone for the night."

"Before ten." I counted back on my fingers. "That means we have to leave here by five?"

"Four would be better. My grays will be tired after the effort of yesterday and we won't be able to make the time we made today."

"Four o'clock. How delightful," I said faintly.

"You can sleep the day away once we're home," he said unfeelingly. "The important thing now is to get you home before anyone knows that you have been away."

Even though I was exhausted, I didn't sleep very well that night. When Lord Winterdale knocked on my door at four in the morning, I struggled out of bed in the cold bedroom whose paltry fire had long since gone out. Dressing was easy. Since I had slept in my dress, all I had to do was put on my shoes. I went down the pine staircase, with its intricately carved designs of all different kinds of fruits, and found Lord Winterdale in the dining room having coffee and more of the cold beef we had been served last evening.

"Eat something," he commanded me. "I don't want you fainting on me again."

I struggled to get some of the roast beef down, but I have never been one to eat meat for breakfast. I watched Lord Winterdale spread horseradish liberally over his beef and repressed a shudder.

By four o'clock we were back in the phaeton and heading for the highway. The sun had not yet come up and the early-morning air was cold. Lord Winterdale had commandeered a blanket for me from Lord Marsh's butler, and I wrapped it around my shoulders like an old peasant woman. I knew I looked awful. My eyes had circles under them, my braids had long strands of hair sliding out of them, and my dress was wrinkled beyond repair.

"If Mr. Stanhope could see me now, he'd break our engagement for certain," I said glumly as we drove along in the cold gray morning air. "I look like a hag."

"He will have far more cause to break your engagement than your looks if this little adventure ever becomes known to him," Lord Winterdale returned coolly.

I sighed and scrubbed my eyes with my fingers.

"What are we going to do about Lord Marsh?" I asked.

"I have been thinking about that," came the very grim reply.

"You can't call him out," I said. "If you do, people will think that I am the one involved, not Anna, and that will certainly put off Mr. Stanhope."

"That thought has crossed my mind."

I looked at him, and said earnestly, "Anna's welfare has to be paramount. You do see that, don't you, my lord?"

The sun was just beginning to rise above the horizon now, streaking the sky with bands of rose and gold.

I think it was because I was so tired and so emotionally wrung out, that I found myself talking to him in a way that I had never talked to anyone before.

"It is so hard to be a woman," I said. "One never has control of one's own life. I look around me at the parties I have been going to all Season long, and I see all these young girls, most of whom are loved and spoiled and lapped in luxury, and I see that one man, a husband, stands between them and homelessness. It is utterly terrifying."

His glance was a flash of blue in the growing light. "Surely homelessness is too strong a word," he said.

The sun was brighter now, and the hedgerows along the side of the road were beginning to cast shadows on the roadway.

"Perhaps," I said. "But it is not too strong a word for me and Anna."

He was silent. The grays trotted steadily on. They were not being pushed to canter today.

"What would you have done if you didn't have Anna to look after?" he asked after a while. "Would you have married the squire's son?"

"I don't know," I said. I tried to laugh, but all I managed to produce was a watery chuckle. "Perhaps I would have run away and become a circus equestrienne."

"I doubt that," he replied drily.

I sighed. "You are probably right." I sat up straighter. "To return to my original question, my lord. What can we do about Lord Marsh? Obviously we must do something to keep him from repeating his kidnapping attempt, but at the same time we don't want any scandal."

He said with a bitterness that shocked me, "This everlasting concern about scandal. The only good thing I can say about my upbringing was that my father was never concerned about scandal." He paused, as if trying to get his emotions under control. "Much as I would like to call that bastard Marsh out and put a bullet through him, you are right. We *can't* afford the scandal. Instead, I shall call upon him and threaten him with exposure should he ever try to lay hands upon Anna again. As it is now, his acceptance in polite society hangs by the merest thread. If there is any more scandal about him, that thread will be cut. He doesn't want that."

I digested what he had said. "Are you sure you can really assure Anna's safety that way?"

"I am sure. I only wish I could assure the safety of all the other children upon whom he preys." His voice was very harsh as he added, "I agree with you, Miss Newbury, that in some ways it is very hard to be a woman."

CHAPTER
fourteen

WE REACHED LONDON BY TEN AND WERE INSIDE Mansfield House by ten-fifteen. Anna threw herself into my arms, weeping hysterically, and I took her upstairs, leaving Lord Winterdale to make explanations to his aunt. After I had got Anna calmed down, I left her with Nanny and went next door to my own room. I desperately wanted a bath and a hair wash and, as the tub was being brought to my room, Catherine came in the door.

She said, "I won't stay more than a minute, but are you all right, Georgie?"

I ran to give her a huge hug. "Thanks to you, Catherine, darling, I am fine, and Anna is, too. Thank you, thank you, thank you! If you had not been there when Lord Marsh's carriage went by, or if you had not decided to follow it . . ."

I could not control the shudder that went through me at this thought.

Catherine hugged me back tightly. "You must thank Williams as well, Georgie. He was the one who saw Anna in the first place."

"I will be certain to do that," I said fervently.

The tub had been set up in front of the fireplace and Betty came in the door now with two maids trailing behind her carrying cans of hot water, which they proceeded to empty into the tub. When the three of them had left to return to the kitchen to fetch more water, I said to Catherine, "I slept in my clothes last night, and I don't believe I have ever felt more grimy in all my life."

"Philip told Mama that you both spent the night at Marsh Hall," Catherine said.

I nodded. "I froze all night long in an icy-cold bedroom, and then we left at four in the morning so that we could be back in London before anyone could suspect that we had been gone."

"What a dreadful experience," she said feelingly.

"Not as dreadful as it would have been if Marsh had got his hands on Anna," I assured her.

"Well, that is certainly true." It was her turn to shudder. "Poor child, did you know that she had been half-drugged to keep her quiet?"

At that point, the parade of maids with the water cans came once more in my door and Catherine left, saying that she would see me later, after my bath.

The hot water and hair wash revived me somewhat, and I spent the rest of the morning by the fire in my bedroom, letting my hair dry and reading a book. Catherine came upstairs and reported that Lord Winterdale had gone out to show himself around town, which I supposed was a good idea even though I was certain that we were safe.

After all, how was anyone to know that we had been gone together overnight? Under the circumstances, Lord Marsh was scarcely likely to say anything!

There was a ball at the Richwoods' that night, and Lady Winterdale felt that it was imperative for me to attend. I had managed to catch a nap during the course of the afternoon, so I was not as exhausted as I thought I might be as we alighted from the chaise and made our way into Richwood House in Portland Square.

It was halfway through the evening that I noticed that something was wrong. People were looking at me, and one or two men who always asked me to dance did not. In fact, I actually found myself sitting out two dances, something which had never happened to me before.

By the time we left, Lady Winterdale was looking like thunder.

"What has happened, ma'am?" I asked as we rode through the quiet streets on our way home. "Something is obviously wrong."

"Three separate people told me that they have heard a rumor that you and Philip spent the night together," Lady Winterdale said. "I did my best to quell the story, but apparently the two of you were seen returning to London." Her clothes rustled as she turned to glare at me. "This is a most distressing turn of events, Georgiana. I am seriously displeased."

"Good heavens," I said faintly. "But who could have seen us?" It was too late for the late-night carousers to be coming home and too early for those who were paying morning visits to be out and about."

"Apparently Mr. Tunby is in the habit of going for a walk in the morning for his health, and he was walking down Park Lane when you and Philip came driving by. You must admit, Georgiana, that you certainly looked as if you had been out all night." We passed under a streetlamp, and it illuminated a solitary gentleman walking along the pavement in the direction of St. James's Street, where all of the men's clubs were located. Lady Winterdale continued, "I was horrified when I saw the state of your clothes and your hair when you walked into the house this morning."

Catherine reached over and squeezed my hand, which was lying loosely in my lap.

"I cannot imagine what Mr. Stanhope will do when he hears this rumor," Lady Winterdale said with dire foreboding. "No gentleman wishes to marry a woman about whom scandal clings."

"He can't cry off," Catherine said loyally. "No gentleman would."

"The engagement is unofficial; nothing has been put in the papers," Lady Winterdale said, an ominous note in her voice. "He most certainly can cry off." She paused. "Unfortunately."

"I will, of course, explain the entire situation to him," I said quietly. "Surely he will see that I had no choice but to chase after Anna."

"For your sake, Georgiana, I hope that he does," Lady Winterdale said in a tone of voice that indicated she thought this hope was unlikely to be fulfilled. "A marriage announcement at this particular moment would go far toward saving your reputation. If Mr. Stanhope backs off, however, then I fear that your chances of catching another husband will be quite ruined."

Lady Winterdale did not sound as if this result would cause her to shed many tears.

I usually did not pay a great deal of attention to Lady Winterdale's comments, but the fact that Lord Henry Sloan did not pay his usual visit the following morning sent off a warning note to me that perhaps this time her prediction of disaster might not be wrong.

I did not have a chance to speak to Lord Winterdale about what had happened at the Richwood ball, as he was closeted in the library with his steward all morning and then, in the afternoon, he went out and did not return until after I had gone to bed.

The following morning, George Stanhope arrived in

Grosvenor Square and asked to speak to me in private. I took him into the downstairs drawing room and we stood under the chandelier and faced each other across the pink and blue Persian rug.

His usual cool demeanor was definitely ruffled. "Georgiana," he said, "I have heard the most extraordinary story from my sister . . ." He broke off, looking worried and clearly not certain how he should proceed.

I had already decided that the best way to handle this situation was to be completely truthful. In consequence, I told him all about how Lord Marsh had kidnapped Anna. I told him how Lord Winterdale and I had chased them into Hampshire, only to find that it hadn't been necessary after all. I told him that we had stayed at Marsh Hall overnight— in separate rooms—and left for London at four o'clock in the morning in the hope of getting home before anyone knew that we had been gone.

"You can imagine how terrified I was that something dreadful was going to happen to Anna," I said in conclusion. "It is nothing short of a miracle that Catherine was able to save her."

I had expected him to agree with me, to express a reciprocal horror about Anna's kidnapping as well as relief at her rescue. But that is not what happened.

"Whatever possessed you to go with Winderdale, Georgiana?" he demanded in a voice that was certainly not sympathetic. "He was perfectly capable of dealing with the situation without your presence. And I blame him even more for taking you. He must have known that there was no chance of your getting back to London before night fell!"

I stared into his angry green eyes. "But I wanted to go," I said reasonably. "If we had indeed found Anna, she would have needed me."

"Winterdale could have taken her nurse with him," he snapped. "He most certainly should not have taken you!"

I was furious that he was blaming Lord Winterdale for a decision that had been mine.

"I forced him to take me," I said. I lifted my chin. "I told him that I would follow him on horseback if he didn't."

George's answer was prompt. "Then he should have locked you in your room. Really, Georgiana, he has exposed you to all the worst sort of gossip and speculation. . . ."

Locked me in my room! I could feel my eyes flash with outrage. I took a step closer to him, skewered him with my gaze, and said in a steely voice, "Tell me this, George, do you believe me guilty of illicit conduct with Lord Winterdale?"

A flush suffused his pale skin. "Really, Georgiana . . ."

I moved yet a little closer. "Well, do you?"

He said unwillingly, "I certainly do not think that you would enter into such a relationship of your own volition."

A faint red haze began to appear before my eyes. "I see," I said. "So he is supposed to have raped me?"

"Really, Georgiana! Such language does not become you."

At this point, I was beside myself. "Well, let me tell you this, George, such thoughts do not become *you*." We were standing very close, and I had to tip my head back to see beyond his nose. "Nothing happened between me and Lord Winterdale! I did not go to bed with him, either willingly or unwillingly. We went to Hampshire in pursuit of my sister and Lord Marsh, and we returned as soon as we learned that Anna was safe. And that is the entire story."

The flush had subsided from his cheeks, and he was looking even more pale than usual. Close as we were, he made no attempt to reach for me. "Perhaps what you say is true, Georgiana, but that is not what people around town are saying."

I stepped back from him, lowered my chin and tried to speak in a milder voice. "Believe me, George, I have no intention of holding you to our engagement." My temper sparked again. "God forbid that you should attach yourself to one as tainted as I."

He looked at me unhappily. "You make it sound as if I have no feelings for you. That is not true. It is just that I must consider the good name of my family."

"George," I said in the pleasantest voice I could manage to produce, "I wouldn't marry you if you were the last man on earth. I wouldn't trust a coward like you with the welfare of my dog, let alone my innocent little sister. Now will you please go away and leave me alone?"

He hesitated, opened his mouth as if he wanted to say something more, thought better of it, turned, and departed as if the hound of hell was at his heels.

I was still standing there under the chandelier, shaking with anger, when the door opened once more and Lord Winterdale came quietly into the drawing room.

"I passed Mr. Stanhope on his way out," he said. "He did not look happy."

I said stiffly, "We have agreed to sever our connection."

His reckless eyebrows lifted. "Damn," he said. "I was afraid that something like that might happen. Evidently that old busybody Tunby saw us driving down Park Lane the other morning."

I clasped my hands in front of me and nodded. "It is all over town," I said in a stifled voice.

He said, "Come along with me to the library. We had better have a talk."

I followed him out the door of the drawing room and down the hall to his private sanctum. Once we were inside, he went over to his desk, took his usual chair, and waved me to mine. Once we were seated, he regarded me across the neatly piled papers, his face completely shuttered.

He said, "I am afraid there is nothing else for it, Miss Newbury. You are going to have to marry me."

I stared at him in utter astonishment. "W-what did you say?" I stuttered, certain that I could not have heard him correctly.

"I said that you were going to have to marry me."

I stared in silence at the face I had come to know so well: at the black hair, the recklessly slanted eyebrows, the brilliant blue eyes, the hard mouth that at moments could look so heartbreakingly sweet. He looked back at me, his face expressionless, but I had a feeling that he was not as controlled as he appeared to be.

At last I choked, "Are you serious?"

"Of course I am serious," he said irritably. "This is hardly the sort of thing that one makes jokes about." He leaned back in his chair. "If Stanhope had stood by you, then we might have escaped the net. But as it is . . . not only do you have to marry me, but I have to marry you." He lifted an eyebrow. "I really do not care to figure in the eyes of society as a despoiler of innocent maidens."

"Oh," I said. "I see."

He gave me a cool smile. "It won't be so bad," he said. "I will be kind to Anna, and as you have been saying all along, you must marry someone who can take care of her. Winterdale Park in Surrey is a very pleasant estate, and I am quite certain that she will be happy there."

As if from a long way away, I heard my voice say, "I am certain that she will be."

He lined up a pile of papers that were already in perfect order. "Good, that is settled then. I will have a talk with Aunt Agatha and ask her if it will be best to have banns called or if we should get a special license and be married immediately."

"All right," I said in a very small voice.

He gave me a pleasant nod. "Why don't you run along, then, and ask Aunt Agatha to come to see me. Then you can go and break the news to Anna."

I stood up slowly. It occurred to me that perhaps this was the first time in history that a girl had been proposed to across a desk. I walked to the door, opened it, paused, and looked back. He was leaning back in his chair staring at a green-marble paperweight. There was an ineffable weariness in his pose, and I thought once again that he was the loneliest person I had ever known.

I loved him. I loved him, and now I was going to marry him, and I wanted to weep.

Oh Philip, I thought, daring to call him by his first name at last. *If you continue to lock yourself away from me like this, you will break my heart.*

Lady Winterdale thought that we should get a special license and be married within the week in the drawing room at Mansfield House. "We shall have a small wedding breakfast afterward, and then you and Georgiana can go into the country for a few weeks," she informed Lord Winterdale. "We must hope that by the time you return to London, the scandal will have blown over."

"I can't be away from London for more than two weeks," Lord Winterdale said smoothly. "I have appointments that I cannot break."

Not for the first time, I wondered what it was that he did all day long. He might be at his club drinking and gambling during the evening hours, but he was gone from the house for most of the day as well. What appointments did he have? His life was a complete mystery to me, while mine was an open book to him.

This was not a situation that augured well for a successful marriage.

Anna had been surprisingly delighted when I told her that I was going to marry Lord Winterdale.

"Oh good, Georgie," she had said, clapping her hands. "Lord Winterdale is nice. I like him. He plays ball with me sometimes in the garden."

I hadn't known that.

"We will be going to stay at his house in the country. It is called Winterdale Park, and it is supposed to be very pretty. You will like to get away from the city, won't you, darling?"

"Oh yes!" Anna said with enthusiasm. "May I bring Snowball with me, Georgie?"

"I don't see why not," I replied. "I am sure that Lord Winterdale won't mind if we send for him."

When Anna broached this subject to Lord Winterdale at dinner that evening, he gave her one of his rare smiles and said that she was welcome to bring any animals she wanted to Winterdale Park, that there was plenty of room.

Anna regarded him across the table, her eyes very big. "May I have a donkey, Lord Winterdale? I have always wanted a donkey, but Papa would never let me."

"Certainly you may have a donkey," he returned.

"And since we are soon to be brother and sister, I think that you had better begin to call me Philip, Anna."

She gave him her incredibly beautiful smile and clapped her hands with delight. "I would like that," she said. She turned her head to me. "Did you hear that, Georgie? I may have a donkey!"

Ever since Anna had seen a picture book that featured a little Spanish boy and his donkey, having a donkey of her own had been one of her chief ambitions.

"What fun that will be," I said.

Lady Winterdale's autocratic voice interrupted our talk of donkeys. "I have spoken to Lady Jersey, Philip, and she has graciously agreed to attend the wedding ceremony and the breakfast. Her presence will do a great deal toward lending respectability to your union to Georgiana."

"Thank you, Aunt Agatha," Lord Winterdale—or Philip, as I now must call him—said. "I have also spoken to Lord Castlereagh, and he and Lady Castlereagh will attend as well."

Lady Winterdale stared at her nephew in dumb-founded amazement. "The Castlereaghs?" she said on a note of displeasure. "I did not know that you were acquainted with the Castlereaghs, Philip."

Lord Castlereagh was the foreign secretary for the government and Lady Castlereagh was a patroness of Almack's. Together, they were two of the most powerful people in London.

"Oh, I have known Castlereagh for a number of years," Philip said indifferently.

"You never told me that!" Lady Winterdale's pointy nose quivered.

He gave her an ironic look. "I did not realize that I was required to inform you of all my friendships, Aunt."

As usual, she was impervious to insult. "*How* do you know the Castlereaghs?" she demanded.

He hesitated, then obviously realized that she would not let him rest if he did not answer.

"It is Lord Castlereagh with whom I am acquainted, ma'am. As you know, I spent many years on the Continent during the recent war, and I was often in a position to collect information that Castlereagh found useful. Suffice it to say, he owes me a few favors. He will be at the wedding."

I stared at my future husband in amazement. He had been a spy!

Catherine said, "If the Jerseys and the Castlereaghs are in attendance, Mama, people will hardly be able to say that there is anything havey-cavey about the marriage."

Lady Winterdale transferred her look of displeasure to her daughter. "*Havey-cavey?*" she said. "Really, Catherine, I cannot imagine where you have learned such disreputable language."

"I beg your pardon, Mama," said Catherine, who did not look in the least repentant.

Not for the first time I remarked to myself on the change in Catherine, and I thought of those musical afternoons and the Duke of Faircastle's eldest son. While it was wonderful to see her beginning to stand on her own feet, my fear for my friend was that her love was as one-sided as my own.

CHAPTER
fifteen

PHILIP PROCURED A SPECIAL LICENSE FROM THE OFFICE of the Archbishop of Canterbury, which allowed us to be married at any convenient time or place without prior publishing of banns. We set the date for three days after we got the license, and I spent the intervening time getting Anna and Nanny ready to accompany us to Winterdale Park in Surrey after the marriage. They would be making their home there permanently, while after two weeks I would be returning to town with Philip.

"I have business in London that I cannot neglect, and if we wish to avoid any further gossip, you had better come back with me," he told me during the fifteen minutes that we spent together discussing our immediate future. "If people think that I have married you in a hurry and then dumped you in the country . . . well, you can imagine what they will say."

I was intensely curious about this mysterious "business" of his, but I didn't feel as if I could ask him what it was. He kept his life so secret, was so guarded against trespassers, that I knew if I asked him about it, I would be snubbed.

We were going to be married, and all I knew about him was that something terrible must have happened to him to cause him to become the guarded, wary man that he was. I thought that my only hope was that hint of sweetness that

I had caught a glimpse of once or twice. If only I could reach through the layers of distrust he had thrown up around himself, and find that sweetness, then perhaps we could have a marriage.

It was raining on the day that I was wed. A bad omen, I thought, as I dressed in the white-silk high-waisted evening gown with puffed sleeves and long white gloves that I was wearing for the big occasion. The gown was complemented by a veil of fine white lace, which was attached to a small pearl tiara. The veil hung down my back almost to my waist. I had a bouquet of white roses to carry and a string of pearls to wear around my throat.

I was perfectly calm. In fact, I was amazed by how calm I was. I smiled and joked with Catherine, who was my bridesmaid, and I helped Anna arrange her hair in the way she liked the best.

The earl's apartment was at the very end of the passageway on the second floor, and there was a small staircase that went downstairs from those rooms to the anteroom on the floor below, so Philip did not have to pass by my room on his way downstairs. Consequently, I was not aware of when he descended to the first floor.

We were all starting to feel slightly restless when Lady Winterdale finally opened the door of my room and announced that the guests had arrived, the minister had arrived, and it was now time for us to make our own appearance.

Catherine came to straighten the folds of my veil. Anna ran on ahead of us, excited by the party atmosphere and eager to show off her new frock. I picked up my bouquet and walked out into the passageway in front of Catherine.

The wedding breakfast was to be served in the up-stairs drawing room, and the wedding was to be held in the downstairs drawing room. Down the great circular stairway we went, to the green-marble hall, where I could hear the sound of voices coming from within the opened doors of the drawing room.

It was then that my heart began to hammer.

We reached the doorway to the drawing room. Catherine and Anna went in, and I followed.

The room seemed surprisingly full, but the only person I had eyes for was the man who was standing by the fireplace. He was dressed, as I was, in evening clothes, and as I came in our gaze met briefly across the width of the room. Something flared in the deep blue of his eyes that made my breath hurry even faster.

Anna ran up to him and said shyly, "Do you like my new dress, Philip?"

He looked at her. "It is very pretty, Anna," he said. "You look lovely."

She smiled with radiant pleasure.

Then Lady Winterdale said majestically, "Now that everyone is here, I believe we are ready to start."

Philip and I took our places in front of the clergyman and the others arranged themselves behind us. The clergyman, whose name was the Reverend Halmark, opened his book and in a pronouncedly nasal voice began to read the centuries-old marriage ceremony from the Prayer Book, "Dearly beloved, we are gathered here today in the sight of God . . ."

The room was very quiet, and I felt as if all my senses were more acutely tuned than they had ever been before in my life. The scent of the roses from my bouquet filled my nostrils, and I could feel the warmth of Philip's body beside me right through the fine silk of my dress.

The clergyman looked at Philip and in his nasal voice began the ritual question, "Wilt thou have this woman to thy wedded wife . . ."

My heart thudded in my breast. *Thy wedded wife.* Could this really be happening?

Through the drumming in my veins I heard Philip answer firmly, "I will."

Then the Reverend Halmark turned to me and began to speak. When he stopped, I repeated Philip's "I will" in a voice that was mercifully steady.

From behind me I could hear Anna whisper a question to Catherine.

Philip produced a ring from his pocket and turned to me. "I, Philip Robert Edward, take thee, Georgiana Frances, to my wedded Wife . . ."

Those words again, I thought.

Once more Anna whispered something and the sound of her voice steadied me.

I repeated my part after Philip and then he took my hand into his and slipped a circle of plain gold upon my finger.

The familiar shock went through me at his touch.

The nasal voice informed the small gathering of people that we were now man and wife, in the Name of the Father, and of the Son, and of the Holy Ghost. Philip leaned down and kissed me chastely upon my cheek.

The shock went through me again.

Philip and I signed the marriage register, then Catherine and Philip's groomsman signed as witnesses. A few moments later, I found myself following Lady Winterdale up the great staircase to the second floor, where the wedding breakfast was to be served.

Anna crowded in beside me. "Are you married now, Georgie?" she wanted to know.

"Yes," I said numbly. "I rather think that I am."

Lady Winterdale, in her usual lavish fashion when she was spending her nephew's money, had ordered a splendid wedding breakfast. There was an array of fruits and cakes and tartes, as well as more substantial dishes like ham and turkey and lobster. Champagne flowed, and the wedding cake was laid out upon a table between the two front windows, waiting for me to cut it.

I couldn't eat a thing. I talked to Lady Jersey, or rather she talked to me, and I tried not to resent the way her curious eyes darted back and forth between me and Philip, as if she was trying to visualize the wanton acts that had brought about our unlikely union.

Lady Castlereagh, who was known for her arrogance, was surprisingly pleasant to me, talking rather didactically about the paintings she had seen the day before at the Royal Academy.

My new husband and the gentleman who had been his groomsman, a middle-aged, fair-haired man whom I had never seen before and whom Philip had introduced as Captain Thomas Greene, talked with Lord Castlereagh.

Anna ate a great deal of cake.

It was a little past noon when our guests took their departure. We had decided earlier in the week to leave right after the wedding for Winterdale Park. Neither Philip nor I had come right out and articulated our reasons for this decision, but I knew that I did not wish to spend the first night of my marriage under the same roof as Lady Winterdale, and I suspected that Philip felt the same.

The rain had ceased by the time we were ready to leave, but the sky was still heavily overcast. We were using three carriages to transport us into Surrey: the big coach was carrying all of our baggage as well as Betty and Philip's valet; the town chaise was carrying Anna and Nanny and me; and Philip was driving the phaeton.

Nanny stared at me as the chaise pulled away from in front of Mansfield House, worry in her little raisin-dark eyes.

"You don't need to ride with us, Miss Georgiana," she said. "Anna will be fine with me. If you wish to ride with his lordship, then you do that. You can always come back into the chaise if it comes on to rain."

I did not want to tell her that I had not been invited to ride with my husband, so I said merely, "I shall have plenty of opportunity to be with his lordship, Nanny, and I really do not desire to get my new pelisse wet should it begin to rain suddenly."

The worry did not leave Nanny's eyes. She knew very well that I did not care about getting wet.

We left London at two in the afternoon and it was after six by the time we arrived at Winterdale Park near Guildford in Surrey. I had been prepared by Catherine for what I would see, but even with the warning, my first sight of my new home was startling.

Winterdale Park looked like it should be sitting on the corner of a Venetian piazza, not in the middle of the English countryside. Catherine had told me that the present house had been built by her great-great-grandfather to replace the Elizabethan house that had formerly stood upon the site. Her ancestor had been in love with Italian architecture, she had said, and so he had imported the Venetian architect, Giacomo Leoni, to build his new house for him.

"Lord-a-mercy," Nanny squawked as we rolled down the drive and pulled up in front of the mansion's main entrance. The house itself was built of very red brick, but the entrance front was a central pedimented section done in stone, which stood out starkly against the red brick on either side. "This house looks foreign," was Nanny's disapproving comment.

"It was built by an Italian," I told her.

Nanny scowled. She didn't hold with Italians.

Lord Winterdale—Philip!—had given the reins of his horses to one of the footmen, who had come out of the house to greet us, and now he came to open the door of the chaise so that we could alight.

Anna got out first and looked around shyly. Winterdale Park was a much larger, much grander house than anything she had ever seen before.

"It's so big," she said to Philip in a very small voice.

"I know," he returned gently. "But Catherine tells me that there is a very pretty apartment in the back of the house looking out on the gardens that you and Nanny will like very much. The gardens are very pretty as well, and you will be able to watch your donkey grazing on the lawn."

The mention of the donkey perked her up considerably.

I thought of what he had just said—*Catherine tells me there is an apartment.*

He must be almost a stranger to Winterdale Park himself, I thought. He should have grown up here, he should have had the normal life that a boy of his class expected to lead. That life hadn't happened, however. At the age of eight he had been cast out into the ugly world of gambling hells and loose women.

What kind of moral guidance had he had? I wondered.

Exactly how ruthless was he capable of being? I knew that
he had wanted revenge on his aunt, and he had certainly
been willing to pay a huge amount of money to get it.

Yet he was kind to Anna.

I didn't know him at all, and I had just irrevocably
tied my life to his. It was a distinctly sobering thought.

Philip had sent his steward, Mr. Downs, ahead of us to
Winterdale Park in order to make certain that all was in
readiness for our arrival. Upon Philip's orders we were
spared the traditional lineup of servants on the front steps,
but Mr. Downs met us in the front hall along with the butler, Clandon, and the housekeeper, Mrs. Frome.

I spoke civilly to the two chief servants of the house,
but when I went to introduce Anna I could barely get her
attention she was so busy staring at her surroundings.

The magnificent formal marble entrance hall of Winterdale Park rose through two stories, with an array of classical statues set in niches on the first-floor level. The
architecture was definitely Mediterranean in spirit, with
the white walls and white plasterwork ceiling, the marble
floor and intricately carved marble chimneypieces over
two fireplaces all contributing to an impression of light
and space.

One felt that if one stepped outside, one would see the
canals of Venice, not the misty green verdure of England.

Mrs. Frome, the housekeeper, spoke to me. "Would
you like me to show you to your room, my lady? Or would
you like a tour of the house?"

"I think we will go to our rooms first, Mrs. Frome," I
said.

"Certainly, my lady. And when would you like dinner
served?"

Being called by a title was making me feel very strange, and instinctively my eyes went to Philip. "When would you like to eat, my lord?" I asked.

"Seven," he said decisively.

I turned back to Mrs. Frome. "Seven," I repeated.

"Very well, my lady. Now, if you will come with me, I will be happy to show you to your rooms."

"You ladies go along with Mrs. Frome," Philip said easily. "I want a word with Downs here first."

Obediently, the three of us trailed off after Mrs. Frome, down the great hall, past a vast marble-floored room that looked like a grand saloon from an Italian palazzo, to the grand marble staircase that went up to the second story.

When we reached the bottom of the stairs, the housekeeper said, "Would you like me to take you to your own apartment first, my lady? As his lordship requested, I have put Miss Anna and Mrs. Pedigrew upstairs on the third floor."

I said firmly, "I would like to see Miss Anna's apartment first."

The housekeeper's face was inscrutable. "Certainly, my lady."

The three of us followed her upstairs in silence. Anna looked worried, and I knew the size and magnificence of the house was intimidating her.

We reached the third floor. "The nursery faces the front of the house," Mrs. Frome said, gesturing to her right. She turned the other way, however, and went along the passageway to her left. She stopped in front of a door toward the end of the corridor, and held it wide for us to precede her in.

The first thing I saw was a simple red brick fireplace

with a white wood mantel. There was a picture of a King Charles spaniel hanging over the mantel. I looked around and saw that we were in a sitting room. The walls were painted a pale yellow and the chinz-covered furniture looked old and worn and comfortable.

Anna immediately went to look at the picture of the dog.

"There is a bedroom and a dressing room as well," Mrs. Frome said. "Mr. Downs had me change the dressing room into a bedroom for Mrs. Pedigrew."

She walked to the partially opened door that led off the sitting room, and I went to look in.

The bedroom was as large as the sitting room and was furnished as cozily. The apartment was at the end of the house, and the two tall bedroom windows, which were framed by plain white muslin drapes, looked out on the terrace and the garden.

The view was spectacular.

At the very moment that I looked out the window, the sun came out for the first time all day. It glinted off an ornamental lake in the middle of the park and made the grass sparkle as if a million diamonds were sprinkled among it.

Anna said from behind me, "I like these rooms, Georgie. They're pretty."

"They used to belong to Lady Catherine," Mrs. Frome said.

I swung around, and for the first time I noticed the chest piled with music in the corner of the room.

"Do you think Catherine will mind if I use her rooms?" Anna asked me worriedly.

I shook my head. "It was Catherine who told Philip that you should have them," I said.

Anna's brow smoothed out.

I left her gazing out the windows and went to look into the room that was to be Nanny's bedroom. It, too, was a very decent size and looked very comfortable.

Nanny and I stood together in the sitting-room doorway and regarded Anna's back. "What do you think?" I asked in a low voice.

"I think these will suit us very well, Miss Georgiana," Nanny answered decisively. "Anna will be away from the noise and bustle of the second floor if you and his lordship are entertaining, and when you have children, they will be right down the passageway, which she will like very much."

These images of my future married life seemed utterly foreign to me, but I didn't dare say that to Nanny.

"That's true," I managed to mutter weakly. I forced a smile. "Well, I will leave you to help Anna change her dress," I said. "His lordship bespoke dinner for seven."

"It's your wedding day, Miss Georgiana," Nanny said bluntly. "Miss Anna can eat her dinner upstairs tonight." She looked at Mrs. Frome for confirmation.

The housekeeper's stoic expression never changed. "I can most certainly arrange to have Miss Anna's dinner brought upstairs," she said.

I didn't want Anna to eat her dinner upstairs. I didn't want to be left alone with my husband. I didn't have the vaguest notion of what we could talk about.

I also knew that I could hardly admit that this was the case to either Nanny or the housekeeper.

I said weakly, "If you are sure that it will be no trouble, Mrs. Frome."

The housekeeper looked at me. Her eyes were the color of pewter and she had a large flesh-colored mole on the side of her nose. "It will be no trouble, my lady, I assure you," she said.

I realized that I was not sounding very much like a countess and I stuck my chin in the air. "Very well. Then perhaps you will show me to my own rooms," I said.

"Certainly, my lady," the housekeeper said. She moved toward the door.

"I'm going now, darling," I called to Anna. "They are going to bring you your dinner up here, and I will see you in the morning."

She swung around, her face puckered, her mouth open, ready to protest, but before she could say a word, a small King Charles spaniel came racing in the door, yipping hysterically.

"Snowball!" Anna cried, dropping to her knees and holding out her arms. The dog leaped into them.

I looked at the young footman who was standing in the doorway. "His lordship told me to bring him up," he said to me.

I smiled. "Thank you. What is your name?"

"Alfred, my lady."

"Thank you, Alfred."

Nanny said to me in a low voice, "Go now, Miss Georgiana, while she is distracted by the dog."

I nodded and went quietly out the door with the housekeeper.

We did not return to the main staircase but instead went down a small set of stairs that was just outside of Anna's apartment. I had thought that the earl's apartments would be on the second floor with the other bedrooms, like they were at home, but Mrs. Frome took me all the way down to the first floor instead.

The earl's apartments were at the back of the house,

facing the gardens like Anna's, although they were far bigger and more sumptuous than hers. There was one bedroom, with a four-poster bed and matching chairs that Mrs.
Frome told me proudly had been made for the earl who
lived during the reign of King James. Three tall windows
draped with green-and-gold silk looked out upon the magnificent view. Above the white-marble fireplace hung a
landscape of a Venetian canal.

Two doors opened off the bedroom.

"This is the door to your dressing room," Mrs. Frome
told me, moving toward the door on the left wall. "The
other door leads to his lordship's."

Reluctantly, I followed her into the room that for over
twenty years had been the domain of Lady Winterdale. I
hadn't at all minded putting Anna into Catherine's rooms,
but I found that I did mind following in the place of
Philip's aunt.

Betty was waiting for me, and her familiar face helped
to cheer me up. I talked to her in an artificially animated
way all the time that she helped me to change my clothes.

Talking helped me to keep from dwelling on the fact
that this house apparently had only one bedroom for the
master and the mistress, not two.

The dressing room had a cheval glass, which I glanced
into briefly before I went out into the passageway. I was relieved to see that my inner turmoil did not appear to show
on my face.

Nervously, I smoothed down my golden-silk evening
dress and prepared to face my husband over the dining-
room table.

A footman was waiting outside my apartment to escort me to the drawing room. He told me that a number of
the rooms on the ground floor had been put aside for the

use of the family, and that dinner was to be served in the place he called the morning room. I was ineffably relieved to hear that I was going to be spared the feeling that I was dining in an Italian palace.

Philip was waiting for me in a small anteroom which was decorated with three gilded mirrors and one yellow-silk sofa and two chairs. He did not smile when he saw me.

"Is Anna joining us?" he asked.

"No. Nanny said that it would be better if she ate her dinner upstairs tonight."

His eyebrows lifted slightly. Then he said, "The morning room is next door." He came over to me and formally offered me his arm. I rested my hand on it with extreme tentativeness and together we walked into a room that was fully as large as our formal dining room at home in Weldon Hall.

Philip held my chair for me and I took my seat at one end of the polished mahogany table. In the light of the chandelier, Philip's neckcloth looked as white as snow, his eyes as blue as sapphires, his hair as dark as midnight.

There was a lump in my chest that felt as big as a fist.

The soup came in and was put in front of me. I was terribly conscious of the footmen standing at the sideboard.

We can't sit through this entire meal in silence, I thought desperately. *I have to say something*.

I couldn't think of a thing.

In a perfectly ordinary voice, Philip said, "How on earth did that dog come to be given the name of Snowball?"

I was so surprised by the question, and so relieved by its normality, that I actually managed a little laugh. By the time I had finished recounting the story of Snowball, the lump had subsided from my chest, and I had managed to eat my soup.

After dinner was over, I left Philip to drink his port in correct, masculine solitude. Instead of returning to the small anteroom next to the morning room, however, I was conducted by Mrs. Frome to a room she referred to as the green drawing room. This was a large and magnificent room on the family side of the first floor. The walls of the green drawing room were appropriately hung with green silk and an immense Turkish rug covered its polished wood floor. It had French doors that led out onto a terrace that overlooked one of the flower gardens. The scent of roses came once more to my nostrils.

In spite of all this aforementioned splendor, however, what struck the eye the moment one entered the room were two elegant fragile figures of cranes with gilded feathers that were perched on a satinwood table in the middle of the room. When I commented upon them, Mrs. Frome informed me that they were Chinese pieces imported by the late earl's father.

"They're beautiful," I said reverently.

I actually saw a slight smile on her face as she nodded in agreement. "Would you like me to have some tea brought to you, my lady?" she asked.

"No, thank you, Mrs. Frome." I looked around the room once more. It was filled with lovely pieces of furniture, and several more Chinese figures of birds rested on the mantelpiece, but there was no musical instrument.

"Where is Miss Catherine's pianoforte?" I asked curiously.

"Upstairs, in the blue drawing room," Mrs. Frome replied.

"My, this certainly is a large house," I said lightly. "Tomorrow you must give me a tour, Mrs. Frome."

"I am at your disposal, my lady," the woman said, her face back to its usual stoic expression.

She left, and I crossed the Turkish carpet to look at the cranes. I was still standing there, staring rather blindly at the beautiful, delicate creatures, when the door opened once more and Philip came in.

I turned to face him. Outside night had begun to fall and one could not see the garden beyond the terrace. I looked at him gravely and said what was in my heart. "I am so sorry that you had to marry me, Philip. I know that I blackmailed you into presenting me, but truly, I did not mean to force you to marry me." With difficulty, I kept my eyes steady on his face. "It cannot be pleasant for you to be married to a woman you can't respect, and I am sorry."

He gave me a look that was infinitely weary. "Georgiana," he said, and my heart leaped at hearing my name upon his lips, "believe me, it is not I who have been wronged by this marriage. A man like myself has no business marrying an innocent girl like you. I would never have done so if circumstances had not conspired to make it necessary."

I stared at him in astonishment.

"What do you mean, *a man like you?*" I said at last.

"You have no idea of the kind of life that I have led," he returned somberly. "The tale is far too ugly for your ears, but believe me when I tell you that it amounts to a desecration for me to even contemplate touching you. I want you to know that. I want you to understand that I am giving you a choice. If you wish to accept only the protection of my name and dispense with the other aspects of married life, I will understand completely."

I was thunderstruck. This was the last thing I had expected to hear. I didn't know what to say. In truth, I didn't quite understand what he was proposing.

"Are you suggesting that we could live together like . . . like brother and sister?" I asked carefully.

"Yes. If that is what you want, I shall respect your wishes." His voice sounded quite calm, but even though he was on the other side of the room from me, I had become so attuned to him that I could feel his tension. He said, "The last thing I want to do is force myself on a girl like you."

I tried to think clearly, which under the circumstances was extremely difficult. I finally decided that the best approach I could take to this entirely unexpected development was to be practical.

"We cannot do that," I said. "Whatever you may have been in the past, you are the Earl of Winterdale now, and as such you must have an heir. And to be honest, I want children, too, Philip." My voice sounded slightly breathless as I concluded, "In order to achieve those things, we cannot live together like brother and sister, can we?"

His face was stark. "No, we cannot."

"Well then," I said, trying desperately to sound as if I was merely showing common sense about an essentially trivial matter. "I think that our marriage ought to be a real one."

I saw his fists open and close at his sides. "Are you certain about this, Georgiana?" he asked harshly.

"Yes," I said, trying to sound as certain as I was saying I was. "I am."

CHAPTER
sixteen

Betty helped me to get ready for bed. My nightdress was of the finest, thinnest cambric and the scooped neck and long sleeves were trimmed with lace. She brushed my hair vigorously until it hung in a shining pale brown mantle around my shoulders.

When she had finished, I went through the connecting door to my bedroom and got into the big four-poster that had been made during the time of King James.

Earlier, when Philip had offered me my choice about whether or not I wanted to make our marriage a real one, I had not doubted what my reply had to be. Nor was it really the issue of children which had prompted me to answer as I had. It was simply that I had felt in my heart that if I was not close to him in this way, then I would never be close to him in any way at all. And I wanted to be close to him.

All the same, I was definitely apprehensive about what was going to transpire between us on our wedding night.

The bedroom windows had been closed against the chill night air, and the room seemed very quiet. I couldn't hear anyone talking or moving around in the earl's dressing room next door. There was a fire going in the fireplace and I stared at the glowing red coals with intense interest, trying to keep my mind blank and my eyes away from that dressing-room door. The vase on the marquetry table between the windows was filled with a mixed bouquet of flowers, and their sweet scent hung in the air, mingling with the smell of the fire. The lamp next to the bed was lit. I sat up against the pillows, smoothed the coverlet over my pristine white lap, stared fixedly at the fire, and waited.

The latch on the dressing-room door rattled slightly, and my eyes swung around in time to see Philip coming in. He was wearing a black dressing gown and as he crossed the floor toward me with those panther-light steps of his, I could feel a mixture of apprehension and excitement flutter in my stomach.

I thought that he would get in on his side of the bed, but he didn't. Instead he came around to my side, sat down beside me, and took my hands into his. My pulses began to race.

"Do you understand what is going to happen between us tonight, Georgiana?" he asked seriously.

I could feel the hot color flood my face. I had been raised in the country, after all, and I certainly knew the basics of animal reproduction. The picture was not a pretty one, however, and my mind much preferred not to contemplate it. I had been working hard at not contemplating it all week.

My eyes dropped away from his. "I think so," I said.

"Do you understand that I am likely to hurt you?" he said next.

My eyes flew back upward. "Hurt me?" I echoed. I hadn't known about that part.

"In order for me to enter you, I am going to have to break through your virginity, and that will hurt," he said. "I want you to understand this while there is still time for you to change your mind."

I looked up into his face. It looked taut and hard, as if

he were keeping himself under strict control. "Will it always hurt?" I asked.

"No. Just the first time."

"Oh well," I said with a mixture of stoicism and bravado, "then I suppose we had better get it over with, hadn't we?"

For the first time in days, I saw a faint smile touch his lips. "Always so practical," he murmured.

I looked into his incredibly blue eyes and I didn't feel practical at all. I felt dizzy.

I nodded helplessly.

He raised his hand and ran his fingers through my loose hair. My scalp tingled. "You have such beautiful hair," he murmured. His hand tangled in the soft brown fall of it and pulled gently so that my head tilted farther back. He bent his head to mine and began to kiss me.

The power of my own response startled me. I put my arms around his neck and when he slid me from a sitting position to a lying position on the bed, I went without objection. Through the thin cotton of my gown I could feel his fingers begin to caress my breast and I shivered.

It felt so good.

His lips left my mouth and kissed my ear, my throat, the hollow between my breasts.

I was astonished by the sensations that swept through me at his touch. That little *frisson* of awareness that had always leaped in me at his touch was as nothing compared to the feelings that were swamping me now.

He kept kissing me and kissing me until I was so dizzy I couldn't think at all. I don't know at what point he shed his dressing gown, but all of a sudden I realized with dim surprise that he was naked. I ran my hands up and down his arms and felt the strength and power of him under my fingers. It was exciting. He kissed my mouth again, his own mouth hard and urgent, and I opened my lips and was shocked to feel his tongue enter and curl against mine.

His hands came up on either side of my head to hold me in place. I shut my eyes and slowly my tongue began to follow the rhythm of his. My nightdress was already rucked up and I could feel his hand creep up under it and slide along my leg.

Then he touched me.

I quivered with a mixture of shock and delight.

He kept kissing me and rubbing gently with his finger, and my quivering increased.

I could feel the hardness of him pressed against my thigh, and part of me was frightened and part of me was thrilled.

Then he said, in a hoarse voice I scarcely recognized, "All right, Georgie. Hold on, this is it."

The strangest thing was, I wanted him to come into me. I wasn't even thinking about pain, all I was thinking about was the incredibly pleasurable sensations he had created and that I wanted him to come in. That's why the pain, when it came, was such a shock.

He had to push hard to enter, and I went rigid with the unexpected, burning discomfort of it. Then I remembered what he had told me.

But I hadn't expected this. I hadn't expected to be pierced until I bled. I hadn't expected to find myself pinned under him while he slammed in and out of me, hurting me every time he moved. He was so much stronger than I. He not only hurt me, he made me afraid.

When it was all over, and he was lying on top of me, sweating and breathing heavily, it took all of my willpower not to cry.

He lifted himself off of me and looked down into my face, which I quickly averted.

"God. I'm sorry, Georgie," he said. His voice was harsh, and he was still breathing as heavily as if he had been running hard out for half an hour. "I didn't mean it to happen that way."

He rolled away from me and lay on his back, one arm flung across his forehead, his eyes on the ceiling.

"*Christ*," he said.

He sounded so desperate that it pierced through the fog of my own misery. I said in a very small voice, "Did something go wrong?"

"I should have been more gentle," he said grimly. "It didn't have to be like that. I'm afraid I got . . . carried away. I'm sorry."

He should be sorry, I thought miserably.

I shifted away from him slightly and realized that part of my discomfort came from the fact that I was lying in a sticky wet spot on the bed. I put my hand down to investigate the cause, and that was when I found the blood.

"Philip," I said, my voice panicky, "I'm bleeding!"

His hand closed around my wrist, holding my hand high between us, and we stared together at the bright red stuff that stained my fingers.

"It's all right," he said in a very strange voice. "It's just a sign of your virginity, Georgie. It's a sign that you have never belonged to any man but me."

He kept staring at my hand as if he were in a trance, and after a minute I said in a suffocated voice, "I'll have to change my nightdress, and the sheets will have to be changed, too. We can't sleep in these."

He released my wrist and when he spoke his voice sounded normal once again. "I told Betty to wait in your dressing room to help you. Go ahead, I will see to it that the sheets are changed."

I scrambled out of the bed and tried to walk not run to my dressing-room door.

"Here I am, my lady," Betty's comfortable, familiar voice said as I entered my private sanctuary and shut the bedroom door behind me. "You go into the water closet and clean up, then I've got a nice clean nightdress for you to put on."

She didn't appear to be at all shocked by my blood-stained appearance, so I supposed that Philip had been telling the truth when he had said that this was what happened to all virgins on their wedding nights.

I finished my ablutions in the water closet, and Betty slipped another pretty white cotton nightdress over my head. I wasn't bleeding any longer, but I was very sore indeed as I walked reluctantly to the door leading back to my bedroom.

The last thing I wanted to do was to meet the chambermaid as she was in the process of changing those disgusting sheets, so I peeked in the door to see if she was finished. The room was empty. I crept quietly in and got back into my marital bed.

I curled myself into a ball facing away from Philip's side of the bed, shut my eyes tightly and pretended that I was asleep. Sleep was very far away, however, as I lay there in the quiet of the large, elegant room. For some reason, I felt very very sad.

It was then that the tears began to fall.

Ten minutes later, Philip came into the room. I didn't stir, praying that he would think that I was asleep. He blew out the lamp and got into bed beside me. I held myself very still, trying not to move, trying not to let him know that I was crying.

I know I didn't make a sound, but all of a sudden he said, "Please don't cry, Georgie."

His voice had that same desperate note it had held earlier.

He put his hand on my shoulder. "Come here," he said.

I turned around unwillingly and was surprised to find myself gathered close into his arms. At this point I gave up all hope of concealment, buried my face in his shoulder, and wept with abandon.

"I'm sorry, Georgie," he said. I could feel his lips touching my hair. "I'm so sorry."

"It's just that it was so so . . . n-nice at first," I gulped, "and th-then it . . ."

I cried harder.

"I know." He sounded infinitely weary. "Remember how you once told me that life was unfair to women? Well, this is another example for you. A man's first time is usually very exciting, but a woman's hurts."

My tears were slowing now and the regular beat of his heart under my cheek was very soothing. His nightshirt was soaked where I had cried into it, but I thought that this was a small price for him to pay after what he had done to me.

I yawned, suddenly and horrifically.

"Go to sleep, sweetheart," he said. "You must be exhausted." And his arms began to loosen from around me.

I was exhausted, of course, and it was all his fault, but for some odd reason I didn't want him to let me go.

I cuddled closer into his warmth, muttered something

like, "Hold me," and dropped like a stone into the depths of healing sleep.

When I awoke the following morning, bright sunlight was peeking in through the slats of the blinds on the windows. I looked at the clock on the mantelpiece and was horrified to discover that it was ten o'clock in the morning.

I was alone in the bed.

I couldn't remember the last time I had slept until ten in the morning. I had probably never in my life slept until ten in the morning.

How mortifying, I thought. What a slovenly way to start my new life at Winterdale Park.

And where was Philip?

I got out of bed and went to one of the long windows that looked out on the back of the house. I opened the blinds and found myself facing the beautiful park for which Winterdale was justly famous.

The view in the morning sunlight was breathtaking. A broad grass path led from the stone terrace behind the house to a castellated belvedere to a yew-fringed bowling green. Beyond the bowling green the park was planted with beeches, oaks, chestnuts, and cedars surrounding a rather large ornamental lake with a small island in the middle, which was crowned with a pavilion.

Running along the grassy path near the bowling green, a blue ribbon in her golden hair and her dog at her heels, was Anna. She was laughing.

A lump came into my throat.

"Ah, you're awake, my lady." It was Betty, coming into the room with a tray of chocolate and some toast.

I swung around to face her. "I'm so embarrassed,

Betty. I've never slept this late in my life. You should have awakened me."

"Well now, you had cause, my lady," my maid replied comfortably, "and his lordship said to let you sleep, so I did."

I drank my chocolate, ate my toast, dressed in a pretty pale yellow morning dress and went downstairs to meet the housekeeper.

I spent the rest of the morning with Mrs. Frome being given a tour of the house. To a girl who had lived all her life in a simple brick gentleman's house, the state apartments of Winterdale Park were intimidatingly magnificent. I don't believe I had ever seen so much marble in all my life.

Fortunately, the family rooms were more comfortable. The green drawing room downstairs, the one with the Chinese figures, was very formal, but there were two smaller drawing rooms on the second floor that were more comfortable-looking. It was in one of those rooms that I saw Catherine's pianoforte.

Seventeenth-century Italian landscapes and great gilt mirrors predominated as wall decorations in most of the rooms I viewed.

It was almost lunchtime when I finished my tour, and I thanked Mrs. Frome for her time and went out onto the terrace to see if Anna was still in the park. She and Nanny were just coming in.

"Georgie, Georgie, Georgie!" Anna called to me excitedly. "Do you know what Philip had made for me?"

"No," I said. "What?"

"A swing!"

My eyes swung to Nanny. "A swing?"

Anna's nurse nodded. "That is right, Miss Georgiana . . . that is to say, *my lady*."

"Don't you dare to call me my lady," I said fiercely. "I shall always be Miss Georgiana to you, Nanny. Is that clear?"

She smiled at me, her raisinlike eyes twinkling. "Aye. It's clear." Her smile grew more radiant. "It's true. His lordship is having a part of the garden made over especially for Miss Anna's use. The swing is already there, and there will be a small barn for her donkey, and he has said that if she wants any other animals, he will have housing built for them, too."

I felt tears sting behind my eyes. "Oh Nanny," I said. "Isn't that wonderful?"

She nodded vigorously. "He's a kind lad, Miss Georgiana. You made a good choice."

I thought of what had happened between us last night and didn't think I would exactly call him either kind or a lad. There could be no doubt, however, that he was being excessively good to Anna.

And wasn't that why I had married him?

I had my luncheon in solitary splendor, as Nanny once more insisted that Anna eat upstairs with her. Philip came in as I was finishing, however, and asked if I would like to take a drive around the estate with him. I accepted, of course, and went upstairs to change out of my morning dress.

The afternoon was as beautiful as the morning had been, and I commented on this fact rather extensively as the phaeton went down the wide, graveled drive behind two of Philip's grays half an hour later. Truth to tell, I was feeling rather shy of being alone with him, and I wasn't quite sure of what to say.

My voice finally petered out as we left the wide lawns and stately trees that marked the entrance to Winterdale Park, and he asked courteously as he turned his horses down the road, "Did Mrs. Frome show you around this morning?"

"Yes, she did." I turned to look at him, happy to have a topic to talk about besides the weather. "I must confess, I was quite overcome. What on earth was your ancestor thinking when he built this house? Did he have a delusion that he was a Venetian doge, not an English earl?"

He grinned. I was enchanted. I had never seen that boyish expression on his face before.

"Overwhelming, isn't it?" he asked. "And it's freezing in the winter. All that marble may be fine in Italy, where it keeps one cool, but in our English climate . . ."

He shook his head at the folly of it all.

I said tentatively, "It hasn't been well kept up, either. I'm surprised that Lady Winterdale wasn't a better house-keeper."

He shot me a surprised look. "What do you mean?"

"Well, the drapes and the upholstery in my dressing room are very shabby, for one thing. And as Mrs. Frome took me around, I couldn't help noticing that there are other things that need replacing. It just struck me as odd, that in so wealthy a household . . ."

My voice petered out. He was frowning, and I had a sudden fear that he thought I would next be asking him for money to make repairs.

"Not that I care, my lord," I said hastily. "It is nothing to me if the drapes look shabby. Truly. I don't want you to think that I am asking you to refurbish the house."

"It's all right," he said. The thin line between his brows was still there. "I don't think that. I am just surprised, I suppose. I never noticed anything wrong with the house, you see. But I certainly noticed that there were serious things wrong with the land."

It was a moment before his words registered with me. Then I said, "Ah."

"Yes," he said. "Ah, indeed."

"That is why your uncle was cheating at cards," I said. "He needed the money."

"He needed money badly," Philip said. "His man of business and I have spent almost a year trying to work out a recovery plan. It has not been easy, I can tell you that. My uncle's investments were disastrous."

I thought of all the paperwork that was constantly on his desk and began to understand.

"But Lady Winterdale doesn't seem to be in financial difficulties," I said. "Catherine told me that they have been living in Bath since her father died and that Lady Winterdale has rented a house in the nicest part of town."

Philip said, "The money for my aunt's jointure was secured to her when she married. My uncle couldn't touch it, thank God." A single eyebrow flew. "The thought of having to support my Aunt Agatha is not a pleasant one to me."

I could perfectly understand that.

A little silence fell between us, and I contemplated with pleasure the peaceful Surrey countryside on either side of the road. Little golden leaves sprang on the poplars that lined the road to our left and at the end of the field to our right the oak trees were misted a pinky brown. Bluebells and wild hyacinths grew in the grassy margin on either side of the road. The air was warm and smelled of spring and earth and growing things.

A thought struck me and I frowned. "If your uncle's estate was so encumbered, where did you get the money to pay for a Season for Catherine and me? It must have cost a fortune!"

Philip's eyes were focused between the gray ears of his horses, and all I could see of his face was his profile. "I paid for it out of my own money," he said.

Silence fell between us as I digested this piece of information.

"Your own money?" I said tentatively.

His profile didn't change. I noticed that his nose had the faintest, aquiline curve to it. That must be what gave him that arrogant look he could sometimes wear.

He replied in an even voice, "Yes, my own money. Just as I am using my own money to try to get this estate back to where it should be. The tenant farms have been woefully neglected for at least fifteen years. Perhaps longer."

I wanted desperately to know where he had got so much money, but I didn't feel that I had the right to ask. I clutched my hands together in my lap and was grimly silent.

He said, "Don't you want to know where my money came from?"

I turned my whole body around on my seat so I could look at him directly. "Yes," I said.

The reckless look that was so dangerously attractive came over his face. He said, "I won it playing E.O. In Italy. In a gaming establishment that was housed in a marble palazzo not unlike Winterdale Park."

I could feel my heart sink. I had been right all along. He was a gambler like Papa. I felt unutterably depressed.

He was going on. "I was twenty-three years old at the time, and unlike my uncle, I took my money and made some shrewd investments with it. I tripled it, in fact, and the money is still growing. I won't be able to do everything that needs to be done here at Winterdale immediately, of course, but I can foresee that the next five to ten years will see a vast improvement on the estate."

This sounded like very hopeful news. I said eagerly, "Does this mean that you don't gamble anymore, Philip?"

"No more than is necessary to keep from looking like a pinch-purse," he said. "I get my thrill these days from my stocks, not from playing E.O."

I was so happy that I actually bounced on the seat, like Anna.

"Oh, Philip, you cannot know how that news has set my mind at rest."

He replied soberly, "I understand perfectly well, which is why I have told you all this. I understand how fearful you are of losing your home, and I want you to know that that will never happen."

I gave him a radiant smile, which he didn't see as his eyes were facing front. It occurred to me as I looked at his grave profile, that in this way Philip was not very different from me. After all those transient years, I didn't think that he wanted to lose his home either.

As we drove around the estate, I was struck by how popular Philip appeared to be with his people. Men laboring in the field would stop and take off their caps as we drove by, and I could see the smiles that lit their weatherworn faces. A few times, when there was someone working in a plowed row that was near the side of the road, Philip would pull up and the man would come over to be introduced to me.

A typical exchange ran something like this:

"Is the new roof finished yet, Grimes?"

"That it is, my lord, and it's that grand. No more pots for the wife to put out every time it rains!"

"Heavens," I said, as we turned for home, "I think we had better live with the shabby curtains for a few more years. You really are spending a fortune on the land."

He laughed, and once more I felt that stab of delight that I had made him happy.

He had talked to me this morning as he had never talked to me before. He had actually confided in me. Deep in my heart, I knew that it was because of what had happened between us last night. I knew that the physical joining between us was what had precipitated this other kind of closeness, and that if I wanted to keep this kind of a bond, then I would have to allow the other.

He had told me it wouldn't hurt after the first time, I reminded myself bravely. Perhaps the second time wouldn't be so bad.

I hadn't noticed the food at dinner last night because I had been in such an emotional knot, but I noticed it tonight. If one were being kind, one would call it mediocre. After I left Philip to his port, I sent for the butler, Clandon, and asked him what the cook meant by sending up such an ill-cooked meal. Clandon's face was wooden as he replied, "The dowager Lady Winterdale took the former cook with her when she removed to Bath, my lady. The undercook took over when he left."

"Well, the undercook is not adequate, Clandon," I said. "His lordship cannot be expected to eat overcooked roasts and undercooked potatoes. He left half his meal on his plate tonight."

"Yes, my lady," the butler said.

"Find another cook," I recommended. "The present cook may stay on in his original capacity."

"Yes, my lady."

"Did the Dowager Lady Winterdale abscond with any of the other servants?" I asked curiously.

A glimmer of amusement came and went in the butler's eyes. "No, my lady. She only took the cook and her dresser."

Philip came into the room as Clandon was leaving, and I told him about looking for a new cook.

"Haven't you noticed how dreadful the meals are here at Winterdale?" I asked.

"Actually, I have noticed. I just have had too many other things on my mind to do anything about it."

"Well, now that you have a wife you don't have to do anything about it," I said. "I will."

He gave me an assessing look. "If I had known how convenient a wife would be, perhaps I would have married sooner."

I could feel color flush into my face. I couldn't think of an answer.

He said, "Do you know how to play chess?"

I stared at him in astonishment. "No."

"Would you like to learn?"

"Why . . . yes. That would be fun."

"Good," he said, moving over to a satinwood table with an inlaid chessboard. A set of elegant carved ivory pieces were already set in place on the board. "Come along, and I'll teach you."

I moved slowly toward the board, not quite sure what to think.

He looked at my face. "You're too sore to do anything else tonight, Georgie," he said gently. "Let's play chess."

I felt as if a stone had rolled off of my chest. I smiled, took my seat across from him, and looked intently at the carved pieces, determined to astonish him with my intelligence.

"Now," he began, lifting the smallest piece on the board, "these are the pawns. . . ."

The chess game was fun. Philip played without his queen and his knights, and he still beat me, but I was pleased that I got the feel of how the pieces moved around on the board. I could see why people liked the game. It made one think.

I spent a good part of the following day with Anna, who appeared to be adjusting to life at Winterdale more swiftly than I dared to hope. The promised donkey had arrived, and with it a small cart that Anna could use to drive around the pathways that ran through the large fifty-acre park that stretched out behind the house. These paths wound through the foliage and the open glades of the park, which had little buildings like the summerhouse and the Italian pavilion and even a marble campanile.

The donkey Philip had found was both adorable and docile. No matter how Anna slapped the reins, he never moved out of a walk. And Philip had assigned one of the footmen to keep a constant eye on Anna when she was out of doors.

"I have had Edward checked out thoroughly, and he is perfectly trustworthy," Philip told me. "He will keep Anna within his sights all the time that she is in the garden."

"Is that really necessary?" I asked doubtfully. "Nanny was perfectly capable of watching her when she was at home."

But Philip shook his head. "There are a large number of servants in this house, and I cannot vouch for the integrity of all of them. Anna is extremely vulnerable,

Georgie. She is incapable of protecting herself, and her beauty is enough to tempt any man to do something he should not." His mouth had looked very hard. "Believe me, I have seen more of the world than you have, and I will not be comfortable unless I know that Anna has protection."

Edward was a big, friendly boy, the son of one of Winterdale's tenant farmers, and Anna liked him very much, so I didn't put up an objection. In truth, after what had happened with Lord Marsh, I myself was inclined to be more cautious than I had been in the past about my little sister.

Clandon had hired a London agency to find us a cook, but until that goal was accomplished we were forced to put up with the inadequacies of the present denizen of our kitchen. In consequence, I ordered one of the simplest meals that I could think of: a plain consommé, no fish, roasted chicken, roast potatoes, green beans, and ice cream for dessert. It was quite tolerable and I was happy to see that Philip ate all of his portion. I had thought for a long time that he was too thin.

After dinner we played chess in the drawing room for an hour, and then Philip suggested that I get ready for bed.

The getting-ready part was a nightmare repeat of my wedding night. Betty helped me undress and I entered my bedroom with a sickening feeling of fear and apprehension in the pit of my stomach. I got into my marital bed, and after a few minutes Philip came in from his dressing room.

He got into the bed beside me, leaned up on his left elbow, and gently smoothed the hair off my forehead with the fingers of his right hand. He said softly, "Relax, sweetheart. It will be different tonight, I promise you."

Easy for him to say, I thought bitterly. No matter what

he might try to tell me, my body could not easily forget that painful violation of two nights ago.

"Just kiss me," he said, and slowly he bent his head to my mouth. His lips felt warm and soft and comforting against mine, not brutally hard and demanding as they had been before. After a few minutes, when I had actually began to feel easier, the tip of his tongue slid gently between my lips. I went very still, wary of what would come next, but he didn't thrust any deeper. After a few minutes of this, very tentatively, I touched his tongue with my own. Very very gradually our kiss deepened, and of my own volition, I found myself taking his tongue deeper and deeper into my mouth.

He put his hands on either side of my face, caressed my temples and ears with gentle fingers, and the rest of my body began to flood with lovely warm sensations.

After a while his mouth left mine to trail a rain of soft kisses all the way down my throat. My nightdress was cut low and he pushed the neck down, continuing to move his lips slowly and caressingly down my throat until finally he arrived at my breast. As he took my nipple between his lips and began to play with it with his tongue, I could feel the first waves of sensation begin to ripple through the lower part of my body. His hands slowly stroked over my waist, my hips, and down to my legs. He began to push up my nightdress.

My breath caught on a harsh, fearful sob.

He stopped immediately and smiled down at me. "It will be all right, sweetheart," he said again. "Trust me. I won't fail you this time."

It was the rare, sweet smile that had always melted my heart.

"What if we do this?" he continued. "If ever you want me to stop doing something, just say so and I will."

I stared up at him, my eyes wide. "You will?"

"I promise."

I believed him, and slowly the fear that had once more begun to build up inside of me drained away. I let myself reach out and touch his thick, raven black hair.

His fingers came up and caressed the soft skin of my inner thighs. I began to quiver. His mouth came back to mine. He kissed me and kissed me and moved his finger up to touch me between my legs. I quivered harder, my body growing tauter and tauter, like a bow waiting to be shot. I opened my legs wider to give him better access.

This went on for a while, and it never once occurred to me to tell him to stop.

When finally he moved between my thighs, I was so lost in sensation that I actually lifted my legs for him. Slowly, with infinite care, he eased inside me, giving me a chance to stretch and accommodate him without pain.

Then he was all the way in, and the feeling of having him there was indescribable.

He looked down into my face, his eyes blazingly blue. "All right, sweetheart?"

My reply was husky and breathless. "All right."

I reached up my arms and held him tight. Inside I was totally open to him. Slowly, he began to move, back and forth, back and forth, and I followed his movements, holding on to him frantically, seeking the release that I needed so desperately.

I shifted, so that my legs were high around his waist and my hips were tilted up. That was when he began to drive.

"Philip," I said. "Oh God. Philip."

I didn't know what was happening to me, and I didn't think I could stand it if it went on much longer. If it did, I thought, I would surely die.

As if from a great distance I heard him saying my name, over and over and over.

And then it happened, a great earth-shattering explosion of physical ecstasy that was so intense it was almost paralyzing. Almost at the same time I felt Philip shudder and groan, and I knew that he was experiencing the same intense eruption of pleasure that I was.

We hung on to each other with ferocious intensity, two people in one body, as we flew together through the spheres.

I don't know how much time passed before I actually felt the heavy weight of his naked, sweaty body on mine, as it had been two days before, but tonight I didn't mind at all. I rejoiced in it, in fact. I held him close, my lips against the black hair that was pressed against my cheek, and I reveled in the heavy sound of his thudding heart against my own.

At last he said, "I'm too heavy for you," and rolled away, but he kept one of his arms flung across my stomach just beneath my breasts. He closed his eyes, dozing, and I turned my head and feasted my eyes on his face.

I could not believe what had happened between us tonight. I could not believe that the ugly, frightening encounter of my wedding night had been transformed into this shatteringly sensual experience that left every nerve in my body quivering with awareness and pleasure.

He had been so good to me tonight. He had taken such care not to hurt me, to make certain that this second experience was wonderful. I looked at his darkly handsome face, at his disordered black hair, at his strong, perfect body, and tears came to my eyes.

I love him so, I thought. *Please, please, God. Make him love me, too.*

As if he had heard my thoughts, his eyes opened.

"Did I go to sleep on you?" he asked softly.

I looked at him with my heart in my eyes. "Oh, Philip," I said. "I think you're wonderful."

The faintest trace of grimness appeared around his mouth. "I'm not, you know," he said. And then he reached out and gathered me like a belonging into his arms.

We had two weeks at Winterdale Park before we returned to London. When I am an old old lady, with all of my passions long since dead, I shall still remember those two weeks.

We lived to be with each other. On the surface, we led the lives one would expect to be led by the master and mistress of an estate as large and as demanding as Winterdale Park. But beneath the surface, we hungered only for each other.

We would make a date to meet in our bedroom in the middle of the afternoon and spend an hour making love, only to arise and dress and go about our duties as if no interruption had occurred. Then, that very same night, we would fall upon each other as if we hadn't held each other in a year.

I didn't care what the servants thought. I didn't care who knew about those afternoon assignations, or who saw our knees and fingers touching as we sat over the chessboard at night. I had no shame. My body felt free and shameless and beautiful. Everything about me felt beautiful, because Philip had told me that I was.

Only one tiny dark cloud existed to cast a shadow over my happiness. I had given myself wholly, body and soul, to Philip, but I knew that there was a part of him that he had not given to me.

When we made love, then I had all of him. I could feel it. He was there with me, every part of him, body to body, mind to mind, spirit to spirit. But when our bodies parted, then something inside him went away, too.

I told myself that I was a fool to fret about this. I had a marriage that would be the envy of any other woman in the world. I told myself not to be greedy.

But I had discovered hidden depths of possessiveness in myself, at least where Philip was concerned. I wanted all of him, and I worried about the part that was missing.

CHAPTER
seventeen

WE RETURNED TO LONDON ON A PERFECT MAY morning when a soft warm breeze was blowing from the south and the cuckoos were calling in the trees. Everything seemed to be in bloom at once: the lilacs, the roses, the pale pink tulips that marched in rows across the front lawn. The red and white hawthornes were out all along the roads and in the pastures the newly weaned lambs alternately played and cried for their lost mothers.

I was riding beside Philip on the front seat of the phaeton, and now I inhaled the fresh spring air, turned to him, and said regretfully, "I hate to go back to the city on a day like this. The countryside is so beautiful."

"Can't be helped," he returned. "I have to see my man of business."

I knew that, of course. I even thought that Philip himself regretted that we couldn't remain longer in Surrey. In London, the world would inevitably intrude upon our intense sensual isolation. In London we would become social beings once more.

I was not looking forward to the change. While we were at Winterdale Park, I had had Philip all to myself. Once we arrived in London, his other life—the life of clubs and boxing saloons and men of business—would claim his attention. I knew it was unreasonable of me to expect that we could live all our lives in the haze of newly married bliss. But the fact of the matter was, I did want that. Or at least I wanted it for a little while longer.

But the grays were moving forward with their usual efficient, ground-eating strides, taking us ever closer to London, and Mansfield House, and Lady Winterdale.

"It is going to be so awkward having two Lady Winterdales in the house," I murmured.

Philip clucked to his left wheeler to step up. "It's only for another few weeks. Then the Season will be over and Aunt Agatha and Catherine will be moving back to Bath."

I brightened. "And then can we return to Winderdale?"

He turned his head to look at me. His eyes narrowed very slightly at the corners. "Yes. Then we can return to Winterdale."

I could feel my lips curve in the kind of smile they had never worn before these weeks I had spent with Philip. "Good," I said softly.

The glitter in his narrowed blue eyes was hard and hungry, and I absolutely loved it. My smiled deepened.

His eyes focused once again on his horses, and he said sternly, "You are a minx."

"Yes," I replied with a combination of surprise and pleasure. "I rather think that I am."

Catherine was in the green-marble hall when I came in the front door of Mansfield House.

"Georgie!" she cried in welcome, and came flying to give me a hug.

I hugged her back. Then, as we separated, I looked in amazement at her changed countenance. "You've cut your hair."

"Yes." She shot a small defiant glance at Lady Winterdale, who had come into the hall from the drawing room. "Do you like it?"

"I think it is excessively becoming," I said emphatically. "It shows off your cheekbones. It makes you look . . . elegant."

Color stained the high cheekbones that the short, feathery cut had so effectively highlighted. "Do you really think so?"

"I certainly do."

The front door had been left open behind me so that our bags could be brought in from the town chaise that had followed us home. As I talked to Catherine I recognized the sound of the footmen's steps behind me as they carried the luggage, then Betty's steps came, then those of Philip's valet. I didn't hear Philip's step, he trod so lightly, but I knew nevertheless the exact second when he came up behind me.

I turned to him with a smile. "Look at Catherine's new haircut, Philip," I said. "Doesn't she look pretty?"

"Very pretty," he said courteously.

The color along Catherine's cheekbones deepened.

Lady Winterdale came forward with measured steps. "Georgiana. Philip. I trust you had a pleasant stay at Winterdale Park?"

The expression on her face was sour, and for the first time since I had met her she refused to meet my eyes.

She had to have known about her husband's financial problems, I thought, and she was afraid that now I knew about them also.

To my amazement, I realized that Lady Winterdale was embarrassed.

I said, "We had a wonderful time. The country this time of year is so lovely. And the house is magnificent,

Lady Winterdale. I quite thought I was staying in a Venetian palace."

Her eyes lifted, and she shot me a single sharp look. "I have always been very fond of it myself," she said cautiously. "So fond, in fact, that I scarcely made any changes since the time I went there as a bride."

I gave her a sunny smile and nodded as if I perfectly understood.

Catherine said, "How is Anna? Has she settled in comfortably?"

"She has settled in extremely well. Thank you so much for suggesting that she have your old apartment, Catherine. It is just the thing for her and Nanny."

Catherine looked pleased.

Lady Winterdale said austerely, "Dinner is in an hour, Georgiana. If you and Philip are to change into evening dress, you had better retire to your rooms at once."

"Come along, Georgie," Philip said, taking me by the arm and turning me in the direction of the staircase. "Aunt Agatha is right. You ate scarcely anything at the inn we stopped at for luncheon. You must be hungry."

I let him escort me up the stairs, and as we went by the door to the bedroom that I had occupied for the whole of my previous visit to Mansfield House, I had the strangest sensation. I think that for the first time I truly comprehended what had happened to me. For the first time I truly understood that no longer was I Miss Georgiana Newbury; instead I was the Countess of Winterdale.

The days I had spent at Winterdale Park had seemed almost like a fairy tale, but this house was real. Tonight I would sleep in the earl's apartments, not in my old room. It was I, not Lady Winterdale, who would sit opposite Philip at the dinner table. It was I who would be the one to consult with the cook about the dinner menus and with the house-keeper about the servants.

It was I who was the countess now.

Of course, there was still another Countess of Winterdale in residence, and I had a feeling that the relationship between me and Lady Winterdale, which had never been comfortable, was about to become even more strained.

The earl's apartment was at the very end of the corridor, and the bedroom and both dressing rooms had large windows that looked out upon the small back garden. I stood with Philip in the bedroom and looked around at the graceful four-poster bed draped with pale blue tapestry hangings, at the comfortable silk-upholstered chaise longue and the well-appointed writing table. Pretty landscapes decorated the walls and over the chimneypiece hung a portrait of an eighteenth-century lady with high, powdered hair and a patch on her cheek.

From the dressing rooms that opened off either side of the bedroom I could hear the sound of servants unpacking our bags.

I said to Philip, "I cannot quite believe that this has happened. I feel as if I belong back down the hall in my old bedroom, not here. Suddenly, I am having a very hard time picturing myself as Lady Winterdale."

"You will soon grow accustomed to your new role," he replied. "Catherine knows you and loves you. The servants know you and respect you. With you it is not a case of the pariah come home, as it was when I became the earl." He walked over to the window and stood looking out at the terrace and garden, his hands clasped loosely behind his back.

The pariah come home.

My heart was wrung for him. Was that how it had been?

I answered my own question. Yes, that must have been exactly how it had been.

I went to him, slipped my arms around his waist, and leaned my cheek against his shoulder. "We're two of a kind, then," I said lightly. "A blackmailer and a pariah. Clearly a match made in heaven."

At that, he chuckled. I loved it when I could make him laugh.

He said, turning to face me, "I don't know about you, but I am quite extravagantly hungry. Shall we get dressed for dinner?"

I dropped my arms and stepped back. "An excellent idea, my lord. And after dinner, will you be going out to your club?"

"No," he said, "I believe I will remain at home this evening. The trip from Surrey was rather tiring."

"Oh, what a shame," I murmured demurely.

"But not too tiring," he said.

I smiled.

"Go get dressed, Georgie," he said dangerously, "or I promise you, you won't get any dinner at all."

"I'm going, I'm going," I said, scuttling hastily through the door to my dressing room, where Betty waited to help me change into an evening dress for dinner.

Dinner was rather as I had expected it to be. Lady Winterdale was relegated to my old place, which she knew was proper but which made her excessively unhappy. She expressed her unhappiness by being even more condescending than was her usual wont, but Philip and I—and even Catherine—pretended to listen to her while letting her barbs pass harmlessly over our heads.

It occurred to me that something was definitely going on in Catherine's life to have made her so much more confident. The frightened little mouse she had been when first I came to London had almost disappeared. I wondered if Lord Rotheram had anything to do with this transformation, and I felt a twinge of concern. I didn't know what Lord Rotheram's situation was, and I didn't want Catherine to be hurt.

After dinner, Lady Winterdale and Catherine went out to a ball and Philip and I remained at home. We played chess for a while in the upstairs drawing room. I thought I was actually becoming quite proficient at the game. Philip now gave up only his queen, one of his knights and two pawns when we played.

Of course, I hadn't beaten him yet, but to my glee I had actually got him in check twice. I had hopes for the future.

In the weeks to come I would look back with pain and longing on that first night we spent together in Mansfield House as man and wife. Everything between us was as it had been at Winterdale Park. I was so attuned to him that my body ignited with passion the moment he touched me. He kissed me and I opened my lips and kissed him back. I lifted myself to take him inside me, and he penetrated deeply, moving back and forth, lifting me to the heights of mindless ecstasy.

Afterward, as we lay clasped in each other's arms, I felt the sweet protectiveness of his embrace and thought about how desperately I loved him and about how I might break through that last invisible barrier that I sensed still lay between us.

The next day Frank Stanton arrived at Mansfield House, and everything between Philip and me was changed.

It was late in the morning. Philip had left for the offices of one of his business associates and I was preparing to go out to the circulating library with Catherine, when Mason came to tell me that a Captain Frank Stanton had called to see me.

I was taken completely by surprise. Frank was supposed to be with his regiment in Ireland.

I said to Mason, "Please show Captain Stanton into the drawing room, Mason. I will be right down."

Catherine gave me a curious look. "Who is this Captain Stanton, Georgie?"

"An old friend from home," I replied. "His father is the local squire."

"Oh yes, I believe I've heard Anna talk about him."

"Won't you come and meet him?" I asked cravenly. I must confess I was not looking forward to facing Frank by myself.

"Oh no, you will want to see such an old friend without a stranger looking on," Catherine said. "She gave me a grin. "One of the nice things about being a married lady is that one can actually be by oneself in the same room with an unmarried gentleman."

I could not hide from myself my own reluctance as I went down the great circular staircase. It was not that I did not want to see Frank, I told myself. I just did not want to see a Frank who was angry and hurt, and I was very much afraid that this was the Frank I was going to see.

He was staring into the alabaster fireplace when I walked into the downstairs drawing room, and for a moment I stood in silence contemplating his familiar broad back and smooth sandy hair. Then he sensed my presence and swung around to face me.

"Georgie," he said. His pleasant tenor voice was raspy. His level gray eyes were too bright. "I heard from my father that you were to marry Winterdale," he said. "I came as soon as I could get leave from my regiment, but I see that I am too late. It's true, then? You are Lady Winterdale."

"Yes, it's true, Frank." I advanced into the room toward him, smiling as serenely as I could. "Now please don't look as if the world has ended. You know that there was never any possibility of a match between the two of us, and this marriage is exactly the thing for Anna. We have just returned from Winterdale Park in Surrey, where Anna is to make her home, and I can assure you that she will be very happy there. You know how worried I have been about her future, and now that particular problem is solved. She will have a home for the rest of her life."

He left the fireplace and came toward me. "And what about your life, Georgie?" he said intensely. "I've heard stories about Winterdale. I know some fellows who knew him when he was younger. He cut his teeth in every brothel and gaming hell in Europe. It makes me positively *sick* to think of you married to a man like that." He was close enough now for me to see that he was actually trembling. "Dear God, Georgie, why wouldn't you marry me? Anything would have been better than this!"

I could feel hot anger sweeping through me. "Philip is my husband, Frank," I said, trying to keep my voice quiet. "I do not think you should speak about him to me like that."

"You don't know what kind of man he is, Georgie . . ."

Frank was beginning desperately, when I heard a step at the door.

"Mason tells me that we have company, my love," Philip's voice said. "You must introduce me to your friend."

He had never called me *my love* before. My heart leaped at the words, even though I knew instinctively that they had been said solely to irritate Frank.

I turned to look at my husband and was shocked by the icy look on his face. I wondered how long he had been standing in the doorway before he had made his presence known by that deliberately loud step.

I said in a voice that was not quite steady, "My lord, may I present Captain Frank Stanton, an old childhood friend from Sussex."

Frank bowed stiffly from the waist. "Lord Winterdale."

Philip barely nodded in return.

An exceedingly uncomfortable silence fell, which neither of the men made any attempt to break.

I asked Frank where he was staying.

"A friend of mine, George Thomas, has a bachelor apartment in Jermyn Street," he replied. "I'm staying with him."

"And for how long do you plan to remain in town?" Philip asked, in a voice that made it quite plain he hoped it would not be for very long at all.

"I have a month's leave," Frank replied. His gray eyes glinted like steel. "And I believe I will spend most of it in London."

The atmosphere in my drawing room was growing tenser by the minute. I understood why Frank was so out of humor. He was upset and wounded because I had married someone else. But I could not understand my husband. Why on earth should he be behaving so nastily to poor Frank?

Philip had to have heard Frank's unfortunate comment about his notorious career in Europe.

It was a shame, I thought, but Frank was going to have to accustom himself to the idea that I was indeed married and find himself another girl.

After another few excruciatingly uncomfortable minutes, while I babbled on like an idiot and the men said nothing, Philip abruptly excused himself and once more left me alone with Frank.

"Will you go for a ride with me this afternoon, Georgie?" Frank asked as soon as the door had closed behind my husband. "I have the use of a rather nice hack that belongs to my friend Thomas."

I didn't want to go out with Frank and I felt horribly guilty about my reluctance. He was one of my oldest friends, after all, and the hurt look in his eyes made me feel so wretched.

"I should love to go for a ride with you," I said. "The fashionable hour is five, in case you did not know."

He gave me the travesty of a smile. "I shall pick you up at five, then."

"Wonderful," I said, more warmly than I felt.

After Frank had gone, Catherine and I set off together for the circulating library. The shop was quite crowded and among the people we encountered there were Lady Anstly and Mrs. Henley, two of society's biggest gossips. The sharp, knowing glances they bestowed upon me rather set my back up. I held my temper, however, and was as sweet and charming as I could manage under the circumstances. I knew there was scandal attached to my marriage, and I did not want Philip's reputation to suffer.

The two women were distantly cool, but they did not

cut me, a sign that our marriage was going to be accepted, albeit reluctantly.

I sent a silent thank-you to Lady Jersey and Lady Castlereagh, whose presence at the marriage ceremony was quite probably the reason that Philip and I were not going to find ourselves ostracized.

Catherine and I collected our new books and walked home, shadowed by one of the Winterdale footmen. I had checked out a novel that Catherine recommended, a book called *Pride and Prejudice*, as well as two collections of poems, and I brought the three books up to my bedroom before I returned back downstairs for luncheon.

It was when I was depositing the books on the small writing table in my bedroom that I noticed the edge of a piece of paper sticking out of the novel. I pulled it out and there, in bold black script, were the words:

> *You may have blackmailed Winterdale into marriage, but your career will end there. Hand over the evidence or die.*

I stopped breathing. Then, as the full significance of what was in front of me sunk into my brain, my heart began to pound.

I had thought it was all finished with. I had thought that my marriage to Philip would reassure all of my father's victims that I was no longer in need of money. But it seemed that this was not the case. It seemed instead that the marriage had actually exacerbated someone's fears that I was indeed holding powerful information.

I pressed my trembling hands to my cheeks.

Where is Philip? I thought frantically. *I've got to show him this paper.*

CHAPTER
eighteen

Philip didn't come home for the entire afternoon, and so I was forced to go for my ride with Frank
without having a chance to talk to my husband. I was riding Cato, as usual. Philip had had my beloved mare, Corina, brought to Winterdale Park from Weldon Hall, but
we had left her in the country since I still didn't want her
in the confinement of a city stable.

At this hour, the park was crowded as usual. I was
preoccupied with the threatening note I had received and
consequently was paying little attention either to Frank or
to the people who nodded greetings to me as we rode along
the path beside the Serpentine when, out of nowhere, Cato
let out a high-pitched whinny and exploded into a series of
high, arching, stiff-legged bucks. I maintained my seat for
the first few bucks, but when he planted his front feet,
ducked his head and kicked out high behind, I sailed over
his head. The last thing I saw just before I hit the ground
was the oncoming carriage into whose path I had been
thrown. Then I struck the ground hard and everything went
black.

When I opened my eyes, Frank's face was peering
down into mine. Even though I could not see him very
clearly, I could tell that he was deathly white.

"Are you all right, Georgie?" he asked hoarsely.

My head hurt dreadfully. Cautiously, I moved my arms and my legs. "I think so," I said. "My head hurts."

"How about your back?" Frank asked.

I moved a little. "It's all right, too." I stared up at Frank in bewilderment and fear. I realized I must have come off Cato, but I couldn't remember the sequence of events. "What happened? Did I fall?"

"Your horse began to buck and he threw you."

"Cato?" I asked incredulously.

Frank said, "Georgie, I need to get you home. You hit your head rather hard when you landed, and I'm afraid you might have a concussion."

I thought I might have one, too. My head hurt abominably, and I was very dizzy.

A female voice said, "My husband and I will take Lady Winterdale, sir. We have our barouche in the park today and there is easily room for a third person."

"Thank you," Frank said in a relieved voice. I was certain he had been wondering how the devil he was going to get me back up on a horse again. It wasn't until he had lifted me in his arms, and was carrying me toward the barouche, that I realized who my rescuers were: Sir Henry Farringdon, one of Papa's victims, and his wife, the homely heiress.

I opened my mouth to protest, then closed it again. Even in my befuddled state, I recognized that no matter what Sir Henry's intentions toward me might be, I was certainly safe in the presence of his wife.

Frank deposited me in the seat of the barouche as carefully as if I had been made of glass and told me that he would follow me to Mansfield House leading Cato. Someone had caught the gelding and was holding him. Even with my blurred vision I could see that the poor animal was soaked with sweat and trembling all over.

Something bad had happened to make Cato throw me. I was sure of it, but my head hurt too much to concentrate. I nodded weakly at Frank, leaned my head gratefully against the barouche cushions, and closed my eyes.

Lady Farringdon talked the entire way home. Her voice was shrill, and every single word drilled like a bullet into my brain. She wondered in great detail what could have set my horse off in such a fashion. She commented in extensive detail upon the excellence of the Earl of Lowry's driving. Apparently it was he who had been driving the oncoming vehicle into whose path I had been thrown, and it was only his quick reflexes and strength that had saved me from being trampled to death.

She wondered what my new husband would say when he learned how close to death his bride had come.

If I had had a knife I would have stabbed her to death by the time we arrived at the Mansfield House door.

Frank turned both his horse and Cato over to a groom and lifted me down from the barouche. I shut my eyes as I listened to him make his calm thank-yous to Sir Henry and Lady Farringdon. By this time, my head was a storm of pain.

As Frank walked with me in the front door of Mansfield House I could hold only one thought in my pain-wracked head.

I want Philip.

And then he was there.

"What happened?" I heard him ask Frank sharply.

Frank started to answer but I just held out my arms to my husband. "My head hurts, Philip," I said. "I want to go to bed."

He took me away from Frank and thankfully I laid my

cheek against his shoulder. I heard him say sharply to some-one, "Send for a doctor." And then we were going up the stairs and along the hallway toward our bedroom.

"It will be all right shortly, sweetheart," he said as he laid me on the bed. "The doctor is coming."

I whispered, "This is what happened to Anna."

"No, it's not." He sat on the side of the bed and took my hand into his. "Anna was unconscious for days. I know it hurts, Georgie, but you are going to be all right."

I looked up at him.

"There are two of you," I said unsteadily.

He smiled, and said, "Lucky you."

Some of the fear that had been building inside me re-laxed. It couldn't be so bad if he could make a joke about it.

I told him what I knew about what had happened in the park, and then I said, "Someone sent me a note, Philip. It's in the book over there."

He got off the bed and went over to the table. I heard the sound of paper crinkling.

"I see," he said quietly.

There came a knock at the door and Catherine said, "Is there anything I can do, Philip?"

Philip went to open the door. "Yes. Get Georgie out of that dress and make her more comfortable before the doctor gets here. I want to take a look at Cato."

"Of course," Catherine said. She came over to my bedside, and the door closed behind Philip.

When the doctor arrived and examined me he found bruises on my shoulders and back and he confirmed the di-agnosis of concussion.

"You'll be all right in a few days, Lady Winterdale,"

he said, "but you cannot get out of bed until the double vision is gone. And even then I want you to take it easy for a few more days. Your brain has had a shock. You must give it time to recover."

I did not argue with him. For one thing, I truly was feeling wretched, and for another, as Anna's sister, I was scarcely the person to take a head injury lightly.

When Philip came in to see me after the doctor had left, I asked him to tell me precisely what had happened.

"With no warning, Cato went completely berserk," he said. "According to Stanton, he was bucking like a maniac. He threw you right in front of Lowry's oncoming phaeton. Thank God Lowry was able to avoid you. Stanton says he doesn't know how he did it without at least running over you with a wheel."

I plucked nervously at the counterpane. "There was that note I found in my library book," I said. "Philip, do you think someone might have done something to Cato?"

He was silent for just a fraction too long. Then he said, "I don't see how it would have been possible, Georgie. He was tacked up by Fiske himself."

I squinted at my husband, trying to see him clearly through my blurred vision. "What did you find when you went to the stable to look at him?"

"Nothing for you to worry about. Just get some rest, sweetheart. You will feel better in the morning."

I said fretfully, "I won't get any rest if I am wondering about what you found. I want to know, Philip."

There was a pause, as if he was deliberating about what was the best thing to do. Then he said, "All right. There was a small open wound on Cato's right flank. It looked to me as if he might have been struck with a sharpened stone."

My breath caught in my throat. "But the park was crowded, Philip! How could someone throw a stone and not be seen?"

"Stanton tells me you were going past that area of trees where there are no walking paths. Someone could have been hiding in there and used a slingshot to hit Cato."

I said incredulously, "I simply cannot imagine any of the men on Papa's list lurking in the bushes to shoot a slingshot at me."

"They wouldn't have had to do it themselves," Philip said in a very grim voice. "God knows, there are villains enough for hire in the back alleys of London."

He was right. If Cato had indeed erupted into a bucking frenzy, then the scenario Philip had just described to me was an all-too-likely explanation.

I expelled my breath in a huff and said, "I'm glad you told me. I would have fretted myself to death wondering."

"That's what I was afraid of." He came over to pick up my hand and give it a brief squeeze. "Don't worry, sweetheart. I'll find out who is at the bottom of these attacks."

All of a sudden my head hurt too much even to talk. I nodded, closed my eyes, and curled up on my pillow. The ringing in my ears was so loud that I didn't even hear when he left the room.

It was four days before I was able to get out of bed. By then, even though I still had a slight headache, my vision was clear and the ringing in my ears had stopped and I was so sick of my room that even the sight of Lady Winterdale sitting alone in the dining room when I went in didn't dismay me.

"Georgiana," she said with a gracious smile. "How nice it is to see you out of your bed."

To my surprise, she actually sounded sincere.

"Thank you, Lady Winterdale," I said. "I am feeling much better today."

"I hope you don't mind, but I have taken it upon myself to draw up the menus for the week," she said. "I did not wish to disturb you while you were indisposed."

"Of course I don't mind," I said. "Thank you for your thoughtfulness."

I went to the sideboard to help myself to coffee and an egg.

"Captain Stanton has come by faithfully every day to ask about you," Lady Winterdale said.

"Yes," I replied. "Betty brought me his flowers."

A bouquet of spring flowers from Frank had arrived regularly in my bedroom every morning since the accident.

I looked up from my egg and caught Lady Winterdale regarding me with a speculative gleam in her eyes. I found myself saying defensively, "I have known Captain Stanton since we were children."

"Allow me to give you a word to the wise, Georgiana," Lady Winterdale said. "When handsome young military men pay such close attention to a newly married woman, it can be a cause for gossip."

My nostrils quivered in anger and I retorted, "Let me tell you, Lady Winterdale, that I am heartily tired of hearing about the *ton*'s propensity for gossip. If my husband doesn't object to my friendship with Frank, it's nobody else's business!"

Lady Winterdale looked at me over her coffee cup, her pointy nose particularly evident in this posture. "Ah," she said. "And who says that your husband does not object?"

"Of course he doesn't object," I said. "There is nothing to object to."

Lady Winterdale said bluntly, "You came to London with nothing to recommend you but a pretty face and a winning smile, Georgiana, and you have ended up a countess. Don't be fool enough to alienate Philip over an old flame."

"Frank is not an old flame!" I said hotly. "Philip has no cause to be jealous of me, and he knows it!"

"Does he?" Lady Winterdale said ironically. She put down her coffee cup and rose from the table. "Think about what I have said, my dear. I realize that marriage to a man like Philip might have proved a shock to an innocent young girl like you, but if your marriage is not what you thought it would be, then it is your duty to put a good face on it. At all costs, the Winterdale name must be preserved."

A man like Philip? This was the second time that someone had said that to me. What was she talking about? Did she think that Philip had raped me?

I sat seething over my egg as the door closed behind Lady Winterdale.

The woman was impossible, I thought. She had not a genuine feeling in her whole body. All she thought about was appearances.

And she was completely wrong about Philip.

At least she was wrong about my reaction to our marriage.

Was she wrong, though, about Philip's reaction to Frank?

I pushed my egg away, took a sip of my coffee, and thought back on the past four days.

I had been sick and so Philip had slept on the bed in his dressing room. He had said that this was because he did not wish to disturb me. I had objected, had said that I would sleep better if he were beside me, but he hadn't listened.

In truth, I had been a little hurt that he had left me.

He couldn't possibly think that I cared about Frank.

Well, I was perfectly healthy today, I thought. There was no longer any excuse for him to sleep in his dressing room. I would wait and see what he would do tonight.

I pushed my coffee aside and wished desperately that we had never had to leave Winterdale Park.

That afternoon I accompanied Catherine to the Duchess of Faircastle's weekly musicale. The first person I saw as we came into the music room was Lord Rotheram. It was hard to miss him, as he was bearing down on us with a determination that didn't look as if it would be swayed by a cavalry charge.

"Lady Catherine," he said as he came up in front of us. "How wonderful to see you again." The light in his hazel eyes was unmistakable. Seeing it, a weight was lifted from my heart.

"Lord Rotheram," Catherine replied. I looked at her. She was radiant.

Well, well, well, I thought. It looked to me that when Lord Rotheram's period of mourning was over, Catherine would be receiving an offer of marriage.

From a future duke!

"You remember my friend, Lady Winterdale," Catherine was saying.

"Certainly." The future duke bowed to me. "When last we met, however, you were still Miss Newbury. Allow me to wish you very happy, Lady Winterdale."

"Thank you, my lord," I said.

"My mother has invited a few extra people today to hear you play, Lady Catherine," Lord Rotheram said. "Come and let me introduce you to them."

I looked at the couple whom we were approaching and immediately recognized Charles Howard, the man on Papa's list who had been forced to borrow from the money-lenders.

Lord Rotheram made the introductions. "Lady Winterdale, Lady Catherine, may I introduce Mr. and Mrs. Howard." He looked at Catherine. "Mrs. Howard, in particular, is a great music lover and expressed a special desire to hear you play, Lady Catherine."

Catherine flushed with pleasure.

Charles Howard and I looked at each other while the other three exchanged conversation about the piece that Catherine was to perform that afternoon.

"Have you quite recovered from your accident, Lady Winterdale?" he asked me in a low voice. I could not mistake the malice that glittered in his droopy blue eyes.

"Yes, thank you," I replied evenly.

"You lead a dangerous life, do you not?" he went on in the same intimate tone.

I could feel myself stiffen. "I wouldn't say that."

"Wouldn't you?" He smoothed an imaginary wrinkle out of his sleeve. "Think about it, after all. Just two weeks after you forced Winterdale to marry you, you are almost thrown under the wheels of a carriage."

I stared at him incredulously. "What are you suggesting?"

"Nothing that isn't being suggested by other people in town, Lady Winterdale," he returned spitefully.

"Charles," said Mrs. Howard, "I think it is time for us to take our seats. The music is about to begin."

I stood for a moment and watched the thin, fair young man and his wife find seats in the middle row of gilt chairs, then I turned to Catherine and Lord Rotheram.

"I have saved some seats for us in the front row," he said to me. "Come and sit down. I believe Mrs. Robinson is going to begin with a recital upon the harp."

I sat through the ensuing concert in a state of growing distress. Could it possibly be true that rumors were starting that Philip was the one responsible for my accident?

If it was true, I thought, then the rumor had to have been started by the real culprit.

He was setting Philip up to take the blame if he was successful in carrying out his threat to do away with me.

It was frightening to think that I was up against someone that diabolically clever.

I had to get home and talk to Philip, I thought. There had to be a way we could combat this kind of insidious campaign.

Philip was closeted in the library with his man of business when Catherine and I returned to Mansfield House, and so I went upstairs with Catherine and invited myself into her dressing room.

"All right, Catherine," I said, "the time has come to tell. What is going on between you and Lord Rotheram?"

Her cheeks were pink. Her eyes were like stars. "Oh Georgie, he has asked me to marry him!"

I enveloped her in a huge hug. "I am so happy for you, darling," I said. "He seems like such a nice man."

"He is, he is. And he suffered so dreadfully for so many years. His wife was very ill, you know. I realize that it might seem callous of him to be wanting to marry so soon after her death, but their last years together were dreadfully painful. He deserves some happiness. And—oh, Georgie, I love him so much!"

"I am sure that you will make him very happy," I said. "And he seems just the sort of thoughtful, deep-feeling man who will make you happy, too."

She gave me a smile that made her look utterly beautiful.

"What has your mother to say about all of this?" I asked. "She must be in heaven that one day you will be a duchess."

Catherine gave me a mischievous look. "Both Edward and I decided that it would be best to wait until his mourning period is officially over before we break the news to our parents. I don't think the duchess will be very surprised, but I think Mama will be."

I chuckled. "She will be unbearable," I said.

Catherine rolled her eyes. "I know."

I sobered. "Catherine, have you heard any rumors that Philip might have been the one responsible for my accident?"

She looked appalled. "No, I've heard nothing like that. Why? Are there such rumors going around?"

"Someone told me that there were."

"That's insane," Catherine said. "Why would Philip want to harm you?"

"Apparently the story is that I forced him to marry me and that he wants to get rid of me."

Catherine looked distressed. "I don't believe it," she said. But she did not sound quite certain.

Dear God, I thought. If Catherine could find that such a story had a hint of credibility . . .

"No one should believe it," I said. "Philip would no more harm me than Lord Rotheram would harm you."

There was a definite tartness in my voice. I had to confess that I was annoyed with Catherine for that lack of certainty.

I had been sitting on the chaise longue, and now I stood up. "I'm a little tired," I said. "I believe I will take a short nap before dinner."

"A good idea, Georgie," she said warmly. "You don't want to overdo things on your first day out of bed."

I smiled, and wished her happy once more, and went on down the passageway to my own bedroom. I sat down at the writing desk and wrote a note to Philip, which I asked one of the footmen to take to him in the library. I couldn't risk his going out again without seeing me. It was imperative that the two of us have a talk.

CHAPTER
nineteen

I WAS RECLINING ON THE CHAISE LONGUE IN OUR bedroom, staring at the formal bed of tulips in the small garden behind the house, when Philip came in.

"You wanted to see me?" he asked.

I turned my head from the window to look at my husband. There was a deep, tense line between his flying black eyebrows and his blue eyes were guarded.

I said without preamble, "I went to the Duchess of Faircastle's musicale this afternoon with Catherine, and Charles Howard was there. He made a nasty insinuation that there were rumors going around town that you were responsible for my accident in the park. Is it true about the rumors, Philip?"

He came farther in the room, but not in my direction. Instead he crossed to the mantel and leaned one shoulder against it. "There's always gossip in this town," he said. "It's the way people in London live."

I said, "Do you realize that somebody started that rumor, and that it was probably the man who really was responsible for my accident?"

He didn't answer, just continued to regard me with that disturbingly guarded look.

"For heaven's sake," I said, jumping to my feet. "Don't you see what's happening here? If this maniac does succeed in making away with me, you are the one who will take the blame!"

"I see it quite clearly," he said.

As he was making no motion toward approaching me, I crossed the floor to the fireplace, slid my arms around his waist, rested my cheek against his shoulder, and said, "Well then, don't you think that we had better make quite certain that nothing happens to me?"

His arms came up and circled me as lightly as if I were made of porcelain.

"I have every intention of doing that," he said.

His breath stirred my hair and I closed my eyes and leaned the length of my body against him. I said, "You look exhausted. You can't have been sleeping properly on that narrow bed in your dressing room. You had better come back into your own bed tonight."

I was so close to him that he could not disguise the way his heartbeat accelerated at my words. However, when he spoke his voice was quiet and calm. "Do you think so?"

"Yes," I said. "I most certainly do."

By dinnertime I was feeling more fatigued than I had expected to, and when Philip told me that he had to go out for a short while, I decided to go upstairs and wait for him in bed.

I fell asleep and when I awoke in the small hours of the morning, Philip was not beside me. I felt a flash of anger. If he was sleeping in his dressing room again, I was going to demand an explanation.

But when I opened his dressing-room door, the room was empty. Nor was the single bed turned down in preparation for an occupant.

It was four in the morning, and Philip simply had not come home.

I was hurt and insulted and angry. Surely I had been

as blatant as it was possible to be this afternoon. What was wrong with him, anyway? He had been hungry enough for me while we were at Winterdale Park.

Was it that now that we were back in London he had other women friends to assuage his desire, and he did not want me in that way any longer?

This was a terrible, terrible thought, and I tried valiantly to push it from my mind. But it would not be banished.

For another half an hour I lay wide-awake in my darkened bedroom, and then finally I heard the sound of someone entering the room next door. Philip had come home.

I would give him fifteen minutes, I thought grimly. Then I was going to go into his dressing room, and if he was lying in that little bed, I was going to want to know the reason why.

Ten minutes crept by, then the door between the bedroom and Philip's dressing room opened and Philip came in. It was as if an iron hand that had been clasped about my heart suddenly relaxed its grip.

I looked at him in the light of the candle he was carrying. The front lock of his hair was dripping wet, and so were his eyelashes, as if he had hastily splashed quite a lot of water on his face and neglected to dry it properly. The collar of his nightshirt was rucked under and twisted to one side. He was not walking quite steadily. Or rather, he was walking with such slow and conscious steadiness that it looked suspicious.

I had seen that kind of a walk before on my father. I sat bolt upright in bed. "Philip," I said accusingly, "you're drunk!"

My voice evidently surprised him, for he jumped, and the candle in his hand flickered alarmingly.

"Jesus," he said. "I might have started a fire, Georgie. Don't startle me like that."

His voice was very faintly slurred.

"Don't blaspheme," I snapped. "And you have so been drinking. You can't deny it."

"I have no intention of denying it." Moving cautiously, he put the candle on the bedside table and got into the four-poster beside me.

I was profoundly disappointed and beginning to be angry. "Were you at your club?" I asked.

He drawled in that barely slurred tone of voice, "No. Actually I was meeting with an old acquaintance of mine, someone who has a great deal of influence in the London criminal world. I was hoping he might be able to find out who was hired to shoot that slingshot at you the other day."

I thought about this for a minute.

"And did he have any ideas?" I asked at last.

"He is going to make inquiries," Philip replied.

In the light of the candle he had not yet blown out, I could see his strong chest exposed by the twisted neck of his nightshirt. A drop of the water he had splashed himself with to try to sober up dripped off his eyelash onto his cheek. He did not appear to notice.

I said, "I gather that this . . . acquaintance . . . is not overly respectable?"

Philip gave a short, hard laugh. "He is not respectable at all. But he is a powerful man in his own right. If anyone can discover the information I need, it is he."

Even though Philip was lying on his own pillow, on his own side of the bed, I could smell the rich aroma of brandy on his breath. I said austerely, "Was it really necessary to get drunk with him?"

He turned his head to look at me. His blue eyes looked very heavy under his wet lashes. "Unfortunately, it was. He refused any kind of payment, all he wanted to do was to engage in a drinking contest with me. It took a long time. Claven has an enormous capacity."

I stared at him in astonishment. "A drinking contest? Why on earth would he want to do that?"

Philip's voice was bitter. "Because in my wild youth, I acquired an unfortunate reputation for having the hardest head in Europe. It has led to all sorts of problems for me. Claven simply wanted to see if he could drink me under the table. If he could, then I would have to pay him to look for our perpetrator; if he couldn't, he would do it for nothing. Believe me, I would have been more than happy just to pay, but he wouldn't have it."

In my wild youth.

He was twenty-six.

I said gently, "I gather you succeeded in putting him under the table first."

"Yes. I did."

I remembered the state of my papa after an all-night drinking bout. "You are going to feel wretched in the morning," I predicted.

He groaned. "I already feel wretched, Georgie. Can we please stop talking now so that I can try to get some sleep?"

"Of course," I said kindly. I was feeling quite in charity with him since learning that his lateness and his carousing had all been done for my benefit. I leaned over and kissed his cheek. The stubble of his beard prickled my lips. "Good night, Philip," I said.

"Good night," he mumbled.

I tucked the coverlet around his shoulder and left him to his slumber.

He was still asleep when I awoke at eight, and I left him sleeping while I dressed in my dressing room. I breakfasted with Catherine and when I learned that she and Lady Winterdale were attending a ball at the Mintons' that evening, I decided that I would go also and that I would insist that Philip accompany me. I thought it was important that we be seen together, and even more importantly, that we be seen to be on good terms.

After lunch, I confronted Philip in the library, where he was once more going over papers.

He looked like a man with a headache.

"Do you feel up to going to the Minton ball with me this evening, Philip?" I asked. "I know you can't be feeling well, but, in the light of this nasty rumor that is going round, I think it is important for us to be seen together."

He raised his eyes from the ledger in front of him and regarded me. He looked haggard. "If you're going, I'm going," he said. "I'm not trusting you out of my sight until we've found out who is responsible for these accidents of yours."

I said righteously, "I have never been able to understand why gentlemen drink when it leaves them feeling so wretched the following morning."

He sighed. "I'm not up to arguing that point with you right now, Georgie. What time do you wish to leave?"

"After dinner," I said.

He shuddered at the mention of food.

I turned away to leave the library.

"Are you going out this afternoon?" he asked sharply.

I hesitated. "Frank is coming over to visit here at the

house," I said. "He has been so nice about coming to ask about my health, and sending me flowers, that I thought it would be only polite to see him."

His eyes dropped once more to his ledger. "Just don't go out with him," he said.

It was an order, not a request.

I bit my lip. Then, "All right," I said. I walked to the door, opened it, and closed it softly behind me so as not to jar his aching head.

By dinnertime Philip's headache seemed to be improved, even though he ate very little of the food that Lady Winterdale had ordered for our meal that evening.

It occurred to me that he could not have been doing a great deal of drinking during the weeks I had stayed at Winterdale House before our marriage, for I had certainly never seen him as under the weather as this.

Of course, this morning he had as good as told me that he didn't drink the way he used to in his wild youth.

I thought that this was very good news indeed.

There was a line of carriages in front of Minton House in Berkeley Square, and we had to wait twenty minutes before our chaise pulled up to the front door and we could alight. It was raining, and the Minton footmen were out with huge umbrellas to escort the guests from the street to the brilliantly lit white-marble front hall.

The ball was being held on the second floor, in the largest of the drawing rooms, and as Philip and I were announced I could have sworn that at least half the heads in the room turned to look at us.

I immediately slipped my arm through Philip's and smiled up at him brilliantly.

The reckless eyebrows lifted. "Don't overdo it, Georgie," he advised dryly.

"Nonsense. We've just returned from our wedding trip. I should look like a radiant bride."

I batted my eyes at him.

The corner of his mouth quirked.

Lord Henry Sloan came up to stand in front of us. "Lady Winterdale," he said to me with his infectious smile. "How lovely to have you back among us again. You have been missed." He nodded to Philip. "Winterdale. How are you?"

"Very well," Philip said tersely.

Lord Henry turned back to me. "You have recovered from your accident, then, Lady Winterdale?"

I smiled into my ex-beau's curious hazel eyes. "Yes, thank you. The stupidest thing, you know. My poor Cato was stung by a bee."

"Indeed?" Sir Henry looked thoughtful. "So that is what happened."

I had invented this excuse earlier, and I thought it was very clever of me. Philip said nothing.

At this moment, the orchestra struck up a waltz. Philip took my hand. "My dear?"

Once more I bestowed upon him my radiant new-bride look. "I should love to."

As we circled the room, I could feel people watching us.

"I don't like this at all," I muttered.

"Neither do I," said my husband. "If the villain has gone to all this trouble to plant suspicion about me, then he must be serious indeed." I saw a muscle clench in his jaw. "Damn! Claven had better be able to find out something for me. If he doesn't, I shall be forced to kill all of the men on your father's list, and that could be rather awkward."

"Philip!" I stared up at him in shock and horror. "You wouldn't kill innocent men."

He gave me a very bleak look. "Why not? I've killed an innocent man before."

I could feel my heart accelerate. "What do you mean?"

Before he could answer me, however, the music stopped, and we found ourselves standing next to Catherine and Lord Henry Sloan, who had danced the waltz together.

Lord Henry grinned at me, and said, "I have the strictest orders from my brother Rotheram to engage Lady Catherine for all the waltzes. He is deathly afraid that someone is going to steal her away from him before he can officially claim her for himself."

Catherine turned deliciously pink.

"I see that you are in your brother's confidence, Lord Henry," I said.

"Yes. He told me out of necessity, and enjoined me strictly to keep my tongue in my head." Another grin. "A very difficult task for me. You know how I love to gossip."

He bowed and left us.

Philip looked at Catherine. "Rotheram? Am I to wish you happy, Catherine?"

She looked a little distressed. "Henry is such a rattlepate. He was not supposed to say anything. But, yes, Philip, Rotheram has asked me to marry him after his mourning period is over."

Philip flew one black eyebrow. "Does your mother know?"

"Not yet."

The other eyebrow joined the first. "A future duke," he said. "She will be delighted."

Catherine retorted, "She will be unbearable, and you

know it. It can't be helped, however. Edward is who he is. I would love him if he were an apothecary's assistant."

Philip grinned his rare, boy's grin. "I do wish you happy, Cousin," he said. "You deserve it."

Catherine looked first surprised, then delighted. She smiled back.

A dreadfully familiar creak sounded in my ears. "Lady Winterdale," said Mr. George Asherton. "It is such a pleasure to see you back in London."

I could feel the sudden tension in Philip. He said coldly, "I do not believe I know this gentleman, my dear."

He knew perfectly well who Asherton was, and he knew that Asherton was one of the men on Papa's list, but I said, "My lord, may I present Mr. George Asherton. He was a friend of my late father's."

Mr. Asherton bowed. "Lord Winterdale. I am pleased to make your acquaintance, sir."

Philip looked at him icily. "How do you do," he said.

Undeterred by my husband's unwelcoming behavior, Mr. Asherton said, "May I request the honor of your hand for this dance, Lady Winterdale?"

I said quickly, before Philip could snub him, "Certainly, Mr. Asherton." I smiled up into my husband's rigid face. "Will you excuse us, my lord?"

He gave me an exceedingly hard look, which I ignored. I wanted to talk to George Asherton. Specifically, I wanted to allow him to talk to me. He might let something fall that would give me a clue as to whether or not he was the author of that threatening letter.

The dance was a country dance and as we walked toward the floor Mr. Asherton asked me if I wouldn't rather sit it out. He looked a little surprised when I agreed, but he escorted me to a chair along the wall and went to fetch two glasses of punch for us. Philip and Catherine had moved to a place on the other side of the room, almost directly opposite to my chair, and as I glanced at them I noticed how the blazing wall sconce shone on my husband's raven head and sparkled off Catherine's diamond earrings and her spectacles.

It was quite clear that Philip meant to keep me under close surveillance, and I found this thought to be extremely comforting.

Mr. Asherton came back with the punch and sat down on a gilt chair next to mine. He shifted his weight, and the chair creaked in tune with his corset.

"I was so sorry to hear about your accident the other day, Lady Winterdale," Mr. Asherton began. He did not look sorry at all. "I understand that you took an ugly fall from your horse."

"Yes," I said. "He was stung by a bee, and he threw me."

Asherton regarded me with watery blue eyes. "Stung by a bee?"

I sipped my punch and nodded.

He cleared his throat in a loud, disgusting manner. "One would be more inclined to believe that tale if one hadn't heard of other unaccountable accidents befalling you, Lady Winterdale."

My head snapped around, and I stared at him. The sconce above us illuminated a bald patch in the middle of his head. "What other accidents?" I demanded.

"For example, I heard just yesterday that a few weeks ago you fell into the lion's cage at the Tower." Asherton's pudgy face was hard to read since it was so unnaturally smooth and unlined for a man of his age. "Is that true?"

"Where did you hear that?" I demanded.

He shrugged and once more his corset creaked. "I don't recollect specifically. It was the talk of White's, however." He narrowed his eyes, and for a moment his fat face actually managed to look dangerous. "A blackmailer's existence is extremely hazardous, Lady Winterdale," he warned. "Look at your own father. He was stabbed to death on the streets of London, was he not? Now you yourself have first fallen into a lion's den, and then been thrown into the path of a horse and carriage in Hyde Park. Don't you think it would be wise of you to give up your evidence and put an end to your nefarious career?"

The blood ran cold in my veins at his words about Papa.

It had never before occurred to me that Papa might have died at the hands of one of his victims.

I managed to say in a voice that did not shake, "Are you responsible for the accidents that have befallen my family, Mr. Asherton? You appear to know a great deal about them."

He bared his teeth at me. They were very small teeth for such a big man. "Someone is responsible, Lady Winterdale. I do not fool myself that I am the only one whom your late father was blackmailing. I do not know who the others were—except, of course, for Winterdale, who is obvious. But someone is out to stop you from following in your father's footsteps, my dear. It may be Winterdale, whom you have entrapped into marriage, or it may be someone else. But my advice to you is to give up your evidence. It is the only way you can assure your own safety."

"I destroyed the evidence," I said grimly. "I do not know how many times I have told you that."

"If you destroyed the evidence, then why did Winterdale take you in and pay a huge amount of money to give you a Season? Why did he marry you?"

This, of course, was the unanswerable question. I could hardly say that Philip had done it to get back at his aunt. Even I could not wish that kind of a scandal on Lady Winterdale. And it was unlikely any of Papa's victims would believe such an explanation.

"He knew my circumstances, and he felt sorry for me," I said lamely.

"Winterdale?" Mr. Asherton stared at me as if I were mad. "Winterdale never felt sorry for anyone in his life," he said. "Do you know how he got his money? He won his entire fortune from a young Italian count, who went out immediately after the game in which he lost all his possessions to Winterdale, including his family villa, and killed himself. At the time, Lady Winterdale, Count Ferria was all of twenty-three years old."

I could feel myself go pale.

I've killed an innocent man before, Philip had said.

I set my jaw. "And how old was my husband?" I asked Mr. Asherton.

"Oh, he was about the same age, I suppose," Asherton replied impatiently. "But at twenty-three, Winterdale was a man of the world. Ferria was still a babe in arms."

I said grimly, "Was the game fair?"

Asherton glared at me. "I suppose it was fair. I never heard that it wasn't."

"Then that Italian count was a fool," I said stoutly. "Gentlemen shouldn't play when they can't afford to lose." I glared back at my companion. "As you, of all people, should know, Mr. Asherton."

Mercifully, the music was ending and I got to my feet.

I looked around for Philip and saw him coming across the floor in my direction.

"Allow me to tell you that I find you to be an excessively unpleasant man, Mr. Asherton," I said. "I shall make a bargain with you. I will stay away from you if you will stay away from me."

Philip arrived at my side and gratefully I put my hand upon his sleeve. I said, "This punch I have been drinking is warm, my lord. Do you think we might go into the supper room and have another glass?"

"Of course," he replied.

As we crossed the floor together in the direction of the door, I could feel the eyes watching us.

I was going to have to tell Philip about the fact that news had got out about my fall into the lion's den at the Tower, but I decided to keep my suspicions about my father's death to myself.

CHAPTER
twenty

WE LEFT THE BALL EARLY AND ALL THE WAY HOME in the chaise, Lady Winterdale complained to Catherine about her giving so many dances to Lord Henry Sloan. Lord Henry, as a younger son, might have been a perfectly adequate suitor for me, but Lady Winterdale had set her sights higher for her daughter.

While Catherine murmured innocuous responses to her mother, I sat with my eyes half-closed, listening to the sound of the rain bouncing off the top of the town chaise. Philip sat beside me in silence, staring moodily out the rain-drenched window.

It was midnight when I entered my dressing room to get ready for bed. Betty was waiting for me, and she unbuttoned all the small covered buttons at the back of my pale rose evening gown and helped me into my nightdress. She unbraided my hair and brushed it so that it fell smoothly between my shoulder blades. Then I put on my green-velvet dressing gown and went into my bedroom next door.

The coal fire was blazing in the fireplace, and a brass candelabra on the writing desk between the two big windows cast its yellow light across the rug. I took off my dressing gown, got into bed, and strained my ears to hear through the walls into the room next door.

The faint rumble of male voices floated to my ears.

Philip was talking to his valet. He must indeed be coming to bed.

I leaned back against my pillows and smiled with a mixture of anticipation and relief.

Five minutes later he came through the door, blew out the three candles in the candelabra, and joined me in bed.

Our lovemaking that night was both the same as it had been at Winterdale Park, and different. Philip's need for me was the same, as was his heart-stopping tenderness. And the swelling surge of my own response, the thrilling convulsion of pleasure that his driving desire gave to me, this too was the same.

And afterward, when he lay breathless on top of me, his heart pounding, and I held him tightly in my arms, so deeply loved that I never wanted to let him go, that too was the same.

But when I awoke in the early hours of the morning, I was dismayed to find that Philip was not beside me in the bed. The rain had stopped and a faint glow of moonlight showed me his figure at the window. He had put on his dressing gown, and he was standing there, his forehead pressed against the glass, staring out at the empty garden.

He looked so desolate, so unbearably lonely.

Anguish struck my heart. In my foolish lovesickness, I had thought that marriage to me would put an end to that isolation of his. I had thought that now that he had a wife who loved him, he would never wear that look again.

And indeed, at Winterdale Park, it had seemed as if we had joined together in a way that was deeply personal, in a way that went well beyond the merely physical attraction that was so obviously between us.

Things had changed since we returned to London.

And what, after all, did I really know of him, I asked

myself tonight. In truth, he had shared very little of his thoughts and feelings with me. He was a man who had learned to live his life alone, relying on his own resources and his own talents and his own wits.

Was I refining too much on the fact that he was a good lover? He had made love to many women; I was aware of that. Why should I be of any more importance to him than any of the other female bodies into which he had poured his passion and his seed?

I lay there in the dark, and looked at my husband, and felt more unhappy than I think I had ever felt before in my life.

He was a mystery to me. He had lived a life that was utterly foreign to the world in which I had been brought up. He had known many women, he had caused a man's death, and he talked of killing with a casualness that frightened me.

But I could not forget that he had been cast into that ugly, rapacious world as a boy and been forced to survive largely on his own. How could I blame him for what he was? How could anyone blame him?

Indeed, it seemed to me that he could have been far worse.

He was gentle with Anna.

He was kind to Nanny.

I looked at his back, at those wide shoulders that managed to look so untouchable, and quelled my urge to get out of bed and go to him. He wouldn't welcome my presence now. Instinctively, I sensed that. So I lay perfectly still and waited for him to come back to bed on his own.

It took him fifteen more minutes before he turned away from the window and came back to our bed. His movements looked unutterably weary.

But what is the matter, Philip?

I longed to cry those words out to him. I longed to reach my arms around him, and hold him close to me and give him the comfort of my body.

But he didn't want me. He had wanted me earlier, but not now.

He punched his pillow into shape and turned away from me and settled once more to sleep.

I lay awake for a long time, the tears seeping silently out of my eyes, trying to understand what bitter and divisive thing might be keeping us apart.

I woke with a headache.

"Too much champagne punch," Philip said when he came in at ten o'clock to find me lying heavy-eyed in bed.

He was dressed in riding clothes and there was fresh color in his cheeks. He did not look like a man who had spent half the night staring out the bedroom window.

"Have you been to the park?" I asked wistfully.

"Yes, Isabelle and I had a nice long gallop."

I shut my eyes. It was not the champagne punch which had given me the headache, and I knew it.

He said, "Georgie, I have had a letter this morning from my agent about problems with the canal at Winterdale Park. I am going to have to go down there to have a look at it and make some decisions."

I said quietly, "Do you want me to go with you?"

He frowned at me. "I do, because I don't like the idea of letting you out from under my sight. On the other hand, I plan to be back tomorrow, and there seems little point in forcing you to make the trip back and forth for such a short stay, particularly if you are not feeling well."

I sighed. "I think it would upset Anna to have me come and go as quickly as that."

"Well then, that answers the question, doesn't it?"

"I suppose it does," I replied glumly.

He was holding his tan leather riding gloves and now he slapped them decisively against his thigh. "Very well, then. I will be gone overnight and during that time I want you to keep to the house."

"Good heavens, Philip," I said impatiently. "There is no reason to make me a prisoner. As long as I exercise sensible precautions, I don't see any reason for me to have to stay within-doors."

"You may not see any reason, but I do," he replied. "You will obey me in this, Georgianna. There have already been two attempts made on your life, remember."

"I promise not to go near any more menageries," I said with an attempt at humor.

He favored me with an extremely hard blue stare. "Stay indoors. Do you hear me?"

I slid down in the bed. I stuck out my lower lip. "Yes, Philip," I said ungraciously. "I hear you."

"Good. I will be leaving within the hour. You may expect me back sometime late tomorrow." He came to bestow a chaste kiss upon my forehead. "I hope your head feels better," he said.

"Thank you," I said. "Goodbye."

He went out the door. With difficulty, I refrained from throwing something after him.

Sometimes, I thought, he could be a very difficult man to love.

I went back to sleep for another hour and when I awoke the second time, I felt better. As I was getting dressed, Catherine came into my dressing room and asked to talk to me privately. I told Betty to have some tea brought up to us and invited Catherine to sit down in one of the worn, chintz-covered chairs. I took the chaise longue.

After some casual chitchat about the previous night's ball, she finally came out with the real reason for her visit. "I have a favor to ask of you, Georgie. Do you think you might accompany me to Vauxhall tonight?"

"Vauxhall?" I was astonished. "Is Lady Winterdale allowing you to go to Vauxhall, Catherine?"

Vauxhall pleasure gardens were a very popular entertainment venue with the *ton*, but Lady Winterdale did not consider them entirely respectable for an unmarried girl, and consequently neither Catherine nor I had ever been there. From what I could gather, the reason for Lady Winterdale's disapproval was that the punch served at Vauxhall was extremely potent, and many of the young bucks who attended the entertainments there tended to get rather boisterous. A few had even been known to pull an innocent young miss off one of the pleasure-garden paths and into the woods for an illicit kiss.

"There is to be a concert this evening, and the Duchess of Faircastle has invited me to accompany her party," Catherine explained. Her eyes shone behind her spectacles. "Edward is going to be there, too, Georgie. We will be able to have supper together in one of the booths, and perhaps we can even go for a walk together down one of the paths . . ."

Her voice trailed off, and she looked at me imploringly.

The poor girl, I thought. She and Rotheram had probably never once had a chance to be alone together.

"I thought Rotheram was still in mourning," I said.

"He is, but it is perfectly proper to dress in a domino

and mask when one goes to Vauxhall, you know. The duchess's party is all going to dress in masquerade, so no one will know who Edward is. He will not scandalize anyone by his attendance."

"But will your mama let you go?" I asked doubtfully. "You know she has never approved of Vauxhall, Catherine."

Catherine sighed. "I had to hint to her that there was a chance that something might develop between Rotheram and me, and that has quite changed her attitude about my attending Vauxhall with the duchess. She insists, however, that I must have a chaperone other than the duchess, who will probably be too occupied with her own lover to do her duty by me."

I had been quite scandalized when first I learned that the Duchess of Faircastle had a long-standing lover in Lord Margate, who was one of the regulars at her weekly musicales. He had also been regularly in attendance upon the duchess at all of the other occasions upon which our paths had crossed. In fact, as far as I knew, the duchess's husband, the Duke of Faircastle, had not made a single appearance in London during the course of the present Season.

Catherine was going on, "Unfortunately, Mama herself is not up to accompanying us this evening, as she was ill for most of the night with a stomach ailment. So will you please come with me, Georgie?"

I stared at her with a mixture of amazement and amusement. "Do I really qualify as a chaperone, Catherine?"

"Of course you do. You are married to my cousin, are you not?"

A thought struck me, and I narrowed my eyes. "By

any chance, did you and Rotheram wait until you knew Lady Winterdale would be unable to accompany you before you arranged this little expedition, Catherine?"

She looked a little sheepish. "If Mama came, you know she would never let me out of her sight, Georgie. You are not so old-fashioned."

I smiled. "That is true."

I thought of Philip's strictures about staying home. He would be furious if I went to Vauxhall. I looked once again at Catherine and knew that I didn't have the heart to disappoint her.

I thought of a compromise.

"Would you mind if I invited Captain Stanton to come with me?" I asked. "I feel bad that I have been able to see him so rarely since he came to London."

"Of course you may invite Captain Stanton," Catherine replied promptly. She looked at me anxiously. "Then you will do it, Georgie? You will come?"

I took a deep breath. Frank would protect me, I thought. After all, he was a Peninsula veteran.

I would have Frank. I would be wearing a domino, which would afford me a disguise. In a burst of inspiration I decided that, as an additional precaution, I would ask Betty to sew a pocket into my domino. It wouldn't hurt to carry a little extra protection with me in case I needed it.

"Yes," I said to Catherine. "I will come with you to Vauxhall."

There were eight of us in the Duchess of Faircastle's party that evening: the duchess and Lord Margate; Lord Rotheram and Catherine; Mr. Fergus MacDonald and Lady Laura Rinsdale; and Frank and I. Vauxhall itself was situated south of the Thames and to get there we first took two carriages to Westminster, where we boarded a boat to cross the river.

The evening was beautiful and clear, and the setting sun cast shades of red, orange, and vermillion on the waters of the river. Suddenly I wished with all my heart that it was Philip sitting close beside me in the boat, and not Frank.

Our party disembarked on the south side of the river, and we entered the gardens by way of the famous Grand Walk. I thought that the long nine-hundred-foot pathway, lined with elms and blazing lanterns, made the place look like the enchanted land in a childhood story my mother used to tell. Couple by couple, the duchess's party proceeded along the Grand Walk, until we reached a large open space in the middle of the gardens, where refreshment booths were arranged in two wide semicircles. These booths were well lit and adorned with bright scenes painted on their backs. The duchess had hired one of the booths for the evening, and we located it by her name, which was discreetly posted on a card on the booth door.

We all eight of us took our seats in the booth, which was decorated by a painting of a maypole dance, and I looked curiously at the scene around me.

In the middle of the open space left by the circle of boxes, an orchestra was playing, and couples were strolling about the area to meet and greet acquaintances. The booths were low enough for those dining within to lean over and shake hands with the people whom they knew. Farther down the Grand Walk was a big rotunda, where dancing was going on.

I gestured to the orchestra. "Is this the concert?" I

queried Catherine, who was seated next to me. She was wearing a blue-silk domino and a matching mask.

"No. Mr. Hook is to play the organ later."

"Oh."

"I say, this is quite a place, Georgie," Frank said from my other side. Like the other gentlemen in our party, he was wearing a black-silk domino over his evening clothes.

"You have never been to Vauxhall, Captain?" the duchess asked graciously. The duchess's domino was lavender, as was her mask.

"No, your grace."

"You will quite enjoy it," the duchess predicted. "You and Lady Winterdale must take the opportunity to explore some of the more famous paths. The South Walk, for instance, has three marvelous archways that simulate the ruins of Palmyra. They are quite realistic, I believe."

"Duchess, is that you? I saw your name on the booth." A middle-aged woman whose cheeks were too obviously painted, was standing in front of our booth looking up curiously. "How nice to see you here."

As the two women engaged in light conversation, I looked slowly around the open arena in front of me at the strolling couples.

It occurred to me that a great many of the unmasked pairs who peopled the scene were married, but not to each other.

This was an extremely depressing observation, particularly in the light of my thoughts about my own husband earlier this morning. I looked now at Catherine and Lord Rotheram. His head was bent to hers, and he was listening intently to something she was saying. Would his feelings for Catherine last, I wondered, or would the corrupt morals of his mother and her lover, and the world they inhabited, subvert the purity of his feeling for Catherine and eventually send him off to find someone more worldly and less vulnerable than she?

I looked once again at Rotheram's partially masked face. I remembered the lines that pain had engraved at the sides of his eyes, and the fear for Catherine that had gripped my heart loosened. Catherine was safe with her Edward, I thought. He was a man who had learned the hard way to value what was important in life.

Frank murmured in my ear, "Georgie, will you dance with me?"

I didn't think I should leave the booth, but I also realized that this was the only chance Frank was likely to get to dance with me during his stay in London. I had invited him to accompany me here, I thought. I owed it to him to give him a dance.

"Of course," I said lightly, and let him lead me to the rotunda, where a waltz was being played.

Frank put his arms around me and we stepped off together.

He began to talk immediately. "I have been trying desperately to get you alone, Georgie. Do you have any idea of the innuendos that are going around town about your accident in the park?"

My pink domino swung out behind me as we made a turn. "I know exactly what is being said, Frank, and none of it is true. Philip is not trying to do away with me, I can promise you that."

"Is it true that you fell into the lion's cage at the Tower?" he demanded.

"Yes."

He shut his eyes. The part of his face that was revealed by his mask was very pale. "Georgie, I think you ought to let me take you back to Sussex to stay with my parents."

I decided then and there that I had better tell him the whole story. After all, he was my oldest friend. I knew that he loved me. It wasn't fair to allow him to think that I was married to a man who wanted to kill me.

I said, "Frank, after this dance is over, let us go for a walk. I have a long and rather ugly story to tell you. It doesn't put me in a very good light, I'm afraid, but at least it will make you understand that I have nothing to fear from Philip."

He hesitated, and then he said, "All right."

We danced in silence until the music had ended and then we turned to leave the floor together. At the edge of the rotunda, we almost literally ran into Lord Marsh, who stopped me by the simple expedient of stepping in front of me.

"Lady Winterdale," he said with every evidence of pleasure.

I was still wearing my mask and I demanded, "How did you know who I was?"

"I recognized your hair," he said with that nasty amusement that never touched his eyes. "If you wish to disguise yourself, you would do well to exchange your braids for curls."

I said fiercely, "Step out of my way, if you please." I had no intention of even pretending civility to the man.

Lord Marsh sighed. "Such rudeness," he said sadly. "I am shocked, Lady Winterdale."

I replied in an icy voice, "I am quite certain that nothing is capable of shocking you, Lord Marsh. Now please let me pass."

After a moment, he stepped out of my way and I

brushed past him, ostentatiously holding my skirts aside in order to make certain that they did not touch him.

"Good God," said Frank, once we were out of Marsh's earshot. "What was that all about, Georgie?"

"I plan to tell you," I said. "Come, let us go for a walk."

It was growing dark so we chose the South Walk, which was well lit and fairly crowded with couples. I began my tale by telling Frank about how I had found out about Papa's blackmailing scheme, and I carried on from there with how I had followed up by blackmailing Philip. I left very little out and when I had finished, I said, "So you see, it is I who have behaved very badly, Frank, and Philip who has behaved very well."

He was silent as we walked away from the third arch that simulated the ruins of Palmyra. Then he said gruffly, "He could still be at the bottom of these attacks, Georgie. From what you have described to me, he was forced to marry you after all."

"I was pushed into the menagerie before we married," I pointed out. "And really, Frank, I don't think I am such an antidote that my husband needs to go to such horrific lengths as murdering me in order to be rid of me!"

He let out a long sigh. "Of course you're not an antidote, Georgie. I suppose I want to think the worst of Winterdale because I'm jealous of him." We had taken off our masks as the crowd on the walk had thinned out and now he turned to look at me, a very worried look in his steady gray eyes. "But if Winterdale isn't the one who is responsible for these accidents, then who is?"

"Philip is trying to find that out."

Frank said, "Have you seen anyone on that list here tonight besides Marsh?"

"No."

"Of course, that doesn't mean anything," he said worriedly. "This place is full of people wearing dominos and masks. God knows who could be stalking you, Georgie. You should never have come here."

I patted his sleeve. "I had to come for Catherine's sake. And since Philip was out of town, I asked you for protection, Frank. I shall be perfectly safe as long as we stay together."

By this time we were almost at the very end of the South Walk. It ended with a Greek temple, which I understood was lit with an artificial fountain on gala nights at Vauxhall. Tonight, however, the temple was dark and deserted, and the path around us was deserted as well. Frank and I had been so deeply involved in our conversation that we had not realized how far we had come from the crowds that filled most of the pleasure garden.

In fact, right now we were the only couple at this end of the South Walk.

Frank looked around him and then said authoritatively, "Come along, Georgie. Let us return to the rest of our party immediately."

I agreed and the two of us turned to retrace our way back to the supper boxes.

We had not gone above a dozen steps when I heard the sound of steps behind us coming from the direction of the Greek temple.

"*Run, Georgie!*" Frank yelled at me as he whirled with fists raised to confront the four men who were rushing at us.

I screamed and tried to go to his aid, but a large, callused hand seemed to come out of nowhere to close over my mouth and pull my head back against a man's coat. I struggled, trying to kick my attacker, and someone swore, and I felt the sharp crack of a fist on my chin, and then blackness descended.

CHAPTER
twenty=one

I WOKE IN A SMALL, DIRTY ROOM THAT SMELLED LIKE cabbage and beer and urine. My jaw ached something fierce. I was lying on a filthy straw mattress on the floor. Two men were standing at the foot of the mattress, arguing.

"We've bin paid t'snuff her, Alf. I say we do the job, collect our blunt, and be done wi' it."

"I ain't sayin' we don't do that, Jem. I just say we have our bit o' fun wi' her first. A fancy lady like that—when 'r you likely to get a bit o' muslin like that come your way agin, eh?"

Even in my semidazed state, it didn't take me long to realize what they were talking about. They were going to kill me, but if the one called Alf had his way, they would rape me first.

I lay very still, with my eyes shut, and tried desperately to remember what had happened.

I remembered going to Vauxhall with Catherine and Frank. Then I remembered the pocket I had had Betty sew into my domino. Moving very slowly, I slid my fingers across my dress. The silky smoothness I touched told me I was still wearing the pink cape.

Thank God.

I opened my eyes a slit so that I could see the two arguing men. Then, slowly and carefully, I reached my fingers inside the domino to the pocket. The small knife I had hidden there slid into my hand.

The room I was being held in was very small, and the arguing men at the foot of the bed were blocking my way to the door.

My heart was pounding and my blood was singing in my ears. My head pulsed with pain. The smell in the room was so bad that I felt like throwing up.

I had not been this frightened even in the lion's den.

I had to get out of here.

I summoned up all my courage and moaned.

Immediately the men fell silent.

I tossed my head from one side to another, and moaned again.

"She's wakin' up," the man called Jem said. "I say we do 'er now."

"Go and see if the alley is clear," the man called Alf ordered. "We don't want no one to see us when we dump 'er. I hear'd Claven bin askin' questions about that slingshot in 'yde Park. We don't want Claven down on us, Jem."

"Ye're right about that," the other said fervently. I heard the door open and close and steps clattered on the stairs. Then I heard Alf's step as he came over to the bed. My eyes were closed but I could feel him looking down at me.

"Ye might be a fine lidy, but I'll bet ye're just the same under your skirts as any doxy from the street," he said. He put his hand on the neck of my evening dress and began to rip it.

I brought the knife up fast and stabbed him deep in his left shoulder.

He howled.

Blood gushed out of the wound. He clutched at it and tried to grab the knife.

I pulled the knife out of the wound, inflicting more damage I hoped, rolled off the bed, and ran like a maniac for the door.

Outside I found myself on a small landing, with stairs that only went down, not up. Evidently we were on the top floor. I held up my skirts and raced downward, praying that I would reach the ground floor before Jem came back from his job of checking the alley.

I had just made it past the second landing when the front door to the narrow, stinking building opened and someone came in below me. I couldn't take a chance that it would be Jem, so I turned and ran back up again to the second floor.

There was no place behind the staircase to hide, only two rickety doors on the narrow landing. Desperately I tried one of the doors only to find it locked. I tried the other one and it opened. I ducked inside.

The room was dark and it smelled just as badly as the room upstairs where I had been held. I was not alone in the darkness, however, as the sound of a creaking bed and the unmistakable grunts of a man in the final throes of sexual pleasure made clear.

"Who's that?" a rough, female voice asked through the thick, stinking blackness.

The walls were so thin that it was easy for me to hear the sound of Jem's feet tramping past the door and beginning to mount the steps to the next landing.

"Oh dear," I said brightly. "I thought that this was the Smith residence."

The man on the bed, who was obviously now finished with his business, cursed foully.

"Sorry," I said to the couple I had so rudely inter-rupted. "I'll go."

I slipped out of the room, tore down the stairs and out onto a dark, narrow, and excessively smelly street.

I had no idea where I was. Mayfair was the only sec-tion of London with which I was familiar, and clearly this was not Mayfair. One thing I did know, however. I had to get out of this neighborhood before Alf and Jem found me again.

I began to run.

Someone shouted at me from an alleyway.

I stepped ankle-deep in something I didn't even want to think about.

Then I heard the sound of heavy steps in pursuit.

I ran even harder, looking around desperately to see if I could find a hackney to take me back to Grosvenor Square. But evidently hackneys did not frequent this sec-tion of London. I thought of how my father had been killed, and ran faster. But my breath and my legs were beginning to give out.

All of a sudden a woman's voice from a doorway said urgently, "In here."

I didn't even think, I just blindly obeyed the com-mand, ducked into the doorway, and allowed myself to be propelled up a flight of narrow stairs and into a room. The door closed behind me and I stood still, my breath ratchet-ing in my lungs, my legs trembling with the effort of my run.

The woman lit a single tallow candle, illuminating a bed, a scarred old dresser, and a baby's cot in the corner. A tattered rag rug was on the floor, and muslin curtains hung on the windows. A single wooden chair faced the cold fire-place.

The room smelled like turnips and baby.

"Are you hurt?" my rescuer asked me in a voice that had a heart-warming burr that I recognized.

I shook my head, still breathing too hard to talk.

"There's blood all over you," the woman insisted.

"It's not mine," I managed to say. I realized that I was still holding the knife in my hand, and I held up its bloody point to show her. "That man who was chasing me was trying to attack me. I stabbed him."

"Sit you down," she said, pointing to the chair, and I dropped into it, grateful to get off my shaking legs.

"The man who was chasing me," I panted. "Has he gone?"

She went to the window and peered out between the curtains. "I din't see him." In the dim light of the single candle I saw her back stiffen. "Wait a minute, here he be now."

"Oh God," I muttered. "Did anyone see me come in here?"

"I din't think so," she replied. "It's sommat quiet out there tonight. I was standing in the doorway for two hours and only got one customer."

For the first time I realized that I had been rescued by a whore.

We waited in silence for what seemed to me a very long time. Then she turned, and said to me, "It be all right now. He's gone."

The tension went out of my lungs in a whoosh. "Thank God." I rubbed my hands together, like Lady Macbeth trying to wash off Duncan's blood, and said shakily, "I don't know what I would have done if you hadn't been good enough to call to me. The man who was chasing me was going to kill me."

She turned completely away from the window and surveyed me from the tips of my feet to the top of my head. I knew I must look terrible. My shoes were filthy from the streets, my hair had come undone and was tumbling down my back, and my clothes and my hands were streaked with Alf's blood. But I was wearing a silk domino and under the cape was a dress that I was certain must have cost more than this woman could earn in five years.

The baby in the cot began to cry. The woman went over and picked him up and cradled him tenderly in her arms.

"He's hungry," she said and matter-of-factly she unfastened the front of her dress and began to nurse her child.

It was my turn to look at her.

She was very young and appallingly thin. I thought she would have been pretty if she were not so thin. Her blue muslin dress was threadbare, but clean.

The whole room, in fact, looked clean. It smelled, of course, but not the way the rest of the rooms I had been in that night had smelled.

"Why was someone trying to kill you?" she asked me in a matter-of-fact voice. "Did you get some gent's wife angry at you?"

It was then that I realized she had mistaken me for a fellow whore.

I said, "No, I'm afraid it's a little more complicated than that. In fact, my husband is going to be very upset when he discovers that I'm missing."

"You got a husband?"

"I do indeed have a husband." I gave her my friendliest smile. "I am Georgiana Mansfield," I said, "and my husband is the Earl of Winterdale."

She jerked, and her baby lost her nipple. He yelled

with outrage and she connected him back to his food supply. "You ain't serious?" she said. "You ain't no countess?"

Once more I gave her my friendly smile. "I am afraid that I am. And what is your name?"

"Maria," came the mumbled reply.

"Are you from Sussex, Maria?" I asked gently.

Once again her head jerked around to look at me. "How'd you know?"

"I am from Sussex also. I recognized your accent."

The girl heaved a heartfelt sigh. "I wish I was still in Sussex," she confessed. "I thought I was so smart, coming up to Lunnon. Sussex wasn't good enough for the likes of *me*, I thought. No, I was going to get a job as a milliner's assistant. No life as a farmer's wife for the likes o' Maria Sarton, I thought." She snorted. "What a fool I was."

"What gave you the idea of becoming a milliner's assistant?" I asked curiously. It was not a thought that would normally occur to a Sussex farmgirl, which clearly is what Maria had been.

"Some woman stopped me one day when I was comin' home from minding the sheep," Maria said. "Told me she was looking for a pretty girl like me to work in her shop. Fool that I was, I believed her. I took her money and sneaked away on the stage. Only thing was, when I got to Lunnon and looked the lady up, it turns out she was Ma Nightingale, the worst abbess in London."

"Abbess?" I queried.

"She run a brothel, my lady," came the brutal reply. "And that was where she put me to work, not at no milliner's shop."

I stared at the young woman, appalled. "But that is a

horrendous story, Maria. Couldn't you have gone back home to your family?"

"I din't have no money, my lady. Ma Nightingale made bloody well sure of that. Nor did my folks know where I'd gone to, so they couldn't come lookin' for me. Not that they would have. My ma and pa had six other mouths to feed. They were probably just as glad to get shut of me."

I was horrified by this tale, told so simply and in such a matter-of-fact tone of voice. I said a little hesitantly, "Are you still working in this brothel?"

"No, my lady. When I got myself in the family way, Ma Nightingale threw me out. I can tell you, it's been hard goin' for me ever since. I've had to stand in doorways and get my business from passersby."

Maria's story was getting more and more frightful. I remembered the terror that I had felt at the thought that Alf and Jem might lay their hands on me, and this poor girl had it happen to her every night.

"Well today is your lucky day, Maria," I said to her firmly. "If you will help me to get back to my husband, I can promise you that you will never want for money again."

She sat in silence, holding her child to her breast. Then she said, in a small, tentative, heartbreaking voice, "Do you really mean that, my lady?"

"I most certainly do. If it had not been for you taking compassion upon me tonight, I would have been dead. I owe you my life, Maria, and I am not a person who forgets her debts. You and your baby will be taken care of from now on. I give you my word on it."

She pressed her lips against her baby's head. "Oh my God," she said. "Oh my God."

Tears stung my eyes, and I blinked them away. It wouldn't do to get maudlin, I thought. I had to get back to Philip before I could do anything to help Maria.

"How can we get a message to Grosvenor Square?" I asked her. "Is it possible to get a hackney cab in this neighborhood?"

She laughed shakily. "No, my lady, that it is not."

It was cold in the room, and I could see that Maria was shivering. So was I. I looked at the empty grate.

"Do you have any coal?" I asked.

"No, my lady. I used my last scoop yesterday."

I tried not to think about my creature comforts and concentrated instead on my immediate future. "What about in the morning?" I asked. "Could we get a cab in the morning?"

"Not here, my lady. We'd have to walk toward the river."

I was afraid to venture forth in the daylight. I was certain that Alf and Jem would still be on the lookout for me.

How was I going to get back home?

I meditated for a minute and a name surfaced in my mind. "By any chance do you know someone named Claven?" I asked.

She stiffened, and once again the baby yelled with indignation at being cut off from his milk supply. "I should think so! That is, I don't know him, but I know of him, certainly. Everyone does." She frowned at me. "How do you know Claven, my lady?"

"I don't know him at all. My husband does. Is it possible for you to get in touch with Claven, Maria?"

"It might be," she replied cautiously. "The man upstairs is a messenger, and he works for Claven some-times."

"If I can reach Claven, then I'm certain that he will make it possible for me to get home safely," I told Maria. "Is this upstairs neighbor of yours at home, do you think?"

"I'll go and look," Maria said. The baby had finished nursing and fallen asleep, and she went to lay him in his cot. I noticed that she had a woolen blanket that she folded and put over the child while there was only a thin cotton blanket on her own bed. After she had left the room I went over to the window and stood behind the clean, worn curtain to peer out at the street.

What a horrible place, I thought, shuddering. I was sure there were rats running through the gutters.

It was outrageous that women had to bring up their babies in places like this.

Well, Maria was not going to have to bring up her baby here, I vowed. I would make Philip give her a nice cottage at Winterdale Park, where she could eat healthy food and drink plenty of milk and enjoy the warm Surrey sunshine.

"He ain't there." It was Maria coming back in the door. "Probably out on business. I reckon we'll have to wait for the morning to catch him."

I wanted badly to get home. I knew that Frank and Catherine would be frantic with worry about me. But I didn't seem to have any choice. It would be foolish in the extreme for me to venture forth unprotected upon the streets again. I had been saved once. I couldn't count upon God providing a second miracle.

"All right," I said, resigned to the fact that I was

going to have to spend the rest of the night in this freezing room.

"You take the bed, my lady," Maria said. "I can sit up in the chair."

"I wouldn't dream of taking your bed from you, Maria," I said firmly.

This was not merely politeness on my part. Doubtless I was being a prude, but the thought of what must have transpired in that bed truly disgusted me. I would rather freeze by the empty grate than lay amidst the scene of all those sexual horrors.

"You don't know anyone from whom you could borrow a little coal at this hour, do you?" I asked hopefully.

"I am afraid not, my lady."

"Oh well," I said heartily. "I have my domino, Maria. I shall be just fine. Don't even think about me, just get into your own bed and get some rest. We'll try to catch your neighbor in the morning."

After a few more protests, she saw that I meant what I said and we all settled down for the night.

The chair I was sitting in was hard, and a silk domino provides no warmth when it is worn over a short-sleeved, half-torn evening gown. I shivered for hours. I don't think I have ever been so glad to see the sky beginning to lighten with the coming day as I was that morning.

The baby woke Maria, crying to be fed. After she had taken care of him she went upstairs to see if her neighbor had returned home yet. She returned with a wizened little man who had a gimpy leg and a nasty scar on his right cheek.

"This is my neighbor, Colin Tregrew," Maria said to me. "Colin, this lady is the Countess of Winterdale."

"I need to get in touch with a man called Claven, Mr. Tregrew," I said. "Can you do that for me?"

"I reckon I can," he returned cautiously. "What is it that you wants me to tell him, my lady?"

"Just tell him that Lord Winterdale's wife was attacked at Vauxhall last night and begs his assistance in being returned to her home in Grosvenor Square."

The little man looked me up and down with sharp, glittering, dark eyes. The blood had dried on my domino leaving ugly rusty-colored stains. I kept it pulled together over my dress so that he could not see the tear that exposed my breasts. I was quite sure that my nose was red as a cherry from the cold. It was certainly running, and I could not disguise the fact that I was shivering badly.

"All right," he said slowly. "I'll tell him that." He turned to Maria. "I can let you have a wee bit of coal first before I go."

"That would be wonderful!" I said. I had gotten to the point where I didn't think I would ever be warm again.

The blessed Mr. Tregrew returned with the promised coal and started a fire for us before he took his departure. I stood in front of the grate and toasted myself while Maria took care of the baby.

Maria said, "I usually go out to buy some bread for breakfast. Would you care for something to eat, my lady?"

"I lost my reticule when I was attacked last night or I would give you the money to get breakfast, Maria," I said regretfully. "Are you sure you have enough to get something for me, too?"

"I will if I use my supper money, too," she replied.

"You won't need your supper money as you will be

coming home with me," I promised her. "Go ahead and get us some breakfast."

I was starving.

While Maria was gone, the baby began to cry, and I picked him up from his cot and walked him around the room, patting him on the back. He heaved a huge burp, and stopped crying. I didn't put him back into his cot immediately, though. It was a very nice feeling to hold a baby in one's arms, I thought.

Perhaps one day soon I would be holding a baby of my own.

Maria returned with the promised bread, I put the baby back into his cot, and we stood in front of the fire to eat.

The bread was so hard and so stale that I could scarcely chew it.

Maria chewed it, though. The poor girl ate that dreadful stale bread as if it was a dish from the Prince Regent's kitchen. I pretended not to be very hungry and gave her mine, and she ate that, too.

I was standing in front of the fire, hungry but warmer, when there came a knock upon the door.

"Maria, it's me. Colin."

Maria ran to open the door and there in the doorway stood the hugest man I had ever seen in my life.

Mr. Tregrew said, "This here is Mr. Claven. He's come to meet Lady Winterdale."

I stepped forward. "I am Lady Winterdale. Come in, Mr. Claven. I am very grateful to you for coming to see me."

The giant ducked his head and came into the room, which immediately seemed half the size. He had shoulders that were as wide as my armspan and he had to be six feet four inches in height. He was immense.

He looked at me and immediately noticed the bloodstains on my domino. He didn't ask about them immediately, however, First he said, "How did you know to send for me?"

"My husband told me that you were helping him to find out who was trying to harm me," I said.

He had thick light brown hair and thick light brown eyebrows and he frowned at me now and said, "It's not like Philip to mention my name."

His speech was curiously accentless, as if he had worked very hard to remove any traces of his origin from it. He reminded me of a lion—not the poor scruffy one whom I had encountered at the Tower, but a sleek, powerful lion in the full strength of his maturity and health.

"He was quite drunk when he told me," I said coolly. "That was your fault, I believe."

He grinned suddenly, and the menace I had sensed in his presence disappeared.

"It took me two days to recover from that night," he said. "Becoming respectable hasn't softened Philip's head one little bit."

It occurred to me that my husband appeared to be on a first-name basis with every scoundrel in London.

Claven's face once again became serious and he said, "All right, then, Lady Winterdale. You'd better tell me exactly what happened."

I told him everything, starting from Frank and I being attacked at Vauxhall to my rescue by Maria.

"Alf and Jem," he said thoughtfully.

"Ain't they the coves that worked for Lamey?" Mr. Tregrew asked.

"I believe so," Claven said. "Have them picked up, will you Colin? I want to talk to them."

On the surface he sounded calm and reasonable, but for some reason, I shuddered.

He looked at me. "The first thing we need to do, Lady Winterdale, is to see that you get home. Philip will murder me if anything happens to you. I'm surprised he wasn't banging down the door of my office last night."

It seemed so odd to hear this man, who was evidently the king of the London underworld, talking about his "office," just as if he were a respectable barrister.

"My husband went to Winterdale Park yesterday so he doesn't know about my abduction," I explained. "But he should be back in London this afternoon."

"I see." Claven gave me a look that was almost as intimidating as Philip's blue stare could be. "May I give you some advice, Lady Winterdale? Don't leave your husband's sight until we get this little puzzle resolved. It was very stupid of you to go to Vauxhall alone last night."

"I didn't go alone," I protested. "I went with friends. One of them is a Peninsula veteran, for heaven's sake!"

"Fighting in a war is one thing; street fighting is something else. As I have just told you, don't go anywhere without your husband."

Claven turned to Mr. Tregrew. "Get a hackney to come along here, will you, Colin? Then you can put out the word for Alf and Jem."

CHAPTER
twenty-two

CLAVEN HIMSELF ESCORTED MARIA AND ME BACK TO Grosvenor Square. Catherine and Frank came running into the hall from the drawing room as soon as they heard Mason say my name, and Catherine flung her arms around me and held me tight.

"Is his lordship at home?" I heard Claven asking Mason.

"His lordship is from home at present," Mason answered icily. Apparently, even though Claven was dressed in proper morning clothes of blue coat and fawn-colored breeches, and even though his voice bore no traces of dialect, the butler had decided that the huge man was not worthy of being addressed as a gentleman.

I loosened Catherine's arms from their grip around me and ignored Frank's urgent questions about my well-being to go shake Claven's hand.

"Thank you, Mr. Claven, for your assistance," I said fervently. "I will tell my husband how you helped me to get home."

"Tell Philip to come and see me as soon as he returns," Claven recommended. He gave me an admonitory look. "And don't go anywhere without him."

"I won't," I promised.

As Claven turned to leave, the slender forms of Maria and her baby, who had been sheltering behind him, were revealed to the rest of the people in the hall. I went to put an arm around my rescuer and bring her forward. "Come and meet my friends, Maria," I said. "I want them to know how much I owe you."

Maria pressed against me. I saw the frightened and awed look she cast around the vast marble hall, and my mind went back to my first visit to Mansfield House. I knew exactly how intimidated she was feeling.

I said to Catherine and Frank, "This is the girl who saved my life. Her name is Maria Sarton. And this is her son, Reggie."

Catherine, whose essential kindness one could always count on, responded immediately. "We shall be eternally grateful to you, Maria. We have been terrified for Georgie ever since she was kidnapped from Vauxhall."

"That is so," Frank agreed. For the first time I noticed that he had a swollen eye and a puffed-up lip. Once again he asked urgently, "Are you all right, Georgie? Nothing . . . terrible . . . happened to you?"

"Nothing," I said firmly. "Thanks to Maria."

"I want to hear the whole story," Frank said grimly.

"I will tell you, but first Maria and I want to get warm and to eat. We're starving." I looked around for Mason, who appeared as if by magic. I was certain that he had been listening avidly from some secret post of his own.

"Mason, have some food brought to my dressing room," I said. "A nice spread, if you please. Cold meat, eggs, muffins, chocolate, coffee . . ."

"Yes, my lady," Mason said.

I steered Maria toward Mansfield House's magnificent circular staircase. I was taking her to my dressing room because it was the coziest room I could think of, and I wanted her to be comfortable. I knew she would be extremely uncomfortable in the grandeur of the dining room, and I did not want to expose her to the haughtiness of the servants in the kitchen, who would most certainly treat her with less respect than we would.

I also thought that my dressing room was one place where we would be safe from Lady Winterdale.

"You can come, too, Frank," I said over my shoulder.

And so all of us filed up the stairs and into the privacy of my dressing room. We settled the baby on the chaise longue, with Maria beside him, and the rest of us took the three other chairs in the room.

I proceeded to tell my tale to Catherine and Frank.

The food was delivered and Maria and I ate. I continued to talk, but Maria ate silently and seriously and we all left her alone to concentrate on filling a stomach that quite obviously had not been properly filled in a very long time.

Frank was bitterly angry with himself for having been careless enough to put me in danger and then for not being capable of protecting me.

Catherine was upset that it was she who had coaxed me into going to Vauxhall in the first place. And then she said, with a very uneasy look in her eyes, "It appears that Philip is acquainted with this man Claven, Georgie." She bit her lip nervously. "You don't think that Philip had anything to do with your abduction, do you?"

I went up in flames.

"How can you even suggest such an outrageous thing?" I said furiously. "Claven is the person who rescued me, Catherine! Philip is working with Claven to try to find out who is responsible for all these attacks on me." I glared at her. "I can't believe that you, of all people, could be so stupid."

She continued to bite her lip and look miserable. "I'm

sorry, Georgie. It's just that I don't understand why these things should be happening to you. It doesn't make sense. You aren't a threat to anyone. Why should someone want to kill you?"

Frank and I were sitting opposite each other on either side of the fireplace and now we looked at each other. I had told Frank about my father's blackmailing scheme, but I did not want to tell Catherine. After all, her father had been one of my father's victims. I had never got the impression that Catherine was overly fond of her father, but one never likes to discover that one's parent was a cheat.

Also, selfishly, I didn't want to ruin Catherine's good opinion of me. She had become such a dear friend, and I didn't want to lose her regard.

I looked at her. She was perched on the small white beechwood chair that belonged to the dressing table, and I could see from the look on her face that she was not convinced of Philip's innocence.

Regretfully, I decided that Catherine's regard for both her father and for me was going to have to be sacrificed. I could not have her blaming Philip for something that was not his fault.

I sighed and said, "I see that I shall have to tell you all. This is not a pretty story, Catherine, so prepare yourself." And I launched into the all-too-familiar tale.

When I finished, Catherine's eyes were huge behind her spectacles.

"Papa had money troubles?" she said in amazement. "I never knew that."

"Philip found it out when he inherited. That is why he spends so much time with all of these business people. He is trying to bring the Winterdale estate back to what it should be."

"I always thought that Papa was just mean," Catherine said with wonder.

"No, he was broke. Then he tried to acquire some money by cheating at cards, and my papa caught him."

Catherine leaned toward me, reaching out her hand. I put mine into hers and she squeezed it. "I am so sorry, Georgie," she said. "It must have been a terrible shock to you to discover that your papa was a blackmailer."

I stared at my friend. "Catherine, my father was blackmailing your father! Don't you hate me for that?"

"Of course I don't hate you," she returned. "What does anything our fathers did have to do with you and me?"

I took my hand away from hers. "Didn't you just hear me? After my father died, I came here and blackmailed Philip. That is why he presented me. I was just as bad as my father."

"Not at all," she returned serenely. "You did it for Anna, not for yourself. If it was not for Anna, you would have married Frank and not blackmailed anyone. Isn't that true?"

Frank made a sound indicative of extreme pain.

I winced. I might have said such a thing once, but I was horribly afraid that Catherine's remark was making the wrong impression on Frank.

At this point, Reggie began to cry. I turned to Maria, who was sitting on the chaise longue, holding her son, and listening to us with a mixture of bewilderment and wonder.

"I imagine the baby is hungry, too," I said to her with a smile.

"That he is, my lady."

I had been thinking about where to put Maria and I decided now that for this night she could have Anna's old room. Lady Winterdale and the housekeeper would have a fit, but I didn't care. I wasn't putting Maria in with the servants, who I was certain would treat her like a whore.

Well, she was a whore, but it wasn't her fault.

As soon as Philip returned to London, I would talk to him about sending Maria into the country.

I stood up. "Come along with me, Maria, and I will show you to your room, and you will be able to feed Reggie in peace."

Philip got back to Mansfield House at six o'clock that evening. I was in my dressing room getting ready for dinner when he came in the door, exuding such an aura of danger that he made poor Betty drop the hairbrush she had been holding. It clattered to the top of the dressing table and we both jumped.

"That will be all for now, Betty," he said in a clipped voice. "I want to talk to her ladyship alone."

"Yes, my lord," Betty said, and she scuttled out the door as quickly as she could.

The door wasn't even closed behind her before Philip demanded, still in that same clipped voice, "All right. What happened?"

I swung around on the beechwood chair and faced him bravely. "What have you heard?" I asked.

"My aunt met me with the news that you went to Vauxhall with Catherine and Frank, that you disappeared for the night and are now harboring a 'young person of dubious respectability,'" he replied grimly.

"Your aunt is a menace, Philip," I said hotly. "She is forever poking her nose into my business. This was for me to tell you about, not her!"

He folded his arms. There was a white line about his mouth. "Then tell me about it, Georgie," he said.

"I have every intention of doing so," I replied with dignity. Then I told him the whole story. The only thing I left out was the bit about Alf's desire to rape me. I had a feeling that that little extra might be the final spark that would cause Philip to ignite.

When I had finished he skewered me with his coldest, bluest stare. "I strictly forbade you to leave this house while I was gone."

I tried a placating smile. "I know you did, Philip, but I couldn't find it in my heart to deny Catherine. She desperately needed me as a chaperone. And I took Frank along. Good God, he's been through a war! I thought he would be sufficient protection."

"Well he wasn't, was he?"

I sighed and shook my head. "The poor man looks as if he took a sad pummeling. I feel bad. It was all my fault."

By now there was a white line around his nostrils as well as his mouth. "It certainly was your fault. If you had obeyed me and remained at home, none of this would have happened."

All of this talk about commanding and obeying was beginning to set my back up.

"I'm not your dog, Philip," I said irritably. "In retrospect, I agree with you that it was not wise of me to have gone to Vauxhall, but at the time it didn't seem like such a dreadful thing to do."

His eyes narrowed. I added hastily, before he could say or do anything else, "Claven said he wants to see you. He was going to try to put his hands on Alf and Jem to find out for whom they were working."

A little silence fell between us. He still had that white

look that made me nervous. I plucked at the muslin skirt of my dress and bravely held his gaze.

"I'm sorry," I said.

He said, "Did you even think to tell Catherine not to mention to anyone that you would be going to Vauxhall with her?"

I bit my lip. I shook my head. I felt like an idiot.

"So not only did you make the foolish decision to go to an open, unprotected place such as Vauxhall, but you took no precautions to make certain that no one would know you were going to be there."

I was feeling more stupid with every passing minute.

"No," I said glumly.

At last he moved away from the door, going over to the fireplace and resting his hands on the mantel. With his back to me, he stared down into the glowing coals, and said, "From what you are telling me, then, the only person who is responsible for the fact that you did not find yourself raped and murdered and dumped in an alley is this young woman my aunt was holding her nose about."

I hadn't said anything about rape, but I suppose he knew the type of men I had been dealing with.

"Yes," I said.

His hands clenched on the mantelpiece turning his knuckles white with pressure.

"Where is she?" he asked.

"I put her in Anna's old bedroom. I did not want to expose her to the snobbery of the servants."

He turned to face me once more. A lock of black hair fell forward across his forehead. "You can't keep her in Anna's bedroom forever. It won't be comfortable either for her or for us."

"I know. I was thinking—perhaps you could find a

nice little cottage for her at Winterdale Park? She is from the country originally." I leaned forward in my chair. "She told me the most horror-filled story, Philip. You cannot imagine what has happened to that poor girl."

His face was bleak. "I can imagine very well," he said.

"No, but listen . . ." And I told him everything that Maria had told me.

"It happens every day, Georgie," he said wearily.

"What kind of man would take advantage of a poor, helpless girl like that?" I asked in disgust. "I don't understand it at all."

He didn't answer.

"And that part of London where I was being held!" I shuddered. "It isn't right, Philip, that some people should live so luxuriously while others live surrounded by such dreadful filth and poverty."

"The world is not an easy place to live in, Georgie. And if one expects to encounter justice in this life, then one is a fool."

There was so much bitterness in his voice that I winced. His face was hard and shuttered.

"Well . . . will you find a cottage for Maria?" I asked helplessly.

"Yes."

He turned to go. He had not touched me once.

"Philip?" I said in a small voice.

He turned back. I stood up and ran to fling myself into his arms. "I'm sorry," I said into his shoulder. "I didn't mean to put myself into danger, truly I didn't."

His arms came up to hold me, and for just one moment he pressed me so tightly against him that I thought my ribs would crack.

Then he let me go.

"I know, sweetheart," he said. "Let us hope that Claven has some information that will help us to put this matter to rest."

And he was gone.

Philip left the house immediately after our conversation and he did not return to Grosvenor Square until two in the morning. When he came into the bedroom I knew immediately that he had been drinking.

I pushed myself into a sitting position and stared at him. I could see his face in the light of the candle he was carrying, and his eyes looked heavy-lidded.

"Did Claven find anything out?" I asked.

"Oh, are you still awake, Georgie?" he asked in a too-carefully articulated voice.

I was definitely annoyed. Actually, I was more than annoyed. I was furious.

"Can't you and Claven ever get together without drinking yourselves into a stupor?" I snapped.

He put the candlestick cautiously on the bedside table and got into bed beside me. "Claven managed to get ahold of the two men who kidnapped you, but all they knew was that they had been hired by a fellow who makes a business out of hiring out profeshional—professional—villains."

"That must be Lamey," I said.

He turned to look at me. His eyes were a much darker blue than they usually were. "How did you know his name?"

"I heard it mentioned. Can't Claven find out from Lamey who the man who hired him was?"

"Lamey runs his own operation. He and Claven pretty well let each other alone."

"How delightful. Does this mean that Claven can't help us?"

He grunted. "Looks that way."

"Well, you're a great help, Philip," I said sarcastically. "You go away and leave me so that you can inspect a stupid canal, then, when I'm almost raped and killed, you can't even find out who kidnapped me! All you can do is go off with your disreputable friends and get drunk!"

He blew out the candle plunging us into darkness. "I'm not drunk," he said.

"You are, too," I hissed. "And I don't believe that Claven challenged you to a drinking contest this time, either."

"We had a few glasses of blue ruin while we were disscushing your problem," he said.

"You had more than a few glasses," I returned bitterly.

"I did not."

"You did, too!"

He pulled up the coverlet. "I will talk to you in the morning, when you are more reasonable."

"I think you are disgusting," I said.

Silence. In a few minutes I heard the sound of a gentle snore.

Tears pricked my eyes. I had desperately wanted him to make love to me, and instead he had come home drunk. Our marriage, which had started so gloriously at Winterdale Park, had been going downhill ever since we returned to London.

I don't know what upset me more, the fact that I was the target of a murderer or the unraveling of my marriage.

As I lay there thinking, it occurred to me that my second problem was inextricably linked to the first. If I could solve the mystery of who it was who was trying to kill me, then Philip would cease hanging about with Claven (who was obviously a bad influence) and perhaps he would come back to me. So far I had been rather passive about the situation that confronted me. I had been leaving it to Philip to handle.

From now on, I determined, I would take a hand.

I needed to put this would-be murderer into a position where he had to try to kill me himself. That was the only way to find out which of the four men I had so foolishly written to was responsible for all of my accidents.

For a moment I remembered my recent episode with Alf and Jem, and my heart quailed. Then I recited to myself the lines of poetry that had become my talisman:

> He either fears his fate too much
> Or his deserts are small,
> That puts it not unto the touch
> To win or lose it all.

The Marquis of Montrose had known what he was talking about when he wrote those lines, I thought.

I gave Philip a push to make him turn over and stop snoring, and began to plot.

CHAPTER
twenty-three

It wasn't until the following morning, when I was going through the invitations that had arrived during the week, that I hit upon the scheme that I needed. I was sitting at the breakfast table with Catherine and Lady Winterdale, sipping coffee and looking through the cards that were piled next to my plate, when I picked up one from the Marquess and Marchioness of Amberly.

It was an invitation to a garden party at their home on the River Thames, some miles above Hampton Court.

I tapped the card on the table thoughtfully and said to Lady Winterdale, "I see that Philip and I have received an invitation to a garden party at Thames House. What exactly is Thames House like, my lady? I've been told that it is situated directly on the river. Is that indeed so?"

Lady Winterdale's whole face pinched up as if she were eating an extremely sour pickle. Finally she managed to articulate the words that were making her so miserable. "Since you are now my nephew's wife, Georgiana, I think it would be proper for you to call me 'Aunt Agatha.'"

I goggled at her.

She shot me a distinctly irritated look and snapped, "Do try not to look more of a fool than nature intended you to be, Georgiana."

"Yes, my . . . ah, Aunt Agatha."

Her face twitched as I spoke the dreaded words.

Hastily, she answered my question, "Thames House is indeed situated on the Thames. It is, in fact, famous for its setting. Its gardens and woods are extensive and afford splendid views of the river in all of its majestic beauty."

This guide-book-type description afforded me deep satisfaction, not because I was anxious to enjoy the undoubted beauty of Thames House, but because it sounded like Vauxhall—just the sort of place where a murderer would find it convenient to hide and then to strike.

"Is this garden party usually well attended?" I asked.

Lady Winterdale returned her delicate china teacup to its saucer. "It is always one of the biggest events of the Season," she informed me. "As I believe I mentioned before, the gardens are extensive. The Amberlys invite the world."

"It sounds perfect," I said sincerely. "I shall write immediately to say that we shall come."

Needless to say, the "we" was entirely spurious. I had no intention of letting Philip know that I planned to offer myself as bait to trap a murderer. He would have a fit if he learned that I planned to go to Thames House.

Catherine frowned at me from across the table. "I don't think it is a good idea for you to go to a garden party, Georgie," she said. "The grounds at Thames House will be too open, too unprotected."

Those were exactly the reasons why I wanted to go, of course.

Even Aunt Agatha was regarding me with some dismay. "Really, Georgiana, these extraordinary things that have been happening to you of late are causing talk. I do not think it is wise for you to place yourself in a position where something else might befall you. It could cause a scandal."

I was touched by her concern for my personal safety.

"Mama!" Catherine protested.

Aunt Agatha sniffed. "It is true, Catherine. People are talking. I do not like it. People have never before talked about the Winterdales." She picked up her cup, took another sip of tea, and added with a distinct trace of bitterness, "Of course, when someone like Philip becomes the earl, I suppose one cannot count on any semblance of propriety."

Icy-cold anger swept through me, chilling me to the bone. I said, "For someone who has accepted his hospitality, and allowed him to fund her daughter's come out, I think that is an utterly vile thing to say."

Aunt Agatha looked at me in surprise. Usually I allowed her barbs to slide off my back, but she was going to learn that I would not allow her to say anything against Philip.

"Say you're sorry," I demanded.

She straightened her already-straight back. "Philip's disreputable career is well-known throughout the whole of Europe, Georgiana. I am not saying anything that has not already been said by dozens of other people."

"Dozens of other people are not the person who refused to take him in when he was a motherless boy," I said fiercely. I hid my hands in my lap so that she would not see that they were clenched into fists. I scowled at her. "Say you're sorry."

She stared at me and, surprisingly, was perceptive enough to realize that I was deadly serious. If she didn't apologize, I was perfectly prepared to tell her to pack her bags and get out of my house.

"I beg your pardon, Georgiana," she said acidly. "I did not mean to criticize your precious husband." She stood up. "If you will excuse me, I have finished my breakfast."

Catherine and I sat in thick silence as Lady Winterdale swept out of the room. When the door had closed behind her, I looked at Catherine.

"I'm sorry," I said, "but she made me furious."

Catherine shook her head. "It's all right, Georgie. I don't blame you." She frowned. "But do you really mean to go to the garden party at Thames House?"

"Yes." I told her why I was going to do so.

Catherine's first reaction was negative. "You could easily get yourself killed, Georgie, and that wouldn't solve anything at all." She gave me a very sober look. "Just think of the scandal Philip will have to face if his wife should turn up dead."

Clever Catherine. She knew where I was vulnerable all right.

"I have no intention of turning up dead," I assured her loftily. "Don't you see, the whole point of this expedition is to protect Philip? People are blaming him for these accidents, and I can't have that, Catherine. His reputation is already too vulnerable, and it's very important to him to be respectable. He's lived on the fringes of society for too long."

Catherine still disagreed. "It's too dangerous, Georgie."

"Wouldn't you feel the same way if it were Rotheram who were in the situation that Philip is in? Wouldn't you put yourself in danger to protect him?"

Silence.

At last, "You are diabolical, Georgie," Catherine said wryly.

I grinned and explained, "It isn't as bad as it sounds. I

am not planning to go into this situation completely unprotected. I am going to make certain that I have a bodyguard."

"And who is this bodyguard going to be?" Catherine
asked with resignation. "Frank?"

"No," I replied. "If you will agree, it is going to be
you."

Later that afternoon, I asked Maria if she would like
to live in a cottage on the Winterdale estate, and she accepted with alacrity.

"I didn't like the country when I was younger, but that
was before I knew what it was like to live in Lunnon," she
said sadly.

"His lordship's steward will find you a nice cottage,
and before you know it, I'll wager you will find yourself in-
undated with offers of marriage," I assured her.

Privately, I intended to make certain that Maria was so
economically desirable that she would be beating men off
with a stick.

She gave me a look of amazement. "Ain't no one
going to want to marry me, my lady. Not after what I've
bin."

I agreed that Maria's past would probably prove an in-
superable obstacle to her future happiness if she let it. Men
were such hypocrites. They could make use of the women
in brothels and still consider themselves worthy of marriage, but it certainly wasn't the same case for the poor
women whom they had used. And the women were the
ones who didn't have any choice!

Here was one more example of how unfair life was to
the female sex, I thought.

"Don't tell anyone about your life in London, Maria,"

I recommended. "We will say that you came from my home village in Sussex, that your husband recently died, and that you wanted to get away from the area to recover from your grief."

She looked at me in wonder. "Do you really think I could do that, my lady?"

"Yes, I do. Generally speaking, I am not in favor of lying, but your circumstances are extraordinary. You deserve some happiness in your life, Maria. Don't be afraid to reach for it."

She looked doubtful.

"And don't forget, there is Reggie to consider as well," I continued. "You don't want him to know the real circumstances of his birth, do you?"

At that, she shook her head vehemently.

"I will back up your story," I promised. "We will say that we knew each other as children and that I am helping you because of our old friendship."

Her thin face broke into a particularly sweet and lovely smile. "Thank you, my lady," she said. "I'll take yer advice."

Philip wouldn't let me leave the house, so I sent Catherine shopping with Maria to buy some of the things that the young mother would need in her new life. They came home laden with packages of clothes for Maria and for the baby, as well as household linens and some pretty pottery items. We had an enjoyable afternoon in Maria's room looking over everything that she had purchased, and then Philip called me down to the library to talk to his steward, who had come from Winterdale Park at Philip's summons to discuss a home for Maria.

The two of them had already decided on the cottage

they were going to give her and the repairs that needed to be made to it. The house and grounds actually sounded more like a small farm than a cottage, which I thought was all to the good. The more land Maria had, the more desirable as a wife she would be.

The two men also informed me that Mr. Downs, Philip's steward, would take Maria and Reggie down to Winterdale Park the following day, and I went back upstairs to relate the good news to Catherine and Maria with a spring in my step.

I dressed for dinner with especial care that evening, determined to catch Philip's eye and (hopefully) stimulate his lust.

He did not make an appearance in the dining room.

I stared at his empty chair in a state of shock. He had said nothing to me about missing dinner while we were meeting in the library. I didn't have even the vaguest idea where he might have gone.

Something was very wrong with him, and I didn't think it was just the attacks on me. If it was simply that I was in danger, I should think that he would be spending as much time with me as he possibly could, trying to protect me. Instead, he was clearly avoiding me.

I wasn't even angry with him anymore. I was merely very very worried.

Catherine and Lady Winterdale went out to a ball and I stayed home alone. The hours after dinner crawled by. I tried to read a book, but I couldn't concentrate on the words in front of my eyes.

What the devil was going on in Philip's mind? What could have caused him to withdraw from me like this?

Had I mistaken the passion we had shared at Winterdale Park for more than it really was?

I thought about it, and thought about it, and I didn't think so. I remembered those afternoon trysts in our sunny bedroom. I remembered the time we had actually made love outdoors in a hidden lakeside glade.

Philip had never told me that he loved me in so many words, but I like to think that I am a sensitive person. I had felt his love. It was not just lust that had brought that warmth, that possessiveness to his eyes whenever he looked at me.

He did not look at me like that anymore.

Why?

I did not know.

I had to get him back, I thought. If I didn't, my heart would surely break.

He never came home that night at all. In fact, he still was not home as I dressed to go to the garden party at Thames House.

One benefit of his absence was that he wasn't able to put a stop to my plans, but I was getting more and more upset.

Where was he? Was he hanging around with Claven somewhere in the slums of London?

When I see him, I will kill him, I thought grimly. Then, *Please God, let me see him again soon*.

The Amberlys had hired a whole fleet of boats to leave from Westminster and take their guests up the river to Thames House, and Catherine and I and Lady Winterdale shared a boat with Lord Henry Sloan; his mother, the Duchess of Faircastle; and her lover, Lord Margate.

It was a lovely spring afternoon, and the sun sparkled on the dark green water of the river. The dark color was due to the algae, which made the water almost opaque, and when I trailed my hand in it, it was still cold from the winter ice.

As one came upstream, Thames House was hidden from view around a bend in the river. Then, as the boat rounded the bend, and one saw the house soaring high on a chalk terrace over the river, it literally took one's breath away it was so beautiful. The boatmen tied up at the dock, and the Amberlys had footmen stationed there to help their guests out of the boats and onto the steadiness of the wooden landing. We then proceeded up through the gardens to the grass terrace, where the Marquess and Marchioness were receiving their guests.

The house itself dated from the Restoration period, and Lady Winterdale had told me it was built by William Winde, but the real beauty of Thames House was the grounds. The terrace where we stood waiting to greet our hosts was made up of closely scythed grass on which beds of lavender fringed with box hedges and punctuated by clipped yews formed a geometrical parterre. There was a band, and people were dancing on the parterre. There were beautiful gardens, like the long shady yew walks which wound above the river to the west of the house, in which gentlemen and ladies might stroll. Scattered among the grounds were three garden buildings, which Lady Winterdale loftily informed me were built by the Venetian Giacomo Leoni, the same architect who had built Winterdale Park.

The grounds could not have been better for my purposes. There were literally dozens of places where someone could lie in wait for me and catch me alone.

Let me hasten to assure you that I was not quite as brave as I might sound about this clever plan of mine. The thought of confronting a murderer was far from pleasant. It was just that I did not know what else to do. And I was growing more and more convinced that if I did not do something, I was going to lose my husband.

I was not totally unprepared. I had had Betty sew another pocket into my dress, and once more I was carrying my trusty knife. Catherine was similarly armed. I had thought that she might be a bit squeamish about stabbing someone, but she had proved to be delightfully bloodthirsty.

"It would afford me great pleasure to stick a knife into the person who has been trying to kill you, Georgie," she had said ruthlessly. "Never fear that I will fail you."

Catherine had come a long way from the little mouse that I had met upon my first arrival at Mansfield House. It is amazing the transformations that love can work.

Our original plan was for Catherine to keep me within her range of vision while concealing herself from the view of anyone else. This way, if one of our four suspects tried to cut me out of the crowd, she would be able to see what was happening and insinuate herself into a position to hear what was going on.

Our idea was that if an actual attack was made upon me, Catherine would scream for help. Even if I was knocked unconscious (which I devoutly hoped would not happen, considering the pain my poor head had suffered during my last two mishaps), Catherine would still be free to summon aid. There might be hidden areas in the gardens of Thames House, but people would still be close by.

I thought that this was an extremely sensible plan and one that had every chance of success. The fact that it went awry was most certainly not due to any lack of preparation on my part.

*   *   *

The first part of the afternoon went by quite smoothly. Catherine and I managed to slough off Aunt Agatha by commandeering Lord Henry Sloan to be our escort, and with him we toured every area of the extensive gardens, in particular reconnoitering the garden buildings. Lord Henry kept wanting to stop and talk to people, but we ruthlessly dragged him along in our wake. I wanted to make very certain that I was seen to be present.

"Don't you ladies realize that the purpose of a party such as this is to socialize?" Lord Henry complained at last.

"It is just that we are so interested in examining the beauties of nature," Catherine said innocently. "The setting here is so magnificent, isn't it, Georgie? Look at that view of the river!"

"It is perfectly splendid," I said with perhaps too much enthusiasm.

"Well, I should think by now you have seen every blade of grass the place has to offer," Lord Henry grumbled good-naturedly.

A silky soft voice said from behind my back, "Lady Winterdale. What a surprise to see you here without your husband. What is wrong with Philip that he has allowed you go out so unprotected?"

I knew that voice, and it sent shivers up and down my spine. I turned my chin slightly so that I could look at Lord Marsh. "My husband will be here shortly," I lied. "What a surprise to see *you* here, my lord. I should think a garden party such as this would be a tame entertainment for someone of your . . . exotic . . . tastes."

His strange, pale gray-green eyes glittered at my words.

"I rather doubt that Philip will make it to Thames House this afternoon, my dear," he said much too gently.

"The last I saw of him he was drunk as an emperor in some gaming hell in St. James's Square."

He was an utterly hateful man, and I wanted very badly to stab him with my knife.

I said nastily, "Aren't my cousin and I rather ancient to be the subject of your interest like this, my lord?"

The look in his eyes now said quite clearly that he would like to stab me fully as much as I would like to stab him.

He said in an icy voice, "If I were you, I shouldn't frequent such unprotected places without the escort of your husband."

At this point, Lord Henry said huffily, "I say, Marsh, perhaps you may not have noticed, but *I* am here to give my protection to Lady Winterdale."

Lord Marsh looked at him. Then he looked away. Nothing could have been more insulting.

"Lady Winterdale." Marsh bowed to me. "Lady Catherine." A bow to Catherine. And he walked away.

Lord Henry was both shaken and infuriated. Catherine and I spent a good ten minutes calming him down. I thought that Lord Marsh was probably right about Lord Henry's qualifications as a bodyguard, but I certainly wasn't going to say that to my ruffled former beau. He was a very amiable, very amusing young man, but there was no weight to him. His world had been too pleasant, too easy. In all his life, he had scarcely ever had to make a decision. I rather thought that that was why he had never offered for me. A marriage proposal would have required him to make up his mind about something, would have required him to think about his future. Lord Henry did not want to be bothered to do that, not when his present circumstances were so easy and enjoyable.

The appearance of Lord Marsh had assured me of one
thing, however. My scheme was successful in one way:
every one of my suspects was present at Thames House this
afternoon.

Now it was my job to see that one of them came forward to try to kill me.

CHAPTER
twenty-four

IN ORDER TO SET MY PLAN INTO MOTION, THE FIRST thing Catherine and I had to do was to detach ourselves from Lord Henry. This we did by returning to the grass terrace at the back of the house, where a long, linen-covered table laden with a magnificent banquet had been set up. There, Catherine and I were easily able to shed Lord Henry as we wandered from group to group, our gauzy white frocks floating around us in the delightful breeze from the river.

People were straying all over the gardens, some were playing lawn tennis, and some were drifting on boats on the river. Catherine and I spent at least half an hour on the terrace, and during that time I saw Mr. Howard, the young man who was in debt to the moneylenders; Sir Henry Farringdon, the young man who was afraid I'd snitch to his rich wife about his mistress; and chubby Mr. George Asherton, who had poured the most money of all into Papa's bottomless coffers. The last of Papa's victims to arrive on the terrace was the Earl of Marsh, who stood by himself next to the champagne table, drinking glass after glass of the sparkling wine.

Splendid, I thought, resolutely ignoring the sickly, nervous flutter that had started in my stomach.

Catherine and I went into the house to the ladies' withdrawing room and I told her about the last-minute change in my plan.

"I think it would be best if I wandered alone out to one of the little garden buildings," I said, as we sat huddled on two chairs in the corner of the large room that had been put aside for the ladies' use. "If you will go before me, and conceal yourself somewhere in the surrounding shrubbery, then you will be ready to leap to my rescue when I need you."

Catherine was evidently having second thoughts about the whole scheme, because she said, "Do you know, Georgie, I wonder if this is a good idea after all. There are so many things that could go wrong."

I had been thinking the same thing myself, but now that someone else had questioned my judgment, I felt called upon to defend myself.

"What could possibly go wrong?" I demanded. "No one is going to kill me in the garden building, for heaven's sake! There is too great a possibility that someone might have seen him follow me in."

Catherine chewed on her lip in a way I had not seem her do in weeks. "But suppose he is willing to take that chance? Suppose he shoots you or something before I am able to rescue you? I think we ought to wait, Georgie. Philip will uncover the identity of this evil man. Philip is very competent."

I didn't doubt Philip's competence. It was other things that worried me about Philip.

I said stubbornly, "No one is going to shoot me. I want to go ahead with the scheme, Catherine. If you don't want to help me, then I shall just have to do it on my own."

There was a deeply troubled look in the blue eyes that were so close to mine, but at last she said reluctantly, "All right, Georgie. I said that I would help you, and I will."

I gave her a relieved smile. "Thank you, Catherine. I knew I could count on you."

She continued to chew her lip worriedly, and merely nodded.

I pulled my chair a fraction closer to hers. "This is what we will do," I said in a low voice. "The little temple with the green copper roof is the most isolated of all the garden buildings, so that is the one we will use. I will give you a fifteen-minute start to get out there and get into position, and then I will follow you. Keep a sharp eye out, and as soon as you see one of our targets enter the building after me, come to the door after him, and listen. I will try to make him confess that he is the one who has been trying to kill me, and once he has done that you can show yourself."

"Georgie," Catherine said doubtfully, "suppose he has a gun?"

"No one can walk around a garden party for hours with a gun concealed on his person," I said positively.

She rubbed her forehead as if she had a headache. "I suppose you are right."

I said jokingly, trying to instill some bravado into the both of us, "You do realize that the most difficult part of this whole enterprise will be for the two of us to disappear by ourselves for more than ten minutes without your mother instituting a major search?"

She managed to smile back, but I could see that her heart wasn't in it.

In the end, however, she went.

I hadn't been completely joking about Lady Winterdale, and sure enough, five minutes after Catherine had disappeared she came up to me wanting to know her daughter's whereabouts.

"She went back into the house, Aunt Agatha," I said guilelessly. "I think something she ate disagreed with her."

Aunt Agatha glared direfully. "Really, Georgiana, I should think you would have had the courtesy to accompany her."

"She didn't want me, Aunt Agatha. She said she might lie down for a while."

"If Catherine is not feeling well, then we should leave," Lady Agatha pronounced.

"Perhaps you ought to go and talk to her yourself," I suggested.

"I will do that," she said, peering down her pointy nose at me. "I am seriously displeased by your lack of attention, Georgiana."

"I am sorry, Aunt Agatha," I said.

Catherine's mother sailed off to check on her daughter. As soon as her back was turned, I made my exit from the terrace. I had no idea which of my suspects was present, but I had to assume that the guilty party would be keeping me under watch if he did indeed intend to make an attempt on my life that day.

I set off through the beech woods in the direction of the temple. As I walked briskly along, I told myself that everything would go according to plan, that the would-be murderer would be caught, and that I would get Philip back again. The woods were almost in full leaf this time of year without having that fullness of foliage that blocks one's view, and from the path I caught tantalizing glimpses of the river with the sun sparkling off its deep green water. On the floor of the woods on either side of me, I saw violets, wood anemones, wood sorrel, and the brilliant blue speedwell that always reminded me of Philip's eyes.

A particularly striking purple violet caught my attention, and I stopped to look at it more closely when an arm circled me from behind and pulled me up and back against a hard thin masculine body.

I hadn't heard a single footstep coming behind me.

"Don't make a sound, Lady Winterdale," a familiar voice said in my ear. "I have a pistol in my other hand."

The voice belonged to Charles Howard, the young man who was in the clutches of the moneylenders.

My heart began to race wildly.

"That is impossible," I managed to say. "You cannot have been walking around this garden party all afternoon with a pistol concealed on your person!"

His laugh was very ugly and I felt the pressure of something small and round thrust against my ribs with bruising pressure. "It is a very small pistol, but at this range, I can assure you that it will be quite effective."

I looked desperately ahead through the woods. We were too far from the temple for Catherine to see us.

"You are the one who has been trying to kill me," I said bravely.

Waves of rage flowed from him so that I could literally feel the heat of them. "That is right. You deserve to die, Lady Winterdale. People like you are scum. You have ruined me. I have had to mortgage my estate, and I am in debt to those bloodsucking moneylenders. And it's all because of you!"

"But *I* have done nothing to you!" I said despairingly. "In fact, I tried to help you. I destroyed all my father's evidence against you."

The gun pressed even harder against my ribs. "I don't believe you, Lady Winterdale. You blackmailed Winterdale into marrying you. What is to say that you won't start on me next?"

"I did not blackmail Winterdale into marrying me!"

"No?" he said. His voice was shaking with fury. "That is not the story going round the *ton*."

I tried to think how I might get through to him.

"If you shoot me, you will be putting yourself into danger as a suspect," I said. "A great number of people saw me leave the terrace, and I must believe that you were seen leaving as well."

The whole time we were speaking he had kept his arm around me, trapping me against him and keeping me from seeing his face. He said now, "I've thought of that. All right, bitch, let's go." And he began to push me forward.

"Where are we going?" I asked, hoping desperately that we would be going to the garden temple.

"We're going out on the river, where we are going to have a little accident," he replied.

My blood ran cold. It had never occurred to me that my attacker might make use of the river.

I couldn't swim.

"No!" I said, but even before I could think of struggling, the gun slammed hard into my ribs.

"I wouldn't, Lady Winterdale," Charles Howard said viciously. "If you force me to shoot you, I will. I am a ruined man anyway, thanks to you."

Somewhere in his twisted mind he had confused me with my father, and I couldn't seem to make him see the difference.

He began to shove me down the path toward the river.

"There must be some way I can make you see that I have no intention of bleeding you for any money," I said despairingly as I stumbled along in front of him.

"There isn't," he said grimly, and I realized that he had reached the state where he was beyond the reach of common sense. The fear and the state of anxiety in which he had been living for so long had had an effect upon his brain and he was incapable of being reasoned with. All he knew was that I was his enemy and as such he must eliminate me.

Not a very hopeful situation for me.

We reached the river's edge, where a boat was tied up to a tree, and I realized that Howard must have planned this execution very carefully.

He shoved me forward and when I turned to look at him, the sun flashed off the small silver-mounted pistol he was holding in his hand. "Get into the boat," he said.

It was get into the boat or get shot.

I didn't have any chance at all with the gun.

I got into the boat.

He followed me in carefully, all the time keeping the pistol trained upon me. Then he pushed off with one oar and we were out on the opaque waters of the Thames.

We were the only boat out on the river now, as all the boatmen employed by the Amberlys had gone into the house to have their tea.

I looked toward the shore, and there was no one there whom I could wave to for help.

Charles Howard put away his pistol. He didn't need it now. I wasn't likely to do anything that would upset the balance of the boat.

"What are you going to do?" I asked fearfully.

"We are going to have a boating accident," he said. "It will horrify all the people at Thames House, I am certain, but you are going to lose something in the water, and as you lean over to try to grab it, the boat will overbalance, sending the two of us into the water. I am able to swim, and I will try my best to rescue you, Lady Winterdale, but alas,

I will be unsuccessful. The current underneath is very strong here, and it will pull your body down and thence along the river bottom all the way to the sea."

I was terrified, but I would not let this insane man see that I was afraid of him.

Howard picked up the two oars and began to pull the boat farther out toward the middle of the river. I sat there helpless. My only hope, I thought, was to grab onto the boat when it was turned over and try to keep afloat until I was rescued.

I didn't have much faith in this plan, but it was the only one I could think of.

At least Anna is taken care of, I thought. *At least I won't be leaving her alone and unprotected in the world.*

Then: *I should have listened to Philip. I should never have tried to solve this problem on my own.*

I shut my eyes for a moment and called his beloved face up before my mind's eye.

The worst thing about dying, I thought, was that I would never see him again.

When I opened my eyes, I saw that another boat had rounded the turn in the river and was coming toward us.

It was as if my dreams had conjured him up, for there in the prow, directly facing us, was Philip. I opened my mouth to call out to him, but Philip's voice cut me off coming clearly across the stretch of water that separated us. "Hi there, Howard. Have you really managed to get her out here alone? Good going, man!"

I sat frozen. Then, after the beat of a second, I managed to choke, "Oh God, here is Winterdale. Now what am I to do?"

I saw Howard smile grimly. In his disordered mind,

he clearly thought that Philip was going to help him kill me.

Philip's boat, rowed by a professional boatman, came on, and Howard didn't do anything. I waited, scarcely breathing, and when finally Philip's boat was within a few feet of us, Howard called out to him. "I am glad to see you, my lord. I have put us into a position to be rid of our nemesis."

Philip did not look at me. The wind from the water was blowing his black hair over his forehead and his eyes were bluer than the intensely blue sky as they looked unwaveringly into the slightly mad eyes of Charles Howard.

"Look at the bank, Howard," he said mildly. "There are a number of people watching us. Do you really think it is wise to attempt anything here?"

Both Charles Howard and I looked involuntarily toward the shore. During the time that it had taken for Philip to reach us, a group of people had indeed gathered there. I could see the sun reflecting off of Catherine's spectacles. When I had not arrived at the temple, she must have run to summon help.

While we were staring at the newly gathered spectators, Philip's boat had pulled even closer to ours. He still had not looked at me. All of his formidable attention was focused on Howard.

"Do you think it possible to make it look like an accident?" he asked Howard.

Howard smiled. "That was precisely my thought."

"What about my boatman?"

"You can buy him off, my lord. You have the money. And you will owe me, too, I think, for helping you to get rid of an unwanted wife."

"I certainly will, Howard," Philip said quietly. He

took an oar from the hands of his clearly horrified boat-man. "Let us do it this way. Pretend to have dropped something overboard and then lean a little out of the boat, as if you are trying to retrieve it. I will pretend to reach with my oar to scoop the object toward you, and in the process of maneuvering with the oar, I will clumsily hit my wife over the head and knock her out of the boat."

Charles Howard looked radiant. Such a plan, of course, would remove all the onus of my death from him and place it on Philip. He was not insane enough to be in-capable of realizing the advantage of that.

"An excellent idea, my lord," he said.

Wasting no time, he mimed the loss of an object overboard and then he leaned over the side of our boat as if to retrieve it.

Philip raised the oar he was holding and hit him over the head, hard. He went into the river like a stone.

Philip sat down and pulled off his Hessian boots.

"Get into the boat with her ladyship and get her to shore," he instructed his boatman tersely, and then he dived into the water after Charles Howard.

"Take the boat after him!" I instructed the boatman hysterically.

I was afraid that when Philip surfaced there would be no boat available to rescue him.

"No need to do that, your ladyship," the boatman said. "Look."

I followed his pointing finger and saw one of the boats from the dock at Thames House being pulled by two of the boatmen whom the Amberlys had employed for the day. Someone must have run to fetch them from their tea.

They swept past us at a far greater rate of speed than we, with but a single man at the oars, could ever achieve.

As my own boat began to return to the shore, I kept my eyes trained on the river. No sleek black head emerged from beneath the water.

Philip. My lips moved and shaped his name, but no sound came out.

Still the river was empty. The rescue boat flew downstream, but there was no one to rescue.

I said to my boatman, "How long can a man stay underwater?"

"A few minutes, my lady," came the gruff reply.

I counted: *One, two, three, four, five. . . .*

I couldn't stand this.

"Is the current bad here?" I asked next.

"It's nae so bad on the top, but it runs strong deep under."

I remembered Charles Howard's words: *The current will take you along the bottom all the way to the sea.*

Philip had dived from the boat into the water. He had gone in deep.

I could not bear it. We had reached the shore, and hands reached out to help me out of the boat, but I refused to move. As long as I kept watching that river, I thought, then Philip wasn't gone.

"Let me alone," I said sharply, and shook off a hand.

From far down the river, much farther than I had thought it possible, a black dot appeared in the water.

I squinted into the sun. The rescue boat changed the course of its direction and began to row in the direction of the dot.

It was Philip.

I began to cry.

"It's all right, Georgie," Catherine said. "You can get out of the boat now. He's all right."

I stumbled into the arms of my friend.

The person who had sent for the rescue boat was, of all people, Lord Marsh. It seems that he had seen Charles Howard leave the terrace and follow me. Marsh had known, of course, that I was the target of previous attacks, and he had decided it wouldn't be a bad idea to keep me within his sight. He had arrived on the bank too late to prevent my getting into the boat with Howard, but he had run all the way back to the house to get the boatmen to launch a boat to rescue me.

Of course, in the end the boat had ended up rescuing Philip.

The incident on the river had taken place while most of the Amberlys' guests were eating or playing lawn tennis, so only a relatively few people had seen the "accident" that had sent Charles Howard into the water. Those people, about twenty of them, were gathered on the Thames House dock, but Philip's boat came into shore at the place where Catherine, Lord Marsh, the boatman and I were standing. Philip jumped out of the boat in his stocking feet, and I ran to him.

He grabbed me by the shoulders and held me at arm's length away.

"Don't, Georgie. I'm soaked. You'll ruin your frock."

"I don't care about my frock," I said fiercely.

"Well, you'll get all wet, and then you'll take a chill and become ill."

His hands on my shoulders were quite firm. He really did not want to hold me.

I swallowed and stepped back from him.

"Thank God you are safe," I said.

He gave me a strained smile. His hair was still dripping, and in the full sunlight of the river bank I saw that there was a stripped austerity about him that had not been there before our return to London. Shadows of sleeplessness marred the taut skin beneath his eyes.

Lord Marsh said, "Surely it wasn't necessary to go in after him to finish the job, Philip. From here it looked as if you had been quite effective enough with the oar."

Philip looked at him. "One always likes to be certain," he said expressionlessly.

"Well, you almost got yourself killed making certain." Marsh's strange light eyes looked curious. "Did you get your hands on him underwater?"

"No. I was too late. By the time I got in he had been swept too far away for me to see him."

I stood there with Catherine and listened to Lord Marsh congratulate my husband on making sure of the demise of my attacker.

I could not help but think that Charles Howard had a wife and three small children.

Philip looked exhausted. "Who sent for the rescue boat?" he asked. "I would never have made it back to shore if it hadn't been there."

"I did," said Lord Marsh.

The two men looked at each other.

"I think we can say that at last I've repaid you that favor, can't we, Philip?" Marsh said softly.

Philip nodded wearily. "We're even, Richard. From now on, let us agree to stay out of each other's way, shall we?"

Lord Marsh gave his eerie, humorless smile. "Just as you wish, dear boy. Just as you wish."

He turned and walked away though the trees.

Philip had started to shiver. "Let's go up to the house," I said gently. "I'm sure the marquess will be glad to lend you some clothing so that you can get home without catching your death."

He looked cynical. "I can assure you, Georgie, I have been in far worse straits than this."

I didn't think his shivering was just from the cold. "Come along," I said with a bit more authority.

He shook his head. "I don't want to face all those people and all those questions. I'm not ready yet, Georgie."

There was the faintest trace of desperation in his voice, and I knew I had to listen to it.

"All right," I said, "but I am coming back with you."

He didn't want me. I could see it in his face. But I was adamant, and I supposed he could see that in mine. I turned to Catherine, and said, "Will you tell your mother that I have gone home with Philip, Catherine? And tell the Amberlys and Mrs. Howard that of course we will be willing to answer questions about what happened on the river this afternoon, but . . . not today."

"Of course," she said gently.

I took her hand and squeezed it. "Thank you, Catherine."

Philip merely nodded coldly. We both knew that he was furious that she had allowed me to come with her to Thames House.

He'll get over it, I mouthed to her, and she gave me a strained smile in response.

Philip and I got into the boat he had just come upriver in, and the boatman pushed off.

It was a silent ride back to Westminster. Philip dried
off a little in the sun and the breeze, but he continued to
shiver all the way back home.

My mind was preoccupied with what had happened
this afternoon. Foremost, of course, were joy and relief that
we were both alive. But I had to confess that I was deeply
disturbed about the ruthlessness that Philip had shown in
getting rid of Charles Howard.

Hitting Howard over the head with the oar to save me
had been one thing. But deliberately to try to drown him
was something quite else.

We took a cab from Westminster to Mansfield House,
and Philip went into his dressing room to change out of his
wet clothes.

"I want to see you," I told him as we went upstairs.
"Come into my dressing room when you are dry. It is imperative that we have a talk."

He looked wary and reluctant, but under the circumstances he could hardly plead a prior engagement. I didn't
even bother to change out of my garden-party dress, but
forced myself to sit on the chaise longue and wait patiently.
It took him twenty minutes to come in. He was wearing a
dressing gown.

"They're filling a tub for me, so I can't stay long," he
said. He sat down on the edge of one of the fireside chairs.
"What is it that you want to talk to me about, Georgie?"

I looked at him. I saw the finely drawn look of him,
the strain around his eyes, and I remembered Lord Marsh's
disturbing comment about his attempt to make certain that
Charles Howard was dead.

A charge that Philip had not denied.

Like a blazing comet lighting up the blackness of the
night sky, the truth dawned on me.

"You didn't try to drown Charles Howard this afternoon, did you?" I demanded. "You tried to rescue him."

He looked at me and didn't answer.

"You hit him over the head because you had to get him out of the boat with me, but then you went after him and almost got yourself killed in the process."

A little of the strain left the corners of his eyes. "I was too late. You can't see in the water of the Thames, and by the time I got into the river he was gone."

"But you kept on looking for him, didn't you, Philip? That's why you were underwater for so long."

He rubbed his hand across his eyes. "I thought about leaving him. He had tried to kill you, after all."

I smiled at him, trying to bridge the chasm that still yawned between us. "I'm glad you tried to rescue him, Philip. I'm proud of you."

He looked ineffably bleak. "Don't be proud of me, Georgie. That is a mistake."

I got up from the chaise longue and went over to stand directly in front of him, too close for him to get up without bumping into me.

"I want you to tell me what is wrong, Philip."

He started to say something, but I cut him off. "Don't try to deny it. Something is very wrong with you. You have been avoiding me lately as if I had the bubonic plague. If you don't like me anymore, if you don't find me desirable, then please just say so. I can't bear this situation where I am left feeling rejected and I don't even know why."

"Not find you desirable?" His laugh was painfully harsh. "Why do you think I haven't been coming home? It's because I can't bear to lie next to you in that bed and not make love to you."

"But why can't you make love to me, Philip? Have I

said or done anything to indicate to you that I don't like it when you make love to me?"

"No."

His face was stark.

I put my hands on his shoulders. Under the heavy silk of his dressing gown, the tension in them was palpable. I asked reasonably, "Then what is the problem?"

He drew a deep, unsteady breath. "Do you remember, when you were telling me about Maria, how you said that you couldn't understand how men could take advantage of poor young girls like her?"

"Yes."

"Georgie." He looked up and met my eyes. His own were clouded with pain. "My father took me to my first brothel when I was fourteen years old. I am one of those men whom you so rightly despise. How could I possibly touch you when I knew that? I didn't have the right."

I stared back into the dense, pain-filled blue of my husband's eyes. Dear God, I thought. Fourteen years old. What kind of a monster had he had for a father?

I ran my thumbs caressingly along his cheekbones. "Philip," I said gently, "you are not to blame for what happened to you when you were fourteen years old."

"But it continued," he said. "Don't you see, Georgie? It became a way of life with me."

A little silence fell between us as I contemplated his words. So this was the cause of the distance that had always lain between us, I thought. This sense of his own unworthiness.

I tipped his face up, so that he had to look at me, and said, gravely, "Philip, if I forgive you for the sins of your youth, will you promise me that you will forgive yourself?"

He didn't say anything.

"You had a wretched upbringing. You had no one to teach you right from wrong, no one to teach you the importance of being kind. I think it is nothing short of a miracle that you have turned into the kind of man who can be gentle to Anna, the kind of man who can risk his life to rescue a would-be murderer like Howard. I admire you more than any man I have ever known. And I love you. If you don't love me back, I will surely die."

"Georgie," he groaned. "Oh God, Georgie."

He clamped his arms around my waist and pressed his face against my breast. I held him close to me, my lips buried in his midnight-dark hair.

We remained like that for many moments.

Then he said, "I have felt so desperate. I wanted you so badly."

"Well, you made me thoroughly miserable," I returned. "I was beginning to think you had a mistress somewhere."

At that, he lifted his head from my breast and looked up at me incredulously. "A mistress? Are you serious?"

"Well, what else was I to think?" I asked reasonably. "We were so close at Winterdale Park, and then, when we returned to London, you didn't seem to want me anymore. You acted as if I was polluted or something. I didn't understand."

He reached up, pulled me down so that I was half-sitting, half-reclining on his lap, and then he kissed me. Thoroughly. Dizzily. Wildly. When finally he lifted his mouth, my head was lying limply against his shoulder and his hand was lying possessively upon my breast, gently massaging my nipple.

"I love you so much, Georgie," he said. "I thought I should go mad this last week."

My heart rang like a bell at the sound of those longed-for words.

I wiggled a little on his lap. "When did you first know you loved me?" I asked, eager for more confidences.

"The day you walked into my library and said that you were there to blackmail me," he returned promptly.

My eyes flew wide open. "What?"

He grinned at me, that boyish grin I loved so much. "You stood there, and looked at me out of those huge brown eyes, and you were so brave and so sweet and so determined." He kissed my nose. "Surely you don't think I spent all that money just to get back at Aunt Agatha?"

"You're joking," I squeaked.

"Not at all."

"You were horridly rude to me."

"Of course I was rude. I knew I couldn't marry you myself, and I had no intention of torturing myself by fostering any kind of a friendship between us."

By now I realized why he thought he couldn't marry me.

He was such a wonderful idiot.

"It took me a little longer to fall in love with you," I offered. "It was seeing you with Anna that did it, I think. I knew then that you were not the cold-hearted man you liked to pretend you were."

I reached up and smoothed his hair. I smiled at him. "Oh, Philip, I am so happy."

"In a very short time, you are going to be happier still," he growled in my ear.

"I am?"

The words were scarcely articulated before his mouth was on mine once again: hard, probing, seeking, wildly erotic.

My whole body went up in flames. I wanted him so badly that it frightened me. I wanted to taste him, to touch him, to fill my senses with him. I wanted him to enter me, to possess me, to be one with me, as only he would ever be. I wanted us both to climb together to the heights of volcanic passion, and afterward I wanted us to lie together in each other's arms, fulfilled and quiet and at peace.

Philip lifted his mouth from mine long enough to say, "Come to bed with me?"

"Yes," I said wholeheartedly. "Oh, yes."

EPILOGUE

I[T WAS A WARM SUMMER AFTERNOON, AND N[ANNY]
and I sat on two lawn chairs under the wide-spreading oak
and watched my three-year-old son play with Anna. We
were in the section of Winterdale Park that my husband had
created as a play area for the children, although Marcus,
our one-year-old, was not yet grown enough to take advantage of all the exciting opportunities that this small domain
afforded. He was still perfectly content to sit on the grass in
front of me and dig in the dirt and hunt for worms.

Robin, on the other hand, was perched on the wooden
platform of the tree house. It terrified me every time he
climbed to that high perch, but I forced my fear down and
made myself be content with watching him like a hawk. I
knew that I was inclined to be overprotective of my children because of what had happened to my sister, but I could
not seem to help it. I had nightmares sometimes of Robin
tumbling to the ground from that damn tree house and striking his head.

I had been angry with Philip when he had had it built.
He had paid no attention to me, however, and as I watched
both Robin and Anna scramble nimbly up and down the
ladder that led up to the platform, I reluctantly admitted
that my husband had been right. The tree house was an
enormous success, and kept not only Robin and Anna, but
any visiting children, busy for hours on end.

Now that I was a mother, I found it hard to forget all the dangers that stalked our seemingly innocent world. I had only to look at my sister, trapped in her eternal childhood, to know that fate was not always kind to children.

All of a sudden Robin's clear, childish treble came piping through the air from the heights of the tree house. "Papa's home, Mama! I can see him coming from the stable!"

I smiled. There had been an important debate in the House of Lords that Philip had gone up to London to attend, and while he was in the city he had planned to see his man of business. I had not expected him home for at least another day.

Robin and Anna both scrambled out of the tree house and disappeared in the direction of the stable. The dogs followed them, woofing excitedly.

"His lordship is back early," Nanny said comfortably.

"Yes," I replied. "The debate must have been over sooner than he anticipated."

My husband came around the corner of the donkey barn. He had Robin riding on his shoulders and Anna skipping at his side. The dogs trailed behind, tails wagging eagerly. He came over to me, lifted Robin down, bent to kiss me lightly on the mouth, and said hello to Nanny.

Robin said eagerly, "Did you bring me anything, Papa?"

I said, "Robin, it is very rude to ask people for presents."

Robin said, "Papa isn't *people*, Mama. He's *Papa!*"

"An incontrovertible fact," Philip said gravely. He reached inside his rust-colored coat and came out with a small carved figure of a pony for Robin and two dyed red ostrich feathers for Anna.

"One day soon we will get you a pony just like that one," he said to Robin.

Robin yelled with delight. He held the pony in front of him and began to gallop around the play area, making loud whinnying noises.

Anna jumped up and down, and said, "Please, Nanny, may I go and put my feathers in my hair?"

"Go along with you," Nanny said.

As Anna fled toward the house and a mirror, I looked at my husband. "You know she will wear those feathers like bunny ears, Philip."

"But she will love them."

She would.

He bent down and picked up the baby, who had been lifting his arms to him. "How's my best little boy?" Philip said. Then he tossed Marcus into the air.

The baby shrieked with delight.

Philip tossed him again. Once more Marcus shrieked.

I hated it when he did this, but I forced myself to say nothing. Philip took such obvious delight in his children, was so interested in their lives, was so clearly determined to be different from his own father, that I felt I had no right to let my fears interfere in this precious relationship.

After the third toss, Nanny mercifully said, "That's enough now, my lord. You're going to make him sick."

She held out her arms for the baby, and Philip obediently handed over his son.

He looked at me. "Come for a walk?"

I stood up, put my hand on his arm, and we left the children under Nanny's guardianship while we went along the path that led to the lake. We ended up in our favorite spot, a small sheltered glade that looked out over the water and the island and the temple. I sat with my back against a large oak tree and Philip flung himself down next to me and laid his head in my lap.

"So what happened?" I asked.

His eyes were shut. "The Lords voted to commence the trial of the Queen on August 17."

The Prince Regent, newly crowned as George IV, was suing his wife for divorce, which required an Act of Parliament.

"Oh no," I moaned.

He sighed. "Oh yes. It is going to be utterly hellish. London is in a state of chaos." His eyes opened and looked up at me. "I will have to attend, unfortunately, but you and the children are to remain here at Winterdale. There is already great unrest in London. The populace is disgusted with both the King and the Queen, neither of whom is exactly blameless in this situation."

In fact, the history of adultery on the part of both the King and Caroline was extensive and disgusting.

"What a wretched situation," I said.

"It certainly is," he returned feelingly.

I ran my fingers through his thick black hair, and his eyes closed again. Silence fell. I looked down at Philip's relaxed face. His long lashes lay quietly on his cheeks. He was clearly enjoying the touch of my hand.

"Has anything happened here since I've been gone?" he murmured.

I told him a funny story about Robin. He opened his eyes, looked up, and gave me the sweet smile that always made my insides turn into liquid. He picked up my hand and kissed it.

"I know it's difficult for you to let him run free," he said. "You're a brave girl, Georgie."

Tears stung behind my eyes.

"I try, Philip, really I do."

"I know you do, sweetheart. And it's not going to get any easier."

I sniffed. "It won't if you get him a pony! He's only three, Philip."

His eyes closed again. "He's three and a half, and I'll make sure it's a quiet pony."

Robin was actually a month short of three and a half, but I bit my lip and said nothing.

As I changed for dinner, I thought about what Philip had said about the Queen's trial. It was likely to last for months and if he meant what he had said about my not going to London, I wouldn't be seeing much of him for a while.

I did not like this idea at all.

It wasn't that I would miss London. We had managed to weather the scandal that had attached itself to the death of Mr. Howard, but it hadn't been a pleasant time. I had told the authorities how Howard had confessed to me about trying to kill me, and then Claven had brought forward a man who had sworn that Howard had tried to employ him to murder my father. Then the revelation about Papa's blackmailing the unfortunate young man had been borne out by the moneylenders, who had descended upon the widowed Mrs. Howard like parasites.

It had been very ugly and Philip and I had been very glad to come down to the peace and quiet of Winterdale Park. The scandal had eventually blown over, however, and now we were able to return to London with perfect respectability. Philip attended Parliament when there was a bill pending that interested him, and we always attended a few social affairs during the Season. I also went up to London to shop; there were no shops in Surrey that could match the shops in London.

Otherwise, most of our social life centered around the neighborhood in Surrey where we lived. We had made a number of very nice friends among the neighboring gentry, and though Winterdale Park was certainly the "great house" of the area, neither Philip nor I was too high in the instep to enjoy the company of good-natured, well-bred people who were not of the nobility.

We entertained or went on visits to Catherine and Lord Rotheram at least four times a year. Catherine had a little boy six months younger than Robin, and the two children were fast friends. She was expecting another child soon, and I had promised her that I would be with her when her time came.

Lady Winterdale was queening it over the dowagers in Bath. We never saw her, which suited us just fine.

But it looked as if this business of the Queen was going to disturb the pleasant tenor of my days.

I asked Philip as we sat together over dinner, "How long do you think this trial is going to last?"

He blew lightly on his soup to cool it. "Too long."

"Will it mean that I won't see you?"

He shook his head. "I'll get home, Georgie. The trial won't go on every day, and we're fortunate that Winterdale Park is within driving distance of London. The poor souls who live in the north and the west are the ones who will really be stuck."

"I could come up to London without the children," I said tentatively.

He shook his head decisively. "You don't know what is going on. London is almost on the verge of a revolution. Nearly every day a procession, as large as that which provoked the Peterloo massacre, marches through the streets, flaunting banners. Day and night the streets resound with shouts of 'No Queen, No King!' " He shook his head again. "I do not want you in London."

He had that look on his face which told me he meant what he said.

I loved my husband dearly, but there were still a few flaws in his character that I was working on. One was his tendency to order me around. The other was his tendency to retreat into himself when something was bothering him. Even after five and a half years of marriage, I still had to pry things out of him.

I supposed the habits of a lifetime were hard to break.

"Oh, all right," I said grumpily. "I'll stay at Winterdale Park. But I expect you to get home when you can."

His eyes glinted at me across the table. "You can count on that, sweetheart," he said.

I shot a glance at the footmen who were standing next to the sideboard, then dropped my glance to my soup so that no one should see the response in my own eyes.

After dinner we took our usual walk in the park with the dogs. Then we played a game of chess before the tea tray came in. Then it was bedtime.

This was the time for us to assert our union in the deepest, most intimate way that was possible. As we clung together in the big four poster, where we had made our two beautiful children, I felt the unutterably precious joy of a woman who is happy and who knows it.

I felt him kiss my throat and my collarbone.

I sighed deeply. "Happiness is such a complicated thing," I murmured.

"Not at all." He sounded very sleepy. Philip was always sleepy after he made love.

"It's not?"

"No." We had blown out the candles because the moonlight was streaming in through the open window. I heard him yawn. "Happiness is actually very simple," he said.

"What is it, Philip?" I asked curiously.

His voice was really drowsy now. "Happiness is Georgie," he said.

Tears filled my eyes. What a lovely thing for him to say. I reached over to kiss his cheek and all I heard was a gentle *wuffle*.

I looked at my husband in the moonlight. He was lying on his back, his hair very dark against the white pillow. His shoulders took up almost the whole of his side of the bed.

Why did he always have to go to sleep on his back? He snored when he was on his back.

I kissed his hard, bare bicep, gave him a shove to make him turn over, and settled myself to sleep as well.

CHAPTER ONE

It was three o'clock in the afternoon, on a beautiful but blowy day in mid-May, and I was, as usual, in the office of the stables of the Earl of Cambridge talking with his Head Groom. I was lounging in my chair, in a most unladylike posture, when there came the sound of a carriage being driven rather precipitously into the stableyard.

Clark jumped to his feet like a shot. "Lord Almighty, Miss, could that be his lordship?"

I said a little dryly, "Since I don't know anyone else who comes sweeping in here quite so grandly, I rather imagine that it is."

Clark disappeared out the door. I slid down a little farther on my spine and idly wondered what could be bringing the Earl of Cambridge back to his ancestral home in the midst of the London Season.

A brilliant ray of May sunshine came slanting in through the small office window and rested on the top of my head. It had been a cold April and the heat felt delightful. I closed my eyes to savor it.

"You here, Deb?" a familiar voice asked, and I opened my eyes to regard the man who had just come in. The Most Noble George Adolphus Henry Lambeth, Earl of Cambridge, Baron Reeve of Ormsby and Baron Thornton of Ware, stood in the door looking at me out of his famous dark eyes.

"I'm always here," I returned mildly. "Where else am I to be—at home with Mother, gardening?"

He flashed me a swift, charming grin. "Well, since you put it like that . . ."

He came into the room and sat on the edge of the desk, facing my chair and swinging his leg.

"The really interesting question is what are you doing here?" I asked. "Isn't the Season still in full swing?"

"I'm going over to Newmarket tomorrow to take a look at Highflyer," he said. "The Derby is in a few weeks, and I want to make certain that he's training well."

I bolted straight up in my chair. "May I come with you?"

He sighed. "You know you can't do that, Deb. It ain't proper for an unmarried young lady to be alone all day with a twenty-four-year-old man."

"Fiddle," I said vigorously. "You and I have been friends forever, Reeve. No one will think anything odd of me going to see your racehorse."

He snorted. "Won't they? My reputation is not exactly spotless, Deb, and I am *not* going to besmirch yours. You can't come with me, and that is final."

I glared at him. "But it is so boring here, Reeve. The only thing the local girls do is giggle about boys and talk about getting married. It is enough to make one go stark raving mad. If I didn't have Clark to talk to, I think I *should go* mad."

He looked like a dark angel as he sat there, swinging his booted leg and looking at me out of enigmatic eyes. "You ought to think of getting married yourself, Deb. You can't spend the rest of your life as a spinster, after all."

I could feel my face take on what my mother calls its stubborn look. "No one wants to marry me, Reeve."

"Don't be ridiculous," he said.

"It's true," I insisted. "For one thing, I'm too tall."

3

"You're not too tall." His straight black brows drew together. "Stand up," he commanded.

"No."

Two strong hands closed around my wrists and dragged to my feet.

"Hah!" he said. "The top of your head only comes up to my mouth. That's a perfectly good height for a woman."

I was annoyed. "Reeve, you are several inches over six feet. I don't know if you have ever noticed, but most men are not quite as tall as that. They like girls whom they can look down upon."

His eyes flicked over me. "They also like girls who wear something more feminine than ancient riding skirts and jackets that look as if they were rejected by the local orphanage."

I scowled up at him.

"It's not as if you were a Valkyrie, for God's sake," he said. "If anything, you're too thin. I could probably fit my hands around your waist."

"Well don't try it," I warned. I backed away from him and folded my arms across my breast. "How did we get started on this conversation in the first place?"

"You started it."

"I did not."

"Yes, you did. You were complaining that all the local girls are on the catch for a husband."

I leaned my hip against the desk that he had stepped away from. I shrugged. I hated to admit that I was wrong.

"It's perfectly normal for girls to want husbands," Reeve went on. "I don't know why you should find the topic so boring, Deb."

"It's not only boring, it's fruitless," I said. "Not only am I too tall, but I have no money. Don't forget that little fact, Reeve. Gentlemen are not inclined to marry a girl who is virtually destitute, which is what Mama and I are. We are lucky to have a roof over our heads." I shook my head. "No, I fear I am doomed to a life of spinsterhood."

I must admit I was not as unhappy as perhaps I should have been about this situation. My long legs might have made some of the shorter local swains uncomfortable, but they gave me a distinct advantage in the saddle. In point of fact, except for Reeve himself, I had the best seat in the entire countryside. This was the reason that I had the free rein of Reeve's stables, of course. He knew his horses were in good hands when I took them out.

Realizing that he was getting nowhere with his discussion of marriage, Reeve changed the subject. "It looks as if Highflyer is going to be the favorite for the Derby," he said smugly. "What do you think about that?"

"I think it is wonderful," I replied slowly. "But what does Lord Bradford, your trustee, think?"

Reeve scowled. "Bernard is a spoil sport," he said. "All he does is spout prosy speeches about the evils of racing. He has no understanding that racing is something that all real gentlemen do. He lives on that boring little estate in Sussex and does nothing but see to his farms and his flocks of geese. Wait until Highflyer wins. Then he'll see the value of keeping a racehorse!"

I said carefully, "Reeve, where are you getting the money to have Highflyer trained?"

"Oh, Benton loaned it to me," he replied carelessly. "I'm to repay him as soon as Highflyer wins the Derby."

A note of foreboding struck my heart. "And what if he doesn't win?"

That earned me the famous Cambridge glare. "Of course he'll win! He's by far the best horse in the race. That's why he's the favorite!"

He picked up an iron paperweight in the shape of a rearing horse and slammed it down on the copy of the *Stud Book* that Clark and I had been looking through. "Damn Bernard, anyway. Why does he have to make my life so difficult?"

It was a question I couldn't answer.

Reeve raked his hand through his dark overly long hair. "You don't think I should have borrowed the money from Benton?" he challenged me.

I looked back at him, taking a minute to think before I answered. Even Reeve's glower could do nothing to disguise the classical purity of his face's bone structure. The only thing that saved him from being outright beautiful was the bump in what had once been a perfectly straight nose. He had broken it when he was twelve. Someone had been riding too close behind him over a fence and crowded his horse, and both Reeve and the horse had come down. He had been laid up for weeks with broken ribs and a broken collarbone as well as the nose.

I had known Reeve since I was seven, however, and I was so accustomed to his dark splendor that it rarely got in the way of my reading the inner man. So I knew now that under the bravado he too was nervous about the money he had borrowed. I also knew that he would never admit it.

"It is just that I would hate to see the relationship between you and Lord Bradford deteriorate further than it already has," I said carefully.

Reeve gave a short bark of humorless laughter. "I should think that is impossible, Deb," he said.

There was no answer to that so I pushed away from the desk. "It's time I was going home," I said.

6

"Mother will be looking for me."

He nodded. "I really wish I could take you to see Highflyer, Deb, but even if you could find a chaperone, I'm not coming back here after Newmarket."

"That's all right, Reeve," I said resignedly.

"Give my best to your mother."

"I will."

And so we parted.

Highflyer lost the Derby. He stumbled on his way up the last hill and pulled up with the lower part of his leg dangling. He had snapped his canon bone. They put him down right on the Epsom course.

"Oh my God," I moaned when I read the account of the race in the *Morning Post* the following day. "This is terrible. Poor Reeve. What incredibly rotten luck."

"Let me see." Mother reached across the breakfast table to take the paper from me.

"Oh dear, that is too bad," she said in distress when she had finished reading the article. "Lord Bradford will be very annoyed when he learns that he has to pay out training money and now Reeve doesn't even have a horse he can sell."

"It isn't just the training money, either," I said gloomily. "Can you see Reeve not betting on his own horse? A horse that is the Derby *favorite*?"

"Oh dear," Mama said again. She knew Reeve well enough to recognize the truth of what I had just said.

I didn't see him for two weeks after the Derby fiasco. Then, one hazy June morning, as I was helping Mama in her garden, which fed us for most of the summer and half of the winter, he drove his phaeton up to the front of our cottage, pulled up with his usual flourish, and jumped down. I wiped my hands on my skirt and walked over to greet him.

"Hello Reeve," I said. "How are you?"

"I've been better," he replied shortly.

In fact, he looked ill. He had lost weight, which made his high, classical cheekbones more prominent than usual, and there were noticeable shadows under his eyes.

"I was so sorry to hear about Highflyer," I said gently. "What a terrible way to lose a good horse."

He nodded tersely. Reeve had never been very good about dealing with his own feelings.

At that point, my mother came up. She patted him gently on the arm and said, "It's good to see you, Reeve."

She too knew him well enough to realize that an excess of sympathy would not be welcome.

"I've come to ask Deb to go for a drive with me," Reeve said to Mama. "Will that be all right, Mrs. Woodly?"

"Of course," Mama said. "Change your dress first, Deborah. You cannot be seen abroad in that dirty old gown."

"She looks fine," Reeve said impatiently.

"If you don't mind, I would like to wash my hands at least," I said mildly. "I won't be long."

He gave me a very somber look. "All right."

Good heavens, I thought, as I went into the cottage. Something must be very wrong indeed. Could Lord Bradford have refused to pay his debts?

A cold chill struck my heart. Surely Reeve had not gone to the moneylenders? He would not be that stupid!

I washed my hands and face, brushed off my dress, and was back downstairs in ten minutes. Reeve was standing beside his horses, talking with Mama and looking tense.

"I'm ready," I said lightly and let him take my hand to help me up to the high seat of the phaeton.

As we rolled away down the country lane, Reeve was very silent, ostensibly concentrating on driving his matched pair of bays. I didn't say anything either. He had obviously sought me out for a purpose, and from past experience I knew I was going to have to be patient until he was ready to bring it out.

Reeve steered the phaeton away from the well-kept paths and splendid gardens of Ambersley and aimed instead toward the river, following one of the local country roads that at this season were lined with leafy trees and small grassy meadows filled with wildflowers. At last he pulled off the road and stopped the horses in a small glade that was hidden from the road by a stand of graceful beech trees.

He loosened his reins so the horses could stretch their necks and turned to look at me.

I could hold my tongue no longer. "Whatever is the matter, Reeve?" I asked. "Did Lord Bradford refuse to cover what you owed on the Derby?"

Dark color flushed into his cheeks. "If I live to be a hundred, Deb, I do not ever want to spend another hour such as the one I spent with Bernard after that race. He is such a clod. Do you know what he said to me? He said that raceowners were a congregation of the worst blackguards in the country mixed with the greatest fools. That is what he thinks me. A fool!"

Reeve's eyes were glittering dangerously and there was a white line around his mouth.

"Lord Bradford is a very conservative man," I said carefully.

"You won't credit this, Deb, but he seems to have no understanding that what I owe on the Derby are debts of honor." Reeve thrust his fingers through

9

his dark hair. "I shall be drummed out of the Jockey Club if I do not pay up on my bets, do you realize that?"

"Of course you must pay your debts," I said. I added carefully, "Er . . . how much exactly do you owe, Reeve?"

He scowled. "I bet sixty thousand pounds on Highflyer to win. Then, of course, there is the money I borrowed from Benton for training fees. That is another ten."

My heart sank. Seventy thousand pounds!

"And has Lord Bradford refused to meet your obligations?" I asked.

"He has said that he will meet them, but he has made a stipulation."

For the first time he looked away from me, averting his face and staring out over the shining dappled brown backs of his standing horses.

I looked in puzzlement at his profile, which was shaded by the overhanging canopy of leaves from the beeches. There was a single stripe of sunlight on the left shoulder of his rust-colored coat.

"And what is this stipulation?" I prompted when it didn't seem as if he were going to continue.

I could see a muscle jump in his jaw as he clenched his teeth. "I have to get maried."

I was dumbfounded.

"Married?" I echoed. "But what does getting married have to do with your debts?"

He didn't answer immediately and the truth slowly dawned on me. "Oh, I see. He has found you an heiress."

Reeve's reply was bitter. "I don't need an heiress, Deb. Even Bernard knows that." He turned around to look at me directly once again. "It seems that my esteemed cousin and trustee is a great believer in the settling effect of matrimony on a man. He has hopes that if I take a wife, and begin to set up my nursery, then my wildness will disappear. In fact, he has promised to give me access to half of my money when I marry and the other half if I can maintain what he calls a 'decent life' for a year."

"Good heavens," I said faintly. "Can he do that? I thought your father's will stipulated that you could not come into your inheritance until you were twenty-six."

"Apparently he left it to Bernard's judgment to put forward the time if he felt I showed sufficient 'maturity.' " Reeve's gloved fingers opened and closed on the loosened reins he was holding. He added grimly, "A stipulation that Bernard has not seen fit to inform me of until the present."

I stared at his clenched fingers and tried to make sense of what he was saying. "Lord Bradford told you he will not pay your debts unless you marry?"

"That is what he said."

Here was just another example of the way Lord Bradford constantly mishandled his cousin, I thought angrily. One of the worst mistakes one could make with Reeve was to put him in a position where his back was to the wall. And Lord Bradford was very good at putting him in that position.

I said, "What are you going to do?"

He growled.

I looked at him with compassion. "If you want your debts paid, it looks as if you are going to have to get married."

He growled more ferociously than before. "I don't want to get married."

"Surely it won't be so bad," I said encouragingly. "I read the papers. According to the gossip columns, there are dozens of young ladies who would welcome a proposal from the handsome Earl of

11

Cambridge. You will have to marry some day, Reeve. Why not sooner rather than later?"

He moved a little closer to me on the seat of the phaeton. Feeling his movement, his off leader tossed his head. The bit jingled in the warm June air.

Reeve said, "The young ladies you talk about are the silliest collection of twittering idiots I have ever met in my entire life. It would drive me mad to have to spend my entire life leg-shackled to one of them."

I watched as he moved another inch on the seat, intruding into my space. I felt like a mare about to be herded. He bestowed upon me his most charming smile, all white teeth and glinting dark eyes.

I regarded him warily. I never trusted that smile. I had seen too many times how unscrupulously he could use it to get his own way.

His voice deepened. "I have been thinking about this situation I find myself in, Deb, and I have come up with a splendid idea. Why don't you and I become engaged?"

I stared up at him in utter shock. "Are you mad?" I finally managed to sputter.

"You wouldn't really have to marry me," he said reassuringly. "Once Bernard hears that I am engaged, he will pay off my Derby debts. Why, if I play my cards right, I might even get him to sign over half of my money to me before the marriage takes place. After all, he can't expect us to tie the knot immediately. Weddings take time to plan, don't they?"

"I have no idea," I said firmly. "And, much as I would like to help you out, Reeve, this scheme of yours is impossible."

He moved another inch closer to me. "Why?"

I moved an inch in the opposite direction. "For one thing, Lord Bradford will not consider me a suitable wife for you. You are a Peer of the Realm,

12

Reeve, and I live in a cottage!"

"There's nothing at all wrong with your birth, Deb," he returned. "You're the daughter of a baronet, aren't you? You don't need to have money. God knows, I have money enough to support the entire county if Bernard would only give me control of it!"

I shook my head and repeated, "Lord Bradford would not consider me a suitable wife for a man of your station."

"The hell with what Bernard will consider suitable," Reeve said. His dark eyes flashed dangerously. "He didn't say that I had to marry a duke's daughter. All he said was that I had to marry."

He was bearing down on me with the full force of his personality, which was considerable.

"Stop trying to push me off the side of this phaeton," I said crossly. "I am not going to marry you."

"You won't have to marry me. I promise you that faithfully, Deb. All you will have to do is pretend to become engaged to me. We will inform Bernard, send out an announcement to the *Morning Post*, and then, according to his promise, Bernard will pay my Derby debts."

"And how are we to sever this engagement, pray tell?"

As soon as I said the words, I knew I had made a mistake. I had opened a wedge and Reeve was sure to leap right in.

He did.

"Well, I think it would be a good idea to keep the masquerade going for a few months, Deb. If Bernard thinks that I am really serious about getting married, he might sign over to me the control of half of my money before the deed is actually done."

I folded my arms across my chest. "You didn't

answer my question. How are we to sever this engagement?"

He returned promptly, "We will discover that we don't suit."

I frowned. "I don't know, Reeve. It sounds . . . dishonest."

"I'm only trying to get control of my own money," he pointed out. "How can that be dishonest?"

My hair was in its usual style, a single braid down my back, and I chewed on the end of it worriedly while I looked at him, trying to make up my mind.

He picked up my bare hand in his gloved fingers. "Help me out, Deb," he said coaxingly. "There isn't anyone else I could ask to do this for me."

"Mother will not like it."

He snorted. "The last time you listened to your mother you were eight years old."

Still I hesitated.

"Deb," he said, "if you don't help me out I'm going to have to sell off my stable."

I stared at him, appalled.

"I have to find the money to pay my debts somewhere. The hunters will have to go."

His eyes glittered. He had me, and he knew it.

I let perhaps ten seconds of silence elapse. Then I said tightly, "All right, Reeve, I'll pretend to become engaged to you."

He put his arm around my shoulder and gave me a brief, hard hug. "You're a great gun, Deb. I knew I could count on you."

"You blackmailed me," I accused as he shortened his reins and backed the horses in preparation to leaving the glade.

He chuckled.

Oh well, I thought, what we were doing

couldn't be so very terrible. I had always thought that Reeve's father had done him a terrible injustice in making that will.

And it was certainly nice to see Reeve looking cheerful again.

I made Reeve come with me to break the news of what we were planning to do to Mama. As I had predicted, she was utterly opposed to the scheme.

"It is deceitful," she said. "I cannot like it."

"It isn't really, Mrs. Woodly," Reeve assured her. "All I have to do is assure my cousin that I am engaged, and he will pay my Derby debts."

"But you are not engaged," Mama said distressfully.

"Yes we are," Reeve returned. "We just don't plan to *remain* engaged, that's all."

He looked at me for confirmation and I rolled my eyes.

We were sitting in the parlor of our cottage, Mama and I on the settee that was perpendicular to the fireplace, and Reeve on one of the two straight-backed chairs that faced the settee. He always looked absurdly large in this small room.

Mama said next, "It is not as simple as you are making it out to be, Reeve. For one thing, Lord Bradford will most certainly expect to be introduced to Deborah."

Reeve waved his hand like a magician. "No reason for him not to be."

I looked at my dress and thought of the rest of my wardrobe. "Reeve," I said, "I look like a pauper. Mama is right. This idea of yours is simply not going to work."

"Yes it will," he said, "and I am going to tell

15

you why it will work. I had a run of luck at Watiers two nights ago."

I stifled a groan at this news. Watiers was one of the most expensive of the gambling clubs in London, and I hated to hear that Reeve was patronizing it. He surprised me, however, by concluding, "I actually got out of the game with ten thousand pounds in my pocket."

Ten thousand pounds was a huge sum of money to me, but for a man like Reeve, who owed seventy thousand, it was pin money. I was surprised that he had not tried to increase the money he had won by continuing in the game. He was not known for getting out early.

"Do you know what I am going to do with that money?" he asked me now.

I shook my head, mystified.

"Take you to London and buy you a decent wardrobe," he said smugly.

"What!"

"You heard what I said."

"I cannot allow you to do that for Deborah, Reeve," Mama said firmly. "It wouldn't be proper."

"Nonsense," Reeve said. "I look at it as a ten-thousand-dollar investment that will net me much more money in return. "

"Just a moment, here," I said. "When I agreed to pose as your promised wife, I did not bargain on a trip to London and a new wardrobe."

Reeve stretched his legs out in front of him so that one polished boot rested on the ankle of the other. "Deb, I've said there's nothing wrong with your birth, and there isn't, but there sure is a hell of a lot wrong with your wardrobe."

I scowled at him. "This masquerade is getting a lot more complicated than you originally said it would be."

He gave me a patronizing smile. "Just remember those hunters, Deb."

"Deborah," Mama said, "I forbid you to do this."

I remembered the hunters.

"I have to, Mama," I said piously. "I can't leave poor Reeve in the lurch. It would be terribly unfair."

He gave me a wicked grin. "Now that's the attitude a man likes to hear from his promised wife."

With difficulty, I restrained myself from throwing something at his supremely self-satisfied face.